THE PREMAR EXPERIMENTS

THE PREMAR

EXPERIMENTS

A Novel by
ROBERT RIMMER

Crown Publishers, Inc., New York

Published simultaneously in Canada by General Publishing Company Limited

Library of Congress Cataloging in Publication Data

Rimmer, Robert H.   1917-
   The Premar experiments.

   Includes bibliographical references.
   I.   Title.
PZ4.R577Pp   [PS3568.I4]   813'.5'4   75-4540
ISBN 0-517-52148-2

ACKNOWLEDGMENTS

The architectural drawing of Topham's Corner and Confamiliaum #1 was prepared by Charles Giles Associates, 11 Ridgeway Road, Medford, Massachusetts 02155.

The author wishes to express his thanks for permission to quote from the following:

"Human Nature Is Still Evolving," by Elisabeth Mann Borgese: Reprinted from the April, 1973, issue of *The Center Magazine,* a publication of the Center for the Study of Democratic Institutions, Santa Barbara, California.

"Sexuality in a Zero Growth Society," by Alexander Comfort: Reprinted from the December, 1972, issue of the *Center Report,* a publication of the Center for the Study of Democratic Institutions, Santa Barbara, California.

Ellis, Albert, *Humanistic Psychotherapy.* New York: Julian Press, 1973; McGraw-Hill, paperback, 1975.

Goldstein, Al, "First Interview with Linda Lovelace," from *Screw,* Milky Way Productions, P.O. Box 432, Old Chelsea Station, New York, New York 10011.

The Transparent Self by Sidney Jourard, © 1968. Reprinted by permission of D. Van Nostrand Company, New York.

Shane, Harold, *The Educational Significance of the Future,* Phi Delta Kappa Educational Foundation, Bloomington, Indiana, 1973.

Das Energi written by Paul Williams, used by permission of Elektra/Asylum/Nonesuch Records, New York, © 1973. All rights reserved.

The Anatomy of Human Destructiveness by Erich Fromm. Copyright © 1973 by Erich Fromm. Reprinted by permission of Holt, Rinehart and Winston, Publishers.

THE PREMAR EXPERIMENTS

For Release to
Associated Press and
United Press International.

Dr. Phillip Tenhausen, of Harrad College, stated today
that a consortium of twenty-six small colleges and major
universities located in or near the urban areas of every
major city in the United States has joined the American
Association of Marriage Counselors and the American Association of Sex Educators and Counselors to offer, beginning with the fall term, a unique premarital living and educational program in three separate divisions.

Division One will consist of incoming freshmen,
male and female, who will be accepted at the institutions in much the same pattern as at present, except
that within the particular university or college, special
dormitories will be set aside where single students of
opposite sexes will room together. Roommates in
these dormitories will have been paired by the National Premar Selection Committee, composed of the
heads of the psychology, sociology, and religion departments at each location. Pairing will be made by
matching programs similar to those now used by dat-
ing services, balanced by a wide range of knowledge
gained from personal interviews with guidance counselors and testing procedures. Half of the students in
all divisions will be matched on the basis of common
interests and approaches to life. The other fifty percent will room with students having strikingly dissimi-
lar interests and approaches. It will be understood by
the incoming students that their roommates have
been chosen as one potential marriage partner, although marriage will be discouraged during the four-
year experiment.

1

Division Two will be based on a similar male-female roommate relationship, but it will be geared to the university-without-walls concept. Students accepted into Division Two will live together in communal houses or apartments in the nearest large-city core area in the vicinity of the sponsoring universities or colleges. Rooming arrangements will be as in Division One, but unlike Division One, students who may be fully or partially supported by their families and/or by loans, Division Two students will pay for their education as they go. These students will complete the requirements for an undergraduate degree in eight periods of thirteen weeks, alternated with eight thirteen-week working periods. During the 104 work weeks to be completed within four to six years, students will work in industry or service jobs at a guaranteed weekly income of not less than one hundred dollars a week net. Seventy-five dollars of this wage will be paid directly, or pledged by the employer, to the Premar commune, apartment, or home, which wil be mortgaged to National Premar Communes, Inc., an organization owned jointly by the universities and colleges involved in the program.

Thus, a premarital unit, comprising one male and one female, will contribute from its earnings approximately four thousand dollars annually to the commune, which will in turn pay the commune mortgage, supply the food, and pay the tuition bills of the students. Tuition costs are being reduced temporarily by participating institutions to one thousand dollars per student annually, but will respond, as will the pay of the students, to inflationary needs. Administration of the Premar commune will be handled by one male and female graduate student (house parents), who will allocate funds to a house council of elected students responsible for the delegation of house maintenance and food preparation.

House parents will receive twenty-five dollars per week in addition to room and board and tuition for their graduate courses. House parents will initially be chosen on the basis of their graduate study programs in the areas of religion, psychology, sociology, and guidance counseling, as well as the results of tests of their ability to handle interpersonal relationships in the Premar commune.

House parents will lead a continuing three- or four-year overview seminar in Human Values. Later, if the experiment becomes permanent policy, house parents will be chosen from graduate students who have experienced their undergraduate training in Division One or Division Two. House parents will be married monogamously and will agree to defer any postmarital experimentation, such as group marriage, or other alternate life styles, while acting in the capacity of student leaders.

A group of college and university faculty members working with the Association of Marriage Counselors and the American Association of Sex Educators will assist house parents in formulating and conducting the four-year Human-Values Seminar and will maintain a constant surveillance of the content and effectiveness of the Human-Values seminar, in which all students must participate.

Division Three students will comprise male and female high school graduates who have taken high school vocational courses which were not oriented to regular college admission requirements. They will live in Premar communes together with Division Two students and will take continuing education in their career areas for at least two years. After two years, Division Three students, even though they may be working full time, will remain in the Premar commune so long as they are unmarried and will take the Human-Values seminar over a four-year period.

For the first four to six years of the experiment, each participating institution in the consortium has agreed to establish at least two Premar communes with twenty-four couples in each. The physical premises of these communes will be remodeled housing in peripheral urban areas. Such areas will be low-income neighborhoods within a radius of four or five miles of downtown core-city areas. They will be close enough to the participating institutions to make the use of public transportation possible.

"We realize this will require adaptation of derelict housing in areas that are now often ethnically oriented," Dr. Tenhausen said, "but we will be working with youngsters who come from comparable environments in the urban areas of other cities, or low-income areas in suburbia. Premar students will be the children of families of median and low income. The original Harrad concept will continue to reflect upward income mobility, but with Premar we will be working mostly with youngsters who ordinarily would not have the opportunity to experience an undergraduate environment. While this separation reflects 'class' based on money, it is necessary because we are often working with different value structures in different income groups. Eventually, we believe, Premar will be able to break down the separateness that this society creates between those with money and those without. In the American tradition, these students will be expected not only to participate in the building, painting, and maintenance of their dormitories, but will also be paying for their own education. Ultimately, we expect that many children of upper-income parents may prefer the community-related aspects of Premar over Harrad-style undergraduate environments, which tend to be isolated from the mainstream of life.

"We hold that the survival of democracy depends on a new kind of structural liberal education beyond high school for *all* citizens. In a sense, we are expanding the former Carnegie Commission approaches to higher education by redefining them. Undergraduate liberal-arts or science degrees are not the prime goal of Premar. Instead, we aim to open the entire interpersonal and extrapersonal world to young people in a total learning and self-discovery process. With Premar, and the coordinating courses in Human Values, we will provide a true education, and an exploration of each person's potential that will, finally, broaden his vocational training. On the level of man and woman and life styles, and philosophy of life, our goal will be to give all men a common ground for intercommunication, and it will not matter whether an individual's specialty is law, medicine, nursing, running a beauty shop or data processing equipment, bricklaying, or pipe fitting."

Dr. Tenhausen explained the approaches of Premar with a quotation from A. S. Neil. "Montessori," he said, "had been describing to Neil the achievements of his mother in teaching the children of illiterate parents to read. 'It's beyond me,' Neil told Montessori, 'because you're talking about education, the three R's and science, and I'm thinking about the dynamics of life, the dynamics of a child and how we are going to prevent the child from becoming a Gestapo, or becoming a color hater. The sickness of the world. I'm interested in what we're going to do *for* the children to stop them from becoming anti-life.' "

Asked if he was suggesting that Premar would be using Skinnerian approaches and conditioning the students, Dr. Tenhausen chuckled. "Our whole society is conditioning young people from birth," he said. "We're going to *decondition* them. Take competitive sports. George Leonard, in his book *Transformations*, says, 'If varsity and professional competitive sports build character, it's the character fit for a criminal.'

"Since most Premar students—all those in Divisions Two and Three—will be supporting themselves, they will not have time for varsity sports. Beyond that, as one example of our Human-Values approaches, we will reveal the social fallacy of teaching unrestrained competitiveness in sports or of extolling sports that exclude the female. We believe that conditioning a human being for antisocial competitiveness is counter to normal human responses. Carried to extremes, sharpening hockey sticks, fistfights between teams, or gouging, biting, or elbowing in competitive football—the whole professional sports scene depends on an underlying brutality—whets the appetite of the viewer for mayhem. Such a ruthlessly competitive approach to life, whether in sports, business, or education, builds a psychic case against human cooperation. To return to A. S. Neil, Joseph Featherstone, commenting on Neil's theories, described Summerhill as an experiment in community living, and stated, 'This may be more important than education.'

"We believe that four years of Premar will give all young people an education in how to live joyously," Dr. Tenhausen said, "and in the process we hope to make millions of people aware that there are only two basic reasons for *any* schooling—to learn how to live, and to learn how to love and to gain the necessary skills to do a socially useful job. Because many educators have never fully understood this, the first sixteen years of education in America has become a wasteland of nonsense."

Dr. Tenhausen provided a generalized description of Premar communes. "Keep in mind that we expect to remodel existing urban structures. We want Premars to be living in a particular community as well as experiencing each other in a premarital and educational setting. We hope that within any one building we will be able to accommodate twelve to sixteen couples, with separate rooms for each couple. Thus, a Premar unit of forty-eight youngsters could be in three or four adjoining buildings. Within these structures, in addition to the separate rooms, there will be six privacy rooms that can be used by a student for an hour or much longer, as needed. On approval of the house parents, students who for one reason or another cannot adjust to their roommates will be permitted to live alone in one of these for a time. In a sense, a meditation cell for personal reevaluation, should this become necessary.

"Within each commune of forty-eight youngsters, we will have a communal dayroom for the daily Human-Values seminars, as well as communal parties, and so on. Each commune will have one large communal bath, Japanese style, with tubs. Each commune will also have an office and private sleeping quarters for the two couples who will function as house parents."

Dr. Tenhausen pointed out that while it was likely that other universities and colleges would eventually join the experiment, particularly in later years, the initial program would include over two thousand students nationally and would continue until five full classes, or over ten thousand students, had had the full four-to-six-year Premar experience. Full evaluation and a decision to continue the program will be made before the acceptance of the fifth freshman class.

A minimum of fifteen percent of the students admitted to each Premar commune would be black. Initial room assignments will group blacks with blacks and whites with whites, but the impetus of the Human-Values seminar would be to encourage all Premars to room later on a racially integrated basis. "We expect to create a total living situation where black and white students are completely intermixed," Dr. Tenhausen said. "We realize that attempting this within the urban environment would cause some misgivings among both black and white people, but we feel that we must face up to the fact that in most colleges and universities black youngsters have simply given up and have withdrawn into their own campus enclaves. While many more blacks are attending colleges and universities, their contact with the white students is peripheral. The next really great revolution in America will be widespread socially approved intermarriage between blacks and whites. Premar intends to do everything possible to make that revolution succeed."

Asked whether applicants for the Premar program would require parental permission, Dr. Tenhausen said, "Youngsters eighteen or over do not really need parental approval to live their own lives, but since many Premars will not pass their eighteenth birthday until they are well into our program, we hope we will be able to convince parents of the merits of Premar. Fortunately, many parents have become adjusted to the inevitability of premarital sex, and since so many of these are aware of their own inexperience and deficiencies in interpersonal relationships, we believe that the simple act of sex, or the experiencing of several other human beings in a controlled, permissive environment, will be widely accepted as a part of education; especially so, since the main thrust of Premar is not sexual mechanics but the development of value judgments based on love for other human beings. In this regard Premar reflects all religious thinking."

Tenhausen said that an effort would be made to see that all high school students are given full information on Premar by their guidance counselors. "Our approaches, until our political leaders realize the importance of national funding, must still be selective. In the beginning we will accept a number of academically qualified candidates for admission who, because of family income limitations, could not ordinarily afford to attend any college other than state universities. In addition, we will select youngsters from low-income families who would never have a chance to earn an undergraduate degree or to pursue vocational training beyond high school.

"All youngsters will be fully tested and measured, and we will know their backgrounds. If the program develops as we hope, we are going to create a whole new category of in-depth learning, and a need for a million students pursuing graduate study. The house parents, in a very real sense, will be learning as they teach. Eventually the flow of Premar-trained teachers will work its way back into the secondary schools. Alive, aware teachers there and in the grade schools will then be the order of the day. In twenty or thirty years we will have reordered the nation's social priorities."

He said the Premar communes are to be economic entities, and that indiscriminate sexual relations among the members will be discouraged. "We believe that meaningful sexual expression between human beings must always be a one-to-one experience. Group sexual adventures, from troilism to mass sex orgies, ultimately devalue the sexual act, depriving it of communion and deep intimacy."

In a discussion of the plans for outside employment of Premar students, Dr. Tenhausen was asked if the net pay of one hundred dollars a week to young, inexperienced Premars seemed unrealistic.

"Not at all," he replied. "If inflation continues we will adjust upward in this area. If a study were made of people who are doing a large portion of the service jobs today in the United States, or the prat jobs in industry, you'd find most are young people. There are millions of these jobs that must be done and which technology can never displace. What better approach to living is there than the assurance, for all young people, that society has been structured so that they can independently pay for their own education, while earning a fair wage for doing the necessary menial jobs. We will explain to Premars that if their job assignment during some work periods involves low-level manual work, whether it be garbage collecting or waiting on tables, this does not matter. Jobs will be rotated, in any case. Under an experimental agreement with the Department of Health, Education and Welfare and the National Education Foundation, industry or service organizations employing Premars may apply for a federal subsidy for the difference between the national minimum wage and the initial guaranteed Premar net wage of one hundred dollars a week. Right now, in every major city, graduate students are signing up cooperating employers.

"Our prediction is that new kinds of cities will emerge which will have practically no manufacturing within five to ten miles of the core. While keeping their banking, insurance, investment, sales, and administrative functions, the cities will slowly reemerge as the centers of education, arts, and culture. And the millions of youngsters working and studying in these cities will be their lifeblood. They will no longer be cities that die at night when the commuter goes home. They will once again become young cities—places where humans feel warm and close to one another."

Asked whether the Premar program evolved out of the original Harrad experiment, Tenhausen laughed. "Of course, but the joy of the world is change. Harrad pointed the way. Harrad will continue in Division One until we can erase elitism and class barriers based on money. Premar may do this over the next half-century. You can quote me. The Premar commune is Harrad now!"

Author's Note

A few months before Phil Tenhausen released the story of the National Premar Commune and the Premar Education Program, I suggested to him that if we could eventually view Division Two and Division Three Premar communes through the eyes of both the graduate students who would act as "Compars" (as the house parents have since been named by the students) and the individual Premar students, we would gain broader perspectives on the experiment.

At the first meeting of two hundred Compars in Cambridge last August, the idea was well received. Bren Gattman, with whom Phil was taking some risks, by accepting the possibility of broadening the Premar program with Bren's Confamiliaum proposals, suggested that the Compars should keep their journals on cassette tapes rather than in writing, as required for the first two years for all Premars. In this way, he said, communication between Compars and Premars would be much more complete. Bren's idea was that the Compar tapes would be available in the Premar commune dayrooms, and if the Compars learned to "dare" self-disclosure, they would create new approaches and confidence for the young people in their charge. Since the "how" of self-disclosure and interpersonal communication is the name of the game, Bren's idea was well received. The only negative reaction was that Compars might lose control if they were too open with the Premars. This was essentially the old parent-versus-child controversy. In the case of Compars, however, who would be less than a decade older than the Premars, it was felt that this kind of openness would actually facilitate cooperation.

I have listened to many of the Compar tapes and read

hundreds of journals from Premar communes in various parts of the country, and it is clear to me that Phil Tenhausen's gamble, in daring to become involved with Compars like Bren Gattman and Rais Daemon, paid off in at least one respect. Because Rais and Bren have been unafraid to improve on or challenge the rules, their journals and those of Ellen O'Day and Merle Blanc, and their interaction with the Premars, are probably the most fascinating to the general reader. In a sense, the taped Compar journals are a counterpoint to the Premar journals.

Thus, while the casual observer may feel that Rais Daemon's St. Noir journals may have little to do with the simultaneous happenings at Topham's Corner, in fact the aborted St. Noir uprising, and the conversion of parts of Topham's Corner to a Confamiliaum (or Confam) style of life, as well as the Premar communes themselves, have much in common in their humanistic, life-exalting styles.

The reader should be warned. If he expects a book with balanced climaxes and denouements, or fictionalized non-fiction which raises the question of the honesty of biography and history, or if he hopes for a book which has the closed loop characteristic of data-processing equipment, with all the answers available if he could only find the right software to feed in—forget it! The intermingling of the journals of the Compars with those of the Premars, and the selection of the Premars' journals in a way that leaves the reader wondering what might have happened in certain relationships, is inevitable.

If you are really interested in the ultimate meanings of your life, why not accept the Premar conditioning? There is no beginning, and there is no ending. Premar is continuous, and the Premar solution lies in your own hands.

BOB RIMMER

PART ONE

Premar

There is no university that I know of where experiments are being conducted in alternatives to monogamous suburbs-living family life; where Utopias are subjected to study and testing by people who live in them and people who study them. There is no department of any university that I know of where new ways to be a man and woman, parent and spouse, doctor, lawyer, governor, or even thief are being explored and evaluated. There is no university with a cadre of exemplary "compleat" men and women who can serve as models for emulation, as pioneers along new dimensions of human existence.

—SIDNEY JOURARD
The Transparent Self

Bren Gattman. Prelude to Premar. May. From cassette tapes transcribed by Ellen O'Day.

I'm Bren Gattman. In a kind of joyous meandering of Yiddish, I guess Bren could be translated "burning," "on fire" hence *"fireball."* That was the kind of son Abe Gattman wanted—a guy who'd set the world on fire. A Henry Kissinger, maybe—or at the very least one of those financial geniuses like Saul Steinberg, who, at the age of thirty, had put Leasco together, became a multimillionaire, and nearly took over the Chemical Bank of New York. Or like some other of those conglomerators, Charles Bludhorn or Meshulam Riklis, who built huge international industrial empires, or like Rocky Stone, the guy my sister, Laura, married, who put together Stone-Western Industries and may have more money than any of them.

"Gattman Ford is a stepping-stone for you," Abe used to tell me. "Your sister doesn't need it. I built it for you—the largest Ford dealership in upstate New York. Your Zadie was a poor rabbi. My family—your mother's family—none of them had a dime. I had to claw my way up. You're getting the education, the background. You don't have to sell Fords for a living. Go to a business school. Get in with the big boys. Rocky Stone would take you in. You could make millions. Go to law school—be a senator, or a governor. Be a President! Why not? The first Jewish President!" The tears of joy in Abe's eyes disappeared when I told him that I already was president.

"President of what?" he demanded, suspecting the worst.

"SDS. Students for a Democratic Society."

"Di oi'eren nit vos dos moil redt," Abe groaned. Which means the ears don't hear what the mouth is speaking. Abe is always quoting Yiddish proverbs at me.

Ellen O'Day is listening to my yak. The tape recorder is gobbling up my words. Not that I believe my words are

15

immortal, but as I told Phil Tenhausen last night, tape is not
only quicker than keeping a journal, tape doesn't give you
time for self-reflection, hence it fits perfectly one of the
Premar approaches—learning *the how* of self-disclosure,
being open and defenseless with another human being.

Ellen is half-sitting, half-lying in my bed. Her head is
raised high on three pillows. Her chest is bare. Her breasts
are languid, and kind of helpless-looking. Her warm brown
aureoles and her sleepy deep brown eyes are looking at me.

What are you thinking, Ellen? Are you wondering how
the daughter of Dancer O'Day, city councilor and cham-
pion of law and order, adored by all overweight South
Boston housewives, ever let herself get trapped with a mad
Jewish messiah from upstate New York? Ellen O'Day,
what would your father say? He'd have a stroke if he
could see you now, naked except for your see-through
panties, lying in the bed of that radical, vermin, kike,
Bren Gattman, who less than three years ago helped
occupy the administration offices of Boston University.
One of the famous J&B duo. Jews and black—Bren Gattman and Rais Daemon, who got their asses kicked halfway down Commonwealth Avenue by the Boston fuzz just
because they believed in America with a big A, and no K.

Ellen, you know you can't repress that tiny grin.
Eventually you're going to find your lovely Irish tongue,
and then you'll spout your feelings onto tape. But eventually these tapes, along with hundreds of others I have made,
will disintegrate, and no one will have listened. But we're
learning, Ellen. That's the key! When the Premars arrive
in September, the more we have discovered how to be
human, the better—how to unclench our fists, throw our
arms back, and with palms open, dare to say, "Here I am,
for better or worse. . . . This is me—with all my hopes and
fears. Sometimes I'm brave. Sometimes I'm a coward. But
what I really want most in this world is to love and be
loved." The more we discover how to open ourselves up
like that, the more the kids will dare to be open with us.
And then our real education will begin! Ellen . . . Ellen,
don't look at me with your soul hanging out, with your eyes
drowning me. I can't concentrate!

Everything starts somewhere. Yesterday I read Phil
Tenhausen's news release on the National Premar communes, and lightning struck! I knew I had found the missing
link. I could take Phil Tenhausen's proposal one step fur-

ther and blend it into an idea that Rais Daemon and I had been toying with three years ago when I bought this tenement house. A total scheme that will create new kinds of cities. Urban educational environments that would involve the younger generation with lower-income America. We could blend youth and the unmeltable ethnics into a new, exciting, forward-looking America. But I needed a wife—a real honest-to-God night-in, night-out bedmate. And then, lo and behold, Ellen O'Day, you fell right out of the blue into my arms.

Phil and Margaret Tenhausen liked my idea, Ellen! They really liked it! I wish you could have been with Merle and me last night. I hadn't seen Phil or Margaret for five years. Other than the things that I've read about Harrad, the only time I ever really talked with them was at a lecture and rap session they ran at Boston University. That was a few years ago, when they were just getting the Cambridge Harrad started. Merle thought I was pretty nervy to telephone them like a long-lost friend. But good ideas never get off the ground without some pushing and hauling.

Last night, when Merle and I finally got to the Tenhausens' home in Auburndale, it was about eight-thirty. Phil greeted us at the door naked—reminding us that the poet William Blake often surprised visitors by welcoming them without clothes. It either flipped their brains, or they joined their host, undressed, and discovered that, naked, communication proceeded on a different level. Phil invited us to the screened back porch and introduced us to the Abernathys, Claire and Mark. The porch overlooks their back yard, which is filled with pine trees and birches. You can see the edges of the Charles River in the distance. I shucked out of my jeans and T-shirt in a split-second. Merle wasn't so enthusiastic. She grinned at Claire Abernathy, also naked, and said, "It ain't so easy being black when everyone's white."

"Or being green." Mark Abernathy, who is a psychiatrist, smiled at Merle. He wears a beard that makes him look like a Civil War general. "Don't undress at all if you don't want to," he told her. "Being naked is just that— being. You'll note that Margaret is wearing a dress that just covers her naked behind. Tonight that's being for her. Being sexier, maybe half-undressed. Or maybe she's chilly. We'll have a more sparkling world when we've learned how to enjoy each other, just being, and we don't demand consistency from our friends. Why shouldn't a person's style of being vary from one day to another, to suit his own needs?"

"So that you won't be wondering," Margaret told us, "the Abernathys live next door. We share our things, especially food and automobiles, and switch houses and partners for a few days or a week at a time. Occasionally, a day or two will go by when we don't even see our original spouse. Then we get lonesome for the interaction of the four of us, and we all stay together for a few nights. Our kids—there are five altogether, from eight to fifteen—enjoy the changing scene, and we're much involved with all of them. We're a family of nine. That's more fun and more challenging than a family of four."

On the porch Phil opened bottles of California wine that Stan and Sheila Kowalski had sent them. Phil explained that they had graduated in the first class to finish Harrad, more than twelve years ago. Up in the Sonoma Hills, among other things, they owned a winery that's run by former Harrad students. One of their labels was "Chateau Harrad," a Zinfandel. I sipped it, getting slightly mulled, while I tried to sell my idea to Phil.

"I know the general area where Bren is living," Phil explained to the others. "It's near Topham's Corner in Dorchester. As the crow flies, it's about three miles from the core of Boston—the City Hall and the Government Center. Franklin road bisects it. On one side is a solid concentration of blacks, on the other side are Irish, some Poles and Italians. It was built between 1870 and 1890 in a grid pattern, with cheap wooden three-story tenement houses. Recently some new low-income housing has been built, but the new low-income housing is already in worse shape than the tenements."

"I own one of those tenements," I told them. "I bought it the beginning of my senior year at Boston University for nine thousand dollars. I decided to be slum landlord and rent it to other students. It's right in the heart of blue-collar-Joe country. Rais Daemon, Merle Blanc, Lena Goldman, and I moved in together. Last fall, when Lena got her B.A., she married a lawyer. Lena's a Marjorie Morningstar type. She defied the system for a while, was intrigued by the radical Jewish son whose upper-middle-class father owned an automobile agency. She was sure I would eventually come home again. Finally she became convinced I was a lost cause. She told me my demise would fit my name. If not a burning, a crucifixion. Lena decided that she had had her fling. She's not a change-maker. She wanted the comforts of upper-class suburbia. So what if there were frustrations and upper-income ennui? What would life be like with Bren Gattman when there was no revolution? Or with an Alan Ginsberg, or an Abbie Hoffman or Jerry Rubin? Would starving with old hippies, or living on welfare, be better than eating yourself to death in the Borscht Belt?"

Anyway, Ellen, I told Phil that Rais and I got our master's degrees last year. We still had a low profile in Topham's Corner, but we had some interesting plans. Rais and I decided to stay together. When Rais married Merle, she joined us. Then Rais and I got in that fracas at the university. It was a weary scenario. We really had decided that the old style of revolution was hopeless, anyway. Thrashing-riots-marching were old hat. But, hell, we had to help. A hangover from the days when we believed we could change things—like the draft, or the saturation bombing of Vietnam, or the Pentagon running the universities. Rais slugged one of the pigs who was slugging him—with his own billy club—and he took a few whacks at your fathers' ass, too, Ellen.

Rais got six months in the can. With nothing else to do, he wrote "Walk Before God." It was published in practically every newspaper in the Caribbean. Several publishers are looking for Rais right now, and he could sign a contract with any of them. New American Library wanted him to develop his article into a paperback book. Rais is a hero on the island of St. Noir, where he was born. Four weeks ago, when he was finally released from Walpole Prison, he flew back to try to calm things down. But by this time the natives were all walking around with fuses up their asses, waiting for our hero to light the match. Rais knows the time is *not now*, but I doubt if he can cool them.

"I read Rais' article," Claire Abernathy told Phil. Claire teaches psychology at Brandeis. In contrast to Margaret, who is bright and quick, Claire is kind of drawly and sensuous. I wanted to suggest to Claire that she should teach one of her classes naked, relaxed, and deliberately provocative, just like she was right then. It would be an interesting experiment. But for once I kept a thought to myself.

"As I remember," Claire said, "Rais' writing style seemed unnecessarily inflammatory. If he does come back to Boston, and you persuade this Ellen O'Day to marry you, while you might all qualify for Compars, I think you may be a little too avant-garde."

Margaret agreed. "You must remember, Bren, while the Premar idea has been around for a while, most people still believe Premar communes, if not completely immoral, are pretty close to it. We've sweated blood and tears to bring Premar about, and I'm not sure that at this point we need dewy-eyed dreamers trying to build a bridge between Premars and lower-income groups, or activists like you and Rais stirring up a breeze with ideas like your Confamiliaums. We're pretty much in agreement that graduate students who plan to go into guidance counseling are the best all-around choice for Compars."

"But," I said, "your Division Two Premars, presumably, will be kids from lower-income families. The typical fifty percent who don't get any college training. That's who Rais and I are interested in, too." I didn't want to tackle Margaret on guidance counselors—but it seemed to me, if Premar caught on, it should embrace graduate students seeking their degrees in many different areas.

Mark agreed with Margaret and Claire. "Bren, I don't think Phil expects to win over the parents of lower-income students immediately to his premarital training program. It will take time. While kids at eighteen can make their own decisions, life styles change slowest among the poor, who, of necessity, or for whatever certainty they can hang onto, fight change. We'll convert the parents gradually and mostly through their children who have experienced Premar. It may take fifty years, but lasting change can't be legislated—nor will it come from overt revolution. Not in the twentieth century."

"Besides," Margaret said to me, "after talking with you for a couple of hours, I'm convinced you're even more of a tilter at windmills than Phil. This Ellen O'Day—is she really the daughter of Dancer O'Day? If you manage to commit her to your insanity, how do you know Dancer won't contact one of his Irish buddies or one of his godfather friends? You could all disappear forever into Boston harbor, wearing cement shoes."

I was beginning to think it was a hopeless cause. Merle didn't help by telling Margaret she wasn't too sure that Rais would ever come back to Boston. She was flying to St. Noir in a couple of weeks, after her last classes, to see what Rais was up to; she wasn't sure she would come back, either. She was married to Rais, after all, and not to me.

Then Phil, who had been doodling on a large pad of paper, drawing boxes over and over again, said, "You'd need at least two other houses. Could you get them for under fifteen thousand dollars each in the same area?"

I grinned. "Next door, two are for sale. We'd have to take care of a couple of welfare families living there."

"It could be an interesting side approach to the total effort," said Phil reflectively. "I'm convinced that each Premar communal group should have its own individuality. We've set up a Division Two Premar commune in the South End, but I'm not sure whether we can integrate it into the Puerto Rican community. Let me give it some thought. If we could bring all the pieces together fast—including remodeling the houses—I might persuade the consortium to go along. It would be a hell of a tight schedule. As for Merle and Rais, if they measure up as Compars, I'll wait for them until September." Phil smiled at Merle. "I'd do that, without knowing Rais, on the theory that if you married him, he must be quite a guy."

Ellen, you haven't said a word. Have you been listening? I'm asking you to marry me. Don't look at me as if I'm completely whacked out. I knew I loved you the second I picked you off the sidewalk. You need me! I'm the activist you have to be but can't be. I know you're curious about Merle. The reason that Phil wants Rais and Merle is that he wants good black Compars. I love Merle. But she's like my kid sister. We sleep together because we're both lonesome. She likes me because I love Rais. And she thinks it's kind of chuckly to make love with "the man." She can't believe that she would ever let a whitey call her his "hot chocolate." I told Merle that I have a chocolate deficiency that she helps correct. But she's married to Rais, and loves him, too.

Ellen, Ellen, don't look so sad. I love you. I've lived twenty-eight years, and the only other woman I wanted to marry thought I was too intense. Don't say no. Not yet!

You can't go home today. Give me your answer on tape. Dare to be the Ellen you've been hiding for twenty-four years.

From the journal of Andrea Pillisuk, September, the first year of Premar.

Sure, like a couple of million others I've read *The Harrad Experiment,* but *this,* in the words of Joe McDonald, "is something else again. So different, it could be happening on another planet."

After two days I have to admit I really don't know whether I'm coming or going. I guess, as Bren Gattman told us at the first Human-Values meeting, the "thing to do is to get it all down on paper. Because in a few months the bewilderment will be gone, and one day you'll want to look back and see what kind of a person you were at the beginning. We'll guarantee you: a few months from now, another you is going to surface, and you may never recognize your old self again."

Bren wasn't just kidding. One of the requirements of Premar is that we keep this journal daily, and every week we must turn it into the Compars. The idea is that in this way we'll all get to know what is really happening in each other's heads, and yet we'll dare to put down things we'd be too bashful to say out loud either to Compars or to our roommates.

"We're going to insist on the journals," Ellen told us. "They're an established part of all Premar programs. In exchange—so that we have ultimate communication—all Compars are required to keep a similar journal, but on cassette tapes. If you think that is easy, try it! Some of our tapes are already in the dayroom library, and Premars can listen to them, together or separately. We hope you'll still like us when you discover that we're frightened sometimes—just like you."

Merle Blanc, another Compar, who is black, was listening. She said, "I'll warn you kids, right now, you've got a new kind of listening experience. Ellen and I have been keeping tape journals since July. Bren's and Rais Daemon's tapes go back several years. Whatever else, before you get through Premar, you're going to know us intimately, and what makes a lot of people tick—including yourselves!"

Bren put it another way. "We're going to re-create each other," he said the first night. So far, I'm sure of one thing: In less than a week, Andy Pillisuk is already light-years removed from the girl who said good-bye to her sobbing mother three days ago."

Poor Ma, she kept kissing me and telling me she didn't know whether she was doing the right thing. Letting me go. Seventeen and a half years old, practically a baby, to live alone in a room with a boy. Unmarried, yet. But what could she do? Now kids can vote at eighteen, and drink in bars, and get married whether their parents like it or not. Maybe that's the best thing about this school. She sighed. "At least you won't be screwing around and have to get married at eighteen like I did. Maybe you'll find out, before it's too late, that the bed stuff isn't what it's cracked up to be."

What had marrying my father done for her? She was eighteen, then. A virgin. Five years later my father had disappeared. Run out. Couldn't stand marriage. God knows where he is. And here Ma is thirty-six years old and knocked up again. Babe Dransky is the father, and they're going to get married as soon as her divorce comes through. But she didn't trust Babe. It was just as well that I was going to college, or whatever. Premar undergraduate living! Wow!

I knew what Ma meant and didn't say. Babe isn't a bad guy. But he's got sex on the brain. He's a good plumber—no joke intended—and makes a lot of money, but the way he occasionally looks at me and pats my ass isn't what you'd call fatherly. Ma isn't bad-looking, but she doesn't need competition from me under her own roof.

Anyway, when my high school counselor told me that Premar was a kind of poor kids' Harrad, where you'd have to work part-time to put yourself through, I thought it was a great idea. So here I am! And though I'm not a virgin, and may have to admit it to Joe McDonald, my first roommate—damned if he isn't. A virgin, I mean. Joe doesn't know much about me yet. The day I lost my cherry didn't amount to much, anyway. From the time we were juniors in high school, Tony Sardola had the hots for me. And I knew I had to do it pretty soon, anyway, since I was about the only kid in the class who hadn't screwed at least once.

It happened on one of those mad afternoons when we were puffing a joint together in the cellar of his folks' house. Ugh! What a yucky place to lose it! Still heated by a coal furnace. There was a urine-smelly mattress down there someone had forgotten to throw out, and I let him get me down on it.

I let him go all the way. Four different afternoons we did it on the same mattress—but the other times I put newspapers on it—and Tony's pecker would no sooner get inside me than he'd pop off. "I can't help it"—he'd laugh—"I look at your tits and your pussy, and I'm climbing the wall." So was I, but Tony never read any of those sex books where a man is supposed to wait for the girl to come. His way of making it up to me was to take me downtown to a first-run movie that cost three dollars. I'd rather have seen the same movie a few weeks later for one dollar and discovered what it was like to climax with him doing it to me. I never did with Tony. Masturbating feels okay, and it's one way to make it, but I want it to happen with a guy. The right guy.

Yuck! I'm sure glad I got through that business without getting knocked up. The kissing and hugging was great, but once he came, Tony didn't have much time to be friendly. Can I ever tell Joe? Bren and Ellen, or that pretty black girl, Merle Blanc, will be reading this, and even that gives me the willy wobs.

Was it just three days ago that I arrived in Boston? I took the Greyhound bus from Detroit with fifty-five dollars in my pocketbook. With no money, but good brains—according to my chemistry teacher at Northmont High, if I'd ever use them—I'm going to college for four to six years, depending on how long it takes me to earn and learn. Wow! It's all up to me, I guess.

Ellen and Merle met me at the Park Street bus terminal in an Econoline truck that has seen better days. It turned out I wasn't the only one arriving by bus. There were a bunch of other kids waiting for them. Ellen is about twenty-five, kind of tall, skinny, with dark brown hair and flashing brown eyes and a kind of cheery, oval Irish face.

I guess I was kind of surprised to see Merle. In our neighborhood, everybody is either Polish or Italian. They tried to bus the black kids to our high school, but that practically caused a riot. Even my Ma took to the streets to make sure her daughter stayed lily white and uncontaminated. There was no sense arguing with her. Babe Dransky took her side. Blacks were blacks were blacks. So I guess I never really talked with any black person except a clerk downtown at Hudson's department store.

Merle wears a close-cut afro. She had a kind of uppity, aloof manner. When I mentioned that I'd have to get a job pretty quick because I didn't have any money, she shrugged. "That's the nature of the beast. This isn't Harrad, honey. There's a lot of Harrads around. But mostly, in Divisions Two and Three of Premar, we're all broke." She finally laughed. "Except Bren Gattman, maybe. His grandma left him a bundle. His father is rich, but Bren and his old man don't see eye-to-eye. At the rate he's going, it's just a matter of time before Bren spends his inheritance bailing himself out of jail."

Merle drove the car and Ellen sat beside her, and six of us who arrived at the same time in Boston sat in the back seats. Two were black, one a boy from New York, Bob Jefferson, the other, Cheryl Jones from Atlanta, who's kind of pretty with big brown eyes floating in milk. Her nose is a little too flat and her lips look like chocolate pudding. She looked a little more scared than the others. Rachel Silverman is skinny and kind of overbearing— Jewish. The other girl, Kathy Flaherty, has the prettiest face I've ever seen on a girl, but the poor thing must weigh one hundred and seventy pounds. Maybe the boys will like her big tits. The other boy, Able Anderson from Worcester, couldn't keep his eyes off them. But he's nice, a laughing Swedish boy. We were all talking at once.

Were Merle and Ellen really Compars? They told us they were. Were they married? Well, Merle Blanc was married to Rais Daemon, a West Indian. Rais had gone home to St. Noir, an island in the Caribbean. Hopefully, he'd be back in Boston in the next few weeks.

Ellen smiled at us. "Eventually, we're going to have to ask all of the Premars to keep our secret. As you know from your catalogs, all Premar communes are keyed around housing complexes that can accommodate twenty-four couples, plus four house parents. The regulations provide that house parents, or Compars, must be married so that there are two husband-and-wife teams for each forty-eight kids." Ellen stopped talking for a moment, lost, I guess, in her thoughts.

Merle shrugged. "What Ellen hasn't told you, and what you'll find out if you listen to our tapes, for her own reason, which she may confide in you, Ellen hasn't married Bren. Phil Tenhausen and the National Premar Communes consortium think they're married. Rais and I are married, but at the moment Rais has gone underground. No one knows exactly where he is, though the British are after his scalp for fomenting a revolution. Ellen, Bren, and I are all working for our Ph.D.'s. As your proxy fathers and mothers, we get free housing and pocket money. That's our bag. Bren is convinced that Ellen will eventually marry him. As for me, if and when Rais gets back to the States and gives up his mad daydreams, we'll finally be full-fledged Compars."

Merle sounded as if she wasn't at all sure of Rais Daemon. The truth is, I don't think any of the kids give a damn whether Ellen and Bren are married, or whether Rais shows or not. We soon discovered that Bren goes to bed with both Merle and Ellen. But most of us are so concerned with the sudden naked exposure of our little selves we haven't time to worry about much else.

We didn't even know simple things, like how to react when we drove up in front of our old tenement houses, which aren't much better on the outside than my mother's flat in Detroit, and Ellen said gaily, "Here we are—National Premar Commune, Local Sixty-Three. There are four others in the Boston area."

Bob Jefferson chuckled. "Do they get to sixty-nine?"

Merle burst into laughter. The other kids look mystified. I guess at seventeen and a half, Andrea Pillisuk knew more about some things than her classmates. But that first night, I have to admit, even the most sophisticated of us were a little popeyed.

All the Premars were directed to the dayroom on the first floor of one of the tenement houses. It's a completely open room with only one interior supporting wall. Part of the room, a space about thirty or forty feet, is carpeted in a deep green broadloom. The other part is tiled and has a dining room with about a dozen tables. Along one wall there is a big ceiling-high bookcase full of books and a built-in stereo with a lot of records. Bren Gattman was sitting behind a big card table covered with stand-in files with the records of the Premars. He was handing out mimeographed room and work assignments. Mine read: "Andrea Pillisuk. Room 10, O'Day House. Roommate, September through March, Joseph McDonald. Work assignments: September through December, typist, clerk, Buchanan Manufacturing Corporation; January, breakfast detail; February through March, supper detail."

Typed below this it says: "Twenty-four of the Premars in this commune have work assignments for the next thirteen weeks. Premars on work assignments are not required to perform kitchen duties, which will be handled by Premars during their alternate thirteen-week study programs. Both work and study assignments will be discussed in detail with all Premars during the next few days. Tonight, after dinner, all Premars will meet in the dayroom, *naked*. In each room you will find your own Turkish-towel bathrobe. If your room is in either O'Day House or Blanc House, you must wear this robe to the meeting. If your room assignment is in this building, Gattman House, you can arrive at the meeting without your bathrobe. The communal bath, for all Premars, is in the basement of Blanc House. This bath is Japanese-style. You must wash and hose yourself thoroughly before sitting in the tubs. Premars who do not live in Blanc House must wear their bathrobes going and coming from the baths. Questions will be answered at our first Human Values get-together this evening."

I ate dinner (spaghetti and meat balls) with three other kids, who were talking hilariously about this nuttiness of being naked together. Afterward I sneaked back to the second floor of the O'Day House, just two houses away from the dayroom. Joseph McDonald, thank God, still wasn't in Room 10. My room! *But there was no damned privacy!* Two beds, two desks, two dressers. Down the hall there were three other rooms just like it, and a bathroom with three hoppers with doors on them, three sinks, three washstands, and three urinals. I guess if a girl wanted to watch a guy take a piss she could, but girls still could pull down their pants and sit without being watched. In the front part of the two bedroom floors as you come up the stairs, there's a sitting room with a TV and a few chairs, and a bulletin board with the rules of the house.

1. This sitting room is for television watching. The four couples on this floor may decide by vote, however, to use it as a reading and talking room, and regulate television hours to suit their needs.
2. Housekeeping on each floor is the responsibility of the people living there.
3. Rooms will be inspected by Compars once a week; each resident is responsible for keeping his area reasonably neat.
4. Drinking is neither encouraged nor discouraged. Smoking grass (dope, pot), until the laws are changed, is forbidden. The existence of National Premar Communes with our unmarried roommate system is precarious enough. We ask that you don't jeopardize this unique educational opportunity.

I managed to get out of my clothes and into the bathrobe just as a guy walks into the room and introduces himself as Joe McDonald. I actually felt myself blushing! I just couldn't look straight at him, so I didn't discover until later on that he really looks like a mouse.

"Hi," I said as I was leaving. "See you later. We're supposed to be in the dayroom at seven-thirty—naked! I'm on my way." As I walked into the dayroom in the tenement house next door, clutching my bathrobe around me, wondering what in hell Joe McDonald and I would talk about later, I saw some of the kids had arrived already and were sitting naked on their bathrobes. It wasn't easy, but I let mine slide off and plopped down on it. Soon there were forty-eight of us, all looking silly as hell sitting on the floor leaning on pillows. Watching us arrive were our communal parents, Bren Gattman, Ellen O'Day, and Merle Blanc, naked as jaybirds, too. We were all ready to swoop the first loop on the Premar roller coaster.

Bren was lounging on a little platform that separated the dayroom from the dining room behind it. Ellen and Merle sat on either side of him using pillows and the platform for a back rest. There were a couple of hundred pillows flung around the room. There were no chairs. The way the girls were squirming and clasping their knees together, I knew most of them (including myself) were as uneasy as hell. No matter how you held your legs, some guy could see all the way up between them. The only solution was to stare back at them, or glue your eyes on their penises. It was funny, really. A lot of guys had little erections when they dared to look, and you could tell that most of them were just as jittery as the girls were.

I decided to concentrate on Bren's penis, which is circumcised and kind of thick. At least his seemed more remote than the ones belonging to guys sitting buttock-to-buttock with me. Anyway, it wasn't long before most of us tuned in to Bren's words and were less conscious of our nakedness. In case whoever reads this thinks I'm a genius and remembered everything Bren said, you're wrong. Bren had a tape going, and I copied it all down later to give to Ma. She'll be shocked out of her britches—but she'll love it!

"Welcome to your first night at Premar." Bren grinned at us. "You're the best-looking collection of guys and girls I've ever seen. And thanks to those who had their first crack at the supper detail, the spaghetti and meatballs were pretty fair. We've got a lot of things to cover tonight. You have your room assignments, and most of you've met the party you'll room with the first twenty-six weeks. Tomorrow, Thursday, and Friday we'll go over in detail with you either your work program or your study program. Those of you who are going to try for an A.B. or B.S. degree should be able to make it based on a more or less continuous thirteen weeks study, thirteen weeks work—in about four years. Those who are taking strictly advanced vocational training, whether secretarial, drafting, data processing—you name it—will have completed your courses in less time, but we hope you'll continue to live here for the full four-year period.

"We want to generate as much thinking freedom as possible, and have plans eventually for some study in foreign schools for those who qualify. In any event, we hope that somewhere during the four years we, or Compars who will succeed us, can manage this commune well enough to save enough money to take you all on a tour of the major European countries.

"We have no fixed road map of where we're going. Our function is to run the commune and a continuous seminar in human values in which we expect to learn as much or more than you do. In addition to learning together, we are friends to lean on—the kind of friends who will listen to you, whatever your problems may be. We will not sit in judgment on you.

"First, I want to tell you where you are, and why we are all here together naked. These three-story tenement houses have been named after us, for convenience. There's one more across the street which we hope we can buy eventually, which we'll call Daemon House—if we can ever locate our friend, Rais. He's the missing Compar. We'll tell you more about him later.

"The interiors of these old houses have been rebuilt on a crash program. Thanks to about ten of you, who have been here since July, working with the regular contractors, we've got them livable. But there still is a hell of a lot of work to be done. We want to repaint them and connect them together, if we can convince the fire department. Build sun decks on the roofs and put window boxes in front of all the windows. But you can't use them to grow grass. Pot's out!" Everyone roared with laughter. "We want to give this neighborhood a new lease on life. Make it look as if the people who live here really care about their environment. But Premar isn't a free ride; whatever we do is going to be done on money you generate.

"Most of you, who don't live in Boston, should know that your home for the next four years is located in a very conservative, dirt-poor, ethnic neighborhood, predominantly Irish, with a few Poles and Middle European first- and second-generation people, plus a spillover of black people from Roxbury, who are not welcome but have no other place to go.

"If you have counted the blacks sitting around you, you will discover there are six black girls and six black guys in this commune. In most colleges and universities the blacks and whites live in separate enclaves and go through their undergraduate experience without knowing people of the other race, except as strangers they see in class or on the street. Premar is different. Every one of you, black or white, is eventually going to room, not only with someone of the opposite sex, but with at least one human being of the other color. And we hope you will experience intimate physical love together. When you get to know a black or white intimately, you're going to find we all have one thing in common. We all need to love. Not be loved, but to love. And you'll discover that's what Premar is mostly about.

"Black or white—the people who live in this area of Dorchester are what sociologists call low-income. Many have no income; many families are on welfare. These families, whether their income is low or about average, will be pretty much the same kind of families many of you were raised in. Our neighbors in Topham's Corner are eventually going to be our friends, but that isn't going to happen easily. One thing these people don't do in their homes is walk around naked. Being naked together, for most Americans, is generally associated with having sex, and having sex for your fathers and mothers and your next-door neighbors, here in Dorchester, is something they're not supposed to do until they are married, and then they do it, as a rule, with the lights out, and quickly.

"I'm making a point of this because if our neighbors here could see us now they'd be shocked out of their skins. In fact, Ellen O'Day, whom you've all met, is probably almost as embarrassed at being naked in this group as any of you. Ellen, you're blushing! She is the daughter of Dancer O'Day, one of the city councilors in Boston. Dancer thinks all young people should act *his* age. When he discovers what is really happening at the National Premar Communes, his first reaction may be to summon all the paddy wagons in the area and, with sirens screaming, lug us all off to jail. He's one of many problems we have to keep in mind.

"While I know some of you are a little queasy at being naked for the first time in the presence of the other sex with the lights on, we have good reason for imposing this on you. We're going to make you openly, joyously aware of your wondrous body, and of the amazing and wondrous bodies of your friends of both sexes at Premar. And in the first few weeks of the Human-Values seminar we're going to refocus sex and human loving for you in such a different perspective you'll soon wonder why any people are afraid of discovering each other as complete naked human beings. And when I say 'naked,' I mean stripped bare, literally and figuratively, because we'll also be teaching you to expose your innermost thoughts to one another.

"This is going to raise a problem for us and you. Because gradually you are going to discover that you are strangers in a strange land, and unlike Michael Valentine, in Robert Heinlein's novel, you won't have been raised on another planet, and you won't be able to hide at the bottom of the swimming pool when the going gets rough. From my point of view, the worst thing that can happen to you is that you'll begin to think that people who aren't having this kind of experience are simpletons and fools. I am going to tell you this again and again: If that attitude develops toward the people who live in this neighborhood, people who may be prejudiced and completely pig-headed, but are only trying to survive in this jungle, then we will have lost the first battle, and maybe more.

"So we are asking you to be careful. The only nudity permitted in the National Premar Communes is inside these houses, where we hope it becomes so natural you men may never have to buy a *Playboy* or *Penthouse* or *Oui* magazine again, and guys like Burt Reynolds, who pose naked for *Cosmopolitan,* will go out of business because every male here is just as well endowed, as the girls can see for themselves when your hands aren't covering your penises and testicles."

While Bren was talking, I realized what was happening: Most of us were being hypnotized. Bren has a way of talking to a group of people as if the group doesn't exist, and he personally is talking to you, and he makes you feel warm and loved. No kidding. I asked a couple of other girls, and they felt the same way. Every girl in the commune is in love with him. Bren told us that in the coming weeks we would meet in the dayroom every night for an hour—mostly with our clothes on—and we would begin the process of discovering every aspect of ourselves, including our sexual selves, inside out. But tonight we had some further preliminary business. So that we could anticipate the future, Ellen and Merle would read the names of our present roommates as well as our future roommates, and as our names were called, four different times, we would stand up, turn around, and show ourselves. Before we finished, we would know each other by face, body, and—if we weren't too spellbound—by name.

"The plan, which we can change if it doesn't work," Bren explained, "is that each twenty-six weeks, for the next two years, you will live exclusively with one member of the other sex who has been chosen for you by the National Premar Consortium Selection Program. The plan is that within a period of two years you will have lived intimately and privately with four different members of the other sex, and at least one person of the other race. Since we don't presume that you will jump into bed with each other for at least a week or two, we won't go into contraceptive methods tonight.

"Each of you will be given a thorough physical examination in the next week. We plan to keep you healthy and, hopefully, happy. The important thing to understand in this premarital experience is that being in love with one person will happen to you, not once, but three or four times, at least. That kind of being in love implies responsibility in a number of ways. One responsibility that I'll tell you about right now is that there will be no babies at Premar. What is more, we don't believe in abortion as a birth-control method. We will teach you how to make love joyously, occasionally on the pill, occasionally with an intrauterine device, occasionally with a diaphragm. We aren't happy that the only secure methods of birth control are the female's responsibility, so we'll teach you some other fun things that depend on the male but can be relied on only at certain times in the month. If, despite all our teaching, somebody accidentally becomes pregnant, we will arrange a quick abortion. Or, if the couple wish to get married and leave Premar, that, of course, will be their choice. Mostly, we'll be mad as hell at you if you get pregnant, because it will mean you haven't been responsible to each other.

"Keep in mind," Bren told us, "that while we'll wager that before you leave Premar, you'll find someone you'll want to be legally married to—the kind of person who is not only fun and joyous with you in bed, but who reinforces you as a complete person, better than anyone else— keep in mind that our belief is that this will happen because you have expanded yourself and built a new foundation for *you,* as an educated person. Part of this learning experience will be achieved in the intimate involvements you will have had with more than just one human being. That's what Premar is all about. In your last two years, you may settle in with one person of your choice, but we hope that while you're here, you'll stay unmarried.

"Now, Ellen and Merle will help you say 'Hi' to your roommates, present and future."

By the time Ellen had called my name and I stood up and turned around, naked, and every one else had done the same, I wasn't trembling anymore. It was even kind of funny. In less than an hour I was introduced to four boys who, if I didn't chicken out, would probably make love to me. First, Joe McDonald. I finally took a good look at him. He's awful skinny, kind of frightened-looking, nice blue eyes, a few pimples on his face and behind. I knew his type. Tongue-tied with girls. He probably hasn't even talked with a girl for more than a minute in his whole life. In April, I get Mohamed Hassan. He's nearly six feet, black-black, with wiry bushy hair and an enormous black penis. He looked coolly at me as if he'd just as soon swallow me in one gulp. Next year, Chuck Ventrano, kind of oily-looking. He stared at me from head to foot, as if he already owned me. Finally, Bill Cusik, obviously Polish, like me, blond and beefy-looking, but with a real nice crinkly smile. I'd have preferred to room with Bill first, but to tell the truth, a week ago if any one of them had asked me for a date in Detroit, I'd have turned them all down.

Now it doesn't matter, because I'm falling in love with Ellen O'Day. If you read my journal, Ellen, don't get worried. I only mean that after I listened to you on those tapes in the dayroom, I wanted to hug you. A lot of the other girls feel the same way. I don't know about Merle Blanc—yet. But if I had an older sister, I'd have loved her to be like you.

Ellen O'Day. Prelude to Premar. May. From tapes transcribed by Katherine Flaherty.

The tape recorder on my lap has patiently wound through half of its sixty-minute reel. Staring at it, hypnotized by its implacable, whirling disinterest, I'm sitting here in this rocker like a half-wit groping for words. God knows I have no lack of them. But where to begin?

With Bren? Have I really lived twenty-four years before yesterday? Now, in less than twenty-four hours, the twenty-four years at last seem to have some kind of purpose. Or am I daydreaming? What's happening to me?

A few years ago, when student rebellions and protests were a way of life, Bren was a senior at B.U.—Boston

University—and I was a sophomore. We were studying in the same few acres of classrooms. But up until two weeks ago I've known Bren only like the celebrity you've seen on television; a one-way rapport with a shadow that may leave you feeling more lonely than if it never existed.

Can you be in love with someone you scarcely know? I guess the answer is in how you define love. Bren was me, Ellen, the way I thought I might have been if I'd been a male and had a sound heart. How could Bren Gattman— alive, challenging, rebellious, unaware of death—have any sympathy or involvement with a girl from South Boston? A girl who many a night had taken him to bed with her, in her mind only, not for sex, but as a friend to snuggle with and talk with. Not for sex, because I never expected to marry—or even, unmarried, have a man penetrate me. There were too many females in the world for a man to choose the dubious pleasure of a climax with a sexually hungry one whose heart might give out at the moment of ecstasy. Could a man tell the police his girlfriend died fucking, though not for pleasure? I was a masochist then, and maybe I am now. I wanted to die—fast and clean—to put an end to that plague. The "when-will-it-happen" ques- tion forever flitting through my brain.

But even if it had been physically possible for me to join with my generation by becoming an activist, I'm not at all sure I would have dared to challenge my father's world. Even now, I know I wouldn't be here if Bren hadn't carried me into this old tenement.

I've consoled myself that someday I'd dare to tell peo- ple like Bren and Rais Daemon that some of the silent majority believed in their activism. Someday I'd confront my father and let him know how I felt, too. Unlike many of us, Bren and Rais weren't just sitting and moaning about the state of the world. Operating behind the scenes, in de-facto control of the university's radio station and newspaper, actively in the front lines of the sit-ins and marching with the protesters, they had joined with hun- dreds of others like them, not for revolution, but for a long-overdue reevaluation of man and his purpose and meanings here on earth. The smart-ass establishment could laugh at the idealists who proposed a greening of Amer- ica, and tell them it would never happen—but seething un- derneath, unrecognized by most of the politicians, there were lots of Ellen O'Days. And one day we'd get the nerve to act, and then they'd hear us loud and clear!

If my father had given it any thought, Bren—six-foot-three, with a lithe muscular body—would have been an ideal mate for his only daughter. Especially if Bren had proven his apparent masculinity with some interest in the Red Sox or the Bruins. Fortunately, my father confined most of his reading to the Boston newspapers. "Kid news-papers, run by college commies," didn't interest him. It was just as well. In editorials in the university newspaper, Bren had written that structured athletics engineered by the rich for the masses were modern versions of the Ro-man circuses, and proved that today's mass man was just as easily conned by trumped-up excitement and pseudo-mayhem as his ancestors had been. And my father would have found it just as heretical that anybody like Bren, with his hair growing "like some fruit cake," should stand at least four inches taller than Dancer, who was a Boston po-lice captain at the time, no less, and kept his graying World War II cranium in close-clipped military readiness.

Even today, if Dancer, whose gray hair is now fashion-ably longer, knows he has an audience or is in front of a TV camera during a City Council meeting, he'll slip into one of his hair tirades. Eventually this leads him into problems of law and order. "I brought my kids up know-ing who's a male and who's a female just by looking at them," he said once. "If my two sons at the University of Massachusetts ever came home with hair on their shoul-ders, I'd kick their asses from here to Dublin." Then Dancer smirked at the ladies who, even if they were un-seen, he was sure were cheeing him.

"The whole trouble," Dancer liked to explain to his middle-aged constituents, who believe his every word, "is that these kids were brought up on that Dr. Spock crap. Too much permissiveness. No discipline. No one to make them go to Sunday school and learn the Good Book like you and I had to. They were never taught to respect their elders. So we've reaped the whirlwind. Look at them on Boston Common, those half-witted anarchists, marihuana smokers, and junkies with no damned morals. Run them out of Boston—that's my way! Make it yours!"

"That's my way! Make it yours!" My father's words be-came a campaign slogan.

He startled ward politicians by daring to challenge the

local polls, and he ran for city councilor from our district. Even before his election with an amazing plurality, Dancer O'Day was being heralded by his followers as a potential future mayor, and by his detractors as the Irish Puritan with a Nazi mentality, the man who would really restore law and order to the city of the pilgrims even if he did it over the dead bodies of Negroes, Jews, Puerto Ricans, and much of the younger generation.

Although I mostly don't agree with my father, I've never really dared to challenge him. A female in the family defending the radicals at Boston University wouldn't have done much good anyway. Dancer O'Day was convinced that women, and this included his daughter, existed for the four K's—Küche, Kirche, Kunte and Kinder. Besides, I wasn't too sure how far on a left limb I could comfortably sit. Well, it didn't matter. I was having enough difficulty trying to persuade my parents of my right to drop dead if I wanted to.

Although my mother seemed to understand, I suppose my daily subway round trip between Topham's Corner and Boston is a tribulation to both of them. In the first-floor flat of the tenement house my father bought many years ago when he was a rookie policeman, the subject of Ellen's insane pursuit of education is often the subject of table conversation.

A few weeks ago was typical. Daddy kissed me on the cheek and plopped in front of the ravioli that Gina was serving. Then he said, "Ellen, for Christ's sake, you look as pale as a ghost. When are you going to stop this nonsense? When you got your B.A. degree, I thought you agreed enough was enough."

Mother listened silently. When Dancer embarked on one of his harangues, even though you had heard it all before, there was no sense interrupting.

"Your mother never went to college. I never went to college. I'm not against education for women. But these career females with their never-ending yak-yak about equality would scare any normal male half to death. I'm damned sure they're the kind that's responsible for all the faggots running around. Who wants to live with a woman who's trying to grow balls? Jesus, I read an article in one of these women's magazines your mother subscribes to that predicts in thirty years babies will be born without the female getting pregnant. Instead of lugging the baby around inside them for nine months, they'll be able to watch the kid grow in a fishbowl."

Daddy belched and attributed it to nervous indigestion caused by his anxiety for the future. "What good will a master's degree in city planning do you, Ellen? This city is planned all right—half-assedly by politicians with their fingers in the till. Why waste your time? The long-hair dreamers will never be able to eliminate graft.

"Why did you study Italian for three years? So you could understand your half-assed relatives who never bothered to learn English? So you can listen to Italian opera? Big deal! Will opera support you? If you have a heart operation, and you get married, will your husband listen to opera? All the ginzos with any sense play baseball. Don't let Gina's old lady try to convince you that she was an opera star. Your grandmother doesn't know Turdi, or whatever his name was, from a hole in the ground!"

"The name is Verdi!" Gina came to life when her family was being attacked. "You never heard of an Irishman who wrote an opera. All they sing is "Danny Boy," and then only when they're soused. My mother knows all about opera. When Maria was a girl, she was with La Scala."

"Scrubbing the stairs," Daddy snorted. "Anyway, all I'm asking Ellen is a simple question. Why, with a bum heart, are you bothering your head about the urban mess? We've got the Boston Redevelopment Authority for that crap. Give them a chance and they'll screw the city up good. Urban planners are a lot of airy-fairy intellectuals who don't understand real people at all. If you must keep studying, why not get into something practical, like computers?"

"What Ellen studies is none of your business, Dancer." My mother rarely called my father by his political name. "Why don't you let Ellen alone? She's earned the money to put herself through school. Instead of complaining, you should be proud of her."

Her questioning his pride in his daughter aggravated Daddy. As I slipped away to my room to study, his voice boomed after me. "If Ellen had asked me, I'd have spent every dime I had in the world on her, for education or an operation."

Daddy can't understand why I won't have a heart operation, a commissurotomy. He knew it was a risk. But if it were him, well, goddamnit all, he'd rather take a gamble than live a half-ass life balancing on a high wire. "I talked with Dr. Haynim yesterday," he told Gina. "He says Ellen is crazy to wait any longer. He says that from now on she'll gradually get worse. The opening through her mitral valve is only half the size it should be. Haynim says that every day the operation is getting safer, there's practically no risk."

Lying on my bed listening to him, I reflected that I was an especial thorn in the flesh to an Irishman who had never known a sick day in his life. How could I tell him that I was afraid—that I didn't want to die on an operating table. I knew quite a bit about the operation—the broken ribs, the incision that would run under my breast, down under my arm, and up my back, while my heart was kept pumping by a machine. The doctors would patch up my valve so it would work better for a few more years. But there was no guarantee of how long. The whole thing seemed hopeless and chancy.

Daddy was back on the subject of education. "Really, Gina, all they do in college is teach the kids to share the wealth—put everyone on welfare, give the niggers all the jobs." While the oracle was speaking, my mother didn't dare walk away. "When you and I were kids, only rich boys, and damned few girls, went to college. Even the dean at Harvard admitted the other day that there's too many kids going to college. Instead of studying practical things, or how to make a living, most of the kids are listening to crackpot professors who tell them about the day when the money will fall out of money trees.

"We had a name for daydreamers like that when I was in the army. Goof-offs. Fuck-ups. Look at Ellen. If she ever gets a master's degree, do you think she'll earn one cent more than if she had just continued to work for that law firm? Last summer she was making one hundred and seventy dollars a week, and she gave that up. George Cosgrove told me she was the best secretary he ever hired." I could imagine the look of disgust on my father's face.

"One hundred and seventy dollars a week—that's damned near as much as a policeman makes. Christ! With a family to support I don't even make twice as much. No wonder there's so many crooks. A cop is a sucker not to take a little graft if it comes his way. It was a damned sight easier to make a living when I was on the force.

Now I have to watch my step. But there's plenty of green stuff floating around. . . ."

Of course, Daddy was and is worried about my plans for the future. In his way, he loves me. But I'm a problem. Here I am, nearly twenty-five. When I look at myself in the mirror, what do I see? A girl with tilted brown eyes, high cheekbones, and long legs. I see firm breasts, not too small, on a washboard chest. Well, no one can say that I'm beautiful, but I suppose that if I had led a normal life, some man would have chosen me by now. Several have made the preliminary overtures, but when friendship moved toward intimacy, I rejected them, because I knew that eventually I would have had to tell them the truth, and that would have scared them off. A sexual partner who gasps for breath and who might suddenly die in your arms wouldn't be much fun. I had heard it described as death in the saddle, but that applied to men.

A few years ago I remember Gina telling my father she thought I was waiting to die. She wasn't far wrong. "You, with your good looks and good health, you wouldn't understand that," Mother told him.

"My God! You're crazy! When father was watching television or reading the sports page, he only half-listened to Gina. "How come you know so much of what goes on in Ellen's head?"

I heard my mother sob. "Ellen knows we love her. We did our best. Today most people don't get rheumatic fever. They've got better medicines." Gina's voice trembled. "The trouble with Ellen is that she needs a man. She'd want to live if someone loved her. But no one loves her." Gina couldn't restrain her tears. "And no one loves me."

"For God's sake, Gina, don't give me that crap again. . . . I love you, but I can't help it if I'm not as active as I used to be."

"You're not fooling me," Gina said bitterly. "You're getting it, but not much with me. Probably with that bitch Martha Casey. You don't have to look so innocent. *I know*. My brother told me. Ever since Bill Casey was shot last year by those hoodlums, Martha has been dishing it out. Lennie says she won't be satisfied until she's screwed the whole police force."

"Holy Mother of God!" My father's snort sounded like a wounded bull. "'I haven't seen Martha Casey since last fall. You know what was happening then.

We'd been living on the sidewalks of Boston University. Martha's apartment is only a few blocks away. She invited Timmy O'Hara and me over for a couple of beers, that's all. I wonder what happened to that rabble-rouser Jew—Bren Gattman."

My father slapped the kitchen table. "Jesus. Worse than him was his buddy! I wonder what that refugee from an African jungle, Rais Daemon, is doing now that he's out on parole. It doesn't pay to arrest anyone anymore. They all get out on parole, especially jigs." He was silent a moment. Then, evidently hoping to divert my mother from the subject of Martha Casey, he told a story I had often heard before. "Gina, I swear, that night there were a couple of thousand kids milling around there, blocking traffic and cheering. A bunch of them were occupying the administration offices. They were spitting at us, throwing bricks, calling us pigs. Most of them looked like flophouse bums. They were being egged on by that coon, Rais Daemon, and that Gattman character. Then the jigs started calling us the worst thing of all."

Daddy's voice was hoarse. "Good people like us scarcely know what such words mean. 'Motherfuckers! Motherfuckers!' they yelled. Then all hell broke loose. I was praying that Ellen wasn't around to hear such blasphemy. Motherfucker!"

My father sighed. "Would any real man stand for that? What did they expect? Jamie started clubbing the black troublemaker, but the bastard was so big Jamie didn't have a chance. Before he knew what was happening, Daemon had snatched the billy club right out of his hand and was beating Jaimie with it, and before we got the cuffs on him he even took a few swipes at me. Now, I ask you, Gina, for God's sake, how could I have been whoring around when my ass was nearly broken? Stop crying. I'm going to have a talk with Lennie. Your brother's got a goddamned Sicilian imagination. That's his trouble."

Poor Mother. She had snapshots of Gina Marcello taken in the village in Italy where she was born. The wide-apart brown eyes are all that remain of the young girl who once weighed one hundred and eighteen pounds. The tiny Italian girl Danny O'Day rushed back to Italy to marry after World War II now has a midriff that sticks out farther than her breasts used to. The new Gina slowly discovered that while her husband might enjoy her high-calorie cooking, and grew a little paunch himself, he likes his females stringy and lean.

But the tears flooding my eyes right now aren't for the possible betrayal of my mother. They're because I feel guilty and scared. My God—what if the politicians who hate my father could see Dancer's daughter sitting here in Bren's bed, damned near naked and talking her heart out into his tape recorder?

What if they or Daddy knew? Last night I telephoned my mother and told her I wasn't coming home. Fortunately, Daddy wasn't there. "I'm going to stay with Marie Timilty for the weekend. She has her own apartment," I told the doubting Gina.

"Marie's roommate has gone home for the weekend. I'll be home by Sunday night. Don't worry." I kept saying it over and over again. "I'm all right, Mother, I feel fine." When I put the phone back I wondered what madness had overcome me. But I knew! It was a Bren infection, a disease probably more dangerous than my rheumatic heart. And it hadn't been my fluttery heart that had kept me from daring to live. It was simply that I didn't have the courage of that first mariner, wondering whether he was actually sailing over the edge of the ocean, but trying it anyway.

Rais Daemon. Prelude to Premar. February. From the essay "Walk Before God," recorded in Walpole State Prison and transcribed by Samantha Brown.

I know the white judge was wrestling with his own devils. During the three-day trial he stared at me so hard that I felt he was trying to crawl inside my brain. Maybe he was wondering how the world looked through black eyes. Maybe his cold blue eyes were simply mirrors with no mind; only congealed bone behind them.

I needed time to get my head together. Three months in the pokey for slugging a policeman with his own nightstick seemed sufficient punishment to fit the crime. After all, that Irish cop with a Nazi haircut, James Duffy, had whacked me first, before I grabbed it out of his hand. And I didn't hit him on the head. I just beat his fat ass so he couldn't sit on it for a couple of weeks.

The judge's eyes were opaque. His sorrowful stare seemed unreal. "Rais Daemon," he said, "I've studied your records at Boston University. You are a St. Noirean by birth. Even though you have applied for United States citizenship, during your undergraduate years you have been involved with every subversive, left-wing organization in the Commonwealth of Massachusetts. Because of the conflicting beliefs you have espoused in this courtroom, you have finally hanged yourself on the horns of your own untenable political position. You have tried to characterize yourself as a militant humanist—something that seems a contradiction in terms. In attempting to subvert this courtroom for your own political purposes, you have alienated even your own friends, the factions responsible for the rioting at the university. And you have been found guilty, as charged, by a jury of your peers.

"May I suggest in sentencing you to ten months in the state penitentiary, that you use the time to search your soul. You have great potential as a human being, but perhaps you need to discover whether you love men more than you hate human stupidity."

It was seven months more than I needed. Judge Hugo Overbee missed the point. When those poor silly grunting pigs with their soft brains encased in white helmets drove their cruiser in front of the administration building and ran up the steps, pink-eyed, blustering, yelling at us to go home, I couldn't help laughing. Before he knew what was happening, I had picked up the one who was bleating the loudest, Dancer O'Day, an Irish cop, now a city councilor, probably because I made him famous. Holding him up by his armpits, I shook him a little and grinned into his beady eyes. "Cool it, you motherfucker! No one here is mad at you. We all love you. If you just wait a minute, we'll feed you some swill." That's when his buddy started belting me. What made the scene altogether too sad was both of them were in a state of panic. Not so different from the black man who might have embraced them as brothers if they'd let him.

Not that I pretend to be Jesus. But as I mentioned on the witness stand, had this O'Day character been nice, the pig might have ended up with a kiss on his snout instead of a sore ass. I should have pulled down his trousers and spanked his lily-white buttocks for him.

Prison has one advantage. It's giving me a sabbatical from action. Like a lot of my people, I've been too caught up in the heat of battle. We need a cool time to rethink revolution. What must emerge is evolution. Why, for example, should we have African studies and African history just for the blacks? Now that we've got some of the historical truths out into the light of day, let all men, white and black, demand that the entire history of man be rewritten. Tell it like it really was! History as the painful story of man using his brain to slowly sort his reflexes and emotions into a rational pattern of social behavior. History as the story of man's slow triumph over his self-centered ego. Man slowly becoming aware that his need for self-enhancement is a perversion of his need to give love.

Tell all men the truth. Man was enslaving man long before the white man carried the whole process to a point of no return and enslaved twenty million blacks. The black African slave wasn't the victim of the white man, he was a historical accident occurring during the delayed development of man's brain. Given a few more years of African "freedom," such as it was in those days, and the African kings would have enslaved their own people. Let's look at the truth about man evolving and write a history of man that lays it on the line. A history that doesn't extol the kings, the heroes, the particular culture, the religion, or the politics of any man. A history that reveals the life of man on this planet, not as a cyclical repetition, but a forward motion, however slight that reveals man—black, white, yellow—groping out of the jungle toward a united man. Man *is* a superior animal. Like other domesticated animals, he *can be trained* to be loving—or vicious. Man is the product of his environment. For the first time in history man has it in his grasp to evolve a new environment for all men.

In the process of getting a degree from B.U. I had read damned near everything else, but I had always made it a point to skip the white man's Bible. Anyway, between the ages of five and twenty, I had sopped up most of it by osmosis. In St. Noir going to the white man's Sunday school gives the black kids something to do in the morning. My family and their forebears had been saved—saved?—by the Protestant missionaries. In later years, when the British relaxed their hate-the-Pope attitude, the Catholics made some inroads, but most of my people still give lip service to a mixture of voodoo and Methodistism.

While we haven't held out for a black Jesus, at least we've been spared too much emphasis on his milk-white mother. Even so, our teachers never bothered to tell us much about the Jews, who were responsible for the whole one-God business. Our Sunday-school teachers, white and black, knew the first chapters of Genesis, but they skipped over the whole long history of fucking that presumably brought the world into existence. Too febrile for young imaginations, and maybe productive of too many other questions best left unanswered.

So here I am at Walpole Prison. Last night before the ten-o'clock lights-out, I started with Genesis, and got as far as Chapter 17. I couldn't go to sleep, thinking about that Jewish cat who had written all this genealogical business. Obviously, the begat and begot stories had been cooked up post-facto, several hundred or more years after the event. The historian carving his daydreams of fact and fiction on clay tablets was trying to give a potpourri of Jewish tribes (and particularly the young bucks who probably couldn't have cared less) a sense of continuity, a sense of identity and belonging, just as we blacks have been doing by trying to prove that we have a cultural history that extends back to the beginning of man. It made me smile a little. Instead of telling history like it was, everybody, black or white, democrat or communist, is rewriting history to prove he is somebody. When all the suppressed history of the blacks has been rewritten, then we'll match our somebodies against anybody else's somebodies, and devil take the hindmost.

I suppose that's one way. The other got stuck in my brain. When Abraham was ninety-nine years old, the Lord appeared before him and said, "I am the Almighty God! *Walk before Me, and be thou perfect.*" Was that Jewish historian giving us a little bit of Jewish laughter and insight? To conceive of a ninety-nine-year-old man joyously fornicating for another sixty-five years until a whole nation came into existence goes to show that you have to read history with a sense of humor. But on a more subtle level, I think the old buzzard who wrote about Abraham might have been laughing in his beard. For a moment he forgot the sword-waving Jehovah and dared to think about a warm, laughing God. A God who was both created by man and created man. A God who could whisper in his ear and say, "We're in this together, baby. Don't always rely on me to take your hand. I get tired and confused, too. *You lead the way. Walk before me, and be perfect."*

So, I propose to all men, black and white, stop drinking the bitter tea of the black man's past. Lie on this prison bunk with me and think about man. Not where the black man is going . . . but where man himself is going! Creating an African history, an Afro-American history, seeking black separatism, black power, black religions, demanding reparations from the white man because of the cruel ways of his forebears, bolstering ourselves with the chant that black is beautiful—aren't these simply detours on the path to the inevitable? The day whose tiny glow is on the horizon right now, when finally the cry of men must be: "All men, black, white, yellow, are beautiful."

Black men can spend the next century bemoaning their inheritance. For the next hundred years we can relive the tragedy of the white man enslaving our people. Or we can take the wider perspective of the *new-man.* Man aware for the first time that the gods of the past were the necessary creation of man emerging from the jungle and trying to comprehend the mysteries of this planet. Man trying to plumb the universe that tolerates his existence but will never hand him the secret on a silver platter.

Walk before me, and be thou perfect! *Walk Before God!* Only now, ten thousand or more years removed from our jungle heritage, can we grasp the meaning of these words. Maybe even in this century the words will only be a whisper. But some of us can amplify the whisper into a cry of ecstasy. We, the blacks, the men who still have their roots in the earth, can, if we dare, lead all men into a new kind of world. The *Century of Soul!* The child emerging from the womb, whether black, white, or yellow, re-creates the story of man's struggle for survival. It's there for everyone to see. At first the child is completely self-oriented, autistic, hedonistic. *Without love he will remain that way all his life.* But give him warmth, tenderness affection, and security—give him these, and his psychological struggle for survival in what he thought was a jungle will slowly be replete by the deep joy and satisfaction he discovers in other-directedness and his love for people-involvement.

You are God! I am God! I Am Thou! The comprehension of this truth is beyond creatures still struggling in hostile environments. Their bodily needs force the psyche to the necessities of *Me* first.

Because the black man was enslaved for four hundred years, he has the possibility of providing the insights that come from an ancient oppression. What the Jews did for their people, the black man can do for all men. Can the black man dig into his soul, *Walk Before God*, and dare to understand that man waging wars, enslaving his fellow men, is not the white man, the black man, or the yellow man creating his own hell on earth, but is simply the child human being slowly discovering, as we close in on the twenty-first century, that *because* he is black, because he knows suffering, and has had to look inward, that deep within him lies the fulfilled man that finally can evolve from the child?

From the journal of Joseph McDonald, September, the first year of Premar.

I thumbed up here from Springfield in the middle of August. It wasn't my idea to arrive before the rest of the kids, but after discovering, to my amazement, that I had been accepted, I got this letter from Bren Gattman that asked me to come right away. "We've been studying your background and testing scores," he wrote, "and we're happy that you are going to be with us. Since you're an apprentice carpenter and have worked on home-building jobs with your father, we're pleased to tell you that you will be employed directly by National Premar Communes as a carpenter at one hundred dollars a week, net, for at least the first twenty-six weeks at Premar. If you come early, we can put you on the payroll immediately."

My father didn't say anything when I told him I was going to apply to Premar, but I could tell he was burning. We'd been working on a couple of roofing jobs together. He refused to even talk with me about the insanity of going to college, let alone living with some girl I didn't even know. He married Mom when he was thirty-two, twenty-four years ago. I'm sure that he's never touched another woman before or after. Funny, I have a feeling that Mom, who is ten years younger, took my side on this Premar idea. "Angus," I heard her tell him, "I want Joe to be happier than Maggie. Maybe it won't be so bad if they teach him how to make a woman happy. Look at Maggie. She left Ed and had to go to work, and now her baby is being brought up in a day-care center, and she's living in Greenwich Village with that Jew, and we both know he'll never divorce his wife to marry her. Our daughter is somebody's mistress."

Mom never talked to me directly about Maggie, who is my older sister. When she came home for Easter, she told Mom, right in front of me, she'd bet Mom never had an orgasm. As far as Maggie was concerned, Dad was a male tyrant, and not knowing any better, she had married a man just like him. It was good riddance when she and Ed decided they couldn't stand each other. She made up her mind to raise her own child and to have good sex for a change. "When you aren't married to them," she told Mom, "men are hell-bent to please you. Afterward you can forget it!"

Mom was shocked, especially because I was listening. "You'll find out, young lady," she told Maggie, "orgasms and fancy sex isn't what makes life."

It's hard to tell what makes a life between Mom and Dad. I never heard them talk much with each other except about the high costs of food or Dad's poor relatives in Nova Scotia, whom Mom doesn't like. Sometimes Dad talks on about how he is estimating a particular job. Margie told Mom that she lives her whole life vicariously by watching *Search for Tomorrow* and other soap operas on the tube. *Search for Tomorrow* goes on day after day, and all the women are unhappy with their husbands and having little love affairs that never get anywhere because most of them don't dare to really mess around, or if some woman does, she becomes pregnant by her over or gets caught in the act and then her husband kills the man and afterward is sorry as hell.

Anyway, I don't want to be a carpenter. It was Dad's idea that I follow in his footsteps. He isn't impressed with me going to college, even if he could afford to send me. Funny, though, I sometimes think I was the only guy in my class in high school who read books because he liked to. I was reading stories all the time. Especially science fiction. Guys like Robert Heinlein, Arthur Clarke, Isaac Asimov, Ray Bradbury, really get to me. I kind of thought I'd like to be a writer. But in this world you don't always do what you want to. Even though Dad thought I was stupid to go to college and work twenty-six weeks a year at one hundred dollars a week, when I could go to work with him immediately and get five dollars an hour, I decided to give Premar a whirl.

The idea of actually living with a girl, seeing her naked, making love to her (wow!), was something I couldn't stop daydreaming about. Especially since I've managed to live until nearly nineteen and have never really made out with a girl. The only live woman I've ever seen naked is Maggie, and that wasn't easy. In our house everyone is careful to lock the bathroom door. Mom is always either fully dressed, or if she's wearing a bathrobe, she has plenty of clothes on under it, you can bet! When Maggie lived home she used to flop around her room naked, looking at herself in the mirror, and sometimes she'd lie in front of it with her legs open, her head on a pillow, and play with herself. Trying to watch her through the hot-air vent in the ceiling of her room didn't give me the best view.

Well, damn, I did kiss Millie Walker twice in the school lockerroom, and once I got my hand on her tit. When I was kissing her she'd start to pant like she'd just run the half-mile, and the day I finally touched one of her boobs she was shocked. She didn't care what other girls might let me do, no boy was touching her tits until they were engaged. It's a screwed-up world. In magazines like *Penthouse* and *Oui* you can look at girls naked, practically inviting you to screw them, or pictures of guys touching them. And your tongue is hanging out, and your pants are stretched tight from your hard-on, but the real-life Millie Walkers don't put out. I'll bet those Pets and Bunnies don't put out much either. They just do it for the dough-wiggling in front of a camera like they couldn't wait another minute, when they're probably just like Millie. I wonder if girls really like to do it the way men do, just because they feel horny. Someday I'm going to ask a girl if she ever felt like me. And if she did, then why not do it with a guy and not make such a fuss? Then the guy wouldn't have to jerk himself off, and he'd probably feel better.

Millie wouldn't believe her eyes if she could see my roommate, Andrea Pillisuk. The first night after our session with the Compars, when I discovered that she was the first girl I would live with, I almost couldn't look at any of the rest of the girls on my schedule. There's a Kathy Flaherty, then next fall a tall black girl, Samantha Brown, and if I last (boy, I've just got to) my fourth roommate will be Lainey Franci, an Italian girl almost as skinny as me. She's really flat-chested, but she has a face like one of those madonnas you see in art books. Kathy makes up for her. I guess Kathy weighs about one hundred and sixty. She has great big boobs and a pretty big bum. All the guys were staring at Kathy's tits. She has brown eyes and about the prettiest face I've ever seen on a girl, which kind of makes up for the fact that she really is overweight. A couple of guys I was talking to wanted to room with her, but they didn't. "You could lose yourself between those tits," one of them said. And another just shook his head. "Kathy's too much of a good thing," he said.

I felt kind of bad for Kathy. After all, none of us really knew her. I think she decided to switch the order of her roommates and live with Mohammed Hassan first, just because he looks so mean.

But I can't worry about her right now. I've got Andy, and she's really put together just right. She has the kind of body you want to touch everywhere at once, and a face that isn't too pretty but gets to you because of the wide-eyed, open-mouth way she tells you straight from the shoulder what she's thinking.

"Look," she said when we got back to the room still wearing our bathrobes, "I don't mind rooming with a guy, but I can tell from just looking at you that I'm turning you on too quick."

That didn't require any great smarts. My damned ding-a-ling was pointing my bathrobe into a tent, and other than grabbing it and holding it down, there wasn't much I could do. It sure wasn't listening to my brain.

"You heard Merle and Ellen," Andy said. "A guy can cool himself off if he wants to. The Compars don't believe we should do any heavy lovemaking for a while."

I didn't know what to say. Despite appearances, I didn't want to jump into bed with Andy. I didn't even know her, and I sure didn't feel like telling her I wasn't sure I knew how. It was ten-thirty, and I suppose the thing to do was to turn off the lights and go to sleep. There was a television in the sitting room down the hall, but I didn't want to look at it alone. I watched Andy unpack. She was wearing her bathrobe. She found a small transistor radio and asked if I'd mind if she turned it on. Finally she pulled the covers down on her bed, took off her bathrobe, and put on a light shortie nightgown. Under the covers she looked at me with tears in her eyes. "It's silly, but I kind of miss my mother." She sighed. "But I guess she doesn't miss me much. Have you ever been away from home for long?"

"Summers I camped with the Boy Scouts."

"Then you're used to living different places. Just the same, you look kind of sad, too." Andy was staring right into my eyes. "On the other hand, maybe we'd both feel better if you got in bed with me and we talked. We could read that book *Self-Love* together. Bren expects that all of us will have finished it for tomorrow's H.V. meeting."

Andy slid over in her bed. Wondering if I was going to jump right out of my skin, or reach a climax without even being touched, I got in beside her. At least my full-size erection wasn't so visible under the covers. I lay on my back, kind of rigid, praying somehow I'd calm down before I shot my load all over the sheets.

Andy curled up beside me, and she was grinning. "You're awfully excited, aren't you?"

I nodded. "It'll go away."

"This book *Self-Love* is about masturbation."

"Yeah."

"Have you ever?"

I couldn't look at Andy. "Sure."

"So have I." She was quiet. "I suppose I could hold you."

I really wanted her to, but somehow I began to wonder how many guys Andy had made love with. She obviously knew a lot more about guys than I knew about girls. That did the trick. Ten hours ago, I didn't even know Andrea Pillisuk, and I was already jealous of her. My ding-a-ling got the message and quieted down, for the moment.

By eleven o'clock we had read to each other halfway through the book, and I told Andy I guessed I was learning more in this hour than I'd ever learned in my whole life. I guess she felt the same way, because when she read, she was really glued to the book. "This is really interesting," she said, her eyes reading ahead of her voice. "Listen to this, Joe: 'Why is the sex drive so strong? If the answer is pleasure, then why is it so pleasant? It is over in a split-second. Why, then, will men and women risk life, liberty, marriage, reputation, money, and limb for a single sexual encounter? It's not necessary to sustain life, as are food and water. Why, then, will men and women leave careers, jobs, hearth and home and family for a satisfactory sexual relationship?' "

I read Gordon's answer to her. "Man's basic drive is for unification, to be in one mind and body, to be one with the world, to be one with others, and to resolve the subject-object bifurcation that divides him from others since his birth. The drive for unification is also the mainspring of man's behavior, which is characterized by his search for happiness and ultimate reality.... What do sex, climbing a mountain, running a race, watching a football game, eating a good meal, having a few drinks before dinner, consummating a business deal, making money, getting high on alcohol or narcotics, painting a picture, playing golf or tennis, sneezing, robbing a bank, playing cards, sky-diving, all have in common—there is build-up of tension which is then lowered, relaxed, and discharged.... One thing is clear: *There is no thought at the climax.*"

"I think what he's saying"—Andy put the book down—"is that when you masturbate and when you finally reach a climax, for a moment maybe your brain turns off completely. It isn't possible to think. He believes that men and women spend most of their lives trying to achieve a kind of consciousness where they simply let go and completely forget their egos."

I couldn't help laughing. "I like it when David Gordon says, 'Man is not obsessed by gambling, or the wish to make money, but by the desire to live in the thoughtless, unified state as frequently as and as long as possible, which might be called living a state of orgasm.' I know one thing when I've played with myself, I kept hurrying because I felt so guilty—but I really wanted that second or two before coming to last forever."

Andy snuggled into the pillow, smiling at me sleepily. "'I didn't think I would, but I really like you, Joe. I never really talked with a boy before."

I put my face on the pillow next to hers, and of course in a flash was erect again. Her eyes were closed. "I've made love with a guy a few times," she whispered. "I never reached a climax. Then I read a book and discovered I could do it to myself pretty easily—no sweat at all."

I kissed her nose.

"Want me to do it to you, Joe?"

"Yeah."

"I never did it for a boy." Andrea pushed back the covers and looked at my big ding-a-ling. She grinned. "Close your eyes, and don't watch me."

I felt her fingers like feathers playing with my foreskin and pulling it gently over the top. "The boy I knew was circumcised. How come you're not circumcised?"

"My father thought only Jews got circumcised. He hates Jews."

"Am I doing all right?" Through her nightgown I could feel one of her breasts against my face. I knew I wasn't going to last long.

"I guess this is nicer than doing it alone." Andy's fingers, like a hundred feathers, moved faster, all over me. Why couldn't it last forever and ever? It couldn't. I let go with a wild yell, and opened my eyes to Andrea watching me, completely bemused, like a little girl holding an amazing toy.

"I never touched a girl before," I told her, "but I'll try, if you want."

She wiped me with a Kleenex. "Not tonight, Joe," She sighed. "Just turn out the light. You can put your hand between my legs and hold me in your arms."

Ellen O'Day. Prelude to Premar. May. From tapes transcribed by Katherine Flaherty.

I suppose I should stop indulging myself with the story of my life, but Bren and Merle have listened to my first tapes, and they've both encouraged me.

"Therapy for those *hors de combat,*" I told them.

"Not at all." Bren laughed. "You're learning to be a recording angel. Even if you never marry me, it's important that *you* know where your head is at, and can share your knowledge with the Premars."

"Where my heart is might be more realistic," I replied. "As for Premar—that sounds like a Tenhausen-Gattman daydream."

The first few weeks of my senior year at B.U., I slowly became aware something was missing. Bren had graduated. A new group of young men with new ideas and new issues had taken over. But compared to Bren and Rais they seemed less concerned. The marathon runners were passing on a flickering torch. Daydreams were giving place to individual survival in the economic jungle. The politicians had subtly managed to defuse the idealists by ushering in an era of economy and scarcity.

Even so, while I could transfer my allegiance to those who now sought a subtler revolution, I couldn't transfer my love. I heard rumors that Bren was doing graduate work in sociology, but our paths never crossed. I plodded along in the same dreary routine, determined to achieve the Eldorado of my diploma without knowing why I wanted it. It was like a middle-aged man who hangs onto a boring and uninteresting job, even though he hates and detests it because he senses he has nothing else left in the world going for him; the job has become himself.

Nearly two years passed, and when the image of Bren had pretty well faded, and even in my bedtime thoughts I could only partially reconstruct his face, then, last month (my God, was that only a few *weeks* ago?) I signed up for a seminar in urban planning and discovered to my amazement that Bren was not only involved in the course as a student but was acting as an assistant to Ronald Tavish, head of the department.

At first I maintained a calm distance. What held me back wasn't only the surprise of at last coming to grips with the reality of Bren Gattman; it was also my fascination that I was encountering a different, more mature man than I had supposed him to be. His Dutch-boy haircut had given way to a rough, radial cut, like a shaggy pioneer trail boss might have worn. It was obvious, too, that his involvement with Merle Blanc, a black girl, continued beyond the seminar. But even though I considered both him and Merle almost nauseatingly vocal, I recognized in Bren what I could only describe as a focused rebellion. With his cool certainty, he seemed finally to have harnessed the wild energies of his undergraduate years. Bren had the aura of a man who knew where he was going.

I suppose, from the beginning, I should have entered into some of the seminar discussions, but mostly I was a silent listener (and voyeur?). I suspected that if I challenged some of the ideas Bren was introducing, I would probably do so out of jealousy over his rapport with Merle. Their relationship had become a tantalizing, annoying mystery to me. I was aware that if Bren rounded the balls, Merle wouldn't hesitate to hurl them at Professor Tavish or anyone else who might disagree.

One of the girls in the seminar told me that Merle was Rais Daemon's girl, but Rais had disappeared. She'd bet a dollar that, now, Bren was sleeping with Merle. According to my informant, Bren and Merle were living in a run-down tenement house in the "riot zone," where the black population of Roxbury was overflowing into Dorchester. Rais, Merle, and Bren were said to have moved into this area because they had plans to use the house as a center for the radicalization of the lower-middle class. From such a base, they were certain a revitalized student movement could gain the necessary strength for "the blueing of America"—blue meaning working-class America. But Rais was arrested last fall for assaulting a police officer, and when he was released, three weeks ago, he went home to St. Noir.

Bren, my friend told me, had some new, mad approach to urban living that he called a Confamiliaum, but thus far no one was listening. Since Rais had disappeared, in any case, it was obvious that Bren and Merle were too busy screwing to worry about the fate of mankind.

I only half-listened to Miriam Horney's chatter about Rais, Bren, and Merle, but I was lower-middle-class enough to wonder what went on in the brains of a white man sleeping with a black girl. Strangely, I couldn't wonder what went on in the black girl's mind. Racism has subtleties that most of us have not yet explored, and I simply assumed that black girls were sexier than white girls.

I remembered Rais Daemon. How could I forget him? For weeks my father had talked about no one else. Dancer O'Day finally had had his moment of triumph when Rais was sentenced to ten months in jail. Rais Daemon, as I remembered him, was one of those intense, remote, intractable blacks who view whites from the other side of an unbridgeable chasm. I wondered if he was aware that Bren was sleeping with his woman.

I wondered, too, if Bren and Merle and Rais were so sexually loose that who slept with whom didn't matter. Whenever I thought logically about it, hit-and-run sex seemed the sanest way for anyone who might dare it with me. Any male who seduced Ellen O'Day should have as his password "No Commitment."

It really didn't seem as if I should ever experience the throes of intercourse, and the few times I had caressed myself to a climax were so shockingly violent, and yet so incomplete, that there was really no solution for me except to try to keep my mind away from erotic ideas. But restrained sex will find some outlet. Counterattacks whirled angrily in my mind as, day by day, in the seminar I slowly perceived the absurdities of Bren's proposal for a new urban life style based on some elements of the kibbutzim.

Last week I couldn't help myself. I finally attacked. I was aware that Bren had captured the attention of the class. Instead of just watching his maddening grin, which was always flitting about his lips when he looked in my direction, and making me feel mildly erotic, I was finally hearing his words.

"As most of you know," he said, "a couple of years ago Rais Daemon and I were in the middle of most of the student rebellions and protests at this university. We didn't accomplish miracles. Percentage-wise, even then there weren't many of us. The kids carrying the torch today represent even a smaller minority. It amuses me when the older generation consoles itself that the hard core of dissenters is not over one or two percent of the young people. Isn't that true of the whole damned world? Most people shuffle through life, refusing to become involved. The tiniest fraction of all the people have always led the rest, for better or worse. Trillions of others have simply lived and died without a trace." Bren shrugged. "As for myself, I have no illusions. . . . I am not seeking fame. I simply can't escape an inner commitment. To quote Antonio, 'How I found it or came by it, I know not.' All I know is that without people like me and Merle and Rais Daemon and maybe a dozen or so others on this campus, and maybe ten or twenty thousand others in the whole United States; without the continuity of men and women like us back through history, man would still be swinging from trees."

Suddenly I heard myself interrupting. "Old radicals don't die, they just fade away." and my heart was pounding furiously. "Maybe if it weren't for people like Bren Gattman, with their mad sense of mission, we'd all be happier just swinging from the trees."

I knew that professor Tavish and the class were staring at me, but it was too late to retreat. "We've all been listening to Mr. Gattman's daydreams for the past week," I said, trying to keep my voice level. "Maybe there is some substance in what he is driving at, but so far all I've managed to discover is that Mr. Gattman not only feels that he is an incarnation of Howard Roark or some other Ayn Rand character, but in addition he is obsessed with the idea that before we can improve the cities and revitalize them we've got to change the man who inhabits them. His scheme for revamping human nature is somewhat vague, but that's not all. I don't know his background, but I feel sure he doesn't know the first thing about the psychology of the vast majority of the poor fringe people in this country. Was he born in a tenement? Does he care how many people are still living in these ugly old rectangular boxes? Quite a few million, you can bet on that. Yet the Department of Housing rates them Class B housing. Rundown, but adequate. The white-collar bureaucrats who classify housing don't live in places like that. Does anyone care? The lethargic poor who live in these neighborhoods don't seem to mind. If they did, wouldn't they have joined a mass movement a long time ago to protest a government that manages to tax away a quarter of their meager incomes to build armaments and fly men to planets that have no life on them?

"I hear rumors that Mr. Gattman is living near Topham's Corner in a tenement house he owns. But does he really care about poor people, or is he just planning to exploit them? Is he going to try to use low-income people to accomplish some Utopian intellectual fantasy? Isn't he really dreaming of the kind of housing and fish-globe environment that rich people like to think they can herd poor people into while they carefully expand their own areas of privacy?"

I sounded a little like my father, but while I was shaking violently, I enjoyed playing the devil's advocate. Bren really did irritate me. What's more, I never did believe in the return of the Messiah, even a handsome Jewish one. "If we knew the truth," I said grandiloquently, "like a latter-day Portnoy, Bren Gattman is probably acting out some fantasy imposed on him by an Oedipus complex."

The class responded with a vast belly laugh. Was it amazed that someone had at last dared to puncture the Gattman balloon? Nobody knew they were witnessing the classic case of the female trying to destroy the only one she had ever loved.

Professor Tavish laughed as he suggested that perhaps Bren would like to supply his credentials as a rebel.

For the first time Bren was looking at me as if I really existed, and was still smiling. I had the odd feeling that a female challenging him had an aphrodisiac effect on him. "Miss O'Day—or if you don't mind, I'll call you Ellen—you're right. I live in, and own, a tenement house on Felton Street in North Dorchester. It's only a few blocks from your house. What's more, I am not unaware that your father is Dancer O'Day, one of the nine esteemed councilors in the city of Boston. As you probably know, I was involved in that historic confrontation last fall when Rais Daemon grabbed Sergeant James Duffy's billy club and whacked both your father and Duffy on the behind with it. Until, according to their stories in court, neither your father nor Duffy could sit down for a month.

"I'm also sure that everyone in this seminar knows how your father got elected to the Council. What were his campaign slogans? 'Be tough on junkies and hippies. Clear the Boston Common of bums. Stop the busing to the suburbs. Wipe out sex and pornography, and clamp down on the students and let them know what law and order means.' "

Bren ignored the tears in my eyes. "Dancer touched all bases. But what's more interesting is that since he's been councilor, I've never heard him express the least concern for all the rotting tenements around the core of Boston. Don't you think it's weird that he worries so much about trivia? Or inconsequential things such as whether the nude statue showing the partially aroused penis of a young man should be placed in Boston Common? After your father's shocked ballyhoo, it wasn't. Why is he so fascinated with the morals of the younger generation and the horror of birth control and abortion? How can he ignore the reality of the decaying environment of Dorchester and Topham's Corner?"

Bren paused and smiled at me as if I were the only person in the seminar. "Ellen, I don't dislike your old man. He's just a misdirected fighter, a throwback to the era of city bosses. He knows how to swim in their river of graft without testing the water. But some of us must learn the hard way. A few years ago I played the same game against the opposing team. I called the police pigs, I marched against the Establishment, I helped in the rioting, but I didn't accomplish much. So I have decided that there must be another way. It doesn't involve exterminating my father or yours. You might call it brainwashing."

Bren chuckled. "But I call it reconditioning—even better, reinventing—life styles and then selling the new models to the little guy who desperately needs them.

"For the record, since you have been hinting that I am the typical revolutionist—son of an affluent father—you're right! My father is an automobile dealer in New Hope, New York. He sells Fords and Mustangs. While he has never confided in me, I guess his income is seven to ten times that of a Boston city councilor. The way my father lives, even that's scarcely enough. On the other hand, I've never wanted to destroy him or to go to bed with my mother. Unlike your family, my mother and father have a too-much-of-things problem. They are accursed with their leisure. When making money ceased to be a problem, they didn't have any goals left. My father has his showrooms and maintenance departments running so smoothly they scarcely need his attention. The young Harvard Business School graduate he employs as vice-president is much happier when Abe is off on a trip. The trouble is that Abe and my mother have been everywhere—even to Israel three times. Abe is discovering that he doesn't want to travel anymore. He can't concentrate on anything except his diminishing potency. In the search for his vanished youth, he's been involved with the wives of various prominent citizens of New Hope. My mother told my sister, who, in case you are interested, is married to the millionaire Rocky Stone, that Abe can't get it up with her. But that doesn't seem to bother my mother. I would guess that she has various male friends who would be happy to take care of her."

Bren was ignoring the class now and speaking directly to me. "But I can see that you are shocked by such a blunt exposure of one's family. But don't let it throw you. Despite Kenneth Keniston, and his study of student radicals, I have no psychological scars. My family is typical of hundreds of thousands of others. The truth is that I am sorry for the Abe Gattman's and the Dancer O'Days. We finished off President Nixon, and next to disappear will be the Republican, corporate-controlled state. My only fear is that before some of us manage to create a sounder axis to resolve on, one way or the other these dying dinosaurs of the past, with a last whiplash of their tails, will exterminate us all."

Bren was right. I was shocked. As much as I suspected Daddy's sexual wanderings, I would certainly never have paraded that knowledge in front of strangers. While I didn't want to continue the argument, I was in too deep to back off. "You seem to suggest," I said, "that the average man and woman can unite in the same kind of challenge to authority as the students have been attempting. For example, I understand you have singled out an area like Topham's Corner, and suggested that the residents could restore it to a community square in the European sense of a gathering place with fountains and trees, with the intersecting throughways forbidden to automobiles. To accomplish this, you're implying it's too late to wait for normal legal and government processes. The citizens should simply rip down the neon signs, chop up the roadbeds, and form a cordon against the police. I doubt if you could convince ten residents of Topham's Corner to join you, but if you did, you still wouldn't get away with it. There's millions like my father, who is a Democrat and not a Republican. No matter which, they'll simply build bigger jails and concentration camps and put you out of business."

I had forgotten every warning I had ever been given about getting relaxed. Though I knew I would pay later, the gnawing feeling in my chest was gone, and momentarily my heart was beating evenly. "I'm not too sure that little people like my father aren't basically right," I continued. "The history of revolution proves that when the smoke clears, all that is finally accomplished is the substitution of one ruling clique for another. Man himself doesn't change. There'll always be the wolves and the lambs."

Bren seemed to be seeing into my head as he answered. The students had turned their chairs in a circle around us, each side silently waiting for their favorite contestant to deal the knockout blow. "Ellen," he said. Then he paused dramatically. "Since you think I have dragged in the subject of parents, I want you to know that in one respect you're right. I never could bring my own father around, but I think I could swing the Dancer O'Days of this world to my view. Maybe it's as simple as some of the 'haves' aligning with the 'have-nots.' " Bren's voice was caressingly hypnotic, almost akin to making love. It was a trick I knew he had used on noisy student crowds to quiet them. But the cool underemphasis of his words made them even more febrile. "Let's leave the immediate character of our families aside for the moment. In a sense, they, too, are victims. The dead hands of their fathers and grandfathers still reach out of the grave and dominate their lives with moralities and values that may have worked in a world of a few billion people, and a nation of a hundred million. But we live in the new dimension of a global society which is struggling to eventually keep six billion people alive, and provide them with food and adequate clothing and shelter. Right here in the United States, even with a low birth rate, in less than thirty years we'll have to provide living space for another hundred million people. In the process we'll discover that many of our past values are senseless. One thing is sure. Our generation shouldn't be fighting what we have so blithely termed the Establishment, only to become the New Establishment in our middle years. I may grow old physically, but I will have lost the battle if I ever grow so old mentally that I can't enjoy and abet my children's necessary rebellion—not only against me, but in the continuing, active battle against several centuries of the Industrial Revolution, not to mention the mess created by a laissez-faire philosophy. It may take all our lives and most of our children's lives to shake off the dead hands of the past. But we have to look forward, not behind. And that's how what I've been saying relates to this seminar on urban planning.

"Our problem is: How do we make some order out of the chaos we have inherited? Today millions live in cities which weren't planned. They just grew in accordance with a profit system that continues to produce housing and to rearrange the physical layouts of cities with a complete disregard for the human needs. Low-income housing, for the past hundred and fifty years, has been built with one thing in mind—the personal profit of the builders. Millions of people are living in homes built a century ago by men who laughed at the dreams of a horseless carriage, and who never could have conceived of the sprawling, ugly suburbs that they brought into existence. Now, in the last third of this century, millions of people on the eastern seaboard are crowded into old three-decker houses, built in antisocial grid patterns along miles and miles of congested streets. The low-cost jerry-built houses that gave shelter in the last century are rotting and falling apart. They have outmoded plumbing and wiring, and they're jammed back-to-back and crowded side-by-side so that there are no trees, no grass, no open spaces. This is where blacks and lower-middle-class whites are supposed to raise healthy children. And if this kind of environment isn't sufficient to create a national malaise and sickness, our fathers have responded with something even worse—the modern highrise low-income apartment house. With vast efficiency and with the profit motive dominating every housing concept, they have created impersonal, alienating, cement-and-steel jungles. This is the twentieth-century environment where the little people of this world are supposed to raise healthy, normal children. The same people who build these mazes wonder what happened to the better worlds of the past—the small-town world of their youth, where kids didn't need narcotics to escape an ugly world."

Bren paused for a breath, then continued. "I'm sorry; I'm not really trying to dominate the seminar. Whether she meant to or not, Ellen spilled some gasoline on a smoldering fire."

Tavish suggested that before Bren could motivate the Dancer O'Days in this world, he might have to seduce their daughters. "I do think," he added, "you may be dancing on the periphery of the problem. Our universities and colleges, for four years, and longer for graduate students, provide a unique young people's club, a place where people have a sense of identity with each other, and where they can count on the active or tacit support of their group. Once all of you are no longer protected by the university, once you are actually challenging the little guy who is only trying to make a living, and sounding your call to rebellion, or when you actually try to enlist the troops to fight the status quo, you'll encounter an enormous lethargy, a 'let-George-do-it attitude.' How are you going to find your rallying point then?"

Bren smiled at me, trying, I'm sure, to enlist my friendship, but my heart was doing crazy somersaults, and I ignored him. He shrugged. "Some of us, no matter how tough the odds, have to keep trying. It's our karma."

Ellen O'Day. Prelude to Premar. May. From tapes transcribed by Andrea Pillisuk.

The seminar wasn't over. Professor Tavish directed the class into a study of a type of low-income housing called Infill that had been created by the Boston Housing Authority. But I was too keyed up to pay much attention. At some point I noticed that Merle was tracing her long black fingers along Bren's arm, down to the curve of his hand, which lay between her open, bare thighs. Her short skirt was pushed back to the juncture of her crotch. This scene was hidden from everybody's view except mine by the overhang of the oak table we sat around. I don't know why, but it made my fluttering heart seem as if it had stopped pumping blood altogether. If it were true that Merle and Bren slept together, wasn't the nighttime enough? Did they have to parade their affection to prove that it existed?

Why was I jealous of a man I didn't even know?

My feeling of rejected loneliness didn't last long. I began to know that part of me was watching another Ellen who was going to pass out; I was going to faint. Maybe I was going to die. I kept saying to myself: Not now! Not in front of all these people! Not in front of Bren Gattman! Somehow, watching the hands on the big wall clock creep slowly toward noon, I hung on. I swayed in and out of consciousness, determined that when twelve o'clock finally came, and Tavish dismissed the class, I must hurry to the elevator and be gone before Bren tried to carry on the argument I had begun.

I was in the corridor first, but fate was against me. Frantically I pushed the button for the elevator, but the door refused to open. There was no choice; I would have run down the stairs. Even before I started, I saw Bren and Merle, with others from the class, come into the corridor. I was just lucky I didn't tumble down the stairs. I made it to the second-floor landing and collapsed there. There were yells above me, and the clatter of running feet. Somebody said, "Ellen's fainted!"

I looked up and was engulfed in Bren's brown eyes, wide with sympathy. His arm around me, he raised my head, while Merle, poised over me with a paper cup, tried to get me to sip a little water. I sobbed, "I'm so sorry."

Bren waved away the group of students who surrounded us. "She's all right. Merle and I will drive her home."

He picked me off the landing with surprising ease. "I'll carry you out to my car. Do you feel better now?"

"Please let me down." I was rigid in his arms. All the time, I was thinking: Please leave me before I die. I had a vision of the shock on his face as he realized I had stopped breathing and that he was holding a corpse in his arms. And I was perversely happy at his imagined fear and confusion.

In front of the building, yielding to my insistence that I was all right, Bren let my feet touch the sidewalk. I managed a few steps, tried to wave my thanks and good-bye. I know they were watching closely. I crossed Commonwealth Avenue before the warm, sunny day began to spin gray. As it turned entirely black, I heard the shriek of automobile brakes and Bren's hoarse yell. When I opened my eyes, I was back in Bren's arms. I grinned feebly in response to his worried stare. "I'm sorry." I sighed. "If I could rest somewhere for a few minutes, I'll be all right."

Merle touched my forehead. "You haven't got a fever. We can drive you home, or we can take you to our house. You better tell us what's wrong. Either you aren't eating right, or you've got morning sickness."

Bren smiled at my firm denial of either possibility. "I think it's just a female ploy," he said. "Ellen wants to win the argument she started with me." I could feel the fingers of his right hand, under my skirt, firmly clasped on my behind, but there was nothing I could do. My heart was flipping like a wounded bird.

I stopped protesting, because I knew now that I couldn't have walked. Just before we got to his Volkswagen camper, I confessed the truth. I wasn't pregnant. I wasn't hung over from drinking or smoking grass. I was a cripple. There wasn't much that helped, I said, except digitalis, and maybe I had been taking too much of that.

In the bus, sitting between them, I sobbed my hopelessness into Merle's warm neck while Bren drove us to Dorchester. He ignored my protests that I wanted to go home. I told him I'd be all right if I stayed in bed for a few days. "I guess I should have kept my cool and not tried to argue with you."

Bren grinned. "I loved it. We have an extra bed, Ellen, and we're only a few streets from your Dad's house. Why not stay with us? At least for the rest of the day. Wouldn't it be easier and more comfortable than having your folks fussing over you?"

I knew he was right, but I couldn't repress the feeling that having Dancer O'Day's daughter, helpless in his hands, appealed to Bren's mad sense of humor.

Well, what did it matter? If I survived a few more hours and my heart settled down, I could easily walk home. I let Bren carry me up to the first floor of his tenement house. Passing through the front door, I noticed three solid walls of books and piles of phonograph records, and more books and magazines in helter skelter piles. He lugged me down a narrow hall and into a small bedroom.

Ahead of him, Merle swept some clothing off the bed and pulled down the covers. Puffing, Bren laid me down. "I'm getting out of shape. You can't weigh more than one hundred and ten." Grinning at me, he ruffled my hair. The sympathetic look on his face made it impossible for me to hold back my tears. "I've got a friend who's an M.D.," he said. "Lieb Kahn. He's doing his residency at Boston City Hospital. He'll take a look at you."

My tears weren't so much from pain as my chagrin at being so dependent. "Don't bother him—please! There's nothing he can do. My doctor gave me three choices. Stay put and die later. Run around and die sooner. Have an operation and get better, maybe . . . or maybe just die immejut. Some days I want to live so badly I can taste life. Other days I don't give a damn if I live another minute."

"What about today?" Merle propped pillows behind my back. She pulled down the zipper on the back of my dress. "Take it off, honey. No sense in getting it wrinkled. Besides, it's warm in here."

"Is that your bed?" I asked Bren, who calmly watched Merle lift my dress over my head.

"We don't really have a his-or-hers or mine-and-thine setup. I guess you might say this bed is Merle's, but in the past Rais Daemon shared it. Occasionally Merle doesn't sleep in it at all. When she's lonesome, she comes across the hall and snuggles with me." Bren must have noticed the look of disapproval on my face.

I was conscious that my breasts, my nipples, and my pubic hair were quite visible through the flimsy nylon of my bra and panties. An odd, perverse feeling of sexual excitement played a counterrhythm to the laboring of my heart. I tried to look calmer than I was. "Really, I appreciate your both being so nice. If I could just lie here for an hour, I'm sure I'd get back to normal. Then, if you'll call a taxi, I'll get out of your hair."

Merle disappeared, insisting that she would make some sandwiches and something cool to drink. Bren kicked off his shoes and, to my amazement, lay down beside me.

"Don't say it," he said quietly.

"Don't say what?"

"Don't say all of the middle-class things your father and mother taught you to say. Like it isn't proper to lie on a bed half-naked with a stranger. If you feel like it, you can take off your bra and panties. I'd enjoy seeing you naked."

I felt that Bren was trying to shock me. Why? In retaliation for my attack in the classroom? Did he think that I was acting, that I really wasn't such a mess as I said I was?

"You're right," I said bitterly. "I pulled off the whole business as a cheap trick to see if you were really living with a black girl."

Bren was holding my hand, and I realized he was counting my pulse beats. He leaned over and put his ear against my chest. After a minute or two he got off the bed and brushed his hands over my eyelids. I felt his lips swiftly touch mine. "You rest. I can drive you home later, or you can stay here." He chuckled. "In fact, you can move in with us, if you like. It would be easier to go to class with us than take the bus or subway every day."

Ellen O'Day. Prelude to Premar. May. From tapes transcribed by Andrea Pillisuk.

Drifting to sleep, I could hear their voices from the front rooms. Once Merle tiptoed into the bedroom to leave a plate with a sandwich and a glass tinkling with ice. She held my hand for a second, a touch so filled with feeling that I was at a loss for words. I could only thank her with the tears in my eyes. Vaguely I wondered why a stranger, I, Ellen O'Day, should evoke a sense of caring in them. Caressed by a warm June breeze that flickered uneasily through the bedroom window, I drifted into a restless sleep. When I awoke, the corners of the room were blended with the early-evening shadows. A small alarm clock on Merle's dresser showed quarter of six. If I wasn't home within the next hour, a good portion of the Boston police department, led by Daddy, would be searching for me.

I found Bren sprawled in the living room, his feet resting on the wall above him, his head half-hanging over the edge of the sofa. He was reading a paperback, *The Affair*, by Morton Hunt. Looking at me upside down, he grinned.

"When I read for an extended period, I like to be uncomfortably comfortable." His intense stare made me realize I had forgotten to put on my dress.

"If I don't get home pretty quickly," I said, "or make a phone call, my father will be sure I was attacked on the streets and died trying to preserve my virginity."

"You can't mean it?"

"Mean what?"

"That you've never been penetrated by a throbbing penis."

While I had read conversations like this, I had never engaged in one. My heart was still struggling with a lack of blood, and now my Catholic upbringing was direct fire. I had a mad picture of myself flopping down beside Bren and telling him I was scared and needed him to hug me! Instead I responded stuffily. "I don't think the sexual revolution is here to stay." To divert him, I asked where Merle was.

"She's gone to work. Merle schleps cocktails at the Persian Room in the Sheraton between six and midnight. Dressed in an Oriental harem costume, she looks like a houri. She never gets through an evening without a proposition." Bren pointed at the telephone. "Call your mother. Tell her you're staying overnight with a girlfriend, and then we'll remedy the situation."

"What situation?"

"Your virginity. Ellen, you're trapped with a lecherous monster. I spend all my spare time reading pornography. Now, for the first time, I can act out my frustrations. I can tie you to a chair and have my way with you. Just seeing the careless undulation of your hips, your breasts bobbling indignantly, seeing the telltale engorgement of your pink nipples staring at me, saying touch me, suck me, seeing the wild disarray of your pussy hair beneath your panties and the subtle abandon on your face as you hold your lips slightly parted, obviously gasping for the penis so long denied you—all this has given me a powerful erection that will not be denied."

It was impossible not to laugh. Bren twisted himself into sitting position on the sofa and pulled me down beside him, tossing the paperback in my lap. "Since you're still premarital, you probably aren't interested in postmarital problems. Even so, Hunt's book is good reading. Listen."

Despite my bewilderment at the abruptness of his

switch from insanity to seriousness, he opened the book to a page he had turned down.

> The remedy that lies closest to hand, for boredom and disappointment alike, is extramarital love. It is also Everyman's answer to the impersonality, the disconnectedness, the giantism of modern society. We have lost our names and become numbers, lost touch with our friends and replaced them with people who merely live nearby, lost control of our destinies to governments, industries, and machines that ravish our earth and control our lives. If the individual feels powerless to remake or even salvage this world, he can at least comfort himself by making a world of his own through love. In each of its many forms ranging from casual sexual encounters to the deepest emotional relationships, it (an extramarital affair) gives him a sense of his own uniqueness, a vital connection with some other human being, an area of freedom he can manage, a part of his own destiny. Those who love construct a microcosm of their own, a world in which they are at once Creator and created.

Bren was silent for a moment. "That's a part of what I've been trying to say in class. Hunt is describing the condition, but too few of us have passed beyond diagnosis to the cure." Bren chuckled. "This morning you gave me an idea. I want to meet your father and give him a brand-new campaign slogan."

By this time I was really staring at Bren with my mouth half-open; I had no doubts that my father would think Bren should be locked up. "Of course," Bren was continuing, "to return to our earlier theme. Before I can pursue the will-o'-the-wisp you have offered me—and I do feel a mad compulsion to be the first to introduce you to the pleasures of the bed—I would ask your father and your hand in marriage."

The only one way to survive this kind of madness was to join it. I smiled. "If you change your mind and decide to take me by force, O handsome knight, remember before you do that I have to call my mother. I should also remind you that you've forgotten the reason why poor Nell is still a virgin."

Bren jumped up and looked at the kitchen clock. "I'm

a man of honor and chivalry, fair maid. In exactly twelve minutes the front doorbell will ring. I will open it, and Lieb Kahn, an old-time tribal medicineman in a white coat carrying a portable electrocardiograph machine, will listen to your damaged valves and tell us your chances for survival in the act of love."

I gasped. "Bren Gattman, you're insane! What in hell business of yours is my health or sex life?"

He shrugged. "Well, maybe after Lieb listens to your heart, he should be prepared to snip your hymen. You're probably as unpenetrable physically as you are mentally. While I have a hunch you didn't jump on me in class out of sheer dislike, you must have a pretty good idea that your shelling hit the target." Bren flopped on the sofa and put his head in my lap. He looked at me like a kid in a toy store. "Ellen, I know you can't help it, but you remind me of a starving, stringbean kitten that wandered into our house when I was a kid. After six months my mother said we would have to get rid of her. Evenutally, being unaware that human society believed that animal females should be more circumspect, she would screw herself to death, but by then the Gattman home would be up to its ass in cats. I cried, and my mother relented and told me: All right, we would have the cat fixed. When I discovered what fixed meant, I threw a fit.

"Abe agreed with me. Yenta (that was the cat's name) had fifty or more kittens, and I officiated at most of the births. Yenta was a Yentzer. Someday I'll tell you what that means. Yenta lived a long, productive life with a deep awareness of how to bend human beings and male cats to her will." Bren laughed. "When you look at me the way you are now, you have the same power."

I was careful not to tell him that I had learned some Yiddish slang by the simple process of reading best-sellers.

From the journal of Samantha Brown, October, the first year of Premar.

Samantha Brown—that's me. I'm five-foot-eleven in bare feet. And that ain't—isn't—all. My pa, when he's around, which isn't often, tells Ma that big girls like me used to be called Amazons. Pa didn't know that the Amazons hacked off one of their tits so they could draw an arrow on a bow just like a man. Anyway, Pa figures this going to college and getting mixed up with whitey—in bed, even—just ain't good sense. "It's us against the honky," he tells Ma and me. "Nothin' going to change that in your lifetime, gal. If you're gonna put out, make them pay." Before the Supreme Court said liquor and sex don't mix and nearly wiped out the Combat Zone, Pa worked in one of those go-go places on lower Washington Street. He claimed he could get me a job as a dancer. "Easy work. Just show your money-maker to the man, Samantha, but don't do it for nothin'. A fine stallion like you could make a couple of bills a week."

Ma and I knew that the men who go to those places would try to pay for something else too, and I'd be taking their money—or else! Henry Brown, my pa, isn't too tall, and neither is Ma. My real pa may be alive or dead. I was his only child by Ma, I guess. All my brothers are about five-foot-eight. They don't call Henry Pa, They call him Uncle Willy.

I may be big, but I still got two tits, and whether this Premar jazz works out or not, I've got a whitey roommate, Julian Howe, who can't keep his eyes off them. Right off Julie started calling me Sam. I told him no dice, man. I'm not going around tagged with any boy's name. My ma named me Samantha, and that's who I am.

Julie just laughed. "It'll be hard to say it when I'm making love to you. It would be easier to say Sam-Sam, I adore you." He was sitting on the edge of his bed naked as a jaybird and ready to go. He's about an inch shorter than me, but a lot broader. He's from Connecticut. According to him, there's a lot of rich Howes in Connecticut—but (big pun) his father never discovered how. He sells insurance for the Aetna Insurance Company. Julie's father went to college for a couple of years but dropped out and got married because he had to. Julie has an older brother and no sisters. His ma met another guy, after he was born, and she divorced his father. Julie's family is as screwed-up as mine. He's got a father who raised him, and I got a mother. They should meet. Ha! Ha!

I could tell by the way Julie was watching me that he wanted to lay it on the line. When were we going to screw? While I haven't gone and asked everybody, I guess after three weeks more than half the kids here have done some screwing. Well, I'm not holding out on Julie. Last night, right after supper, I got thinking—since it was Saturday—if Julie did hang around the room, I wanted to be shiny clean, so I decided to go to the tubs. There's usually a half-dozen or more kids in the Japanese-style bath in the basement of the Blanc House. Girls have no trouble getting thoroughly soaped down, hosed off, and soaped down again by some guy eager to feel you up—specially if you're nice and return the favor. After you're clean, you can soak awhile in the tubs with a bunch of kids and have crazy conversations.

Ellen and Merle were the only ones in the tubs when I got there. Ellen was moody, and I guessed she had been crying. "Ellen's daddy is raising hell about Premar," Merle told me. After that we all talked.

When I got back to the room and discovered Julie still there, I was going to tell him about the conversation, and Ellen's fear that the police, on her father's request, might raid Premar. But first thing I knew I was off on one of my sarcastic tacks, saying things just the opposite from what I wanted to say, like, "How come if you're not studying you didn't go into Boston with a gang of the kids, or how come you're not looking at television?" I acted as if I weren't a bit interested in making love. Of course, even a moron could tell how come. Julie wanted to get into me.

He looked at me sadly. "To tell the truth, this Human-Value stuff is coming so fast I'm not sure I can keep up with it. You whizzed through that book, *The Practice of Creativity,* and I haven't even touched it. Between the physics, psychology, and English courses that I'm taking, and all the damned books Bren thinks we should read, I'm going balmy." Julie shrugged. "I told Merle last night that I had made a damned big mistake. Living with a white girl and finding out if we could make it together would be problem enough. But trying to stay sane with an uppity black girl who shakes her ass at you every minute, while all the time she's saying keep off, is enough to drive a guy off his rocker."

"I don't shake it at you!" Instead of admitting there was some truth in Julie's remark, I was getting mad. "I told you we'd screw together when the time was right."

Julie grinned. "I don't want to just screw. I want to make love. And you sure do flip your black ass at me, especially when you know I'm watching. You just better be careful. I might rape you."

"It'll take more than you to rape me," I yelled at him. Then suddenly I couldn't keep the tears out of my eyes. "Anyway, I was raped once. Two years ago. It took four guys to do it."

I decided, what the hell, I might as well tell him. "They dragged me into one of those bombed-out buildings in the South End. I fought them. But they stripped me, and they practically beat the shit out of me. They took turns. Slobbering idiots, with their big white dicks dripping all over me."

I guess that kind of blunt talk stunned Julie. He stared at me as if he might cry, too. "Did you get pregnant?" he finally asked.

"Yeah," I told him. "But not for long. When I dragged my ass home to Ma and she saw what was left of my clothes, she took me to a doctor. When I didn't get my period, the doctor vacuumed me."

"What about the men who did it?"

"They weren't men, they were kids. Puerto Ricans. About a year older than me. I had been going with one of them off and on. Manuel Rochas. All he wanted to do was fuck. When he knew I wasn't going to put out, he and his friends ganged up on me."

Julie didn't say a thing for a while, and since I didn't feel like watching TV in the sitting room, I concentrated on my psych book. I didn't tell Julie why I never could squeal on that rat, Manuel Rochas. I knew if I had, it would have touched off a school riot between the blacks and the spics, and then one of the real tough black kids,

Mikey Harris, for example, would have been the next to try to grab a piece of my ass. Then I'd have ended up in his stable. Either Mikey or Manuel would have written a new career for me.

"How come you agreed to live with a white guy?" Julie looked as if he wanted to take me in his arms and comfort me.

"Why don't you start that book?"

He looked despondent. "Hell, I'm not sure I can go the whole route in this place."

"You mean sticking out the four years and getting a degree?"

"Yeah, maybe Bren should have put me on the work cycle first. I was going to suggest it, but then I would have been living with someone else. Anyway, I was no genius in high school."

"Neither was I." I was beginning to realize that Julie really wanted to room with me. I don't know why, but that made me feel like crying.

Closing my book, I lay down and looked at Julie, who was still flopped on his bed naked. It wasn't that warm in the room; the commune didn't waste heat. Julie's penis wasn't big anymore, and he looked like a big kid who needed to be hugged. I decided what the hell, maybe we can make love gradually, and I won't think about my vulva bleeding and sore, or how awful I felt while those kids fucked me. I took off my bathrobe and pulled down the quilt. I still had white panties on. "Come on, get in with me," I said. "You got goose pimples all over you. You can lie with me, but no fucking."

Julie crawled in beside me. "God, you have nice breasts. Can I kiss them?"

What could I say? "Yeah, but no sucking nipples." I held his head against me.

"Do you feel maternal?" Julie's voice was muffled by my flesh.

"Sure." I chuckled. "I got me a white nigger baby."

"Funny thing." Julie leaned on his elbow and grinned at me. Between sentences he kept kissing my tits. "I was kind of scared to room with you. But when Bren pointed out that first night that there were only six black guys and six black girls and he suggested that the first Premar rule we could stretch, if we wanted to, was the one that said blacks would live with blacks for the first thirteen weeks. I began to figure that, the way things were, with eighteen white guys and six black girls, some of us would never get to live with a black girl."

"Jesus, you sound batty. What's so special about a black girl? You think niggers fuck better, I bet."

"How would I know? I went with a girl in high school for two years, and we made love about four times. It wasn't much fun. We had no place to do it except her family's house, and Sally was so afraid of getting pregnant, or afraid that her folks would catch us, or that the rubbers would break, that I was scarcely in her before it was all over. Maybe you're right. I saw you walking around the dayroom naked, that first night, big and pretty, and looking about fifty times as cool as most of the girls, and I thought maybe you'd know the score and we'd learn how to make love for hours."

"That ain't all you thought," I told him. "You know damned well, you thought: Ha! A black girl will be so happy to have a white guy, she'll jump all over him."

Julie shook his head. "Do you think you'll ever stop thinking black? That thought never entered my head."

"Kee-rist!" I couldn't help laughing. "You've had more experience than me. I've been raped, but no one ever made love to me." I couldn't help it, I suddenly felt kind of warm toward Julie. I kissed his nose. "Anyway, you'd have got me eventually. We were third on each other's list."

"I wonder if they matched me because we're alikes or opposites?"

I didn't tell Julie then, but I really think we're alikes. When Merle asked me if I wanted to switch positions with Mohammed Hassan, who was supposed to be my first roommate, I looked Mohammed over real careful and figured he was a "mad" nigger, and right now, he didn't need a black girl to sing his anger to. Julie looked more like someone I could put down. Funny, every time I have, in the past couple of weeks, I suddenly realize it's not because he's Julie, it's because he's whitey, and I was fighting the same old fight. I guessed right about one thing, though; Julie's parents fought busing and school integration. At the same time, they told him they didn't hate blacks. Sure, just so long as the nigger stays put and don't get into their lily-white neighborhood. Julie believes he isn't prejudiced. If he was, how could he love me?

By now Julie had convinced me we should shove the beds together. One bed was too small for two to be comfortable in. We got giggling over the idea that Premar should have thought about this and provided a crack filler for between the mattresses, because, even when we shoved the beds real close, the only way we could get room enough was to lie in the middle. We rolled up blankets to fill the gap between the beds, but Julie had a better idea. He said that when he had a chance, maybe today, he'd rebuild the frames so we'd have one bed instead of two.

When we finally got back into bed, he told me he loved me and that I was a lot of fun.

"Man, you don't even know me."

"Maybe I haven't been inside you yet, but just holding each other is making love. I know one thing about you—you really like to hug someone."

"It's only nine-thirty," I told him, thinking it was a good thing he didn't know me. I just wanted to hug and kiss all night, every night, maybe for a month. I grabbed his copy of Sidney Jourard's book *The Transparent Self.* "Here, we'll take turns reading it aloud to each other. Bren said the only way we're going to really understand this stuff is to keep talking it over—even while we're making love." We read for about an hour, and while I kept Julie from touching my breasts and belly, and getting both of us too excited, I found out he really understood the book pretty good.

"Jouard says we don't dare to honestly reveal the kinds of persons we really are to each other. We beat around the bush." He laughed. "So I might as well start with being honest with you. If we don't make love tonight, I'll have to jerk off. My balls are aching from the hard-on I've had from most of the last two weeks."

I kissed his mouth and whispered, "Okay, white boy—I'll be honest, I need you, too."

"Supposing I come too fast?"

"Supposing you do?"

He looked very serious. "I guess I'd be embarrassed. I guess that's why they showed us that sex movie last night. No sooner did that guy in the movie get into the girl than he climaxed."

I held up Julie's penis and leaned over and kissed it. Funny damn thing, I never thought I'd do that to any man, let alone a white man, but after three weeks in Premar you learn one thing: Making love is just letting go, and when you do let yourself go, you feel all warm and good, and laughing inside. "You big, white, motherfucking prick," I told Julie's penis. "Don't you shoot your load too quick. If you do, I'll eat you up!"

Then Julie was on top of me, and I guided him in the right direction. "So far, you're doing fine," I gasped. He was in me, and it felt oh so good. "Can you come out and go in again, real slow?" I asked.

"Boy, I don't know, Samantha." Julie was panting a little. "I can feel every bristly hair on your bush. It's like being tickled with a thousand electric shocks."

"Julie, if you come, I'm goin' to get you back!"

"Like the girl in the movie did?"

"Better. I bet I can swallow you better." I couldn't help it. I arched my behind slowly up and down and sideways.

"God, Samantha!" Julie yelled. "I can't stop!"

"Neither can I, Julie . . . Julie, go man! Go! Man, go, go, I love you—ooo!"

So I came, too, and I knew right away I wanted to again. Damned if in about ten minutes, though I must have lapped Julie's jigger for less than a minute, he wasn't ready again!

And he was laughing. "Why do guys worry about coming too fast? All they need is a girl who likes lollipops. This time I'm going to stay inside you forever!"

And he damned near did, and didn't even come out when we were talking and I told him about Ellen O'Day.

Ellen O'Day. Prelude to Premar. May. From tapes transcribed by Andrea Pillisuk.

The actual truth is, the first night I couldn't go home. That isn't exactly true, either. If I wanted to go home, Dr. Lieb Kahn had suggested the best way would be in an ambulance, and if I decided to do that, when I got home I'd have to stay in bed for a week at least. He also thought I should forget the whole business of getting my master's, at least until next year. And he said he wanted me to take preoperative catherization tests immediately. He assured me that there are excellent heart surgeons at the University Hospital who easily could patch me up.

Lieb looked at me wearily as he put away his portable cardiograph machine. "I know that isn't what you want me to say," he said. "I was lying on Merle's bed, watching him. "But it's the truth. Sure, a heart operation is no picnic." He shrugged. "You may even die. But the chances are good that you simply have mitral stenosis, and no complications. The valve can be opened. If you don't do it now, you'll always live a half-life, or you may even get cyanotic one day, and that will be that."

"I want to get my master's," I sobbed. "I want to graduate."

"Why?" Bren demanded.

"Because I want to."

Bren laughed. "Your master's won't help you get rid of the old-maid's degree you've already got."

Why did that make me so angry? I felt like spitting, but instead I tried to look sophisticated. It seemed like a good time to discover if Lieb had the answer to something I really needed to know. "Bren hasn't asked you the question that's bugging him" I said. "What happens to me if I have intercourse with him and have an orgasm."

"Jesus Christ!" Lieb looked at Bren disgustedly. "I thought you two had just met."

Bren was bubbling with delight; he told Lieb the sexual revolution was on. "The trouble with you, Lieb, is you're so involved with medicine you're not keeping up with the world."

In a sarcastic voice I explained to Lieb that before he had arrived, Bren had been trying to convince me that even though we were strangers, if I dared to be defenseless with him and be honestly me, he had offered not only to take care of my overripe virginity, but would introduce me to the joy of making love over a period of three or four hours.

"Blended, I suppose?" Lieb didn't sound convinced.

Bren smiled. "Not necessarily. Naked together, yes. I think Ellen has a problem common to us all—an inability to share loneliness. The comfortable merger of two people gently touching and telling each other, with their eyes and their bodies, meanings beyond words, feelings that can be experienced over and over again without boredom. A man and woman floating in the infinity of their maleness and femaleness. A forever feeling that is indescribably better than all the pills and palliatives that the tribal medicine-man has ever devised."

Lieb shrugged in mock hopelessness. "I didn't have the money to go to college and play house with a female as well as play doctor. In my opinion it's a tough world." He stared at Bren. "No matter how much you may be willing, *you* can't be Ellen with her damaged heart valve. Psychologically, that valve has conditioned her whole approach to life. It has made her fatalistic and introspective."

Lieb asked me when I had had rheumatic fever. I told him sixteen years ago, when I was nine. "That underscores it," he said. "A few decades ago, many family doctors didn't know how to treat rheumatic fever properly. In those days, when they discovered that your mitral valve was damaged, they'd plan your life. You were told you should never exert yourself unduly. That meant you couldn't walk up stairs without reminding yourself that your very ability to breathe hung by a narrow thread." Lieb shook his head. "I don't know about you, Bren, but if I grew up with those kinds of symptoms, two things would have happened to me: I would detest my own dependency and try to hide it in my every encounter with other human beings, and I would withdraw from people to escape their pity. How can you or I ever know, or emote with, the kind of person Ellen has become?"

Bren grinned. "Really, Lieb, one of the true joys of living is to try to infiltrate another person's mind and become that person."

"If you do that with everyone you meet, pretty soon you won't have any identity left. Bren Gattman will disappear." Lieb smiled affectionately; it was easy to tell he enjoyed Bren's idealism.

Bren wasn't shaken. "What will be left will be the essence of all men. A person named Lieb should know what that is."

Lieb patted my cheek. "I'm almost afraid to leave such a lovely Irish girl with such a mad Jewish messiah, but I've got to get back to the hospital. My advice to you is to hang on to your identity. Don't become completely Gatt-manized. To answer Bren's question." Lieb smiled. "Or is it yours, Ellen? If you think you're suffering because you're a virgin, don't try to remedy the situation for a few days at least, or you may be complaining about the view from the cemetery."

"You mean I can never have sexual intercourse." I blurted. I tried to recover my equanimity. "I don't mean particularly with Bren." I blushed at Lieb's quizzical expression, but I still wanted the answer. I had never dared ask Dr. Haynim, who was at least sixty years old and gave the impression that the whole business of sex was highly overrated. "For gosh sakes," I said, "don't look so dumbfounded, I'm only asking a question."

"I'm only an M.D. Ellen, not God." He seemed anxious to leave, but Bren pursued the subject. "I don't know much about physiology," he said, "but I would guess that for Ellen or any male or female, the fear of not being able to respond normally would create its own stresses. These might be just as harmful as the continual need to sublimate. How about that, Lieb?"

"Maybe." Lieb patted my arm. "But if I were the lucky one and had the privilege of introducing you to sex, I wouldn't give you carte blanche. Take my advice, Ellen. Play it cool for the next four or five days. After that, if orgasm sets your heart thumping, keep in mind that it's equivalent to walking up a flight of stairs, but not to climbing a mountain."

Bren followed Lieb to the door. After a while he reappeared in the bedroom with a plate of toast and scrambled eggs. "All you have to do, Ellen, my love, is relax," he told me. "Let me take your bra off, and then I'll feed you." He leaned over and propped pillows behind me.

"Let's get a few things straight," I said, wondering why he assumed I wouldn't get angry at his calm assumption that he could undress me. "Despite your happy-go-lucky attitude, and the fact that my still being here may make you think I've accepted your invitation, I haven't made up my mind. Even if I were feeling fine, I wouldn't jump in the sack with you. On the other hand, maybe deep down I want to, but don't dare. Maybe I am afraid." I tried to keep the tears from my eyes. "All I know is that I do like you."

Before I could stop him, Bren unfastened my bra and lifted it off my shoulders. Very gently, so quickly I could scarcely protest, he kissed my nipples. "See," he said as he held a forkful of eggs toward my mouth, "two things have been accomplished. I've seen your breasts and, behold, they are beautiful—an integral part of you, Ellen. And now, hopefully, you feel less restrained, and if you just laugh a little at the silliness of your fears, you may discover what a very pleasant thing it is to be fed by a man whom you have known less than six hours." As I ate, Bren traced his fingers with a light, shivery touch around the under curve of my breast.

I smiled. "Bren, you're dangerous; you make me forget my defenses and you have a way of pulling me out of my shell. I'm a stranger to you, and yet you make me feel I'm a part of your life. But that doesn't stop the conflicts in my mind. I don't know you, and you don't know me."

He took my hand. "Ellen, even *I* don't know me. But if you dare, when you finish eating, we'll lie together and I'll hold you in my arms. We won't make love ... or, more truthfully, we will make love, but we won't have intercourse. For an hour or two we'll just drift together, enjoying the warmth of our bodies naked against each other. Do we dare to shed the surface selves we live with? In the process, we may discover we really like each other."

I watched him undress. Other than my brothers, on whom I had spied in the bathroom, he was the first man I had actually seen naked. What kind of madness was this? I was sure Lieb wouldn't approve of the way my heart was pounding. Was I taking the first step toward an orgy? Why was I being so foolishly trusting as to attempt this kind of intimacy with a complete stranger? I felt sure my only harvest would be tears of remorse. Not because I had exposed my body, or finally had joined myself with a man, or because I had been immoral by my father's standards, but because I had finally revealed my loneliness and exposed the nakedness of myself to another human being. Because I knew essentially that was Bren's condition of being together, and I wasn't sure I could be so honest. What if he found me empty, childish, just an ordinary shallow female? What would Bren think if I asked him point-blank about Merle? Would Merle approve if she could see us right now? And why was Bren living with a black girl? Did he love her? Why a black girl, when there must be a thousand white girls like myself who would crawl on their knees to a Bren Gattman? I hated my O'Day conditionings, but I couldn't deny them.

From the journal of Mohammed Hassan, October, the first year of Premar.

Sure, I came to Premar with a chip on my shoulder. And, man, I know it doesn't make much sense, but in the last few days I'm slowly beginning to dig this place. Merle told me Friday that I was the last one in the whole damned place not to have turned in a weekly journal. But now I'm getting with it.

"That's not playing the game, Mohammed." She sounded grim. "I know for a fact that you've listened to every tape in the dayroom. You know more about Bren, Ellen, me, and Rais then any of us know about you."

"I don't know much about *you* yet, except that you're married to a brother I'd like to meet." I shrugged. "I listened to Rais Daemon's tapes, 'Walk Before God,' and listened to yours, when you went to meet him in St. Noir, and I know you screw with Bren, but I don't know much else. I can't figure you. Bren's a Jew. Fact is, the Compars seem as screwed-up as the Premars. Do they have a name for the blind leading the blind?"

Merle laughed. "Most of the world is like a new baby that hasn't learned to focus the shadows yet. Bren's a man, not a religion. You've got a Black Muslim name, but your ma baptized you Thomas Jefferson Jones. Your ma evidently couldn't read. Jefferson was no nigger lover."

"I *was* a Black Muslim." I wondered why I didn't smack the fake smile right off her face. "If your name had been Thomas Jefferson, what would you have done?"

"I'd have changed it to Mr. Yacub. He was pretty smart. He created his own enemies."

I couldn't help laughing. I knew Elijah Muhammad's story. How originally all men were black and then Mr. Yacub, a biologist, gradually mated lighter and lighter ones until he got the bleached-out race of whites. "We got about five thousand years left to go," I told her. "Then the blacks will take over again. While I'm waiting, since I like ham sandwiches and pig's feet, I decided to become a Black Panther."

"Why do you have to be a Black something? I'm just myself, Merle Blanc."

I had to admit that her name was almost as nutty as mine had been. A white blackbird. Wow! "Even though I haven't met him yet," I told her, "I'm staying here because of Rais Daemon. He's going to change things. If it weren't for the Compars here—including Bren, who's not so bad—I think I'd split. Most of the kids are pretty naïve. Speaking of names, I looked 'daemon' up in the dictionary. It says. 'Don't confuse with demon'—a daemon is an intermediary between the gods and men."

Merle couldn't stop laughing. "Mohammed, you're a prize. Rais will love you. You discovered his secret ambition. His family name, swiped from some English slaveholder, was Damon. When he was a kid, Rais got some Tom Swift books in Care packages. There was a character named Mr. Damon there who was always saying, "God bless my soul!" Rais detested him as well as Tom Swift."

I wasn't sure that I was with this conversation, but I have to admit that with the exception of me and my roommate, Kathy Big Ass, everyone here, white and black, seems like they've forgot all about color. I was about to tell Merle, among other things, that I wasn't too happy with my job, but she beat me to it. "I hear you're a sanitation engineer," she said. "I knew she was trying to bug me. "Great profession with a great future."

"Very funny. Meet Mohammed Hassan, garbage collector." For that I get one hundred bucks a week, which I never see. On Friday nights the working class and those who don't work for thirteen weeks get fifteen dollars each from the commune. In an emergency, like for clothes, if my ass is showing or if I got a hole in a shoe, I can get a loan. If my roommate shared her loot with me, thirty bucks a week wouldn't be too bad. But Kathy is a waitress in the coffee shop at Howard Johnson's 57 Motor Inn, and she hangs on to her fifteen dollars like it was gold or something."

When I told Bren I couldn't get the smell of garbage out of my nose, he just laughed. "Try shit, Mohammed!" he said. "Shit smells worse, so don't complain. Next cycle you may end up with the sewage department!"

Bren told me the philosophy of Premar is that it doesn't

make a damn bit of difference what you do for a living.
Do it the best you can—maybe even better—just so long
as it gives you time to live. Well, up until last night, when
Kathy and I finally made it, this Premar has been a weird
excuse for living. Really a good way for a horny black kid
to go off his rocker. If you live with a chick for four
weeks, and every day see girls bare-ass all over the house
and in the tubs, and you don't do it, you begin to come
apart.

Every morning, after eating in the communal dining
room, Kathy and I go to work. Kathy takes the subway,
while Jib Kiley picks me up on the corner of Dasson Road
in a Boston garbage truck. Jib is a fat-headed Irishman
who was shocked shitless when I told him his helper sleeps
with an Irish girl named Katherine Flaherty. I know I
shouldn't have told Jib, because Bren warned us not to go
out of our way to advertise what goes on at Premar. Jib
lives near Topham's Corner, and the rumor is already
pretty widespread that a bunch of freaked-out kids have
moved into the neighborhood.

Anyway, I was damn well feeling put upon by Kathy. I
had agreed to room with a girl big enough to carry a rifle
in the Irish Republican Army ... Naw, that's not right.
Kathy is as soft as fresh butter. Well, even though everyone
admits that her face is pretty, I didn't see any of the other
guys rushing to be her roommate. No. That's not the
reason. I wanted to room with Kathy because I hated her.
She's a big white blob of honky flesh. I had a chip on my
shoulder, and I wanted Kathy to knock it off so I could
stomp on her.

Every night, before reading for the Human-Values
course, Kathy shucks herself into her woolly Doctor Den-
ton's so fast I hardly see her white skin disappearing. Even
though I've seen her naked in the tubs plenty of times, she
probably thinks that if she walks around this room undressed, I'll rape her. The fact is, Kathy was scared shitless of me. My Uncle Ed taught me that if you got whitey
on the run, keep him that way; and he's one of the biggest
flesh operators in Detroit, so he ought to know.

Merle told me once that my uncle's philosophy was not
the idea of Premar—but what is, I wasn't sure then.

So last night I was in the TV room reading *Political
Manifesto,* which is next week's book for H.V., and in between commercials watching a hockey game with Bob Jef-

ferson and Able Anderson, a couple of other guys on this floor. Finally I got bored with TV, so I walked back into our room. Kathy was sitting in her chair and had a bathrobe on top of her woollies. Her feet were propped up on the bed. She gave me her warm loving smile, which is her way of proving that she is friendly, just so long as you keep your distance. As I stripped, I started feeling hornier than usual and decided that after four weeks the time had come to make an issue of it.

"I was talking to Chuck Ventrano and Billy Rainbow," I told her, capturing her attention before I dropped my bomb and my underpants. I saw she was listening. "Despite all the sex instruction and shit talk, and the movies we've watched of people making love, Chuck and Billy ran their own little poll. They figure at least half the guys here haven't fucked their roommate yet. What do you think of that?"

Kathy shrugged and glued her eyes to *The Joy of Sex*.

"You read that stuff," I said, "but those pictures are whitey screwing whitey. Fact is, you don't really want to do it with a nigger—ain't it?" I stood next to her chair, my balls and half-erect prick practically in her face.

Looking as if she were going to scream, Kathy squirmed away. "It's not that Mohammed. I'm just not ready."

"You're taking the pill, aren't you?" My disgusted prick was slowly giving up. "Shiiit, you going to make me impotent. So why in hell did you ask to room with me? I think you just wanted to get living with a black man out of the way so you'd never have to do that again."

Kathy shook her head, and I saw she had tears in her eyes. "That's not true. I really like you, sometimes. I like when you told me nothing was going to stop you, that you were going to be a doctor if it took you the rest of your life."

"Sometimes I'm full of crap talk." I knew this was the kind of conversation that the Compars had warned us against. Words parrying words, with no real attempt by either of us to say what we're really thinking—but goddamn, I couldn't help it. If I was mean, it was because of all that gism jammed in back of my pecker. It was a hell of a note just to be waiting for a chance to jerk off in a school that had been started so a guy wouldn't have to in the first place.

Kathy answered me more truthfully. "Sometimes I

think you don't like me. Like maybe you compare me with other girls. I know I'm too fat, and I'm not 'sophisticated like those girls you knew in Detroit. And maybe ... maybe I'm just .. " Kathy hesitated.

"Just what?"

"Just someone to fuck." Kathy blushed. "I'll never get to say that word easily, and I never will be able to make love with someone who resents me. I know you call me 'Fat Ass.' "

"Aw, shit, Kathy, I don't detest you. If I call you Fat Ass it's only in fun." I knew I was going soft, but we were finally communicating in a way. "Fact is, you just don't seem sexy to me. Black girls are sexy as hell." There I was bragging again; why couldn't I be honest? Right there and then, why didn't I tell her I had screwed with two black girls in my life. One was a whore who laughed all the time I was doing it, and the other, my cousin, who is sexy all right, but was on her own fuck-trip, and gave me the feeling it wasn't just me, that any old cock would do. But I couldn't be honest. Not with whitey—not yet. "If I stood near a black gal, naked, like I did with you just now, she'd start breathing hard, and look at me real loving and say, 'Man, I can't wait—shove that big tool into me, honey, I need it so!'"

Kathy stared at me as if I'd flaked out.

Then I went whole hog. "Why, I'll bet you right now if I walked downstairs into Merle's room, naked like this, she'd know what to do."

Kathy was stubborn. "Why don't you? I was talking with her today; she's alone tonight. Bren and Ellen have gone to the movies."

So there I was with my big talk shoved back down my throat. I looked at my watch. Ten-fifteen. I was near as afraid of Merle as Kathy was of me. Merle is a cool sister. Gives me the eerie feeling she's looking right into my brains, and ain't all that pleased with what she sees there. But I had to prove something to Kathy. If I just went down to the baths and poured cold water from the hoses on me, when I came back she wouldn't know whether I had made it with Merle or not.

Wearing just my bathrobe, I walked down to the first floor. I was trying to convince myself that since this stud, Rais Daemon, was off running a revolution, maybe Merle would like a black man as a change from Bren. Anyway, how could she refuse a brother in need?

When I finally got the courage to knock on her door, I had to control my shivering. Merle finally opened it. The only light in the room was a reading light on her desk. Merle's face, in shadow, looked cool, sort of like one of those models who stare at you out of the pages of *Ebony*, and you wonder if she's telling you that you smell bad, and, of course, you know she shits cream puffs.

"Hi, Mohammed, what do you want?" she says. Then I saw there were tears in her eyes.

"Nothing much," I told her. "I was just lonesome." Why couldn't I ask her what was wrong?

She pointed to a chair. "It's kind of late," she said. "You know, you don't look like my man, but you do have the same kind of intensity. I heard from him today, and for better or worse, he's alive. Tomorrow all the Premars can hear his new tapes." Merle pointed to her desk, which was covered with papers. "I'm bookkeeper for the commune. The kids working this first term are paying the tuition for the ones going to school, as well as providing the money for food. Getting more money out of the consortium is almost impossible. Bren is great at organizing some things, even at raising money, but handling pennies isn't his bag. If Rais were here, this would be his job." She wiped her eyes, and I could tell she was trying to divert me. "So everybody's got problems. Those are mine. What's yours, studies or roommate?"

"I guess I got over my snow fever." I looked hard at Merle, hoping she'd get the message. "I like black girls better. Skinny ones, and a little mean."

Merle wasn't tuning in to my vibrations. "I think Kathy Flaherty is kind of pretty," she said. "Have you made love with her yet?"

"Naw, I'm not begging her. Besides, she isn't foxy."

"You mean sexy?"

"Yeah, she's a lump of dough."

"You're only nineteen." Merle laughed. "How many women have you known?"

"In my school, kids were fucking when they were twelve."

"But you weren't?"

"I didn't say that. I've been around."

Merle stared at me for almost a minute, making me

feel very jittery. "Mohammed, why don't you stop playing the mean dude? Kathy Flaherty is a virgin, and I don't think you're far from it."

"Shit, you're crazy," I almost shouted. "I fucked plenty." I knew I wasn't getting anywhere, so I plunged in. "If you think I'm so innocent, why don't you give me some lessons?"

She smiled and said, "Damn, I knew the minute you walked in here what was in your head. You just proved I was right when you sat down with one leg over the chair so that I could see your balls and prick. What'd you think I'd do, lift up my nightgown and say, 'Oh, Mohammed, slip it to me, baby. Hunny, I can't wait'?"

Then we both laughed, and although her words were like she was trying to cut me up, there was this warm understanding look in her eyes. "Well, I guess I blew that one," I said. "See you later, alligator."

Merle sat on the edge of my chair, and she kissed my cheek. "Mohammed, I love you. Any girl would be glad to go to bed with you, if she just had sex on her brain, and that includes me. But if I broke the rules about Compars messing with Premars, it really wouldn't help you, and we'd probably end up screwing up the whole commune."

I shrugged. "I guess I gotta split with Premar. Everywhere is naked chicks and sex talk, and I ain't getting any. Out in the world where it's real and edgy, you may not get it regularly, but you don't think about it so much. If I didn't jerk off, I'd be climbing the walls."

"Did you ever talk with Kathy about her parents?" Merle asked me.

"Not much. I know her father's dead. Her old lady is in the nuthouse."

"Jesus Christ!" Merle shook her head. "The world really needs Premar. How could you two live together four weeks and not break through to each other? Kathy's father was held up and murdered by two nigger kids in the little grocery store he managed for somebody else. Does that get through your thick skull, Mohammed? The reason she wanted to live with you was because she's trying to prove something to herself. Maybe she doesn't want to hate the whole black race because of two kids on junk."

As I walked back upstairs, the scene Merle described to me was spinning in my head: Two kids, my age, swaggering into that store at about eleven-thirty, demanding the cash; Kathy's father, not intimidated by black bastards, swearing at them; the kids, freaked out when he pulls his gun charging him. One of them gets him with a shiv, and he pops one of them with a thirty-eight. Final score: One whitey dead, one nigger dead, one nigger up for life.

And I thought of Merle giving me a big hug. "Be nice to her, Mohammed. Kathy's got guts."

When I opened the door to our room, I couldn't believe my eyes. Kathy was in *my* bed, smiling; her shoulders were bare, her woolly nightgown on the floor.

"I wondered if you were ever coming back," she said. "I'm glad tomorrow is Sunday."

For the first time in my life I didn't have any words. I took off my bathrobe, and Kathy slid over to make room. When I got in beside her, she flung herself into my arms. I could feel her trembling.

Today, as I write this, I'm soaring. I'm a black cloud that's all white inside. I told Kathy I'd let her read my first journal.

"Oh, Mohammed, love me," you sobbed. "Don't hurt me—love me!"

I felt like a clumsy rhinoceros. I was sure I would hurt you, and God knows I didn't want to now. And somehow you and I found a love rhythm. Instead of just ramming it into you and breaking your cherry, I whispered to you to do it to yourself, slowly, with my prick. *And you did.* But first you rubbed me against you so voluptuously—very slowly, and always in the right direction—that I still don't know how I managed not to go off in your hand. I was breathing the warm smell of your tits, and I was sure that my prick must be at least two feet long. And then, like my brain suddenly spun loose, I remembered *The Owl and the Pussycat.* And I whispered it all to you—especially the ending: "What a beautiful pussy you are—you are. What a beautiful pussy you are." And wow! Your doorway opened, and you yelled, and I knew it wasn't pain, because no gal could rock and buck that way and be hurting. And finally, when we were hearing things again and listening to the echoes of our discovery of each other, we couldn't stop laughing, because all the pounding in our heads wasn't ourselves, but Blake Corey and Lainey Fránci pounding on the walls asking if we were killing each other.

"Kathy," I whispered, "you are something special."

And you are. I may live with some other girls before we finish Premar, and you may live with other guys—right now, I'm not sure I can take that—but whatever happens, I'm going to need you, Kathy, the rest of my life.

"I wanted to room with you," you sobbed. "I wanted you to hate me so I could hate you. Ellen says such a person is a masochist. And then I began to realize you might be mixed up the same way. The black kid who killed my father was just as mixed up as the white people who made him that kind of kid."

I was tasting your breasts when you said that, Kathy, and I remembered Ellen in the dayroom showing me some reproduction of paintings by Renoir and Titian. "Men loved their women big in those days, Mohammed. Have you ever really looked at Kathy's body? Her great grandmother probably dug potatoes all day long. She's got strong legs and arms. She can work hard beside the man who loves her."

And I told you what Ellen had told me, and you said, "Oh, God, Mohammed—if you really want a skinny woman, I won't eat until I'm skin and bones."

And I turned you over on your belly, and I massaged your behind and calves and I kissed them. "I love your big ass, honey-pie," I told you. "And you and I promise to keep it in shape, not with food, but with love."

Ellen O'Day. Prelude to Premar. May. From tapes transcribed by Katherine Flaherty.

It was a week ago today that I moved in with Bren and Merle. Monday morning at ten o'clock, when I finally arrived home for a visit, worried that Daddy might have alerted the police to search for his missing daughter—I had been careful not to give my mother any address for Marie Timilty, a girl who actually does exist—I knew I had to face some version of reality. Bren had let me out of his camper at the beginning of Dasson Road. I was sure that by this time that Daddy would be at City Hall.

Mother greeted me with a combination of joy at my return and hostility. Why had forty-eight hours elapsed since my only telephone call? Daddy was convinced that I wasn't staying with any girlfriend. If he were right, and I actually had slept with some young man, he was ashamed of me, and God help the man when he found out who he was.

Over coffee I attempted to explain to her my need to be with other students and people my age. My brothers had gone away to college. I had never really been anywhere. "I'm twenty-five," I said. "I'm going to take a few courses through the summer and meet the requirements for my degree as soon as possible. It's simple, really—some friends of Marie's have an apartment nearby. We'll share the rent. They have a car. I won't have to ride the subway." I patted her hand. "Mother, it isn't as if I'm dying. If I'm ever going to get married, I have to meet boys, and to do that I have to move about."

I didn't dare explain that Bren's tenement house was so close I could walk home. When that bomb exploded, I prayed that by some miracle I could convince my parents that my life in the same house with Bren was really quite innocent.

"If there's boys living in this apartment, your father isn't going to like it." Gina shook her head. "I don't know what's going on in the world. College students living together unmarried! Boys trying to get the best years of a girl's life! They don't marry you, not that kind."

"Mother, I was eight years old when you were twenty-five. When you were my age, you'd been sleeping with a man eight years."

"Maybe so, but you'll find out that sex is overrated."

"What isn't?"

"Family." Gina laughed. "Not Irish families; they're always mad at each other. Italians fight and make up. Anyway, you stay here tonight. You explain it to your father. I'm not going to."

Daddy didn't like the idea. I knew that part of his objection was that I wouldn't be home evenings to listen to his summations of Boston politics. "There's no boys, Daddy," I said. My fingers were firmly crossed. "Before I ever get involved with a boy, you'll meet him."

As I repeated this lie—trying to convince them I was about to enter a convent—the vision of Bren naked, his penis engorged, bobbling in the air, kept dancing in my head. Yet, I was still a virgin in the conventional sense. Merle slept with me Friday night. Saturday night, when she and Bren came back from the Tenhausens', they slept in her room. Did they really want me to live with them? Or was Bren so intent on becoming a leader of Premars that he would do anything to qualify—even marry a girl with one foot in the grave?

Despite their seemingly easy acceptance of me, I'm sure Merle is convinced that Bren is daydreaming. "It's not just that Ellen has her problems," she told Bren. "There's also Rais. I haven't heard a word from him in three weeks. I'm afraid that Gabrielle has convinced him that a party revolution is in the making. If it is, Rais may never come back, especially if Gabby convinces him he can be the next president of St. Noir." Gabrielle is Merle's sister and is editor of the *St. Noir Goat*.

Bren dismissed her fears. "We've got four months until September. If Rais doesn't come back until late fall, I'll forge a letter from him, and the three of us will run things without him. We can handle forty-eight kids." Bren's laughing remark that he would enjoy being a caliph in a black and white harem did not appeal to me; I doubted very much if I was going to welcome his penis into my body on an alternative basis with Merle.

So at least the lie I told Daddy was only a half-lie. Despite the hours in bed with Bren, despite all the crazy, titillating conversation, Bren hadn't attempted to make love to me, though he would say that wasn't true. He had made love to me. He would say that he had intercourse with my brain and found it delightful.

I rode back to Bren's house in a taxi, my clothes in two suitcases I had bought two summers ago for a vacation on the Cape that I hadn't felt good enough to take, my bankbook showing my savings of $2,276, and Gina's insistent ringing in my ears that she would telephone me every day. I had given her Bren's number before I realized that it would be a simple thing for Dancer O'Day to find out the address that went with it. I tried to think sanely. Why was I so anxious to move in with Bren and Merle?

While I told myself it was more than just wanting to be loved, what I kept thinking about was sex with Bren. Given the opportunity, would I succumb to an evening of mad, passionate fucking? With a little snicker I breathed the word I had never dared to say. Fucking. To be honest, I was ready to spend a week, a month, or just forever being like the women I had read about, not only in best-seller fiction, but also in those sleazy paperbacks they sell in "adult" book stores. Was that the kind of woman Bren wanted? If so, I was ready; I was prepared to shake off the mental shackles of my religious training and dare to be the female I suspected was lurking below my frigid exterior. Even if I perished in the attempt.

But exactly what role should I play?

I knew that if I told Bren I wasn't sure whether I should be a passive receptacle for the male (following the advice of Father Tim) or I should be the brash female who sucked his cock, as the porno books put it, he would laugh at me. And, my God, was my mouth big enough? And weren't there less greedy terms, like "jigger tasting"? My brothers had jiggers, not cocks. If I told Bren all these crazy thoughts, he would laugh himself into hiccups. He was more than sex. He was laughter and joy. They bubbled in his eyes, danced on his tongue, and for Ellen O'Day, born of keeners, child of her own sorrow, it was lovely to bask in his sunlight.

While on one level I saw myself seducing Bren (a svelte, knowledgeable Ellen leading him on), on another I was rejecting him with the ferocity of an about-to-be-ravished nun. Could I ever really accept the fact that he cared for Merle, a Negro who was warm, laughing, affectionate too, and maybe even pretty—not standard American pretty, but African pretty—and vibrant with warm, sensuous lips, and crinkly hair (a delight to touch) worn in short bush cut, and then nostrils that could flare wide in disdain—but you guessed at once that nothing was disdainful to Merle.

Friday night, after apologizing for usurping her bed, I watched her undress. Her grace of body as she moved around the room, a naked ballerina, seemed to epitomize her name. She grinned at my compliments . . . crawled into bed with me.

"A few years ago," she said, "when I read Malcolm X's *Autobiography*, I was determined to change my name to Merle X, but to Bren the X was madness. What difference did it make if I couldn't trace my ancestors? He said they were alive in every step I took. He said he'd bet I was the descendant of some African king who sold his people into slavery."

Leaning back on elbow, her breasts warm brown cones topped with black-cherry nipples, Merle looked straight at me. "That made me wonder if my great-great-grand-mother was a king's daughter or wife, how she ended up—in a slave ship."

Merle's eyes twinkled. "Bren's answer to that was that my great-great-granddaddy must have got his comeup-pance. After double-dealing with his own people and sell-ing them to the slavers, some slaver gave the king and his family a shafting and enslaved them, too. Rais and Bren feel that the whole black-slavery business was historically inevitable. Man had enslaved his fellow men for centuries. The Romans did it, the Egyptians did it, the black Afri-cans did it. In the thousands of years before the Ameri-cans turned the black people into a kind of human-robot machinery to harvest cotton, no one, except maybe Spar-tacus, questioned the institution. As in everything else, Americans tend to develop their philosophies to a point of no return. Finally, in the open forum of democracy, they had to question the validity of their actions. The trouble is, even to this day we have leaders who try to vindicate morally evil acts, like when we were bombing North Viet-nam, or hoke them up so the average man can't tell the bad from the good." Merle shrugged. "You seem to be feeling a little better. Did the reincarnation of Karl Marx, or Jesus in his second coming, make love to you?"

Merle laughed. "Don't worry, Ellen, I'm not trying to insult you. Bren and I never think any thoughts we wouldn't tell each other. Bren is Jewish plus Hindu. He firmly believes that he was born before, and not just once, but often. He has lived, he died, and now he's living again. Maybe not as Marx or Jesus, although he does have com-mon cause with them." Merle was watching for my reac-tion, trying, I think, to guess whether I could accept this happy insanity. "Anyway," she added, "if Bren didn't actu-ally make love to you, he most certainly talked your ear off."

I didn't know whether to be completely honest, so I said, "If he did make love to me, would you be angry?"

She gently rubbed my back. "Honey, Bren's loving you won't diminish me in his eyes. Your problem will be to un-derstand that. It's kind of complicated, but Bren hasn't, as yet, made an intellectual truce with a female, at least with any of the white girls he roomed with as an undergraduate. He's always been convinced he would attempt the multiplier effect with people like you. Maybe you'll be his first real conversion."

I frowned. "He wants to play Pygmalion, then?" I was feeling aggrieved and wondering for the hundredth time why I was lying in a black girl's bed discussing her lover as someone we might share.

"No. Don't make the mistake of thinking that Bren wants a reflection of his own ego. He has small patience with minds around him that don't act as a catalyst to his. The reason that he encouraged you to stay here is that you challenged him the other day. If he hasn't already asked you, he is intensely curious as to why you are taking Tavish's seminar in urban planning. It seems so out of character for a girl with a rheumatic heart to care one way or the other about anything except her own survival."

A dozen possible reasons raced through my mind. I had told my family that I hoped my courses might help me get a job with the Boston Redevelopment Authority. Despite my father's bitterness and rearguard fighting against busing and the "Negro invasion," I'm convinced in any case that in a few years the tenements on our street will be at least fifty percent occupied by blacks.

"I guess the truth is, Merle, that I'm interested to know whether something like Rais' ethnic and racial bridges can ever be built. Pluralism can't work if each group digs moats or if people build impenetrable walls around themselves. Maybe Bren is right. If we knew the right approaches, we could begin to bring people really together right here in Topham's Corner with the Irish and the blacks and the Poles and the few Italians who haven't moved away.

Merle shrugged. "There are only about fifty Italian families left in the area, and most of the low-income Jews have already gone. One thing about the Irish—they might not like the blacks, but they stay put when the black wave washes in. Anyway, baby, the ethnics aren't the problem. It's the WASPs." Merle put her arm around me. Out of the corner of my eye, with my face resting on her shoulder, I could contrast my white nose with her smooth brown skin. Not only could I feel the warmth of her bare breast and breathe the sensuous quality of her, but I tried to match the firm rhythm of her heart beat with my own umpty-thump.

"Seems to me there are three basic kinds of families in the United States," she said softly. "There's the Jewish family with its husband and wife and several children. Their religion cements them together and makes it possible for them to bear a tradition of centuries of persecution. They avoid the locked-in boredom of the nuclear family because most Jews maintain such strong kinship relations that every last aunt, uncle, and cousin is involved in the larger family unit. This system gives every member of the family, and all six million Jews in the United States, a feeling that they're involved in an extended family. Every last Jew is a *landsman*, and hence he's related to every other Jew.

"The Italians hold onto some of their involved kinship relationships, as do other ethnic groups that came from Europe, but their Catholic religion doesn't unify them the way Judaism does. Italians kill each other. Jews don't." Merle grinned at me. "The Irish, when they don't make the mistake of marrying Italians, like your father did, often develop extended kinship relationships, but most of them try to substitute the Irish Catholic Church for family, and many of the Irish are seduced by their 'betters.' They can't stop trying to emulate the white Anglo-Saxons who still dominate this country intellectually as well as numerically.

"These Protestant, gentile whites—*the man*—have the second type of family relationship, which is basically money-dominated. Money—how much of it you have—not love, is the key to their behavior. White Anglo-Saxon Protestants." Merle's tone was sarcastic.

"The first WASP philosopher was Martin Luther. He offered them a God and a heaven where the streets are paved with gold. The WASPs may not be the chosen people, but they think they're better than all the others because they just don't sit and wait. They believe that God helps those who help themselves—*to the most*. They believe in Darwin, too. Darwin may never have meant that survival-of-the-fittest jazz, but he got tagged with the idea, and the 'haves' were quick to spread it around the world.

"Their philosophies are only a few centuries old, but they're inbred. The little, middle-income WASP has been conditioned by them—brainwashed. Their children, emulating their fathers and mothers, have produced millions of interchangeable nuclear family units—every last one in business for themselves. They pray to the system to make them rich. They create industries that swap them around the country, like chess pieces, all interchangeable, while at the same time they, and the moneyed Jews, tell us that a transient, junk-accumulating society is the best way of life. They all believe they are special individuals, but even they are finally ground down until they become fungible pieces of the same puzzle. Pick up a piece here, put it over there, and it fits. What's more, each piece believes intensely in doing its own thing, and is completely unaware that its 'I-gotta-be-me' philosophy is surrounded by a billion other pieces, not one of which can afford to let me be me, because, if it does, it can't be it. The senior-citizen center is the Frankenstein monster created by the WASP mentality—and proves the WASPs' inability to care for anyone except themselves.

"Most English and German families are superb examples of the WASP amoeba, divide-and-hate-each-other character. Each particle is so certain of its own infallibility that it can't tolerate any other particle."

Merle laughed at the wonderment in my eyes—not so much at what she was saying, but at my delight that a woman, black or white, dared to philosophize with another woman. I think it is a sad thing that most females I've known avoid ideas.

Merle was effervescent—charged by her awareness that I was intrigued by her thinking. "The third family type in America is the matriarchal, black, extended family, with the mother often taking the whole damned responsibility for her progeny while she maintains contact with an involved network of relatives and friends. Big Daddy pursues his fancies and assumes responsibility only when he's damned good and ready. God! I'm really raving, aren't I?" Merle grinned at me. "But do you want to know something? My bet is that the black style of matriarchy one day will be the most typical family style of all. First, because men, whether they're Jews, Catholics, or blacks, aren't going to marry females who, every day, are getting smarter than they are. A man doesn't want to be responsible for a woman any longer, especially a woman who can earn as much money as he can. What's more, a lot of women don't want men to be responsible for them. If I were a male, a gal demanding her rights and her orgasms would scare me half to death. A man could get to thinking: Maybe I'm going to be a fucking bust in bed. That could be downright embarrassing, especially if the woman yaks about his poor performance. So one day, unless men and women really learn how to love each other, the only kinds of families there'll be in this Western world will be kids eared by their tiger mothers who don't even have tim to lap their asses, but deposit them in day-care cente And we'll produce a whole generation of robots with no family and no roots: eating, sleeping, working, and fucking, with no brains left to ask what's it all about."

Listening to Merle, I wanted to tell her that I suddenly realized that she and Bren had the key to love. It began with daring to wonder with each other—daring to ask *why?* And I suddenly realized why I had fallen in love with Bre nearly four years ago, when I heard him address a Students for a Democratic Society gathering. Both he and Merle—and I was sure it was true of Rais —exuded a bubbling, involved enthusiasm that made it apparent that they *cared*, that they were involved. Before you knew it was happening, they led you into a new awareness of life as an infinite possibility.

But you can't go around for years loving someone who doesn't even know you exist. I tried to tell Merle how I felt about both of them, that it wasn't that I ever wanted to marry Bren. Living with both of them was enough adrenaline for me. But somehow I wanted to help.

Merle grunted at me sleepily. "You may not know it, honey, but you're hooked. From now on you'll never be sure which side of you is up. Whichever, it won't be the dull side!"

Laughing, Merle told me the reason she left a dim light burning on her dresser. "Bren says he can't see me in the dark."

I knew what she meant—that the light was left on when they made love together. Lying beside her, my thoughts began to churn unpleasantly. I tried to convince myself that it didn't matter, that I couldn't be jealous of Merle. I really liked her. Still, my heart was beating an unpleasant gloop-gleep, as if occasionally the gloop couldn't make up its mind. I didn't dare to sleep. If my blood, trying to get through that poor, encrusted valve, was going to give up trying, then I wanted to be awake when it happened. At least I'd be able to say good-bye to whoever had been Ellen O'Day.

Merle Blanc. Prelude to Premar. June. From tapes transcribed by Samantha Brown.

Rais, I'm making this whole tape for you, but I'm not sure that I can talk into this gadget. It would be bad enough on the ground, but flying a couple of miles in the air with the stewardesses looking at me as if I were a CIA agent— well, damn, I got so many thoughts, I can't concentrate. Once, Rais, you told Bren: "One of us should gag Merle for a whole day and make her listen. Maybe then she'd learn how to think before she leaps."

I should have slugged you. But damn, every time I'm burning, you just give me your big sloppy look. You're more effective than Sidney Poitier because you're leaner and sometimes you really look mean, as if you might suddenly change into a tiger about to pounce. With your English accent, Rais, damn you, you give me the tremblies. You make me forget that I'm equal to you, anytime. And I'm a hell of a lot more practical!

If you die before me, which is likely, I promise you I won't go in for suttee, that old Hindu business where they tossed the wife in the grave with her mate. I'll just put you in a wooden box and leave enough room in the hole in the ground so one day they can put me on top of you. When my time comes and I'm dissolving into you, I'll squirm around and give you a metaphysical erection and orgasm. You big dum-dum! Even if you don't know it yet, we're chemically attuned. You'd really fly upside down without me.

Of course, you didn't know that six years ago, when I managed to escape St. Noir, too, and to your surprise followed you to Boston University. I knew your weaknesses. Getting to the States two years ahead of me, you just naturally would discover something more erotic than your black girlfriend from back home. I remember the day you coolly introduced me to her, Lena Goldman, and smoothly told me that if I'd like to have a white roommate, you knew a guy named Bren Gattman. Lena loved Bren, but since she had been unable to tame him, she was practicing on you.

Staring stupidly at Lena, while she gave me the impression I only partially existed, I felt as if I had been kicked in the guts. Even though I have French blood, I felt like nothing but an African field nigger. What chance did I have against long blond hair, milk-white skin, and Polish blue eyes? It wasn't that I was less vocal than Lena; neither of us could ever outtalk the other. It was just that you, Rais, wouldn't listen. You were too busy sticking your black prick into her white cunt, or being amazed that you had managed to get your number-eight-size black head between the legs of Snow White. You didn't actually say it, but I knew what you were thinking: Go away, Merle. You're just like my little sister. I've known you all my life.

How did I get off on that tack? All that's long past. Lena married a lawyer, Sam Greenfield, nearly two years ago. That was the year before she rejoined the Establishment. I told Bren I'd love him all my life, even have his baby, if he wanted; but since Lena was really as much intrigued with him as with you, it would be nice if Bren and you switched girlfriends for a while.

I finally inherited you. For three weeks we slept in the same bedroom, in different beds, circling and sparring like a couple of boxers not daring to land a punch, and then one night—I'll never forget—you grabbed me and held me over your head like a basketball you were ready to sink in the net. You were Atlas holding the world in his hands. Looking in the mirror, you laughed at yourself and me. Screaming and yanking your fuzzy hair, I didn't bother you more than a fly sizzing around your ear. "I'm going to hold you in the air and turn you slowly around and around, until you get so dizzy you'll finally agree to go to bed with me."

"You dumb gorilla!" I screamed. "I've been trying to fuck with you since I was nine years old!"

And a second later, there we were at last, hugging and kissing and admitting that Eldridge Cleaver was right about one thing—the whole secret of the world is prick and pussy power, and the joy of discovering that brains, and the right combination, can motorize that prick and pussy power into a sweetness-and-light trip without equal in this otherwise mad world.

Well, as I learned later, and as I warned Ellen yesterday, females who sit on seesaws with men like you or Bren can expect to find themselves not only with their legs spread, but with acrophobia from being too much on the high end.

What am I doing on this plane? Am I flying to St. Noir to persuade you to come back to Boston? Which is the most impossible dream, the Confamiliaum which you and Bren once thought might change the whole character of urban living for lower-income people, or Bren's sudden brainstorm to combine a new approach to urban community with Phil Tenhausen's ongoing process of undergraduate education? Or is the real insanity the takeover of St. Noir? Rais, I don't care what my sister Gabby is telling you. You can't take on the United States *and* the British. Not at the same time!

All you're going to do is rile up sixty thousand niggers who won't give a damn one way or the other when you lose your life fighting for them. Oh, damn! Rais, you know that I believe in you, but I love you, too. How did I get involved with men like you and Bren? Dreamers chasing after Utopias—charging windmills. One Don Quixote would be enough. I got two. Sure, I love Bren. You know that, Rais. I'm a person who enjoys men—not hundreds, but a couple of special ones. Funny, sometimes when I'm making love and I close my eyes and listen to you talking, if it weren't for your British accent I couldn't tell which of my lovers was inside me. Yes, I could. I just remembered! Rais, your prick is cooler! I mean it literally. I wonder why. When you're inside me, you feel like a big icicle. Will you ever hear this tape? Who gives a shit? I'd rather say it to you in person. I love you!

Taking this tape recorder along wasn't my idea. Bren wants me to persuade you to extemporize on it. "So we'll know what a revolutionist is thinking when he's in the middle of a revolution." But that's not all. Phil Tenhausen telephoned Bren. He's really interested in Bren's idea of setting up a Divisions Two and Three Premar commune in Bren's tenement house and three other tenements that Bren is sure he can buy. Bren was in a quandary. If Phil okays Bren's idea, Phil will insist that there must be at least four of us to function as communal parents. So my mission, after I bring you up-to-date, is to convince you, or, at the very least, to get a tape from you, telling Phil how enthusiastic you are. Which really means that somehow I persuade you that Confams and Premar communes in Dorchester are a beginning. I kept telling Bren that St. Noir probably has more reality for you than the sex life of the white man. But we're practically American citizens, Rais. We escaped! In your heart you know it's true that neither of us can go home again.

You'll like Ellen O'Day. There's something so pathetically honest about her; the way she looks at you kind of grabs you. This morning, wearing one of Bren's shirts, and nothing much else, she appeared in the kitchen, where Bren and I were eating. I think she was happy that I was leaving, but she had tears in her eyes when she kissed my cheek. She said, "I've only known you a week, Merle, but you're my friend. Come back."

I was dawdling over a bowl of oatmeal. "It'll give you time to get acquainted," I told her. "You and Bren can have a honeymoon. Anyway, much as I want to go, this is Bren's dime. He's paying for the trip. You've got twenty-four hours to make up your mind. Phil Tenhausen is coming here tomorrow. If Rais comes back with me, and if you and Bren can show a wedding certificate, the first National Premar Commune in Topham's Corner will be in business."

Ellen looked frightened. "Merle, Bren, I want to be honest with both of you. It won't work. Right now my chest feels like a suitcase that's jammed too tight. What good would I be to you?"

Bren patted Ellen's behind and ran his finger along the separation. "Your tuchas is smiling sideways at me. Stop worrying—you can hold court in your bedroom or in the bathtub, just like Madame de Stael. The kids will love it."

Then Bren seemed to change the subject. He said, "I've been reading every damned thing the Tenhausens have ever written. The key to Premar is simple. Here it is: 'Listen! Listen! Don't pass judgment! Open *your* heart! And *your* mind! *Confidence begets confidence.* Never stop asking why. Ask ten billion questions. Don't be embarrassed to wonder!' If we only manage to teach the kids that much, we'll have given them a fantastic lifelong education. You don't have to be an Olympic star, Ellen, to be that kind of friend as well as teacher."

"Try Bren's oatmeal," I told Ellen. "It'll either kill you or cure you."

Bren waved a spoonful at her. "It's cheap and nourishing. I'm making a study of the cost of feeding people in groups. Amazing what you can do with cooperative buying at wholesale prices. The trick is to make eating together so enjoyable that what you eat doesn't matter. In his *Autobiography*, Benjamin Franklin mentioned he was the thirteenth child. He said he never questioned the food he was served because he was so glad he got anything to eat."

Ellen laughed. "Ben Franklin died of the gout. Overeating French food and wines. If he'd tasted this gluey mess, he'd have gone on a diet."

Bren held Ellen's wrist and counted her pulse rate. "Not too bad," he told her. "But you do look a little washed-out. Are you still wrestling with your guilt devils? You better follow Lieb's advice and stay in the sack today. After a couple of days' rest, you'll be ready for Phil and Margaret."

"I'm not a good bed person." Ellen blushed. "I mean, I can't just lie in bed all day. I get jittery."

Ellen insisted on driving to the airport with us. Before we left, I told her that among Bren's many cassettes she'd find the tape you made of "Walk Before God." "Listen to Rais," I told her, "and to some of those other tapes Bren made. You should know the kind of men you're getting involved with. Rais has bigger dreams than Bren, and I'm really afraid that he thinks he can take over St. Noir. Many of the small Caribbean islands are absolutely dependent on sugar and tourism. Rais wants to expropriate the hotels, take over the buildings and the land, and have them owned by a People's Corporation. Whoever came to the islands in the future would come as a paying guest of all the people, and he'd live with the natives on whatever economic level prevailed. Rich or poor, white people would live intimately with the island people, with no way to exploit them. They'd share *their* sun, and *their* land, and *their* beaches, all at reasonable rates determined by the People's Corporation. A vacation then would become a truly ecological experience as whites discovered the joyous soul of the islanders and enjoyed them, not as a serving class, but as friends."

Driving to the airport with Ellen between himself and me, Bren said he wasn't convinced. "The tourists won't come down to the level of the island people. If St. Noir isn't a playground, and there's no one to wait on them, the rich won't come anymore. Then the islanders will have only their pride to eat. Even black men prefer to sell their souls to the devil who has the green stuff. Look at Cuba. What has Castro really accomplished? You've got to bring Rais back, Merle, because right here is the place for us to take the first step. We can do what Rais can't—at least not now—right here in Topham's Corner. If America, and that includes the Caribbean, is going to change direction, the people who count must see the light first. I mean Joe—whether he's blue-collar Joe or white-collar Joe—all the millions who have been told they're the great silent majority. They still believe in magic. We've got to help them discover that some of the magicians are con artists and slick sideshow barkers performing sleight-of-hand with their money for the magician's benefit. What I like about the Premar communes, as well as the plans Rais and I kicked around for Confamiliaums, is that they're immediately practical. We could organize a Confam now without warfare, without the 'haves' giving a damn one way or the other. Without any big noise, with no one conscious that it's happening, we could kill two birds with one stone. We'll show them a new kind of populist democracy that the little guy, black and white, can empathize with. A truly participatory democracy, a new kind of libertarianism that's so far right, it's really left. We'll use the system constructively in a two-way relationship. It would be a society of smaller communities where Confams working together with common objectives could create deep human involvement. We'll change all the alienated ciphers into wondering, questioning human beings. We'll show blue-collar Joe that God helps those who help themselves. We'll show him that blueing America can make it green."

"You'll have to add yellow." Ellen laughed. "That's me!"

"You better reread Phil Tenhausen's prospectus," I told Ellen. "Communal house parents will be selected from married graduate students. When Phil arrives Friday, what are you going to show him for a wedding certificate? And even if you're crazy enough to marry Bren, there's still no guarantee that I'm coming back with Rais. If I come alone, then there'll be only three of us, and Bren won't be able to go to bed with me. These kids are going to be screwed-up enough, living with a member of the other sex that they're not married to, without giving them the idea that Premar is a tryout for a swinger's heaven." I was teasing him and trying to shock Ellen. Anyway, Bren occasionally needs to have the rug pulled out from under him. "Honestly," I continued, "I can't believe that Phil would ever stick his neck out and get involved with you . . . or Rais."

Bren smiled at Ellen. "Do you understand this conversation?"

She was obviously bewildered. "If you're going to ask me to marry you, don't!" There were tears in her eyes. "You'd get the worse of the bargain, with me fibrillating and my father ready to tear you limb from limb. I'm sure he's discovered already that I'm not living with Marie Timilty. I finally had to tell my mother, and she can't keep a secret."

"We don't actually have to be married." Bren was deep in thought. Driving through the Callahan Tunnel, as usual, he was on the middle of the white line. I wondered if we were going to reach the airport or crack up en route.

"Look, Ellen"—he had such a beseeching expression on his face that he would have convinced Golda Meir that Sadat loved her—"we've got everything to gain. You need a year to get your master's. Rais and I need the year for our doctorates. Merle needs two years. Degrees are a pile of crap, but we've all played the game this far. We might as well finish it. Anyway, you and I and Merle and Rais are the perfect communal parents. *Compars!* Just what the consortium is looking for."

"Some parents." Ellen looked at me and shook her head, but she was unable to restrain a little grin. "We're only seven or eight years older than our prospective children. And you can stop giving me that sad-little-boy look, Bren. God gave me an activist brain, but not the body to go with it. Why don't you face it? I could slump off this seat right now, and not even say good-bye to you."

"No, you couldn't." Bren chuckled. "I'd give you mouth-to-mouth resuscitation. You're not getting rid of me that easily. Besides, now you've got something to live for—me. I need you!"

"Oh, Bren, you are a dreamer. I probably have more hang-ups than the entire freshman class will ever have. You'd be tied to a cripple. Anyway, if I agree to tell Phil we're married, and he buys it, where does that leave Merle?"

I wondered where it left Ellen's father, Dancer O'Day, but I didn't want to open that can of worms. Who would marry them, a priest or a rabbi?

Bren pulled the car up in front of the Air France terminal. I kissed Ellen's cheek. "I got my man, remember?" I told her. "But whether I come back with him, or without him, I'm not sure, Ellen, if you can cope with Bren or Rais—especially together. They're not living in this century. They think they can sleep with either one of us— even have coffee-colored kids—and we, and all the neighbors, would cheer them on because they were good and loving daddies. They'll be determined to seduce you into their cul-de-sac. Whether you expect it to happen or not, Rais would ask Bren if he would mind if he slept with you; and the first thing you know, you'd agree. Maybe I'd be good and mad. Maybe you'd be jealous, but Bren wouldn't comprehend your possessiveness, and Rais would be tickled skinny, studying your reactions as if you were demented. You'd be driven right out of your monogamous mind!"

Bren assured Ellen that I was teasing her. He gave me a good-bye hug. "I'm not sure that you understand Rais," he said. "He's not the kind of guy who would push himself on any woman, let alone a white woman. If the day ever came that he wanted to go to bed with Ellen, it would be because he loved her—really cared for and trusted her. After his experience with Lena, that will take some doing."

"You survived Lena." This was no kind of good-bye conversation, but I couldn't help it.

Bren shrugged. "It wasn't easy. What Rais didn't understand is that she rejected him for the same reason she rejected me. It had nothing to do with Rais' skin color. Christ! Sam Greenfield, the guy she married, is so swarthy he must have some black blood. The difference is that Sam plays only on winning teams. He never, never thinks that occasionally someone should put a spoke in the wheel of the Establishment." Oblivious of the amazed passers-by, Bren kissed me good-bye. "Whatever else you do, Merle, tell that bête noire that I love him and you, too! Come back!"

Phillip and Margaret Tenhausen, and Advisers to the Consortium. June, the first year of Premar. Portion of a two-hour tape transcribed by Ellen O'Day.

This is Bren Gattman. With the permission of our guests, I am recording this meeting for future Premars and for future reference for myself, Ellen O'Day, Merle Blanc, and Rais Daemon, all of whom I believe will be among the best Compars in this unique experiment in premarital living. As I have explained to Phil Tenhausen, my own enthusiasm stems from my conviction that ultimately Premar could be instrumental in creating a total community in Topham's Corner—a community involved in a lifelong growth and communication between age groups and presaging an exciting rebirth of America.

It's two o'clock in the afternoon. The Tenhausens; Dr. James Tamaski, sociologist and architect, who is responsible for the physical environment of Premar housing; Dr. George Salvo, sociologist; Dr. Katherine Pallas, psychiatrist; Dr. Marion Swenson, M.D.; and Harry Littleton, attorney for the consortium—all are present here and all have spent several hours prior to this meeting exploring Topham's Corner.

Welcome! Ellen and I, who are well aware of your various credentials and your current work, are pleased to have you here. Naturally, we hope—now that we have come this far—we earnestly hope that our plan for a National Premar Commune in Topham's Corner has been approved. What have you decided? (Pause.) The suspense is killing us.

PHIL T. Frankly, Bren, a major criticism of you and Rais Daemon—and we have plenty of documentation on your careers—is that you have not convinced us that you can function with us in a team effort. We admire initiative, and God knows there are enough questions to be answered, but we must be sure that major changes in direction, which might involve not only your Confamiliaum approaches (and we are not sure how far we want to travel in that direction) but your total political philosophy, are developed together with and on the approval of the consortium.

MARGARET T. Those of us who are familiar with your own background and Rais Daemon's admire your basic drives and your obvious abilities, but the truth is—and this should amuse you, because we know, Bren, you are an active feminist—the consortium has approved the four of you as Compars mainly because we feel that Ellen's and Merle's pragmatism may serve to cool your wilder enthusiasms. Hopefully, should you lean too far over the brink, they'll save you from drowning. We want your drive and your tendencies to be gadflies, but we're going to be careful not to get stung.

BREN (*laughing*). So Ellen and Merle are to be the caretakers. Without worrying the point, Margaret, I'd like to leave you with the thought that you're perpetuating some presumed differences between the male and female, namely, that the male is the dreamer, while the female's role is to hold the reins on him.

MARGARET (*chuckling*). You have a point. Now, to give you something to think about, I want you to know that we've not had comparable problems in choosing other Compars. Most of our other nominees aren't challenging the entire world in addition to its sex mores.

Phil put in a long-distance call to Rais Daemon yesterday and discovered that Merle Blanc was in St. Noir. He had an enthusiastic conversation with her and a rather noncommittal one with Rais, who, Phil says, sounds on the telephone as if he should be prime minister of England, if not St. Noir. Rais said that Merle had briefed him thoroughly and that he was interested. He also told us that he was trying to cool the situation in St. Noir, which has been getting very adverse reaction in the American press.

PHIL. I gave it to Rais very straight, Bren. He should be here now, if only to familiarize himself with the vast amount of preparation work now going on to make Premar a reality. Because of his master's in sociology, and because he and Merle are black—and we aren't having an easy time recruiting black Compars who have the credentials we want—we gave Rais until October 1. If he isn't on deck and working at that time—and willing to do a great deal of catching up—then we will immediately replace Rais and Merle with other Compars, who may have to be white; we hope not.

As you know, one of the premises of Premar is that interracial marriage, if it could develop in a completely joyous and permissive environment, would not only create a physically healthier America, but in several generations could resolve the black-white problem. Since all Premar communes will provide an environment conducive to interracial love, you can see the importance of getting as many black Compars as possible. Eventually, if Premar survives, we will generate our own Compars, both black and white, who will have been thoroughly conditioned by their own Premar training. Thus, interracially married couples could be the typical Compars of the future.

ELLEN. Your emphasis on conditioning will frighten many people.

KATHERINE P. We're aware of that, but people are being conditioned every day. Millions of dollars are being spent to preserve the corporate culture of America. We prefer to think of Premar as providing a *deconditioning*, a revaluing of one's world and one's society. From what Margaret and Phil have told me about you, you personally are going through a similar, somewhat painful process in your own love life. We are aware of your background, Ellen, and Bren's. We know that Bren has been intimate with Merle Blanc before and after her marriage to Rais. We found out by the very direct process of asking Merle last night when Phil telephoned Rais. You are aware, Ellen, that the consortium insists that all Compars be married monogamously.

ELLEN (*laughing nervously*). I'm not married to Bren, yet. While I have been brought up to believe in monogamous marriage, it seems inconsistent somehow that you're demanding Compars make a commitment to marriage. Not only is monogamous marriage generally under fire, but if youngsters go through four years of Premar, it would seem to me that after living with as many as four different members of the other sex, they will scarcely be ready to forsake all others and marry one person for life.

KATHERINE. Monogamous marriage can work well if the original pair bonding is joyously alive and the two partners reinforce each other both mentally and sexually. That's what Premar is all about. Margaret and I have been involved in a long discussion about you, Ellen. Quite frankly, we're not sure at the age of twenty-five, without the deconditioning that Premar will offer the incoming youngsters, that you can, in the words of Sidney Jourard, "dare to reinvent your life." Margaret feels that while you may be a gamble, your record at Boston University, and the enthusiasm of many of your instructors, convinces her we should take a chance on you. If you can resolve the problem of marrying a Jewish boy, and face the inevitable antagonisms—I'm almost afraid to ask about your father's feelings—you should become a really understanding Compar as well as a real friend to many youngsters, because you will be empathetic with them. When the Premars arrive, they'll find they're not the only "lost souls," treading through a kind of purgatory. Every value they have lived by will be brought into the open and questioned. The wolf will be howling outside their straw houses, too.

PHIL. I want to amplify Katherine's statement about monogamous marriage. We believe that as a result of Premar's deconditioning, youngsters will discover not only how to love, but eventually how to pick unerringly the right person for mutual self-reinforcement. In this process, the primary bond will have a much better chance of surviving a full lifetime in a framework that accepts, understands, and *expects* each partner to have other mental and sexual intimacies, possibly group relationships within defined limits, or parallel relationships, *without* shattering the primary pair bond, around which several families, encompassing several generations, may gravitate in mutual loving and caring.

BREN. While I'm fully aware that Premar is not just a four-year experience in switching sexual partners, these other aspects of this conditioning process are extremely fascinating to me. Since, as Compars, we will be revaluing a youngster's sexual world, we will inevitably be changing his political viewpoints also. Sex is politics. The very emphasis that Premar puts on interpersonal relationships as a primary source of joy in life tacitly places work, religion, and all other aspects of an individual's existence lower on the ladder of human values. How far will Compars be permitted to go in the economic and political reorientation of the Premars?

PHIL. Recently some professors lost their tenure at Harvard because of their radical economic teachings. The Human-Values course must go as far as necessary in developing the youngsters' ability to question every aspect of society. For example, in the process of rebuilding a sound value structure, we must question the pseudo-values being propagated by live television and TV programming—and what happens to individuals and their values when they are overwhelmed with every imaginable conditioning technique whose sole aim is to lead them to purchase products that are, for the most part, valueless. We believe that education for living begins with an understanding of how we are being motivated to act and react by an environment which, in the twentieth century, is largely manmade. Then, using history for the perspective it can give us, we will try to determine how the world arrived at its present human impasse. A youngster who has finished Premar may not have read Shakespeare or studied ancient history, but he will have a clear-cut view of the kind of world he is living in. He will also have resources within himself to protect him against dehumanization by pseudo-values.

I know I'm avoiding a direct answer to your question, Bren. The reason is that we don't want to publicize the ultimate effect of a widespread change in our sexual mores and how this might effect the political and economic directions of our society. The conservatives realize that the so-called "New Left" continues to undermine the old foundations, particularly in the women's equality movement. But they aren't fully aware of the impact that freer and open sexuality, premaritally and postmaritally, will have on human goals and values. If they really understood that the so-called sex revolution foreshadows political and economic revolution, they would do everything possible, by law and executive fiat, to return the country to the old sexual values built on God, Country, Mother, Wife, Family. At the moment, we can scarcely prove to those who resist change that Premar—by telling young people that *they* are the only God they can even know personally, and by pluralizing human relationships and in the process teaching us our common divinity—will create a sounder and healthier and more joyous society.

MARGARET. Two of the sex books that we will be using in Premar are Alex Comfort's *The Joy of Sex*, and *More Joy*. Recently Alex wrote an article for the Center for Democratic Institutions titled "Sexuality in a Zero Growth Society." He says, " . . . the decline of the kinship family has borne excessively hard on the old . . . dependency is rejected, and they become increasingly isolated in a forced 'independence.' Perhaps more than anyone else they would benefit from a 'spreading' of the couple-preoccupied family."

Alex doesn't amplify this, but he could point out that the percentage of the aged in a zero-population-growth society will increase tremendously in the first twenty years of the twenty-first century. In addition, worldwide inflation, caused by previous population growth, cannot be contained and can never be balanced by increased purchasing power, because the expanded population depends too much on a vast productive "nonworking" force comprising government employees and the service industries. Thus politics and economics, as they have in the past, combined to gradually change our life styles.

Alex's summation is pertinent: "I would expect, accordingly," he says, "to see a society in which pair relationships are still central, but initially less permanent, in which childbearing is seen as a special responsibility involving a special life style, and in which settled couples engage openly in a wide range of sexual relations with friends, with other couples and third parties as an expression of social intimacy, without prejudice to the primacy of their own relationship. . . . Such a pattern is coming into existence in America, and it is becoming explicit. Whether it will devalue relationships or only deprive them of neurotic compulsion will depend on the persons involved, and the amount of support they receive from the social ethic. . . . The political implications of universalized kinship are interesting. Marcuse in discussing the eroticization of relationships as a political force was once challenged to 'go eroticize the state of Kansas.' My suggestion is that this may be happening. The family is in fact the microcosm of politics with a one- or two-generation time-lag. Institutional politics today reflects combative paternalism which had its family counterpart in the 1850's. . . . It is possible to overstate the inherently revolutionary potential of 'universal kinship,' but if, as I suggest, it is specifically eroticized it will find a counterpart socially in anarchic community action. . . . The acceptance of sensuality and the widening of its focus to include not one, but many others, would seem in itself to be an emotional technology capable of fitting well into the less compulsive and more gentle world of the twenty-first century. Marcuse is probably right in seeing justice, nonpossession, nonexploitation, ecology, and the wider eroticization of relationships as possible correlates. We may have a rough few years ahead before this pattern emerges, but when and if it does, one could wish to live in those times."

BREN. As I see it, then, the whole effort of Premar will be to provide the emotional and mental technology—as well as the environment—to bring that kind of world into existence. But not flamboyantly, or in the form of a flag-waving crusade—

PHIL (*interrupting*). I want to back up a little. From the beginning we are making it clear to incoming Premars that Premar is considerably different from any style of informal co-ed living that is now being tried in any university or college in the United States. For example, mixed dormitories are quite prevalent, but, for the most part, although young women are living on the same floor with young men their roommates are of the same sex. In some universities there are co-ed suites where one girl or several girls may live with two or more boys. But essentially all these arrangements are goldfish bowls. Everyone is aware of the extent of a particular student's sexual life. There is little time for deep personal involvement with a person of the other sex: Actual intercourse time usually depends on getting rid of one's roommate of the same sex for an hour or two or shrugging off the need for privacy and making love in a voyeuristic situation. Then, too, the young woman may be put in a position where male chauvinists can easily label her as promiscuous.

Of course, many upper classmen live off-campus with a girl or boy of their own choosing, and we know that at some universities there have been attempts at random selection of roommates of the other sex—usually without the knowledge or blessing of the administration—that have made it possible for a young man and woman to live together on campus. But all these probings into what we consider an eventual future style of human mating lack the permissive environmental structure we are proposing. In a Premar commune an incoming Premar will live experimentally, for twenty-six-week periods, one at a time, with four persons of the other sex, *not of their own choosing*.

BREN. You have stated that roommates will be matched based on like as well as opposite characteristics. I'm not a mathematician, but unless you were working with a much larger sample than you are with Premar—perhaps as much as a million students—I would question the validity of your matches based on exactly parallel or opposite characteristics.

PHIL. You're right. We can only hope for general attitude or inner-goal directions as the basis of like matches. But that's not important to our overall view. Most young people picking a mate they will live with, hopefully for life, could not manage the range of selectivity available to a Premar. Nor could they have the opportunity to live in close proximity with a person he or she is not expected to marry or to live with for a lifetime.

Unlike the situation now prevailing at most colleges or universities, where the act of sexual love carries with it overtly, or subtly, the concept of a long-time commitment, the Premar student won't get involved with the trauma of separation. Even if Premars should fall very much in love, and wish ultimately to continue a one-to-one relationship, the environment will conspire to encourage them to explore the alternatives. It will be possible for girls as well as boys to have a variety of intimate relationships without being labeled promiscuous or having an ownership commitment because they have made love. In the third year, a Premar may attempt a longer commitment with someone he or she has previously lived with, or with someone completely new that they may have met in the Premar environment. But this will be done on the student's own initiative, with vastly more than the usual experience in seeking partners. Incidentally, the first Premar program will continue two years before there will be another incoming freshman class. This will give us time for partial appraisal and evaluation.

ELLEN. I guess I'm a little bewildered ... maybe apprehensive. Being a Premar freshman girl would seem pretty scary to me. Would I be expected to go to bed with my roommate even though I thought he was repulsive or just plain stupid? Maybe I wouldn't like him because he was too fat, or too skinny, or had bad breath, or was a drooler, or was too remote, or didn't keep himself clean, or was covered with pimples, or wore double-lens glasses.

MARGARET (*laughing*). How can I begin to answer you? First, all Premars will have monthly physical examinations, and the Premar program is designed to keep them physically healthy. As for personal cleanliness, if Premars haven't been used to taking daily showers, we're pretty certain that the pressures of the commune will make cleanliness a way of life. And the communal baths will be an erotic experience that we expect Premars will look forward to as a daily "funtime." So cleanliness should not be a big problem.

As for having sex with a repulsive stranger, we understand that point of view, which is probably more masculine than feminine. We expect that some Premars will not have sexual intercourse with their roommates, or may be much more involved sexually with one roommate than with another. You Compars will be the first to know when particular Premars haven't made love together. As their counselors, you will help them resolve the interpersonal problems that make sexual intimacy impossible. The Compars will help the youngsters to see their relationships from different perspectives so that each Premar will have the opportunity to see himself through the eyes of his or her roommate. You will enlarge their horizons, and in the sharing process probably expand your own interpersonal growth, too.

As for physical repulsiveness, those who are likely to be repelled by skin color will not come to Premar in the first place. Obviously, we cannot accept Premars who are grossly overweight, or match a midget with a roommate seven feet tall. In other respects, we will ask Premars this key question: "Do you remember yourself as a young child? Can you be as innocent and trusting as you were long ago?"

ELLEN. But we grow older. We learn to hate.

MARGARET. In an interview, Bucky Fuller mentioned the innate necessity of the child to trust. Its very survival depends on trusting. The interviewer asked Bucky, "How do human beings become aggressive vis-à-vis each other?" Bucky's answer was clear and simple: "Violated trust."

Remember that the freshmen will be only about eighteen years old. As a part of the Human-Values conditioning, we are going to decondition them and reconstitute them in an environment that values defenselessness and makes self-disclosure and transparency a way of life. In the process we will restore trust and their ability to surrender to another human being. In essence, Ellen, I'm telling you that in the first few weeks of Premar, if you were a female roommate, you'd gradually discover your "repulsive roommate" in a new light—and while you still might not want to give yourself passionately to him, you both might find it quite natural to snuggle together naked and talk openly to each other, and you'd both *want* to build bridges between your separate islands.

PHIL. B. F. Skinner summed up our goals in *Beyond Freedom and Dignity*. "There are better ways," he said, "and the literature of freedom and dignity are *not* pointing to them . . . [why can't we], now, accept the the fact that all control is exerted by the environment, and proceed to design better environments rather than better men?"

GEORGE S. Since time is limited this afternoon, I think we should stop philosophizing and resolve some immediate problems. We are much further advanced with the rehabilitation of buildings for most of the other Premar communes. The problem here is: Can we catch up? The consortium has agreed to invest a maximum of one hundred thousand dollars in three of this style tenement house. This money must cover both purchase and conversion. If Bren will sell this house, which we believe he owns, to the consortium for fifteen thousand dollars and we can purchase two others next door in the same price area, we'll have fifty-five thousand dollars left for rehabilitation. We not only have a major time problem—we must be ready in less than fourteen weeks—but we realize, too, that the conversion funds are inadequate and that we must, therefore, depend on a "do-it-yourself" approach.

JAMES T. Bren, Ellen, while these three-story boxes are not ideal for our purposes, we are experimenting with two similar locations, one in Chicago and one in San Francisco. I have floor plans here which we think will produce a good community environment. You will note that on all three floors of each building all the internal walls will be removed except for one sustaining wall. In the kitchen area, sinks, stoves, etc., on all floors, will be completely removed. The toilet areas will be maintained, but all the old fixtures will be torn out. A commune toilet area on each floor will consist of two hoppers and two bidets enclosed by doors, two urinals, and an extended lavatory and sink area capable of serving four of the eight people on any one floor at the same time. The balance of each of the two top floors will be partitioned off into four two-person rooms for sleeping and studying; two one-person privacy rooms in the rear of the building; and a communal sitting room in the front.

The first floor in two houses will have a study-room, a bedroom and a commune office for the Compars. The front area on the first floor of two of these houses will be study rooms, and unlike the sitting rooms on the floors above, will have no television. The entire bottom floor in the third house, preferably the middle house, will be a combination dayroom and communal dining room. In the basement of this house will be the communal kitchen, which we hope to be able to outfit with time-saving equipment. The kitchen will be connected to the dining room above it with a dumbwaiter. The basement in one of the other houses will be a communal bath with three large cement tubs. Bathing will be Japanese-style. In the basement of the third house we will have a recreation room with Ping-Pong tables.

You will note that we have generalized separate plans for all three of the houses. While we plan to work closely with you in this conversion, and we will arrange the actual contracting for plumbing, electricity, and heating conversions, all the interior carpentry and painting will be the Compars' responsibility. But one carpenter should be hired to work with and guide capable Premars in the actual building and painting of the interiors. He will probably have to be a nonunion man.

BREN. I understand you plan to get some of the students who will actually participate in the conversion of these houses here before Premar starts. That seems like a tall order. As for the houses themselves, the one next door is empty. The exterior is in pretty bad shape, and there are broken windows and some water damage inside. The house on our left has two families renting from the owner. The third floor is unoccupied. One family is Czech, four children. The mother and father both work. The other family is an old couple on welfare. I know these people, and we get along. If we're permitted to involve the Premars, I'm sure we can easily establish a nice relationship with all of them. There are two empty flats across the street. If we paint them up, and help them to move, there should be no problem. Both buildings are owned by Mort Sadusky, a wealthy slumlord, who bought the buildings to milk them by depreciating them all over again while he squeezed out as much rent as possible, with little or no building maintenance. I recently uncovered some interesting fast dealings that Sadusky had been involved in on a HUD turnkey project. If I can persuade him to sell for ten thousand dollars each, I'll toss this house in at ten thousand dollars. That will give us fifteen thousand dollars more for rehab.

GEORGE. To answer your worry about getting some of the Premars here early, I don't think we'll have any problem. Nationally, we have more potential Premars than we can handle. Those who will be assigned here will be notified by the middle of next month. By the end of July we should have ten to fifteen Premars eager to be employed immediately on the building conversion. Let's remember that just about all these people want summer jobs. They will be paid out of the conversion fund at the esablished rate of one hundred dollars a week, and they can bunk in the buildings they are remodeling.

ELLEN. I suppose it's a small matter, but what about furnishings? Desks, beds, lamps, chairs?

HENRY L. (*laughing*). The Compars running this commune have the original budget of one hundred thousand dollars, and that's all! You'll have to squeeze enough out, not only for the actual conversion, but for an Econo van-style truck capable of carrying ten to twelve Premars. Keep in mind that you will be dealing with youngsters who ordinarily would have been seek'ng year-round employment instead of having this educational opportunity. These kids have never had much to begin with. They'll help you comb the area for all furniture or whatever can be adapted. You can teach Premars how to refinish it.

ELLEN. I'd have to learn how myself.

KATHERINE. That's the general idea. Compars are going to develop a vast number of skills, including carpentry, as well as the handling of the multiple interpersonal problems.

ELLEN. What about the teaching of sex and contraception?

MARION S. I'm the M.D. assigned to this commune. Every Premar will have a thorough medical examination at the out-patient department of one of the Boston hospitals. All the girls will be introduced to the pill regime. Later, as they become experienced in their sexual lives, we will alternate the pill with the diaphragm and the IUD. The Tenhausens have a mechanics-of-sex program which will be supplemented by live demonstrations by volunteer Premars.

MARGARET. In the Human-Values Seminar we will average one book a week. This is going to be a heavy load for many of the youngsters who are not skilled readers, particularly since all of them will also be working either for undergraduate degrees or advanced vocational skills. However, with each book we will provide condensations covering the overall point of view of the author, as well as salient points for discussion. Compars will be very much involved in an ongoing reading process with the Premars at various H.V. sessions, teaching them how to skim and how to share the reading with their roommates, so the roommate who reads all of a particular book will teach the other. Everyone involved in Premar becomes a teacher to everyone else, and the learning-teaching process becomes a way of life that enhances even lovemaking. For the first six weeks, Compars will cover the following books: *Sexual Life Between Blacks and Whites*, by Beth Day; *Self-Love*, by David Cole; *Sexual Symbolism*, by Richard Knight and Thomas Wright; *The Practice of Creativity*, by George Prince; and *The Art of Loving*, by Erich Fromm. Since our goal is to create a new black-white experience, at least ten percent of the books used in the Human-Values seminar will cover the black experience as it now exists, seen through the eyes of the black writers.

PHIL. I want to mention briefly how the Compars will approach the day-to-day Human-Values seminar. This is a very large area in which we will be constantly comparing theories and new approaches. Compars will meet with four couples every other evening, except weekends. Each Compar couple will be guiding three separate groups of Premars. There will be four Premar couples in each group. Compars will switch their three groups on a regular basis, and in any week will be specifically relating to a maximum of three groups. Twice a week all Compars and all Premars will meet in the dayroom for unifying sessions led by Premars. Compars will maintain regular daily one-to-one-consultation hours for Premars who may wish to talk with them personally as nonjudgmental friends. Still, since we will be actively encouraging Premars how to self-disclose in their smaller groups, individual consultation will be discouraged.

For the most part, we are not encouraging the use of any sensitivity or group-encounter techniques. Within the first few weeks Premars will have advanced far beyond the kindergarten approach of much of the so-called human-potential movement. We want to involve them in a much deeper kind of intimacy that comes from sharing and resolving objective problems, rather than concentrating on navel gazing or encouraging any of the do-your-own-thing philosophy which is common to much sensitivity group thinking. We believe that human beings have a natural desire to work together in groups, just so long as this need is balanced by the opportunity to escape the group. They also have a need to demonstrate, in cooperation with others, the ability to solve common problems. So, in addition to putting a great deal of emphasis on learning the ability to disclose oneself to another, we are exploring a small-group approach to learning based on the theories of Synectics. The basic thrust of Synectics is joining people together into problem-stating and problem-solving groups—groups which gain practice in the art of blending seemingly irrelevant and diverse elements into new phenomena and perspectives. Such small groups can simultaneously discover and create an environment of warm affection and intimacy as well as deepen the understanding of roommates for each other, thus making the total environment of the Premar commune a lively and an exciting place to live. We'll use the techniques developed by Synectics, Incorporated, and discussed by George Prince in *The Practice of Creativity*.

MARGARET (*laughing*). And that's a mouthful, sweetie—and a good place to stop.

Ellen O'Day. Prelude to Premar. June. From tapes transcribed by Katherine Flaherty.

Bren insists that expressing one's deepest thoughts on tape can become an important form of interpersonal communication. But it sounds easier than it actually is. To dare to be honest, to verbalize the myriad thoughts that go through one's brain, to disclose yourself, to make yourself known—not to just another potential listener, but to one's own amazed, slowly comprehending self—is a scary business. You slowly begin to discover yourself inside-out.

Besides Bren and Merle, I suppose some of the Premars will listen to these tapes. Do I dare to disclose my fears and frustrations and needs to strangers? It's a kind of openness I never thought I was capable of. But the fat's in the fire. After yesterday's meeting with Phil and Margaret Tenhausen and the people from the consortium, Premar is inevitable.

If you're a Premar and you think this is easy, then you should try it! How much do you dare to reveal about yourself in your written journals? Are you discovering how difficult it is to write a journal and evoke the fleeting feelings, thoughts, and emotions that make you the person you really are? Even if you manage to do it, and you take the big step of letting another person read your journal, you may wonder whether, when your roommate or your closest friend finally discovers the essential frightened little naked you, they will still like you and care for you.

The more you think about it, the more you'll realize how many of the inventions of man are not only changing his physical environment, but hopefully also our ability to communicate ourselves in depth to another person or persons.

Imagine a world where people who in the ordinary course of events would never have written their autobiographies or kept journals, but who have in fact spoken their most intimate thoughts on voice- or videotape.

What kind of a world might it have been if Jesus, Confucius, Lao-Tze, Caeser, Alexander, Cleopatra, Marie Antoinette, George Washington, Napoleon, Hitler, Franklin Roosevelt, and John Kennedy—or your father and mother and their parents—had kept verbal diaries of their deepest feelings and thoughts?

I wonder what was going through my grandmother Kathy's head in the early 1920's when my grandfather Danny O'Day finally convinced her to lift her skirts and she let him put his penis into her. As they lay together in Killarney, did they wonder about the sheer joy of their flesh—their need for each other? What strange forces in the universe made their coupling necessary? Maybe Danny and Kathy couldn't express such thoughts and emotions to each other, but if some of us begin now, isn't it possible that we can improve our interpersonal comprehension of each other, catch it up with our technological abilities, and in the process learn to be more in command of our destinies, and less overwhelmed by thoughts we bury within ourselves?

As I listen to Phil and Margaret and the people they brought here yesterday, I'm really scared to death. How can I measure up to their expectations? Am I the proverbial moth, unable to fly away from the flame? The key to a Premar education for me will not only be to teach but also to learn. Can I be mentally defenseless? Can I learn not to play verbal games with another person? Can I accept the consequences with equanimity?

I love you because you are you, and *not me*—and slowly we both are learning how to love the not-me in each other and the world. How far from this kind of response am I? Sometimes I think I've always been there. But it's only in the past two weeks that I'm really beginning to dare. Mostly I'd like to believe that this Ellen speaking right now has always been me. Yet I know that suddenly, after years of resting on a lonely mountain escarpment, once again I have to start climbing. Maybe the only real joy in life is the struggle toward the top of the mountain. Yet, if you're like me, and occasionally you are panting from exertion, at least you don't have doctors warning you, "Don't climb stairs, Ellen"—and certainly not mountains, literally or figuratively.

I'm not at all sure if I have the courage to stay here, and I can't escape the feeling that I'm going to witness a kind of Gotterdammerung. Any day now, Daddy will discover that his daughter is screwing a man. Only three blocks from her home.

I can't escape the eerie feeling that I was destined to meet Bren Gattman. Even now as I ramble on these tapes, I marvel at the simplicity of the transition. In the space of a few hours, the daydreams of years have come true: I'm living with a boy who dares to make love to me, a man who won't be put off by my fears of sex and death, and my worst fear of all—that nobody really gives a damn, not just about me, but about one another.

The few boys who dated me were really expected to suppress themselves. "Remember, Ellen has heart trouble. We don't want to lose her." That was my mother's standard warning to any young man who penetrated our living room. With serious faces they would nod their sympathetic understanding, wondering, no doubt, how in hell they had gotten into this mess. Ye gods! How do you spend the second or third evening with a hands-off female? Most of them never returned for a second date, and I didn't blame them. It wasn't only the possibility that a boy might find me dead in his arms. The idea of getting married to me, screwing me, must have seemed like mounting the executioner's platform. Even if I lived, I might be an invalid—a helpless wife, not even any good in bed. A burden on some guy's back ... and mind. Ugh!

Last night after the Tenhausens had gone, I felt tiny and protected in Bren's arms, and gaily silly too, as I responded to his pleased examination of my body. I knew he was floating on a high. Premar, at last, was reality, and he was certain that I would be a part of it. He was as curious and frolicsome as a puppy, lapping me and burrowing softly against my breasts and belly. Gently opening my legs, he admired and tasted my middle. Though I was embarrassed and was sure that I must smell bad—I hadn't washed since morning—he insisted that my "Ellen-odor" was erotic. "We're going to make love all night, and talk, and make love some more," he told me. "And whether you believe in marriage or not, for Premar you have to marry me."

"It will be a big sacrifice," I said. "But I guess I have no choice. If I don't marry you, you'll think you can go to bed with all the young female Premars." I couldn't puncture his balloon or saddle him with my fears of being a useless appendage to Premar. Grinning, his eyes peeking merrily at me through my pubic hair, he lay facing me between my spread-eagled legs. "I was reading about a new product," he said. "Orange-, lemon-, and raspberry-flavored douches. The ultimate taste in cunnilingus. My God, this technological society has lost its sense of smell and taste. Is man to be denied the aphrodisiac delights of feminine effluvia?"

"Bren, please," I begged him.

He slid beside me toe-to-toe, cupping my face in his hands. "Ellen, you *are* lovely!" I lay against his chest and felt his joy bubbling in his words. "They call those douches 'Cupid's Quiver.' A dumb product, but a nice name for the vagina. Both a noun and a verb. A quiver is a sheath in which to keep arrows. Ellen's quiver is quivering for Bren's arrow."

There was a lot of truth in that. I tasted his neck, felt his penis big against my belly, and tried to redirect my thoughts into calmer channels.

"You really like to make love a lot, don't you?"

Bren laughed. "Honey, if you think making love is only a penis bulging in a vagina and rubbing an engorged clitoris, both of them finally exploding in an orgasm, then the answer is a qualified yes! But if you believe that being profoundly aware of each other as amazing, fallible human beings is both a human necessity and love, then my answer is an emphatic yes." He put his fingers across my lips. "We really shouldn't talk. Just float together."

But I couldn't. "What about Merle?"

"Why don't you ask the rest of the questions that are bugging you? Are black girls more sexy than white girls? And if Merle is so good in bed, why is Bren lying with me, especially since I may not even know how to wiggle my ass properly when at last somebody shoves his penis into me?"

"Okay." I stifled my sobs and tried to hold back the tears. "Make fun of me if you want, but where I come from girls don't jump into bed with a stranger, particularly when they know he already has another girl."

His fingers were feathery on my back and behind. He didn't answer for a minute, then said softly, "Where you come from, girls who go to bed with boys before they marry them operate on the principle that they are already halfway home."

"Is that so bad?"

"Not really." He brushed his lips against mine. "Ellen, we don't really come from such different worlds. Most of my undergraduate years were a necessary rebellion against my father's world, which is motivated by about the same manners and mores as your father's environment. You might say the only real difference between them is money. Your father, with the same income as mine, would be Abe Gattman's brother; Abe would say 'asshole buddies.' But that difference is crucial. You see, I don't believe the Abe Gattmans can be changed. The drive to preserve their wealth and their status has made them inflexible. Your father has more to gain from revolution—a peaceful revolution. The real problem is: Can people like me come out of their clouds and make people like your father aware of what's happening in this country? Make them realize that wealth and power are in the hands of giant businesses and banks and insurance companies that don't really give a damn about them."

Bren tasted my breast; then he listened briefly to my chest. "Together, Ellen, you and I might put a bridge across the chasm. It's important for me to find out whether I can communicate with your reality. . . ." He sat up. "Your heartbeat sounds like a man chopping down a tree with a blister on his hand."

"You're not helping it much." I swished a tear off my cheek. "I have a feeling that I'm being offered the job of being a guinea pig. You need a wife, and if you don't land one, Phil Tenhausen will destroy your dream. You're still avoiding my questions."

He laughed as he kissed my face with a hundred tiny kisses. "Is it bad that I can love two women?" Bren held my shoulders, sensing I was trying to escape his embrace. "A few years ago, Rais, Merle, and I decided to test an idea we believed in—a plan under which families might live together in closer economic groupings. We had even dreamed up the name 'Confamiliaum.'" Bren grinned at me. "You won't find it in the dictionary. *Con* of course is Latin for 'with.' *Familia* is 'family,' and *um* is the Hindu mantra representing the universe, both the relative and the absolute aspects of life. At least, we're not alone. While he isn't banging our particular drum, I have a good feeling that Phil understands that the Confamiliaum concept goes hand-in-hand with the Premar communes. Perhaps, together they can involve thousands of communities in a joyous lifelong learning process."

But I wasn't really listening. When Merle came back from St. Noir, I knew that I would have to come to grips with reality. Premar was one thing. Sharing a man you loved was something else again.

I moved away, and Bren made no effort to pursue me. I knew I had no right to sound jealous of a man I had known less than ten days. "Bren, I'm sorry," I told him. "You have to understand I'm quite conventional. I keep asking myself: Why am I in bed with you? If I loved a man, I'd accept the fact that he might have had intercourse with other women before we were married, but if he married me and then continued to be a Don Juan, I'd divorce him."

His eyes were dancing with merriment. "Sweetie," he said, "you can take that a step further and say: If I didn't divorce him, I'd make him miserable the rest of his life. Leave aside that you're spouting the presumably normal point of view. You didn't say 'If I were a man.' You said, 'If I love a man.' Yet are you so sure? Because you're obsessed with your physical inadequacy, you're willing to consider the possibility of sex without marriage, aren't you? Even though you've been protesting, I have a feeling that you'd make love with me even though you knew that I might still go to bed with Merle."

"You're right." I tried to slide out of his arms. "I'm way over my head, but at least I've saved myself from drowning. I'm going home."

He was unruffled. "For the past few days I've expected that Dancer would storm up the front stairs, break down the doors, and try to put me in jail for raping a mental minor. Then I'd have to tell him the truth, or at least face it myself. Despite the obvious size of his daughter's breasts and the lush hair on her delta, with those big tears in her eyes, she doesn't look much older than Lolita. You don't have to worry, Ellen, I never go to bed with nymphets."

I couldn't help laughing. "Poor you. Your penis looks eager, even if you aren't. I'm sorry. Making love with a jittery virgin, who might scream when you break her hymen, could be a bore."

Bren smiled. "I just want Ellen O'Day really to enjoy herself the first time she has a man inside her, and I don't want recriminations later. It should be as simple, and yet miraculous, as you and I responding to each other with a complete acceptance of each other as human beings in love with life. So much so that we might even build bridges to our different ways of life and living and really learn to enjoy each other's different perspectives."

"Does Merle have that kind of relationship with you?"

"Yes, but with one exception. She's hung up on the black-and-white thing. Someday I'll convince her I don't think of her as black and me white. I love her because she *thinks*. She's *aware*, she's *alive*. I love her because she's Merle and I'm me. Together we open entirely new worlds to each other."

"I like Merle," I said. "But even she was second choice for you. What would have happened if you had converted Lena Goldman to your insanities?"

"I suppose you want to know about every girl I've ever made love with." Bren sighed. "Lena and I were quite compatible, except for the main axis of living. Lena believes she has only one life to live. She was afraid that she'd become the monkey wrench that I would toss into the machinery. I have a fatal flaw, Ellen. I'm a political animal. I believe if enough of us really want to, we can eat some of the sacred cows, and not get indigestion."

He touched my cheek, then jumped out of bed, and standing next to it, he swung his engorged penis from side to side like a kid proud of his virility. I had an urge to grab hold of it, kiss it, bite it. Suddenly, without words, we sensed a deep understanding of each other. We laughed together hysterically. Perhaps for the first time in my life, I dared to speak my thoughts to another person. I held Bren's penis and said, "I was wondering what he'd feel like if I squeezed him."

He grinned. "Now you know. For me delightful, for you I can't say. Maybe he's a warm salami." He leaned over and kissed me lightly on my cheek. "I'm not encouraging you. I've decided that I'm going to heed Lieb Kahn's warning for one more night and let you sleep."

"Not alone?" I was feeling very sad.

Bren grinned at me. "Honey, one thing you'll have to learn is that a man can't go around with a perpetual erection. I'll sleep with you, but you can't hold him."

I didn't, either. Not until early morning, and then I couldn't help it. Watching Bren sleeping, warm, boyish, trusting, beside me, I knew I was happily lost. My heart beating firmly and easily for the first time in two weeks, I wanted to be Bren. I slid down and kissed his furry belly and tasted his tiny penis, which immediately grew so big I could finally hold it only with my lips. We were both laughing softly, knowingly. I wiggled on top of him and helped aim him into my middle. Slowly I opened. And there was no pain, only joy as he hovered against the flower which opened and ever so slowly enveloped him.

"You'll get pregnant," he said softly.

"No, I won't," I told him. "Merle bought me pills. I've been taking them."

"You could die in my arms."

"Oh, I want to."

Ellen O'Day. Prelude to Premar. July. From tapes transcribed by Katherine Flaherty.

If you live today as if the world will end tomorrow, you can kneel down and pray God will give you forgiveness at the grand finale; or you can become a hedonist and make the most of what remains; or you can try to keep yourself so busy you forget the inevitable.

While the insistent countermotif to my Forty-four-Day Domestic Symphony with Bren foretold the coming doom, I was so involved with my day-to-day responsibilities as the person in charge of purchasing for the Premar tenement rehabilitation, and with the ten boys and three girls who arrived a week ago to begin the conversion of three ugly houses into the Topham's Corner Premar Commune, that I closed my ears to the rumbling notes of disaster. I refused to remember that I was Ellen, daughter of Dancer O'Day, the man who less than a week ago announced that he was going to run for mayor of Boston next year.

Daddy appeared on television yesterday with George Mahoney, the man who painted the showcases of a downtown movie theater with black paint because the manager refused to remove the suggestive advertising of an X-rated movie. "I refuse to see any similarity between George Mahoney and Father Berrigan," Dancer said. "Father Berrigan hates his country. He was sabotaging the only things the Commies fear—our military strength. Like our President, George Mahoney realizes that filthy pornographic movies are undermining family life and destroying the country. The Supreme Court tried to shut down the Combat Zone in this city by refusing to let women show themselves naked where liquor was being served. George Mahoney's act of conscience is only a beginning. We're going to turn the country around and restore Christian morality to this great nation. De Gaulle did it for France. We can do it here!"

Bren smiled as he watched Dancer on the six-o'clock news. "George Mahoney has six children," he said. "Your father should have asked him why he's screwing a woman who works in the lingerie department of the store that he manages on Washington Street."

"You sound as bad as my father," I told Bren. "Whose lies are those?"

"Honest, it's true! Merle worked there a year ago. George is a frustrated cocksman. Ask Merle, she'll tell you."

Merle, sprawled on the floor watching with us, laughed. "George is a sad case. He won't use safes, and his wife won't use the pill. They did it six times, and maybe a lot in between babies for eight years, but now his wife keeps her pants on, and George's tongue is hanging out. He won't let her practice birth control, but all other females are on their own. Five of his six kids are girls. George is going to save them from evil men like himself if it's the last thing he does."

I wondered if she was kidding me. "Did you go to bed with him?" I asked.

"Bed?" Merle guffawed. "You kidding? You don't know George. He likes it fast and quick in the back room. I was bending over one day and he nearly got me right through my pantyhose. Honey, I didn't just quit, I ran!"

Bren wouldn't listen to my premonitions. "I like your old man," he kept saying, and he wouldn't stop kissing my neck and ears. "If, as you say, your mother makes love only with the lights off, he's probably as frustrated as George Mahoney."

Bren was living in a daydream; to him my father was

simply a lovable Irishman; Daddy would come around. Bren didn't seem to realize that Dancer might give that impression to his constituents, but that was his trademark. Dancer O'Day, the product behind it, was a rough-and-tumble hater. The idea of trying to explain to Daddy what I had been doing for the past seven weeks, sleeping under the same roof with a Jew and a black woman, gave me cold shudders.

This morning the telephone rang, and Mother greeted me with all her bomb bays open. "Your father knows!" she exclaimed. "What does Daddy know?" I asked nervously. Could he actually know that last night I reached three climaxes and held Bren's penis in my mouth? Would Daddy call that making love? No, to him it would be "going down on a man," "cocksucking," and he'd detest the woman doing it to him. God, Ellen, I told myself, get a grip on yourself. Nobody but you and Bren and God know the warm sensation of kissing a boy's penis while he kisses you between the legs.

"Your father knows you're not living with Marie Timilty." Mother's voice was shrill.

"But, Mother, why did you tell him? I told you that I'd tell him. Bren and I are going to get married eventually." I didn't tell her that would be when and if I decided we should.

"I didn't have to tell him," she sobbed. "The only person I ever told was Father Tim, and he'd never tell your father. What you've been doing is all over Topham's Corner. Just yesterday Jim McCarthy, at the A&P, asked me what I thought about the sex commune on Felton Street. The Czerniks, who claim you made them move out of their flat to one across the street, told Sally Murphy at the welfare office that you were very nice to them but they're shocked that Dancer's daughter is living in the same house with a Jew and a black girl. And they said that a lot of crazy kids have moved in and are tearing the walls out. Your father is enraged, and he says he's going to introduce a bill to make sex communes illegal. Ellen, Ellen, I beg you, come home before something terrible happens!"

By the time Mother hung up I was crying too. What was going to happen? Bren had gone to Cambridge to a workshop on Premar Human Values, and I couldn't warn him. He probably would have said that I was overreacting anyway.

Merle, wearing nothing but a skirt, bounced into the front room and hugged me. "Whatever's got you down, honey, stop fretting. Premar's coming to life. The way those kids are working, we'll have this three-decker ready in a couple of weeks. Come on upstairs and see what's happening."

I couldn't help grinning at her. "It's a wonder those boys don't saw off their fingers. How can they concentrate when they see you hammering with your breasts swinging? Remember, we're supposed to keep this advanced contingent of Premars virginal until their roommates arrive."

Merle laughed. "The boys like it. Tommy Matthews said it was the first time he'd ever seen female tits. It's so damned hot today, the boys are stripped to the waist, so why not the girls? Lainey Franci took off her bra, but she can't get used to her breasts floating on her chest. Bobby Holiday is working in her slip. Anyway, this is the way my great-great-grandmother worked in Africa before the damned Christians brought her to St. Noir and forced her to put on clothes."

I was about to tell her about my mother's phone call when the front doorbell rang. "Merle," I whispered, "don't answer it!"

The ringing was followed by a pounding, and I heard the kids running down the stairs yelling, "The fuzz are outside!"

Merle shrugged, and paying no attention to my frantic, "Put your shirt on," opened the front door.

My father, God help us! His face flushed red, his white mane flapping, towering over Merle and me and the kids who cowered on the sidelines, he was yelling, "Jesus! Mother of God! Put your clothes on, young ladies. This is indecent exposure!" I was aware of Lainey, terrified, with her arms across her breasts, but Merle just grinned. An African tribeswoman, stepping out of the pages of *The National Geographic* with naked breasts—the kind of pictures my father studied in detail when he was a kid—was challenging his Puritan-Catholic morality.

Daddy shoved her aside and grabbed my arm. "Ellen, get your things! I've got a cruiser out in front. I'm taking you home. And you, young lady," he snapped at Merle, "cover your breasts before I do it for you!"

I don't know where I suddenly got the courage to handle the situation head-on. Maybe it was Daddy's furious expression. A remake of the Salem witch trials flickered through my mind! With tears in his eyes, Daddy was ready to watch me burn at the stake. My heart was boiling furiously. "Daddy, I'm not a child," I said. "You can't bully me. This is my home now, and I'm staying right here. If you want to sit down and talk rationally, I'll tell you what's happening."

Daddy's face was mottled purplish-red and twisted; I wondered if he was going to hit me. "Listen, young lady, I can read." He flung a copy of the Boston *Globe* at me. "When I saw this Premar crap in the paper a month ago, I made a mistake. I thought it was happening in Cambridge. Just the kind of thing you'd expect from Harvard, where all the commies hang out. Now I discover that it's right in my backyard, and my own daughter is involved. Goddamnit, Ellen, what's happened to you? Has that Jew bastard got you on drugs? Don't you know that he was mixed up with that nigger Rais Daemon who tried to kill Jaimie Duffy and me last year in that B.U. riot?"

Daddy stared at Merle, who was standing beside me, watching him with that impassive expression black people hide behind when whitey is badgering them. "I'll tell you one thing, young lady, you may think I'm prejudiced, but the good black people who live around here don't want their people fucking with whites any more than we do."

I was praying that Merle wouldn't introduce herself as "the wife of the nigger who assaulted you." Suddenly she grinned at him, but there was no humor on her face. "Really, Mr. O'Day," she said, "you can't legislate morality. If you care for your daughter, you should leave before she has a heart attack."

Daddy grabbed me by the shoulders. "Ellen, I know you're under stress. The first thing you know, you'll be in bed for weeks. But I'm warning you—this is out of my hands. Leave this house now, before the police raid it. When that happens, even if they put you in jail with your hippie friends, I won't lift a hand to get you out."

"Daddy, I beg you. Please go." I was crying, but not for me—for him and his sudden realization that I was beyond his paternal control. "You make me feel sick to my stomach. I love you . . . but I pray to you, don't harass us. You'll only end up looking like a foolish old man."

I might as well have struck him. He swore at me.

Daddy was right about one thing. I'm in bed again. When Bren came home, Lieb Kahn was here.

I couldn't stop crying. "It's no use, Bren," I told him. "I'm no good to you. I haven't got the physical stamina."

"What you going to do if you go home?" Bren demanded.

"Die in peace."

"You can't. Your head won't let you. If you're going to die, die fighting."

Lieb was shocked.

Bren shrugged. "For a lot of us there comes a time when you can't go home again. Besides, Ellen isn't going to die. She knows I need her too much for her to do that. I've been looking for her most of my conscious life. When she's eighty years old, we're going to be sitting in a rocking chair reminiscing about this, in between kisses."

Lieb finally left, but not without exacting three promises from me. One, I'd stay in the sack for a couple of days. Two, from now on I'd walk away from any situation that could make me blow my top. Three, if I really loved Bren and wanted to be screwing with him on New Year's Eve 2029, before the end of the year I'd check into University Hospital for a commissurotomy.

This morning Bren crawled into bed with me. Knowing I wouldn't stay on my back all day, he told me, "When you get tired of making tapes, explore some of those cassettes in the front room. They'll get your mind off your father. And stop worrying. I talked with Father Tim yesterday, and he's agreeable to marrying us, provided I become a Catholic. I told him, why not? The Church needs a new Jesus."

"You were bugging him!"

"I wasn't." Bren's ear was on my chest, listening to my heartbeat. "And he *will* marry us, Ellen. He said he'd talk to Dancer about it." Bren refused to discuss this wild idea further. Instead he said, "I love you. Remember Socrates' dialogue with Agathon. We're the missing half of each other. You're my anchor to windward."

He looked at me seriously. "Listen to some of those tapes. They'll prove it to you. A few years ago I had a bug on tape recordings. I taped not only my own undying thoughts but those of everyone I came in contact with. Then I realized the folly of it. Beyond listening to a particular tape once, maybe even a second time, or sharing yourself on tape with someone else, a tape recording has limited uses. I discovered that not only have I no time, but I have no inclination to live in the trivia of my own past. It's amusing how Western man has been conned by producers of moving-picture film and snapshot film to document his fleeting present. My father has a closet full of movie films all spliced on four-hundred-foot rolls, recording the years since his marriage. But he's too uninterested or too busy to look back. It would take them a solid month of continuous viewing to look at all that stuff. Every once in a while, during the holidays, sentiment raises its head and we spend an evening viewing Abe and Rivke's happier days—the first years, when my sister and I were just kids and hence controllable. Then one day I realized that those flat images flitting about on the screen weren't me at all. The past recorded in my subconscious: Memories that will snap into rich life at the sound of a seagull's cry, or leaves rustling in a summer breeze, like Marcel Proust's cup of tea, are much richer and fuller than the moving-picture shadows of me at four, ten, or twelve years of age. *I am a man of today and tomorrow . . .* plus a correlating brain, a memory disk containing what I have managed to distill from the vast history of man's past, and my personal experience of living twenty-eight years. Man's total history has value only as a road map of what to avoid in the future, and the joy of occasionally discovering that the thoughts you think aren't so unique. Men long dead have thought many of them before. We should teach history, and learn from the past, only for the light the past may throw on the present and future. Any other approach means reliving death, turning inward instead of living life."

I listened, amazed that Bren's mind could leap out of present problems into abstractions. But he knew my weaknesses. I love to take the high road with him—arguing, of course. "Sometimes, Bren, you scare me. You've got to have sentimental things. Stripped of the past, man would lose his moorings."

Bren smiled. "That's nonsense. The black man, for example, has swallowed it hook, line, and sinker. Ask any

Jew who really dares to think about the past. Jews use history for a purpose, not to extol the past, but to whip their children into gaining knowledge so that the past will never happen to them again. The Irish, the blacks, any people without a long history, try to cook up one, as you just said, for a mooring post. But I disagree; man should dare to untie himself and sail free."

I said, "Your philosophy may be sound, but without historical roots, man can become dangerous—a robot. And I'd like to see movies of my mother and father and my brothers the way we were when we were kids, but we don't have any. Somehow, I remember Daddy as being nicer then. Merle told me that she could scarcely remember her daddy, because he went to sea when she was four. People like you, who do have a strong sense of your origins, can afford to kiss them good-bye."

Bren was kissing my fingers and admiring each one separately. "Did Merle tell you her Daddy had to go to sea? His family was starving because the people in the United States were trying to get skinny and had stopped eating sugar. Each person needs his own fantasies. That's the missing ingredient in old movies and in pornography, too. They're almost always too literal, leaving no room for wonder. I can re-create Merle's world better in my head. I can see her easily, a bright-eyed little West Indian pickaninny with French blood and pigtails. I can imagine the scared look on her mother's face when she thought how the wheel of fortune spins on St. Noir. Her little blackbird would be married at sixteen, lose her teeth in a few years, marry off her kids in her thirties, and be an old lady in her forties. Merle can thank the gods that her mother rebelled against all that and helped her escape."

I'm slowly discovering that life with Bren is continual brain-to-brain combat. After he'd gone with Merle to Cambridge and I sat on the sofa in the book-crowded living room, I had a sense of having at last found my home. Perhaps Bren is right that man can't find his identity in the surface record of his life. Perhaps we can more profitably learn how to explore our subjective memories of time past and thus expand our present, but for me, a stranger from another world, trying to orient myself to the world of Bren, Merle, and Rais, the tapes were a door I could open and walk through into their lives, a record of their value structures and how they came about, and an approach to life that both intrigued me and scared me half to death.

There were hundreds of cassettes, all labeled and dated, some sixty minutes long, some ninety. Lying in bed with several filing cases of them beside me, amazed that after yesterday my heart was once again gaining a confident rhythm, I realized the truth of Bren's parting words: "The trouble is, you can't skim the spoken word. Some of the early tapes are simply recordings of good lectures, while some are attempts to keep a journal on tape, which is an art in itself. It's much harder to verbalize your intimate feelings than to write them down. In one case you can tear up and cross out. A tape can be erased, but it's not so easy. I've tried taping sober, high on alcohol, and stoned on grass, and mostly I've ended up, in the light of sober listening, with pure drivel. It comes to this: The difference between the millions of feelings and emotions that make you react as a human being and the recording of them, in any form whatever, demands the discipline of art, simplification, the elimination of the nonessential. How do you express your loneliness, your need for love, or any emotion, and not let the ineffectual words suffocate the deep feelings within you?"

But it depends on the listener, too. Trying to decide which tapes to snap in the recorder first, I read the labels and dates on all of them. Most were marked not only with dates, but first names, too. Merle, Rais, Bren, Madelena, Abe, and Rivke. I finally discovered the one that intrigued me most. It was marked "Madelena and Bren, finale."

As the tapes slowly turned in their cartridges, I became first the silent participant in the act of love with Bren and Madelena, and then tried to identify with a black man, Rais Daemon, dreaming his dreams aloud. Me, I'm an Irish girl who has never traveled farther from Boston than Washington, D.C., with the Girl Scouts—me, in love with Bren but frightened that I couldn't cope with him or my father. I was mind-adventuring, playing the escapist. I knew that, while I was listening to Bren's tapes on one level, on another I was reliving the episode with Daddy. And I was wondering if Bren and Madelena were right in their own way. No one could really love a *living* Jesus Christ. It would be too lonesome an existence to try to make him understand that I was human, jealous and frightened, and not the perfect loving Ellen he thought I was.

Bren, if I'm able to fight my father, it will be because I can lean on your strength. I'm a one-man woman. I'm not sure I can share you, not even with Merle, whom I really love, too.

*Madelena and Bren. Three years before Premar. Transcribed from tape by Katherine Flaherty.**

"Okay, you're right. I'm mad. Off my rocker. Insane to have ever got mixed up with you, and I knew it four years ago. You walked into the apartment Marge Friedman and I were sharing and you announced we needed a male roommate. At least I had sense enough to escape you in my sophomore and junior years."

"Why did you try one more time, Lena? Honey, relax! Let's go to bed; we talk together better naked. All the time your tongue is saying no, your breasts are saying to your bra, 'Take me off so Bren can kiss us. We haven't been kissed for a week!' "

(*Laughter.*)

"They could have been, but I'm more secure than you are. I don't have to run and hide in every bosom I look at. Be serious. If I had met you in the kind of conventional college environment my mother experienced, I suppose I would have married you and lived uneasily ever after. A nice conservative Jewish girl, everybody would have said, and what once was a conservative Jewish boy. Temporarily a little wild—a little radical—but in three years, give or take, Bren will settle down. He'll become the star salesman in the New Hope Ford Agency, the pride and joy of his wife and father. Boy! How wrong could they have

* In this exact transcription, I have thought it important to indicate in italics where pauses and laughter occur. "*Laughter*" may signify anything from a loud laugh to an appreciative giggle.—BOB RIMMER.

been! Bren Gattman, the uncurable rebel, will be shot dead at twenty-eight."

(*Laughter.*)

"You didn't mention my mother. Besides, after what we've been through, you can't mean it."

"Can't mean what?"

"That you're some kind of Marjorie Morningstar. You know: 'I had my fling. Now I'm living my real life. . . . I have money, a good husband, my family, my security. The rest of the world can go hang.' "

"Why not? Because my mother only cried a little when I told her I planned to experience several males before being married, both in the sack and in day-to-day encounters, didn't mean that as a by-product I've been radicalized by having sex. I can make love with you and still be terrified by what goes on in your brain."

"What about Rais Daemon?"

(*Pause.*)

"All right, I love you. I love Rais. I love Sam Greenfield. I've screwed with four men in four years; Ted Ross was the other one. Two Jews, one gentile, and one black heathen, and I love you all. But in June I'm going to marry Sam Greenfield and help him work his way through law school."

"Why don't you move in with Sam now?"

(*Laughter.*)

"I haven't told him I'm going to marry him yet. Bren! Stop! I have to read five chapters in *The Savage Mind* before tomorrow. And don't think I'm not aware that damned tape recorder is going. All you're trying to prove is that everything I've been saying will just be irrelevant words when I play it back tomorrow or whenever."

(*Laughter.*)

"Why did you take off your pantyhose? Why are you sprawled in that chair with your legs wide open?"

"Verbalizing it all for the tape, aren't you?"

(*Laughter.*)

"Well, its because I'm cooling her. She has no brains, and I'm being practical. Since I don't have sense enough to keep you out of my pants, I took them off. You've ruined enough already. Also in the hope that maybe somehow I could coolly reject you and not be sorry I gave up the opportunity."

"But you won't reject me."

"But I do—at least, until you come up with a good explanation of last weekend."

(*Pause.*)

"If you're rejecting me, why are you nibbling my prick?"

(*Laughter.*)

"Because that's all I can see of you. Turn around! Come inside me! Put him where he belongs before I swallow him."

(*Laughter.*)

"Upside down your behind is very interesting."

"Oh, God, Bren. Stop, stop. Ohhh, Bren, Bren."

(*Pause.*)

"If I bit you, it's your own damned fault. I told you to come inside. My God, I'm shattered. Temporarily.... Uuuuuuu. Someday I would like to screw all day. Every day for a week. No! No more that way. Come inside. I want to feel *you!*"

"Nice! Lena? Don't work. I'm in no hurry. Just drift."

(*Pause.*)

"Okay, I'm listening."

"For what?"

"For your side of the story."

"Why don't you ask Merle? She's mad at me, too."

"I asked her. She said you invited her and Rais to spend the Veterans Day weekend with your folks in New Hope. Rais said he couldn't go. He was trying to write a paper on his ideas for St. Noir."

"I asked you first, Lena. Three weeks ago. Remember? You said that you couldn't get out of the rehearsals for that Ionesco bomb. So what did you think would happen? Everyone cut out on me except Merle."

"Rais and I didn't cut out. We just weren't being honest."

"What do you mean?"

"Rais believed you'd just be using him and Merle to blow tne collective minds of New Hope, N.Y.—not to mention your mother and father's."

"My God! Lena. Your tits taste nice!"

(*Laughter.*)

"Flesh has no taste."

"Yours has. Fresh Lena. An aphrodisiac, too! I couldn't blow Abe and Rivke's minds. I doubt if they have a mind between them. After a year I'm still shocked that Abe accepted the invitation to become the only Jewish member of the Springdale Yacht Club."

"Sounds like progress."

"Bull. They're using him, the same way business organizations hire one or two blacks to prove they're integrated."

"Proving my point. I would have been insane to arrive at your parents' house with Rais and Merle. I figured you were planning to play your trump shocker by sleeping with Merle."

"Are you jealous?"

"No! Yes! Damnit, I don't know. I do know that it would be bad enough to spend the weekend in the Gattman home and have you and me sleep together, unmarried. Upper-class Jews or WASPs don't want integration. Your parents may give lip service to the idea, but they don't want a black daughter-in-law."

(*Pause.*)

"Bren, I have a feeling you're trying to divert me. Just bounce up and down on me, and I'll forget my nitty-gritty problems. Right?"

(*Laughter.*)

"Wrong. I'm not bouncing on you, but you could jiggle a little for me. I love to have you lie on top of me, but every now and then, *without encouragement*, you've got to wiggle your pussy. Either that or you won't be transfixed anymore."

(*Laughter.*)

"Maybe I don't want to be transfixed. Oh, I take it back! I do! I do!"

"Okay, let's coast a minute. Early last Friday, knowing you and Rais would be pissed off at us, Merle and I drove to New Hope. The wind against our faces was Indian-summer hot and sultry. Long before we arrived, Merle said she was glued to her clothes, and she needed a shower. She was obviously fidgety and apprehensive. She wondered why I couldn't forget the whole mad business of bringing a black girl home to my unsuspecting parents. If I arrived with one who stank of sweat, it would only prove what they already suspected about *schvartzers*, that they not only look different, but they smell different, too. This *schvartzer* bit bugged me. I knew that was how Abe referred to blacks when he didn't call them jigs. I interrupted the long argument that we had gotten into—running the gamut of race prejudice—by stopping in a Howard Johnson parking lot just outside of New Hope and sniffing her from head to foot. She smelled great; a little erotic, maybe, but not noticeable unless you put your face exactly where I put mine. Between her legs smelled best—fresh as new-mown hay. But I couldn't convince her. It was either stop at a motel, hire a room, shower and clean up before going to the house, or have Merle decide she was going back to Boston by bus, without me. I guessed she had gotten it in her head that she wouldn't sleep with me in the Gattman house.

"My God, Lena, why in hell is the middle class so hell-bent on making it uncomfortable for its children to snuggle together? I suspected Merle was pushing the motel because then we could go back there instead of staying with my family. A better idea jumped into my head. Abe bought a new fifty-foot Pacemaker last spring, and I knew it would still be in the water. The boat is not only air-conditioned, it sleeps eight and has two staterooms with showers. If it were unoccupied, we could shower and take a swim off a secluded end of the dock. It was warm, and it was so late in the season that the yacht club wouldn't be crowded."

(*Laughter.*)

"You never could have sold me that crock."

"I know. I wasn't too convinced myself. But I was damned if I was going to stay in a motel when Rivke makes such a point of telling me that my room at home is just the way I left it. 'Come home often, Bren. We miss you!' Then, I bring home a female to sleep in my childhood bed, and she's horrified."

"What you really wanted was to say, 'Mommy, Daddy: This is Merle. Your big boy Bren sleeps with her whether you like it or not, because he likes black pussy."

"Is that what Merle told you?"

"No, stupid. I just know you like to wave flags in front of bulls."

"Look, for Christ's sake, I wasn't just being childish. [*Laughter.*] Oh, shit! Maybe I was. Maybe the whole fucking world is grown-up and I'm not. I honestly care for Merle. I told her that it would be fun to invade Squaresville—the Springdale Yacht Club. When we got there, to make sure that Abe and Rivke weren't aboard their boat, I parked the car and reconnoitered the pier.

Well, the coast looked clear. By now Merle was steeling herself and giving a very good impression of a young model who had just walked off the pages of *Ebony*. Instead of ignoring the surprised glances of the members sitting around the pool, I coolly waved to everybody, stopping here and there to converse with such unlikely people as John Parker, president of the New Hope National Bank, who occasionally finances some of Abe's automobile shipments, and Gil Freeman, president of New Hope Plastics, commodore of the yacht club. If they were dumbfounded, it wasn't by Merle, but rather by my unsuspected affability. Behind the appraising glances I could hear them thinking: It just proves our point. Let a Jew become a member of the club, and we're invaded. Look at the beard Abe Gattman's son is wearing."

(*Laughter.*)

"You do look like Rasputin. I don't mind your beard on my face, but every time I make love with you I end up with a pink belly. Anyway, if you'd been my kid, I'd have been pretty mad at you. What were you trying to do, disintegrate the Yacht Club?"

(*Laughter.*)

"Not at all. I introduced Merle as the daughter of the president of St. Noir, and suddenly they saw her as a different kind of black—one with a pedigree—and they loved her. Freeman gave the impression he might even welcome Merle's daddy as a member of the club. Merle reciprocated by inviting all of them to the Nelson Harbor Yacht Club in St. Noir. Nearly hysterical with suppressed laughter, we finally navigated down the pier to Abe's palatial yacht. In the lounge we flung off our clothes, searched the bar, and made ourselves huge drinks of vodka and Seven-Up. Merle was so excited with the luxury of the boat she almost forgot her shower."

"Did you make love?"

"Sure, but we weren't relaxed about it. We had an uneasy feeling the word was out that the prodigal son was home. [*Laughter.*] Why did you ask?"

"A female is always interested if the male she is screwing with recently made love with another female."

"Jesus, you'd think I was Casanova. I haven't had intercourse with anyone except you for six months. Merle isn't a stranger. You know, I did live with her for a year."

"Just asking, chum. I don't like to be compared."

"I never compare. That would lose the moment for a dubious retrospect. Anyway, I really didn't plan it. Merle was in the shower and I was soaping her and tasting her tits and we were feeling sillier by the moment. She kept saying that she wished she had brought her bathing suit, so I told her the hell with bathing suits, the daughter of the president of St. Noir could swim bare-ass at the Springdale Yacht Club anytime. Anyhow, we were both pretty crocked. She ran out on the back deck of the boat with me after her with a huge floppy erection banging against my belly. Just as she dove in the water, a Chris Craft edged its way toward one of the slips farther down the pier. On the deck watching were not only Abe and Rivke and their friends, but my sister, Laura Stone, who is nine years older than me, and whom I rarely see, since she did what Abe and Rivke wished their only son would do—married money. Rocky Stone. Rocky may be fifteen years older than Laura, but Stone-Western Industries, his personal creation, is one of the top five hundred companies in the United States.

"None of them could believe that anyone sane would swim off the floats. The water is too full of shit and piss that the members have flushed through their boat toilets. But Merle didn't know that, and I didn't give a damn. It was a fascinating confrontation. Rivke was waiting with towels when we finally emerged. The cold water had diminished my prick, and Merle, sober and chagrined, had tears in her eyes as she apologized to my family. Being unprejudiced, good fellows, Abe and Rivke had no recourse except to pretend that they were in love with Merle at first sight. What else? She was their number-one choice for a future daughter-in-law. Ha, ha. Rocky and Laura were flying to Nice that night, so we had little conversation, beyond Laura's suggestion that it was time I grew up."

(*Laughter.*)

"My God! I've talked so much I'm limp. Restore me with your magic touch. Hey, have you gone crazy? Come back here. Do you want me to have aching balls?"

"Bren, the world is full of simple people like me who think just the process of learning to live and to love is enough to occupy most of a lifetime. I'm not political. I'm not a revolutionary. Neither were you the first year we roomed together. I knew you were changing, but I didn't want to admit it. You were the first person I ever had intercourse with. I've tried to recapture those idyllic days. I thought maybe you'd have mellowed a little, especially after the riots and the near-miss you had in not going to jail with Rais.

"I can even accept the idea of deeper intimacy between two couples, though not with Merle and Rais. That couldn't work on any lasting basis. I know. You think that shows I'm prejudiced. I'm not. Rais and I enjoy each other in bed. Maybe I couldn't love him exactly the way I love you. He has a remoteness, a lost feeling that I never could break through; but that's not the problem. The hitch is that I'm not the daydreamer you are. And maybe I don't love either of you enough. You both seem to enjoy living in an armed camp of your own making. When you first started getting mixed up with left-wing groups, Merle and I were actively with you, and I didn't even complain when you and Rais were hauled off to jail last spring. Fighting the war, ROTC, demanding black-studies programs—all the things people were fighting for then seemed good and necessary. But now that I'm finishing college, that phase is over. I don't want to live in an environment that's always in danger of blowing up."

"Whether it's New Hope, New York, or Boston University, no matter where you go, Lena, you can't run away. We're the generation that has no place to hide. Not even Sam Greenfield, conservative as he is. Do you think he's going to be happy handling divorce and accident cases while the world explodes around him?"

(*Long pause.*)

"Bren. Oh, God! Bren. You do feel good. Oh, honey! Come with me! Come with me. Right out of this world! What's living really all about except this?"

From the journal of Andrea Pillisuk. November, the first year of Premar.

Yesterday, a notice on all the commune bulletin boards told us that all Premars should come to the H.V. meeting last night, naked. The occasion? Marion Swenson, the commune doctor, would show the girls how to examine their own vaginas. Wow!

I almost feel like sending this journal to my mother. Boy, would her eyes pop! At most of the Human-Values sessions we arrive in whatever clothes we happen to have on. Of course, being naked around the houses is very casual, and eventually in the course of a week you meet all of the kids in the tubs wearing just their skins, or in the playroom most of the kids play Ping-Pong naked. It's kind of fun to watch balls and dorks and titties bobbing in separate rhythms. But it's a different feeling when all fifty of us are flopped around the dayroom together, bare-assed. I enjoy the contrast. It makes us all seem like a bunch of little kids again. Vulnerable—that's what Merle called us—and more human.

Last night we were even more so. Three long folding dining-room tables were set up in the dayroom and covered with sheets and a couple of pillows. Marion Swenson, naked as the rest of us, sat on one of them with her legs swinging over the side. She is about thirty-six, and one of the guys says she's "nicely stacked." She has medium breasts with big pink nipples, really long legs, and blond pubic hair that's a little darker than the rinsed blond hair on her head. We all gathered around her. The boys were especially intrigued at her lack of embarrassment. While she was talking she had flexed one leg onto the table, giving us a clear view of her labia.

She grinned and held up a plastic gadget. "Tonight I'm going to show the girls how to examine their insides with a speculum, a hand mirror. You fellows have always been able to examine your testicles and penises, but most women never get further than seeing the reflection of their labia in a mirror. And you can take bets on it that most of your mothers have never seen their clitorises. What's more, because most parents are still embarrassed when they discover kids examining their own genitals, we have many marriages where women never permit their husbands to enjoy their continued interest in seeing and tasting the female genitals. Many women actually believe that their husbands are kind of kooky or sick if they insist on looking closely at these female mysteries.

"That's why we have magazines like *Playboy*, *Oui*, and *Penthouse*, which owe their existence to photographs of the female crotch. The women shown there aren't real-life human beings who yell and fight with their husbands or boyfriends. They're simply beautiful bodies with complaisant vaginas, hands, and mouths all designed for masculine pleasure. And beyond the men's magazines we have 'adult' bookstores and 'skin' movies whose main business is selling pictures of the female vulva to men. The poor male. He really only wants to see what the female looks like. But since we have a president and a Supreme Court that believe they can legislate morality, and because nudity is loathsome to such people, most of us never see many of the other sex as naked human beings.

"Many people still believe that if women exposed themselves naked on the beaches or front lawn, or even in their homes, wholesome womanhood and sex would be devalued in the male's eyes. Oh, how Victorian we still are! Some men have even been conditioned to get their best erection when looking at a woman who is partially dressed, or who is wearing a sexy see-through bra or panties and nightgowns like those sold by companies that specialize in sexual-come-on clothes.

"We think this is sick. In a natural society no one would be able to sell pictures of the naked male or female, because there would be no buyers. The devaluation of sex and the mystery of human sexuality begins in the printed word and picture. How can being naked, or making love, be rated R or X? In using such a rating system, aren't we really rating our fears and conditionings that making love or being naked is so dirty that one human being can't enjoy another's basic reason for being?

"So tonight you fellows are going to get a special treat. You're not only going to see some twenty-seven living clitorises, but you are going to behold the lovely mystery of the female vagina, the pathway for your penis, and the cervix and uterus, the home where the egg is fertilized. Man may tamper with the human body. He may even succeed in creating artificial wombs—for what purpose, it would be difficult to imagine. But the mystery of life— why you and I are here on earth at this moment—or why some of us will die sooner than some, and all of us sooner or later, will always elude man. In Premar we want to make you conscious of death, not so that you will be afraid that your life will end, but so that you will be deeply aware, humbled, and joyous that you are privileged to participate in living." Marion was so alive and full of laughter that she had us all enthralled. "At the very least, we want you to learn that your genitals, male and female, are lovely, and that your prime purpose in living, whether you ultimately have children or not, is that you are a sexual organism capable of passing on life."

She lay down on the table with her head raised high on the pillows. We gathered around to watch while she bent her knees, spread her legs, opened her labia, and inserted the speculum in her vagina. Those standing behind her could see the reflection of the pink passageway in the mirror she held. The rest of us could see the cervix directly. For a moment I thought everyone in the room was in love with Marion as she softly explained herself to us.

When it was our turn, she helped us and encouraged the boys to examine each of us. "This is the miracle, guys. You have the sword, we have the scabbard. But these are the swords and the scabbards of peace, not of war. Note that the clitoris, like the penis, comes in all sizes and shapes, and also becomes erect during sexual excitation. So there's a point in lovemaking where the man's search should be with very light, feathery fingers. But keep your fingers out of the vagina—that was designed for your penis."

Marion insisted that the girls who were menstruating forget their embarrassment. "No one at Premar should be afraid of menstrual blood," she told Ruth Voight, who was blushing when she pulled out a bright red tampon. "The menstrual cycle is a lovely expression of your earth and sea roots. One of the reasons that modern man is unable to enjoy his own reality is that he has created a synthetic world of metal and plastic which doesn't decay, and is permanent and wholly predictable. He has been taught to prefer the bread that never grows a mold but simply dries into sawdust. We begin to think that the permanence and stability of manmade things is preferable to the never-ceasing change of life. But we soon get caught up in the boredom of manmade things. Instead of being amazed with ourselves and enjoying our ecological involvement with this amazing planet, or instead of being thrilled, we glorify our manmade creations and our puny ingenuity."

The guys were like kids in a candy store, and some of them had tiny erections. One of the kids, Billy Eckman, wondered aloud if all the guys felt as erotic as he did. Bren told him they sure did—and asked Billy to try to express his feeling.

Billy blushed. "Oral, I guess. I look at all the girls with warm breasts and soft hair between their legs, and their eyes sparkling, and I love everyone at Premar, especially the girls." Everyone howled, and Billy looked a little chagrined. "Well, you asked me, and I might as well admit I keep thinking I'd like to taste every girl here."

We laughed with Billy, not at him. I guessed he was trying to express a feeling that was pretty common to all of us. Bren tried to put it into words. "During our first months of life, we discover our world partially by way of our mouths. And we have the instinct to suck and hence gain sustenance and survival. The original joy of living— gained through our mouths—is imprinted on our subconscious. So why shouldn't we be delighted with our primal need to sense a human being we love with our lips and tongue and mouth? To taste the genitals and flesh of the other sex is an expression of the nourishment and protection we seek from each other. As we get older, we are taught shame and embarrassment and we label our needs with old Latin words like 'cunnilingus' and 'fellatio,' which give us a feeling that our needs are somehow evil, or we put down our compulsions with street names like 'cocksucking' and 'cunt-lapping' and so devalue them in each other's eyes."

Marion told us that she didn't want to give the impression that self-examination made it unnecessary for the girls to be examined by experienced gynecologists on occasion. "I don't want to put myself out of business," she told us. "And, of course, a doctor has been trained to see things that a lay person could miss. Venereal disease, for example. I want to reemphasize that sexual relationships within the Premar community include a commitment to this group. If any of you has sexual intercourse with someone outside Premar, then you should tell your roommate and your Compars immediately. Everyone here is free of venereal disease, and we plan to keep you that way."

Marion grinned at our serious faces. "We want all of you to develop a good feeling about your bodies. Healthy naked human beings should feel the joy and laughter in their blood, transformed and almost oozing out of their skin. The real learning experience is to be aware of the mystery of yourself and your individual uniqueness, and then to gradually discover that you can feel the same intimacy toward bodies external to you—the bodies of your friends of both sex.

"For the remainder of this meeting Bren is going to contrast the intimate way we are learning to interact as complete human beings with the hoked-up sexuality of the world outside. When he finishes, I hope you'll all be happy that you are really discovering a world of sex-love that involves you with each other as whole persons."

Bren had an opaque projector ready. "In a few minutes I'm going to project pictures, mostly of dames—first from *Playboy*, *Oui*, and *Penthouse*, and then from *Screw* and *The National Ball*. Before I do, I want to get a general reaction from the guys. I imagine that all of you have looked at the POP trio. POP is a good name for them. They are like old men who dye their hair or wear a toupee to maintain the illusion they are staying young. There are no naked women in these magazines who are over twenty-five years old. Men are portrayed as sexual creatures into old age, but their consorts are always young women. In these pages, women are presumably dead as sexual creatures after thirty. That's something to think about, girls. If you believe POP, most of you have only twelve years left.

"I want to ask the guys the first question. You've been here over eight weeks now. All but a few of you, to our knowledge, are having regular sexual intercourse. In any week you see most of the Premar girls in the tubs, or running around the houses without any clothes on. Now, here's my question, and I know that it isn't fair, because all of us are broke and can't afford many luxuries: Would any of you feel inclined to spend a buck to buy one of these magazines just to look at POP broads?"

When the laughter subsided, Billy Rainbow suggested that Hugh Hefner and the other publishers better watch out. Premar might decide that POP was dead and bury them forever.

"Not really." Bren laughed. "I personally believe that POP could become priests of a new religion which would gradually revalue sex and interpersonal loving as a mystical experience. POP is on the threshold now, but it needs someone to point the way."

Since none of the girls were reacting, I put in my two cents' worth. "Maybe a guy would buy those magazines because the girls have better shapes than most of us."

That really opened up the discussion. Some of the guys openly denied it, but a few admitted that corn-fed, big-titted girls were the American-male fantasy.

"I'm kind of glad that girls come in all sizes and shapes," Chuck Ventrano said. "When you see a whole girl, naked—not just her face or legs—it's amazing how well a particular body fits together."

Lainey Franci, who was holding hands with Chuck, her roommate, has little cupcakes for breasts. She was smiling warmly. "I hope Chuck means me."

"I sure do." Chuck laughed. "Your breasts may be small, but you have the most perfect behind and hips I've ever seen on any girl, and that includes POP girls."

"I'm going to give Bren an assist," Ellen said. "He's always saying that sex and love can be blended into a new religion. I think he should explore that direction."

Merle's eyes were twinkling. "Guys who live in this new world, and are cock-hounds, can now acknowledge their necessities as a way of life."

"What's a cock-hound?" Kathy Flaherty asked, and everyone was bursting with laughter.

Mohammed Hassan hugged her. "A cock-hound is a come-freak, Kathy. By definition, a come-freak loves pussy more than anything else in the world. Bren says we're going to make that a religion. Man, the churches will be filled to overflowing, and not just on Sunday!"

Bren finally got us quieted down and the room lights turned off. He flipped on the opaque projector. "First, we'll take a quick look at Bunny and Pet photographs taken from the pages of the POP magazines. In case you haven't noticed, women's liberation is having its effect. While POP doesn't show too many male genitals yet, particularly erect penises, they're playing down grandfather words like 'Pets' and 'Bunnies'—words which date their thinking and aggravate most women.

"An interesting thing about men who read the POP magazines is that they complain vociferously in letters to the editor when POP runs too many pictures of naked guys making out with the POP girls. Why? Probably because they don't like to think of some other guy touching their fantasy women.

"Now, here are a few pictures from *Viva*, a magazine that Bob Guccione, who publishes one of the POP magazines, has introduced for women. Note that while there are a few nude guys alone, some of the *Viva* pictures show guys and girls together. Evidently women aren't so possessive in their sexual daydreams as men. When *Viva*-style photography takes over POP's pages, POP could be on the road to humanizing sex and taking the first step to becoming priests of a new religion based not on sex worship but on sex wonder and mystery."

While he was talking, Bren was projecting a series of pictures of naked girls on the far wall of the dayroom. "Now we're back to POP pictures again. If you'll look at these photographs carefully, you'll notice the girls are all posed in stylized sexual positions. The cameraman concentrates on the girl's crotch. A few years ago he used to aim at her breasts. A lot of people in other countries used to think this interest in breasts was because Americans hadn't been weaned properly. The real reason was that when your father was a young man it was possible to publish photographs of a woman's breasts, but if you showed genital hair, with the live girl behind it, you'd end up in the jug. Now that POP has survived censorship and can photograph a girl's pussy hair, it was inevitable that the POP girls would have to spread their legs and give the boys a view of the girl's split beaver. Unlike *Screw* and *National Ball,* the POP photographic approach is still an artistic sex tease. You still don't see quite everything. Do any of you guys know what the partially open mouth on the POP girls symbolizes?"

"I think they're suggesting," Julie Howe said, "that they aren't the kind of girl who would screw with just anybody. They're trying to give you a message that *you* are special;

they're silently agreeing with your fantasies. If they could
meet *you*, they'd jump right in the sack with you. But they
know, and you know, that there are seven million other
subscribers who feel the same way. So it's tough luck,
baby."

"That's one point," Bren said, "but there's another, and
that's an interesting use of erotic symbolism. The girl's
open mouth with a glint of white teeth is a stylized way of
suggesting that the female wants the male penis in her
mouth. And have you noticed that many of the girls have
flaring nostrils? Merle will tell you that in ghetto language
'to have one's nose open' indicates sexual excitement."

"Yeah." Merle was lying on the floor supported by her
elbows. The light from the projector danced on the curve
of her brown behind. "Working chicks jive-ass you until
your nose is so wide open you could fly a 747 up it," she
said. "That way the chump is motivated faster, and then
they can get behind the next guy that much quicker."

"My God, Merle!" Ellen laughed. "You'll have to give
us a course in ghetto English. I'm lost."

"Billy Rainbow and Mohammed Hassan can do that
better than me." Merle looked at them. "I'm learning new
words from them every day."

Bren waved. "Okay, okay! We're getting off the main
point. I agree with Ellen that both Yiddish and black English are enriching the language. But to stay on the sub-
jects, POP magazines may be surprised to discover their
real potential in a changing world. Maybe we can phrase
it as what Synectics would call a people's problem. Can we
revalue sex and human loving so that they become the
peak of the hierarchy of human needs, and gradually rein-
vest human sexuality with its original, creative meanings
as the core of religious experience? As an ancillary question: How could magazines like POP, and sex newspapers
like *Screw* and *Ball*, be reoriented to accomplish this?

"But first let's switch to *Screw* and *Ball*, which are
weekly newspapers that could be put out of business any
day because of the wide fear of sexual words and pictures.
Let's hope that doesn't occur. If it does, you can be sure
that Premar will be fighting for its life, too. Neither *Screw*
nor *Ball* has the circulation of the POP magazines, but
Screw in particular tries to be more intellectually honest
and has a unique, wildly unfocused Rabelaisian quality."

Bren projected pictures on the wall of two different girls

sucking, lapping, and swallowing some guys' penises. I was surprised that after only two months at Premar, no one seemed to be shocked. There were a few good-natured chuckles. Joe, who was sitting beside me, whispered, "I like the way you do it better—kind of laughing. They're too serious."

"Now, the unique thing about these two pictures," Bren was saying, "is not that the girls haven't hesitated to identify themselves. Sexual prowess is no longer anonymous. This is Linda Lovelace. Linda was the star of *Deep Throat*, which cannot be shown in most theaters. In the film, Linda discovers that her clitoris is in her throat—a fact which explains her frigidity in vaginal intercourse, but she now can achieve splendid climaxes via fellatio. Linda was interviewed not only by *Screw* but also by *Women's Wear Daily*, *Playboy*, and a number of other so-called 'straight' magazines. Before it was censored, *Newsweek* publicized the movie by reviewing it as serious pornography.

"According to Linda, her boyfriend taught her how to take his erect penis all the way into her mouth and throat. He had learned the technique from a Japanese girl. Here's a portion of the *Screw* interview with Linda and her friend."

> J.R. (*Linda's boyfriend*). It's definitely controlling the involuntary muscle, because the minute something touches your throat, you choke. We worked it out by hypnosis and self-hypnosis. . . .
>
> LINDA. To get it (the penis) down my throat, there are certain positions I have to be in to really do it well. . . . Nobody has ever been too large or too wide or anything. Once your throat opens, your esophagus gets quite wide, like a sword swallower. You've seen some sword swallowers put three-foot swords down. It's the same thing. . . . You have to breathe through your mouth, but whoever is going in my throat has to work in and out. As they come, I take a breath. . . . I like someone in my throat and in my cunt at the same time. That's nice.

Bren chuckled. "Linda's not alone. Here is Tuppy Owen lapping a guy's prick. Tuppy has published a book called *The Sex Maniacs' Diary*, and she's hooked on cock, be it small, smelly, crumpled, pimpled, bent, or black. And there are others, such as Xaviera Hollander, who wrote *The Happy Hooker* and a sequel called *Xaviera!* She goes around the country lecturing on the joys of prostitution. And here's Marilyn Chambers, who was featured as Mother of the Year on the Ivory Snow box until the manufacturer discovered that she was appearing in a movie in which she is holding onto two guys' pricks while she has another in her mouth and a fourth in her vagina. This is Raina Barrett, who wrote *First Your Money, Then Your Clothes* about her experiences with group sex and as an actress in *Oh! Calcutta!* And here we have Germaine Greer, who makes no bones about her sex life and for a long time published a newspaper in Amsterdam called *Suck.* Greer has let herself be photographed with her knees flexed so you can look into her vagina. And there's the Loud family, who appeared on television in *The American Family* and brought you face-to-face with their marital problems and the homosexuality of their oldest boy. This picture shows the Yankee baseball players who swapped wives and families and confessed it all to reporters when it didn't work out. And here's Elliott Roosevelt, who wrote a book about his father, Franklin, and revealed that Franklin had a mistress who lived right in the house with the family. And here finally are pictures of a naked Jackie Onassis, once first lady of the United States. Of course, she didn't pose for these pictures, but she couldn't stop them from being published. Jackie's pictures prove one thing—a woman can still be sexy-looking after forty."

Bren turned off the projector. "So there *is* something new under the sun. We live in an age when people write in detail about their sex lives, and proudly sign their names to confessions. And now in motion pictures, major actors are appearing naked, and are shown copulating. In your parents' youth, there was nothing like this. Authors like Henry Miller and Frank Harris, writing in detail about their love lives, could not be read in the United States. But whether we live in a sexually permissive society, or one that hides sex under the rug, man's approach to sex—both then and now—has a common sickness. The wonder, the joy, the ecstasy, the peak of human experience, the God aspects of sex, are put down and devalued by photographers, artists, writers, and publishers."

Bren showed a dozen more pictures from *Screw* and *The National Ball*. Most were women with their legs open, revealing their wide-open vaginas, and guys hovering over them with erect penises. In one photograph, a girl sitting on the floor with her lips pursed and a hungry, eager look on her face as she clasped the guy's knees and examined his prick and balls hanging above her, was kind of funny, but most of the pictures were sickish-sad.

Sitting on the floor with us, Bren began the discussion. "Occasionally *Screw* has some humor and tries to express the joy of human sexuality, but mostly it's vulgar or crude. *The National Ball* is completely crude, often bestial. The POP magazines try to eroticize the female by suggestion and concealment, and by setting a standard of beauty most females can't compete with. *Screws* blatancy is compensated for by the fact that it comes closer to sexual reality. As you've seen, it tackles copulation and oral-genital sex head-on and does it with photographs of average males and females. But most often than not *Screws* honesty is dishonesty, because, while it extols sex, it depersonalizes the human interaction and relationship or it tries to level it so that it's on a par with pissing and shitting. The premise of Premar is that man's salvation is a return to sexual wonder. If we could learn to worship the ineffable mystery of humanity, and our total ecological relationship to the mysterious forces on this spaceship earth, our perception of each other as amazing humans would revitalize religion and return it to its beginnings—a worship, and joyful awe, but no fear of life, death, and birth and the processes of human existence."

From the corner of the room where she was sprawled against Julie, Samantha Brown said, "The Pope won't get behind you, man. He says, 'We're walking in mud.' He said, 'We're degenerating into limitless corruption.'" Samantha was pushing Bren, but he enjoyed it. "If the Pope saw us all sitting around here stark naked, he'd say this was indecent exhibitionism."

"Do you think it is?" Bren demanded.

"Naw, but some of the brothers and sisters who live around here call us Boojies. They try to tell us this ain't for real, we should cut loose."

"Because you're sleeping with a white guy?"

"They had a program on TV that the Jews finally got off the air. They didn't like it because Bridget, an Irish girl, was married to Bernie, a Jew. Like Ellen marrying you, for instance. The Jews don't cotton to guys marrying into their world, and blacks sure as hell don't think Goldbergs should be sleeping with jigs."

"What you're saying, Samantha, is that you don't think there's much hope for mad idealists." Bren was smiling. "Maybe one aspect of the problem is that neither Christianity nor Judaism has been able to conceptualize birth, death, and the continuous life process in an aura of mysticism for the man and woman of today. They're trying to live by rules that worked for a very different world from ours. Maybe we'll still be discussing it four years from now, but at least in the past twenty years man has seemed to be searching for a religion which doesn't pretend to have the answers, but is deeply aware of the mysterious questions. Really, aren't we all searching for something outside ourselves that we *dare* to lean on? I love you Samantha Brown. In black ghetto language, you're a lovely stallion. You're my soul sister. We can spend a lifetime learning about that kind of loving, which is a lot more than jumping into bed and screwing each other as sex objects. Instead, we could create a new humanism which extols our sexuality."

"I think what Bren's telling us," Ellen said, "is that you don't need pseudo-religions like tarot, I Ching, astrology, witchcraft, or you name them. We don't need Jesus or Hare Krishna or pot or cocaine or heroin or alcohol. If we want to achieve an altered state of consciousness, we can do it through sheer awareness of the other person, and in the process our own ego will dissolve." Ellen smiled softly. "How Bren plans to convince people like my daddy, or how he figures the POP magazines may lead the way, is beyond me, *and I sleep with him.*"

"Don't worry, sweetie—we may not convert POP, but we'll co-opt your daddy." Bren smiled, and it was easy to tell how much he loved Ellen. "Most people are wondering: Now that we have presumably achieved a world of cool sex—cool meaning that no one tries to maintain sexual possession over someone else—where are we going next? Will cool become so cold that hot will look better? In which case we will be simply traveling in circles. If you believe that man's history is a forward movement and we don't repeat all of our mistakes, why can't we conceive of a new religion that relates human sexuality to the majority of cosmic unity? If you try to find out what God means to you, it will lead you back to a concept of the ultimate that is completely inexpressible. The original God of the Jews had no name. The moments in our lives when we are most aware are when we have abandoned ourselves and our little egos and experience a blinding awareness of the unity of all life. Abe Maslow called this a peak experience, but he didn't know how to achieve it at will. We think the how of this kind of surrender, and the Premar approach to education, are what education is all about.

"I don't think we'll find the answers tonight, but the religion we're searching for would restore our wonder and amazement at our sexuality, and our joy in the life-death cycle. If the POP magazines are going to survive, they'll have to change their direction. They're going to lead, as Hugh Hefner once did, and not follow. If they can do this, they'll dare to exalt the mystery of the human body, and our sexuality, and picture men, as well as women, as lovely, aesthetic mirror images of the ultimate. Man and woman, being born, creating life, living life. Man and woman just *being*. Being naked. Man and woman, reevaluated photographically, and in words, by new talented people who discover in the two-dimensional image how to reveal the emotion and feeling beneath the flesh. Men and women knowing each other erotically and sensually, reaching a deep mental rapport. Men and women from youth to old age—fat, skinny, joyfully average, joyfully erotic. That's the only possible religion of the future, and POP and *Screw* could become the important avant-garde priests of that religion."

Bren looked at his watch. "It's ten-fifteen. The subject isn't finished. Hopefully, it never will be, but while I was talking with you, a happy idea flashed through my head. Yesterday I was watching teachers with first-graders. And, God—both the kids and teachers were wonderful, trusting and wanting to learn. Since, by the time you leave Premar, we hope you'll be nearer to your childhood than when you came, Merle will now play the piano—won't you, Merle?—and we'll revert to the first grade, with tunes like 'Farmer in the Dell.' And then we'll play leapfrog. And someday, when the POP magazines wake up, we'll let them come photograph us for what we are—joyous, sexual kids in adult skins."

Mom, honest to God, it was more fun than I've had

since I left kindergarten. All the girls bending on all fours, our asses and bushes in the air, while the boys leaped over us, their balls and penises fluttering against our backs, and gals leaping over guys, laughing, as we could see their balls and penises hanging, and feeling nicely sexy as our breasts flipped against the guys' backs. In ten minutes the dayroom smelled as funky and erotic as hell, and we all beat it naked to the tubs. And as we hosed each other, everybody *really* did like each other.

Later, snuggling in bed with Joe, I told him I wished *you* could have played leapfrog with us, Mom. Maybe it would make you laugh again.

PART TWO

Walk Before God

But these truths were a fire in me, then. Now I can tell them without being burned. The truths do not have to be hurled in men's faces. They are not intended to ignite fervor. I do not trust fervor.

Every time it has burst out somewhere, it has brought fire, famine, misery.... And contempt for man.

Fervor is the weapon of choice for the impotent.

Of those who heat the iron in order to shape it at once, I would prefer to warm man's body and leave him. We might reach this result; mankind retaining this fire through self-combustion.

Mankind set free of the trampoline that is resistance of others and digging into its own flesh to find a meaning.

—FRANTZ FANON
Black Skins White Masks

Rais Daemon. Prelude to Premar. February. From the essay "Walk before God," recorded in Walpole State Prison and transcribed from tapes by Samantha Brown.

A Utopia needs an island to be born on. I begin with my island. St. Noir, in the Caribbean, where I was born, is an island. It is not a Utopia now. Perhaps no place on earth can be a Utopia, but still St. Noir is a place to begin. Man needs to dream, and he needs to try to make some dreams a reality.

Come along with me, and dare to try!

Given: St. Noir is an island in the Caribbean.

Bounded by the Caribbean Sea and the Atlantic Ocean, it has a land area approximately a hundred square miles. It has little rainfall, a year-round temperature of eighty degrees, more than three hundred beaches, and clear ocean that reflects the sun in shimmering turquoise water. It has no exports except sugar. Often the sugar crop is poor. Even when it is good and prices for cane sugar are inflated, very little of the profit ever gets to the worker in the field or the refineries. St. Noir has a population of sixty thousand blacks and about fifteen hundred whites. Many of the blacks are a racial intermixture. Like many other islands in the Caribbean, St. Noir is at the crossroads. Rediscovered within the last fifty years by upper-middle-class Canadians, British, and Americans, the island is being transformed into the American idea of a vacation-land paradise. Whatever cultures and traditions were painfully emerging are rapidly disappearing in the rubble of a Disneyland. In another ten years, with jets bringing four hundred passengers a day, St. Noir will be well on the way to becoming an American honky-tonk. The economists and the government tell their black people this tourist explosion will raise their standard of living. They spend the black people's tax money to encourage the white people.

161

Premise: The black people of St. Noir have only one thing to offer these hordes of white tourists: their personal services.

For the economy to function, the cost of these services must be kept low. The future is easy to predict. Thirty hotels and three gambling casinos are now owned by American, Canadian, and British investors. Thousands of tourists visit the hotels in the winter season. The tourists have no interest in the black native, no interest in his culture, but they need the services of these twentieth-century slaves, who are locked into a system that keeps them barely above subsistence level.

Had the jet been invented in the nineteenth century, this human bomb might not have exploded for many decades. But now that the St. Noirean has been made aware by his black brothers in the United States and Africa of his worth as a black human being, the fuse not only is in place but is smoldering. Constantly exposed to the wealth and values of these transient visitors, the black people of St. Noir, already economically deprived, have lost their identity and are adopting the values of the vacationing segment of the white culture. Those blacks who through luck, training, or sheer acquisitiveness profit most by the tourist dollar have created a separate black power group who, as prat boys, together with the white property owners, control the island. This is the breeding ground for revolution. Since the United States government has already lost one island in the Caribbean, it obviously will not stand by and let the white property owners be dispossessed. Slavery by circumstance. Slavery of the insecure human being will be enforced. The black people of St. Noir will be given the white truth: Without the Yankee dollar, you will starve.

PREMISE: *The questioning of the values and structure of white society by black people separating from the white culture has become a fact of life in the United States.*

This is the inevitable historical result of white racism. On the positive side it has restored to the black people their identity as human beings. Equally important, the struggle of the blacks to free themselves from historical stereotypes has forced on all human beings, for the first time in history, a continuing reexamination of ultimate meanings and purposes of life. Are we born to work, or is work simply a means to control the environment so that we can live a full life? If the latter is true, is there an overriding concept of a full life based on natural law and fundamental values that all men can agree on? Black men acting as gadflies can force the human beast to crawl out of the slough of his inertia. But carried to extreme, the negatives are already grasping for control. Polarity for man, black, white, or yellow—man living in separate cultures, extolling the virtues of his separatism—can only lead to misunderstanding, fear, and hatred. An interacting society cannot tolerate separate human cultures. There must be two-way bridges welcoming continuous cross-traffic. Very few such bridges exist now between the white and black worlds, or between most ethnically oriented worlds.

Many people believe that ethnic differences are valuable for man, since they provide exciting and different approaches to life. Unfortunately, national, cultural, and religious differences are maintained through the creation of an illusion of superiority as between cultures and societies. Is it possible through education to create a new community of men who are aware of all racial, religious, national, and cultural differences? A new breed of man who is simultaneously white, yellow, black, Christian, Jew, Mohammedan, Buddhist, Hindu? A New Man who could joyfully encompass the traditions, the foods, the music, the literature, the arts of all societies? A New Man who retains an awareness of all ethnic origins and loves human beings, not in spite of, but because of their differences?

Premise: Man's obligation to man is to share the economic values he creates.

Historically, individual man has been wedded to group man. In the past century and more we have lived with a philosophy of laissez-faire capitalism, on one extreme, and a Marxist dedication to the state overriding individual man on the other. But now, group man, for the first time in history, is in a position to manipulate entire societies instead of being manipulated by leaders. Unfortunately, the concept of government of the people, by the people, and for the people, which both democratic and communistic societies give lip service to, in actuality has simply assumed the old oligarchic forms. Here there is man, *you and I*, and over there are the leader and his cohorts who govern us and limit our freedom far more than might be arguably necessary. Is there not a better way?

Premise: In four hundred years, the master painter working with a brush dipped in the seed of Carib Indians, Arawaks, Spanish, French, Portuguese, British, and African Bush Negroes has produced a canvas ranging from black-black to cafe-au-lait, with ochers, burnt umbers, and siennas splashed haphazardly so as to warm and blend the extremes.

If there is a God, He has shown Himself so that you can see Him with your own eyes on my island: In your variegated human colors, *You Walk before Me, and You are Perfect*! Black isn't beautiful. White isn't beautiful. The offspring of man copulating with man is beautiful. The island of St. Noir and other islands in the Caribbean have proved the adage "A mixed stewpot makes good soup."

Instead of thinking revolution, let's think evolution. Isn't it possible that the structure of the government that now rules St. Noir could be changed by the people into a People's Corporation of St. Noir, with every person now living there an equal shareholder? The corporation would be run by directors elected by the people, as stockholders, and would function as any modern corporation, not by taxing the people who worked for it and owned it, but by paying the working stockholders in dividends and capital appreciation for the economic wealth they create. Could a leader arise in St. Noir who would dare to use existing mechanisms of society, and by fully democratic means transform the government of St. Noir into a People's Corporation? Can a leader arise who extends, not to the idle rich, but to the average man, an opportunity to create, and become a stockholder in a new kind of society? Could that island, so attractive to tourists escaping from an intemperate climate, be constituted as a bridge between black and white people—a simpler world of man experiencing man instead of machines and a plasticized environment?

Let's play the dream in Western white man's terms. Revolution in the Caribbean is an experience that gives the governments of England and the United States nightmares. *Evolution* from a parliamentary government to a corporate government could be seeded by changing the structure of the island on terms our rich neighbors would understand. Visualize the island of St. Noir valued in terms of the United States dollar. The basis of capitalization established, the new corporate government would take over all privately owned facilities, such as the hotels, the docks, the oil refineries. The present owners would be reimbursed with stock in the corporation. Majority voting-stock control of the corporation, representing the valuation of all the land and buildings, would reside with the present citizens of St. Noir, and be transferable only to children born on the island. The island corporation, basing its earning projections on a new type of vacation home, would offer a hundred million dollars of its stock for sale in units of a maximum of a thousand dollars to nonresident families of St. Noir. Visualize ten thousand especially designed family homes built by the corporation and assigned in two-family units directly to native families who work in this phase of corporate activities.

And now dream the bridge. With the original nonresident stockholder being given priority and stockholders' rate concessions, a vacationing family from the United States, England, or Canada would come to St. Noir and live in an island home constructed in a rectangle that enclosed an inner dining patio. The rear section of the island home would be the permanent housing of two black families who would care for the home, cook the meals, and provide for the guests who would rent the equivalent of two motel rooms built into the rectangle capable of accommodating two vacationing families—white or black. Vacationing families would eat in the patio with resident black families. Food for the unit would be provided by the island corporation, and resident families would be given the housing and moderate wages for their function as hostelers. Vacationers would be assigned their accommodations by the corporation, and would pay their rental to the corporation.

Could St. Noir, one island in the Caribbean, create a new, joyous encounter world where man could rediscover himself and renew himself in a close relationship with sun, sea, and sky? Can man of any color who may eventually cram the world with six billion of his kind permit the few places he has left for renewal to become the shoddy commercial tourist worlds of Miami Beach, and the Grand Bahamas, or the special preserves of the upper-middle-class rich? People of St. Noir, learn the lesson God spoke to Abraham. Let go of God's hand! *Walk before Him!* We may never be perfect, but we will begin to do what all men must learn to do: *Walk Before God!*

Rais Daemon. Parallel to Premar. July to September, the first year. From tapes transcribed by Merle Blanc in October.

A man can travel a long way in twenty-one weeks. Five months ago I was in jail in Walpole. Now I feel I'm in jail again, but this time with a white woman, my own captive, from whom I may never be able to extricate myself—not still wearing my balls. In Massachusetts, my prison cell was cold and damp. Here it's hot and steamy, and the bars aren't metal. They're water—ocean water everywhere, and not a drop to drink. A Devil's Island with strong-arm caretakers; but there's nowhere you could swim and make it.

Even in my wildest dreams I wouldn't have picked the Mons de Cytherea either for incarceration or vacation. Thirty miles southwest of St. Noir, this place is really nothing but a few square miles of volcanic outcroppings, sand desert on the windward side, and a small lush jungle on the leeward. On the survey maps, the Mons is marked "Difficult Access," and warnings are given about the rocky approaches. But the island, a gigantic female lying on her back beneath the surface of the shallow water, her vulva humped in a beguiling invitation, is, like most females, accessible after all. You just have to know where the clitoris is hiding. Once you have discovered it, if you aren't too impatient and will wait for the full tide, the vagina, warm with the spray from encircling rocks, will open and lead you to safety.

The fact of naked humans, a black Adam and a white Eve, huddled together in the twentieth century in this cave overlooking the ocean at the top of the Mons, is unbelievable enough. More so is that the female is Laura Stone, the wife of the millionaire conglomerator and business tycoon Joseph Roche Stoneman, known as Rocky Stone. According to her driver's license, Laura Stone is thirty-eight years old. With dyed blond hair, creamy white breasts, pink nipples, and a hairy brown pussy, Laura is naked, except for a diamond ring that can't be removed from her swollen finger.

Laura is listening as I record this. She's probably the only survivor from the 707 jet that tried to land last night at St. Noir and was evidently ripped apart by a thunderstorm on the approach. Laura is not only listening, she is staring at me; her eyes are dull with hopelessness and repressed fear. She has a temperature; her face is flushed and blotchy. For all I know, she may die, and thus solve my problems. Or she may wish she were dead. Last night you died of shame, didn't you, Mrs. Stone? A big nigger wiped your smelly, diarrhea-covered ass, and while he was washing your behind, he crooned at you and told you to stop sobbing because you weren't going to die. And then the nigger discovered that you were menstruating and had a little bloody string hanging out of you. He took that Tampax out, too. No more cotton to put in your hole, Mrs. Stone. Out here we're back to basics!

What you are thinking? Do you want to say a word on this tape recorder? We may not have many other essentials, but I've got two sets of batteries and ten cassettes, thoughtfully provided by a friend. Here, say a few words into the microphone for posterity, Mrs. Stone. We haven't much to eat, but as long as these batteries last, we can talk our heads off. What's the matter? Are you afraid that this big black nigger is going to fuck you? Maybe he'll shove his prick down your throat. In the long run, that might be safer, since there don't seem to be any pills in your pocketbook. You wouldn't want to be rescued and then discover your white belly full of black pickaninny, would you, Mrs. Stone?

Or maybe this big *schvartzer*. Yeah, Mrs. Stone, I know the Jewish words. If you ever get back to civilization, you can tell your friends at Hadassah, "I was sure the *schvartzer* was going to cut off my finger so he could steal my big rock-candy diamond." Can't wiggle it off, can you, Mrs. Stone? How much is it worth? Twenty-five thousand? Too bad it's not enough to seed a revolution. Does Rocky Stone really think you're worth twenty-five grand? Mrs. Stone, you're obviously a pretty expensive piece of ass.

You don't have to worry, because I've got a better idea. If you don't die from sheer horror at having to roll up in a blanket again tonight with a black man—isn't it amazing that living flesh, whatever the color, can keep you warm?—then I'll ransom you. I'll save one of those tapes, and eventually I'll sail over to Puerto Rico and mail it to your husband. You can sob on it and try to convince him that you really are worth a half-million dollars. You can tell him about the indignities you have suffered.

Of course, you might mention that if it weren't for Rais Daemon, part of you would be in the process of digestion in the bellies of Caribbean sharks. That raw bite on your leg is proof of that. And you might tell your husband that I picked bananas for you, and coconut, and made you chew some lovely raw fish, and I even washed your little cunt. Aha! Laura, I can see, at last, I'm reaching you! Have another shot of rum. Next thing you know, you'll want to live long enough to punch me in the nose. So, listen; I'm only trying to rape your brain, while I preserve this brief moment of my own insanity on tape.

I finally got back to St. Noir, March 26, on an Air Carib jet. A band was playing outside the terminal at Harding Airport, but the St. Noireans weren't celebrating my arrival. It was Carnival time and not coincidentally Independence Day for St. Noir. Scarlet flame trees and blood-red anthrium with their phallus pods fluttered in the sea breeze, along with the new black-and-white flag of St. Noir. Isn't that poetic, Laura ... Mrs. Stone? But, of course, penis symbolism and nationalism have common roots. Politics is a polite way of shafting everyone at once. I had planned my return to arrive during this celebration. Freedom for the blacks? Not quite! White freedom for the blacks. Sure, a chain with a short leash.

In the streets of St. Noir, thirty or more calypso bands were warming up for their competitions. Feet-wiggling music and lyrics sung off the cuff to celebrate everything—independence, the queen of England's beneficence, Sir Crawford Oldham (the former British governor's) wisdom, and the joys of fucking. Please, mister, don't touch my tomato. Yeah, Mrs. Stone, with the big bamboo and the ripe tomato, the St. Noireans (despite the friendly white man who teaches them birth control) are slowly committing population suicide. What else is there to do in St. Noir except harvest sugar a few months a year and fuck? I do sound bitter, but whoever finds these tapes among the vulture-cleaned and desiccated bones of Mrs. Rocky Stone and Rais Daemon should know the truth. I'm really not angry at anyone. In fact, viewed from the right perspective, man's insistence on screwing up his world can only be viewed with cosmic laughter. When there's nothing else left . . . like Zorba, why not dance?

I could only smile as the plane taxied closer to the enthusiastic welcoming committee. St. Noir, as an independent nation, was still just as dependent as it had ever been on white tourism and a sugar crop that often withered in the fields for lack of water. St. Noir exists in a world where the only way to live high off the hog is to be sure other nations owe you more than you owe them. Telling this island speck on the ocean that it can now play in the big-time economic world, in a game even its leaders don't understand, is a typical white man's con game. This kind of independence is like a man with no legs being pushed in a wheelchair where he doesn't want to go. A tongue-tied schoolboy with no cards and a few cents in his pocket trying to play international poker in a trillion-dollar come-on. A philosopher of the poor summed it up: Pride and the right fare will get you a ride on the New York subway. The least you can say, Mrs. Stone, is that the St. Noireans have pride.

Waiting on the runway were the new premier, the Honorable Arthur Granby, black and beaming, standing beside pink-white Sir Crawford Oldham, now adviser-in-residence, whose presence signified that England would still defend St. Noir against its "enemies"—internal or external. Behind them were several black Cadillacs to transport the minor congressional dignitaries and black movie stars from the United States to their rooms in the most pretentious of the island's twenty-nine foreign-owned hotels, all of them basking on the sun-drenched iridescent beaches and nicely sheltered from the soil and ferment of the inner island.

The stewardess, no doubt impressed by my size and my brown-and-orange African dashiki, assumed that I must be an important invited guest. I didn't disillusion her. She actually smiled at me in Nordic complicity as she requested the northern passengers, including the celebrities, to line up behind me. I was first down the debarkation ladder.

Arthur Granby's enthusiastic smile turned to shocked dismay when he saw me. My picture had appeared on the cover of *Ebony* in February, and I knew Gabby Blanc had reprinted it several times, along with bits and pieces of "Walk Before God," in the *St. Noir Goat*. The only reason Arthur didn't alert the police was because he feared to test the crowd's enthusiasm.

He touched and quickly dropped my extended hand. "A bit of political fuck-up, Arthur, my arriving at this time," I said, and grinned at him as he quickly recovered his rubber-faced public image.

"Sir Crawford"—Arthur nudged the shriveled, white-haired Englishman who was staring at me as if I had just landed from the Planet of the Apes—"this is Mr. Rais Daemon, author of 'Walk Before God.' "

Sir Crawford's trembling, bulbous nostrils revealed that he was silently praying for a miracle. Alas, nothing happened; the God of Englishmen must have been dozing in the noonday sun.

Partly because I was aware that there was no hotel room waiting for me, I was tempted to embarrass Arthur and Sir Crawford and follow them with the other celebrities to one of the waiting automobiles. But Merle's sister, Gabrielle, knew a better way to blow Granby's mind.

Last time I saw her, Gabby was thirteen. Now she was fully rounded and ready for living. I heard her screaming an enthusiastic welcome. "Rais! Rais! You've come home!" Struggling against a crowd of spectators trying to watch the movie contingent, Gabby finally wriggled through the police lines, and all five feet two inches of her ran and jumped into my arms. Wiggling her braless tits against me, she puppy-lapped me with wet sloppy kisses.

"You came, *mon singe!* You mad black monkey! Where's Merle? Why isn't she with you? I was going to ask her if I could sleep with my brother-in-law. I'm still a virgin, but it ain't easy." With her legs splayed around my middle, she was shaking and tossing her cropped black head like a stallion in heat. As she yelled and waved at her friends, we wove through the crowd.

Granby's welcoming committee were finding Gabby's performance more intriguing than the arrival of stiff-lipped politicians, while the Uncle Tom movie stars were shading their dazed eyes from the blazing sunlight and looking generally bewildered.

"This is Rais Daemon. He's the man! He wrote it!" Some of the crowd picked up her refrain. *"Walk Before God! Rais Daemon. I love him! You're gonna love him. He's really going to give St. Noir back to St. Noireans!"*

With her legs scissored around me, I found it impossible not to pat her smooth black behind, which was no longer covered by her short shirt. I remembered that a bare ass and screwing are appreciated in easygoing St. Noir. Maybe if men and women in the States enjoyed their sexuality like the blacks do here, marriages wouldn't get so hung up. Merle and Gabby's daddy didn't marry their ma until he was fifty-three. I remember him telling me he had slept with two dozen different women on this island, and he loved them all. What do you think of that, Mrs. Stone?

While most of the spectators seemed to know my name, I knew they didn't really remember me. When a black man or woman escapes this island, the best survival reaction is to put him out of mind; and the hot sun makes forgetting easy. Some who remembered thought I had been lucky, while others were sure I had been a good stud for that white woman who paid for my education. Too bad the entire male population of St. Noir couldn't be drafted to jig-jig with bored white female tourists! Many black mothers, fondling male babies in their arms, would approve the sanity of that escape route. But there was no way out for most of the island females; no white man would adopt them. Even their husbands, sneaking off with black girls who conked their hair or wore wigs and bleached their faces, made it clear to them that white may not be more beautiful than black, but it was a damned sight richer!

I hate to admit it, Mrs. Stone, but you got me worried. Maybe the reason you aren't talking is that you really are in shock. If that's a fact, you're going to force me to make a decision. Should I carry you down to my leaky sloop and sail us both back to St. Noir? Imagine you rising out of the sea like Botticelli's *Venus*. But instead of being supported by a white seashell, there you will be, naked, in the arms of a black man whose hard-on is boring a hole in his dungarees.

Now, I ask you, if you were me, would you do that?
The British troops and Arthur Granby's cohorts would fall
all over each other as they ran to capture that monster of
monsters. They would say that Rais Daemon, the man
who nearly took St. Noir away from them, had now returned as a white slaver.

In that event, I suppose, Laura, they'd probably get
your psyche mended and you'd find your tongue, but I'd
be spending the rest of my life alone in some forgotten
British dungeon. Laura, can't you do anything but cry? I
know you hear me. Twenty hours ago when I pulled you
out of the water, and breathed you back to life, you
stared at me and sobbed, "Why didn't you just let me
die?"

Are you listening? *No one* in this God-forsaken world
believes you're alive. If you don't start talking pretty
quick, first I'm going to beat you, then I'm going to screw
your ass off, and then I'm going to strangle you, after
which I'm going to disembowel you and feed you piece by
piece to the gulls and vultures. Ha! I got through to you!
Was that a smile? Think about it, Laura. Your white ass is
mine. If we don't decide together, what we're going to do
with it, I'll have to make the decision unilaterally.

It didn't take me long to discover Gabby knew the
politics of the island like a chess master knows his op-
ponent's opening game. "There are twelve parishes on
the island," she reminded me as she drove me to the offices
of the *St. Noir Goat*. "In the larger villages we've got
ten trusted men or women for each five hundred of the
population, or well over twelve hundred people who believe in us. If you gave the word tonight, on the first day
of Independence, we could really catch them napping.
Within twenty-four hours the island would be ours."

Maybe I should have listened to Gabby. But I'd been
away from St. Noir for seven years, and Merle's twenty-
year-old virgin sister sounded wet behind the ears. How
could she have learned the ins and outs of a successful
coup d'etat? How could she know whether enough St.
Noireans would really join the cause if they had to do it
with a gun in their hands, and maybe shoot at one of their
black brothers? I believed Gabby when she told me they
had ammunition and one thousand rifles stashed around
the island.

"Look, Gabby, I think we should let the situation jell," I told her. "We can always use force. I want to be sure that you've brainwashed the right people. The kind who won't let us down the minute the going gets rough." That wasn't the truth, but it sounded reasonable. My true feeling was that if we took our time, we could eventually force a new election, particularly if we set the stage so that Granby gradually lost the confidence of the people. He was premier, but only by a coalition with the more radical People's Labor party. The PLP could easily create a stalemate. "If we have the grass-roots backing of twenty-five percent of the workers," I said, "we'll swing it peaceably, before the year's out."

"Shit on your democracy, Rais, you're a dreamer. If you ever do end up premier, you'll be in the same box as Granby. The blacks on this island are too stupid, too scared, or they simply don't give a damn. The only way you'll get your People's Corporation is by a takeover."

Before we got out of the car Gabby gave me a big tongue-tasting kiss, and it didn't seem like the kiss of any virgin. "All right, Rais, we'll show you. Tonight, around seven, before the feasting and dancing, most of the elected officials will gather in St. Michael's Square. There'll be at least ten thousand listening to their speeches. Get ready to make a damned good speech, and when Merle finally arrives, you'll be running this island."

I suspect that Gabby was trying to tell me it didn't matter if Merle ever came back. Gabrielle was ready and able to become the first lady of St. Noir, and Rais Daemon, willy-nilly, was her puppet on a string.

Later, when the square was packed in every direction, Gabby tested her strength. It was an exhilarating experience—damned near overpowering. Arthur Granby was delivering his speech from a platform in the middle of the square. Most of the newly elected officials were seated beside him. Just as Arthur was stressing his faith in the people, and his love of the island, somewhere deep in the crowd steel drums began to talk to each other in a low-keyed "day-o" rhythm. "Rais Daemon, he come back, now we're gonna be home! Rais Daemon, he come back, and we're gonna have home. New Home! Rais Daemon, he come back . . ." Over and over again, growing from a murmur to an intensity that finally drowned out the amplification system. In every direction you looked, torchlighted faces were swaying to the music. Reggae and calypso for the islanders are an effective political weapon. Bewildered, the newly elected officials slowly left the platform and disappeared in the crowd. The singing, now loud and raucous, with everyone dancing and laughing, changed to: "Rais knocked them stone cold dead in the market. Stone cold dead in the market. He ain't killed nobody but Granby. Rais, Rais, Rais, Rais! We want to hear you, Rais!"

"Not long," Gabby yelled at me as I was pushed up on the platform. "Don't talk too long. Just wave your hands at them. Tell them it's going to be a new day. *Savoir St. Noir.* Forget 'Walk Before God.' That's too complicated. *Savoir St. Noir!*" And I did as she told me. Hypnotized by that girl, and the crowd screaming and delirious, I held my arm over my head and yelled, *"Savoir St. Noir!"* Damned if they didn't pick it up like a refrain, and thousands of them were singing a Jamaican-style reggae about a man who finally came home again to his people.

Later, back in her little house in St. Michael's, which she claimed she supported with her earnings from the *St. Noir Goat*, Gabby was elated. "Rais, we're gonna do it, I know it. You've got the charisma. You look like a black messiah." While she was talking, she had slid out of her clothes. Even before I touched her, her nipples were engorged, red-black and demanding. She rubbed her chest against mine. "I've waited a long time, Rais. Merle won't mind. You've got to make love to me."

Whether you minded or not, Merle, the one thing I could agree with Gabby on was that I had to make love to her. Later she admitted she was only a virgin in her head. "But no man ever took me that high, Rais. Before you it was only just fucking. This was ecstasy."

As my blood cooled a little I tried to explain to her that I wasn't a black separatist, and we really weren't vibrating together, at least politically. "The kind of Caribbean I'm proposing would give the black man a unique black identity. I've been down most of the roads, Gabby," I told her while she played with my penis, both of us certain that it wouldn't be long before, once again, it would feel better inside her. "Black Muslimism, rehabilitation of the ghettos by the blacks, black education taught by blacks, Africa-is-my-home, return to tribalism—you name it. They're the wrong way. We've got something better and deeper than 'black is beautiful.' Right now it's only potential, but it's there. Black people being themselves, blacks simply not worrying one way or the other about the white man, other than forcing him to share some of his bread. That kind of black has a pipeline to a new kind of human awareness. Joy and soul blended.

"Look at you," I told Gabby. "You're black but you're French, too. Else, where in hell did you get that thin nose and no puffed lips? Look at me, my mother's got some Spanish blood, but I'm a throwback to Nairobi. Did you see the faces in the crowds tonight? God, I've been in the States so long I'd forgotten. Mostly we see only black and white there. Here we got black-black, cafe-au-lait, ocher, burnt umber, sienna. God must have been chuckling when he said, 'Walk before me and be whole-hearted. . . .' The 'whole heart' is man and woman—loving and copulating and being beautiful, because God made sure that the penises and vaginas fit nicely together, no matter what the color."

But Gabby was listening to her own drummer. For the next few weeks, while I preached moderation, she whipped out editorials flaying the new government every time it fumbled or looked as if it might. *"Savoir St. Noir"* became a rallying call, implying as it did that this special band, the "Daemonite-knowing" (her name for our followers), was more intense and faithful and "more knowing" than our political enemies.

"Sometimes I think you don't really understand the people here, Rais," she told me. "Even most of your lieutenants working for the cause don't understand 'Walk Before God.' Most of them read as little as they can, and all they feel is their toes tingling. But they're bored, and you look like excitement, as if you might shake up things. I can't let them discover the truth about you, that you're really like most politicians, a Mugwump. Your mug is one side of the fence, and your wump is on the other." Gabby was asking me to flatten her. She grinned. "But, Rais, you do have an effective mug. Look at your head. Must be size eight. Look at your flaring nostrils and thick lips. Look at that knife slash on your cheek that your beard won't grow over." She was laughing while I examined myself in the mirror. "Rais, you may be as soft as molasses inside, but, man, you do look mean! You look like the white man's nightmare. A Mau-Mau chieftain who has grown virile by eating the powdered testicles of his white oppressors. Rais, we need you! For Christ's sake, why don't you act and talk the way you look?"

I keep wondering whether Arthur Granby would have arrested me if I had stayed on St. Noir. Of course, he'd have had to. But he could never have kept me imprisoned on the island. As long as Gabby was alive and I was in jail, she'd have used my martyrdom to get the revolution going all over again. The only thing Granby could have done was deport me. But where? Not to the United States. No one in Uncle Sugar would be waiting for Rais Daemon with extended hands.

I'd been a British subject, but now St. Noir was independent. My application for United States citizenship was under the shadow of a jail sentence. Like it or not, for the moment I am the traitorous citizen of a new republic, or more likely a man without a country. The hell with it! Being born somewhere doesn't make it home. Trying to make Africa a homeland, like the Jews did with Israel, doesn't really give one roots either. Malcolm Little became Malcolm X because there was no lineage for a black man. Black men like Arthur Granby don't worry about identity. When you shake it down, playing it cool in Granby's way may be the only sensible approach.

The St. Noir pot finally came to a boil with the strike of the sugarcane harvesters. Arthur Granby invited me to Government House to discuss the situation. "What in hell are you up to, Rais?" he demanded. "You and Gabby Blanc and a few hundred malcontents have put this whole island in a ferment. All this inflammatory stuff that's being printed in the *St. Noir Goat* is unrealistic, and you know it. This isn't Cuba or the Dominican Republic. If that cane rots in the fields, we'll lose a fifth of our annual income."

Arthur was speaking to me like a father trying to bridge a generation gap with his wayward son, and he couldn't conceal the expression of hopelessness on his face. "We've got our independence, Rais; now we've got to go step by step. Without the sugar, without the tourists coming to the hotels, we'd starve. The publicity people who promote St. Noir tourism are already getting the feedback from abroad, and it's hurting us." Arthur sighed. "I know. I sound like an Uncle Tom."

I laughed. "Now that you mention it, yes. I say to hell with Americans who come here expecting that every black man is happy just singing his calypsos or dancing the limbo, or is a drunk and chasing women. Times are not only changing; they have changed. Our people are looking for a better life."

Arthur looked grim. "There's no basis for populism here. We have only a few hundred rich men, and all the other sixty-nine thousand are poor. When you start talking about a People's island, you're talking communism—at least, those who own the wealth think so. I'm warning you, Rais, I've been talking with London and Washington. They've got their ears to the ground, and we'll play ball their way!"

I lighted the cigar that Arthur offered me. "Tell them not to worry," I said. "The Cuban solution isn't for St. Noir, and I'm not the agent of any government. I'm my own man. When I was a boy I worked in most of the hotels on this island, and I thought I was going to get ahead in the world. From slopboy to busboy, to assistant cook, and maybe one day assistant manager, or I'd save up enough money to put a down payment on a taxi. I'd be a capitalist, because I actually owned something."

I smiled at him through a cloud of smoke. "I even dreamed that someday I might be as rich as the white man who comes here and pisses his money away drinking and gambling. I saw them drive through my village on the way to their hotels—through private gates with guards checking the passengers. Down private roads, to luxury and the best beaches on this island. And as they drove through the poverty-stricken parishes, they told each other how colorful the natives were. They haven't changed. They don't stop and smell us. They don't see squalor, and they don't give a damn about the big black bucks standing around with nothing to do except watch television ... *and think*. The damned fool white man wonders why there is such pushing and shoving all over the world. Why doesn't he wake up? No one can flaunt his wealth in front of a poor man and expect him to love him. A century ago, when the rich were smarter, they hid themselves in places like Newport and Palm Beach. Not anymore. In the States they give the poorest blacks Master Charge and urge them to buy televisions so they can see for themselves that there's a lot of cake in the world. Even here, where the people can actually see the contrast every day of their lives, the rich couldn't wait to give them television. All the old crap that was shown on the tube years ago in the States makes some more money here for whitey.

"The glass teat and the big glossy hotels tell the black man the same thing over and over again: This stupid white man, who can't stop fighting wars or spending billions for defense or to walk on the moon, begrudges every dime for the poor. He gives us his white Jesus, and tells us 'Blessed are the meek.' What's he got? His own special hotline to heaven? Well, the news is that the young black man has stopped waiting for the promised land. He wants action—and more."

Arthur pointed to a bottle of rum on the coffee table in front of him. With the luxury of the black leather couches, the Oriental rug, the Havana cigars, Granby's office was designed for tongue loosening.

I shook my head and smiled. "Maybe you think I don't give a damn. Maybe you think that Rais Daemon just wants a piece of the cake for himself, and then he'll shut up?"

Arthur took a different tack. "I'm only fighting you on the how, son—not the whys or even the whens. After ten years, you come back here with a new timetable. Well, St. Noir may be the tortoise, but we're getting there. To change the subject, I hear Merle's coming back. Good! She's calmer than her sister. I hear you and she are married."

I laughed. "Do me a favor, Arthur. Gabby really needs an older man like you. It would steady her. If you took her for a mistress, she'd be rooting for you in her newspaper instead of trying to castrate you every time you pulled a boo-boo."

Arthur poured two glasses of rum. "For the past two years Gabby has been agitating for two political parties on this island, and her belief that neither should be involved with trade unions. You came home, and she got her wish. I still think it's a mistake. Two parties, two trade unions in a population of seventy-thousand people, just creates confusion."

"I agree with you," I told him. "Ultimately, the New Independence party and the People's Labor party will have to merge. When that happens, they'll retire you, Arthur."

"If you want my job and can get it by democratic means, fine. But you'd better face the facts. This island just got off its knees, and there will be no general election for eighteen months. You'll never force it. I don't know or care why you came back, or how you got the money to get here, but I'm not going to let you screw up the island with unreasonable wage demands or a takeover attempt. We've come a long way. The sugar estates have been nationalized, the power company is government-owned. The people have a higher standard of living than they have ever had. . . ."

"Admit it, Arthur, that's for the birds. The wealth is in the hotels, in the industry that you're trying to attract, the oil refineries, the shipping docks. The private investors overseas aren't letting the average St. Noirean dip into *that* private gold mine." I sipped the rum. "You and I have different ideas for the future, and Gabby has hers. She wants me sitting where you are. I'm not interested in NIP, or either of the trade-union approaches, or any of the guardhouse lawyers who think the new union will be better than yours, or that, in the given circumstances, I'd be able to do things one damned bit better than you. I've got a new dream of the future, and it doesn't include more million-dollar hotels or more gambling. The kind of tourism they stand for is coming to a fast end. And sugar won't solve the problem. The price is too high. Anyway, the rum-and-Coca-Cola generation is dead. The new generation is drinking diet colas filled with saccharine. Sugar will give you holes in your head, and I don't mean cavities."

"So what's your way?"

"The world has become too dangerous for anything less than Utopia. All I can tell you right now is I'm not happy with the present situation. 'Walk Before God' didn't light this fire all by itself. It was smoldering before I blew on it. At least, you and I have one thing in common: I don't believe in burning the house down. If there's a revolution, I'll start it at the ballot box."

Merle Blanc. October, the first year of Premar. From tapes transcribed by Samantha Brown.

I need perspective. Maybe if I put on tape just what happened on my St. Noir vacation last June, all of us can share it and possibly find some sense or purpose in the whole business.

Rais is alive! Or at least three weeks ago he was alive, but if I ever get my hands on him, he may be dead after all. It's been three months since we were together on St. Stephen's beach, and not a word from him. And then, yesterday, two cassette tapes arrive, postmarked St. Noir—mailed, I'll bet, by my bitch sister. Two one-hour tapes in a box, and nothing else.

Bren, Ellen, and I listened to them together, and I don't know who was more shocked. It's absolutely insane, unbelievable: Laura Stone is Bren's sister! I met her once. Me naked, her standing there in judgment—cool, sophisticated, remote, with a Jewish superiority that comes from being rich and chosen.

It would be funny if it weren't so tragic. It's one thing to start a revolution, and it's another thing for a black man to keep a rich white woman prisoner. Rais, you big ape, I'll bet you still haven't discovered who Laura Stone is. Even if you have, it's a good thing we, and not Laura's lawyer, have the tapes you made!

Oh, God! I'm assuming you're both alive, but you may be dead. Did you strangle Laura, Rais? At the Human-Values seminar today I suggested that you might have.

Bren laughed. "Ellen, and all of you kids who don't know Rais, I can assure you that my sister couldn't be in better hands. With his beliefs in reincarnation, Rais suffers when he kills a fly that's annoying him. Now, if I were Rais, Laura might have something to worry about. For me, having my sister in my power might be symbolically equivalent to at last having the Establishment under control. I might not kill her, but I'd make her suffer a little."

I flew back from St. Noir on June 28. When I arrived at Logan Airport I telephoned Ellen, who drove in with Mohammed Hassan to get me. Ellen told me that Bren's sister, Laura, had been killed in the 707 jet that crashed in the Caribbean two days earlier. "Bren's gone home for a few days," Ellen said. "His mother is taking it very badly."

I knew about the crash, but I had no reason to connect Laura with Rais. My flight back to Boston had been delayed two days because of the accident. The airport was in shambles anyway, since most of the ground crew had been arrested as conspirators in the Daemonite attempt to take over the island. I wonder if Rais knows that it was scheduled to fly directly to St. Noir, but was diverted toward Puerto Rico because of the uprising. Or that it was diverted again, back toward St. Noir, when the British troops finally radioed that they had things under control. It was after turning back to St. Noir that the 707 crashed in a thunderstorm.

A writer for *Newsweek* emphasized that the worst air tragedy might never have occurred if the flight had gone to St. Noir on schedule. Thus, he suggested, Rais was indirectly responsible for the death of one hundred and sixty-three people. There were no known survivors. Because Laura was Rocky Stone's wife and because certain newspaper columnists suggested she and Rocky were no longer making music together, she was the most newsworthy passenger on board.

When we were discussing the whole mess with the Premars, Bren rejected any idea of Rais' guilt because of the flight delay. "Okay, let's talk about my sister," he told them. "There was very little about Laura worth eulogizing. My sister and I didn't know or care very much about each other. She was nine years older than me. I was a 'change-of-life' baby. I sneaked into Mother's womb when she was at the age when she was sure she couldn't conceive anymore.

"Anyway, while I was growing up Laura was already being conditioned for her role in life. She would be the perfect gift-girl, an adornment, and intellectual prize for her Jewish, and preferably rich, husband. She would be both an extension of her husband and, by some magic, a person in her own right. After graduating from Bennington, Laura met Rocky Stone, who was born Joseph Roche Stoneman. Rocky is above all else a showman. He came from a poor family in Brooklyn, and his middle name was derived from his French grandparents. He thought of himself as being in the Rothschild tradition. He, too, had Continental roots. Despite the fact that Rocky is fifteen years older than Laura, my mother and father were elated. For them, on a lesser scale, it was like a Jackie and Ari Onassis alignment.

"And that's that!" Bren grinned at the kids. "Among other things, Rocky controls a half-dozen theater chains and two film-releasing corporations, so the marriage was held in his villa on the French Riviera, and was timed to coincide with the Cannes film festival. I was only thirteen, but I remember the vulgar display of wealth and power that joined two nebbishes whose prime mission in life was to spend money for self-glorification and self-indulgence. And they finally failed even that. My sister was flying to St. Noir, not because of any interest in the political situation, but because she knew that Rocky's yacht was going to put in to Hamilton dockyard for a few days before sailing to São Paulo.

"Jeb White, the captain of the *Souris*, who plays on both sides of their marital fence, telephoned Laura that Jeanne Mechante, the French actress, was on board. According to my mother, the soul-searing question in my sister's useless mind was whether, in fact, as she knew anyway, it was true that Rocky Stone was fucking Jeanne Mechante. Since anyone who can read between the lines in the jet-set media could have told her that he was, and that Jeanne was not the first whose legs he helped to spread, you'll have to admit that my sister embarked on a useless expedition. Her excuse to my mother was, 'I don't give a damn who Rocky screws, but my daughter and son, *your grandchildren*, are on board, and at their ages their father shouldn't be giving them an education in orgies.' Shulamith and David are seventeen and nineteen." Bren paused, then added, "If Laura had asked me, I'd have told her to enroll them in Premar!"

That particular Human Values session went on most of the night, as the Premars coolly attacked Bren's attitudes and his sister's values. They were also critical of Rais for his larger moral responsibility as he stood by and let his plan for the takeover of St. Noir proceed to the point of futile revolution. The Premars even explored the possibility of cosmic balance, something beyond a personal God, beyond even personal interest in man—a retribution of a kind, which inexorably destroyed anything that threatened to tip the scale of life out of balance.

Bren insisted that we weren't fiddling while Rome burned. "Just catching our breaths," he told Ellen and me, but I wondered. Still, even in the midst of battle you need a calm mind to grasp the entire situation. Lying in bed with Ellen and me, he tried to convince us that the whole business made him believe in God—a loving, jovial one. Only that kind of God, knowing Rais, knowing he had written "Walk Before God," knowing Laura and her generalized feeling about the starving masses—"let them eat cake"—could have played the supreme joke and put them together on a desert island. I was beginning to think even God couldn't comprehend the mess we were in. Rais and Laura were either alive, still on the Mons, or Rais had gone back to St. Noir and was hiding out, which would mean that Laura was dead. But that wasn't all. As all the kids knew, the Topham's Corner Premar Commune, scarcely in existence six weeks, had yet to sail in calm waters.

Less than two weeks ago half the South Boston police came and searched through all three houses looking for marihuana or drugs. They didn't find anything, but Dancer O'Day told Ellen yesterday that he had the leverage to close Premar down, and he'd use it unless she cleared out.

"His police buddies were shocked," Ellen told us. "They told Daddy they found half of us in the communal baths and couldn't believe their ears, or their ogling eyes, when I told them that I was Ellen O'Day. If I hadn't been an O'Day, they'd have carted us all off. But they were afraid to embarrass Dancer."

"It won't embarrass me," Dancer told Ellen. "The next time, if you haven't turned into a pillar of salt, I'll have to save you from this Sodom myself. Don't you know it's against the law for unrelated people to live under one roof? And if it isn't illegal for unmarried kids to sleep together, it should be. I've got lawyers checking it out. It sure as hell must be against some law for fifty kids to be screwing naked in the middle of Dorchester, Massachusetts." He gave Ellen a week to get out of Premar and move back home.

Bren decided that he and Ellen must finally face the old man, so he telephoned Dancer and told him that he'd had a nice talk with Gina, Ellen's mother, and Gina had invited both Ellen and him to dinner. He said that he loved Ellen and wanted to ask for her hand in marriage. Ellen is terrified at the thought of the confrontation. If she doesn't cool it, I'm afraid her heart will act up.

So what happens next? Phil Tenhausen has read the newspaper stories about Rais, but we don't dare tell him about the tapes Rais sent us. Even so, he announced that he has extended himself far enough. Phil doesn't want to, but he says he must find two other Compars to replace Rais and me. Of course, he knows about the police raid, which was kept quiet, and he's aware that a lot of people in Topham's Corner are astounded to discover a Premar commune next door to them. Some are more irritated by the black and white students who have been seen on the streets with their arms around each other than they are about the sexual aspects of Premar.

"We expect some antagonism," Phil said on the phone. "Premar threatens middle-class value systems, but what we intend is a peaceful adaptation to the inevitable, not armed rebellion. Rais is something else. Whatever his convictions, you can't deny he's been involved with overt force." Phil was irritated. "I want to go along with you and Bren—at least until we hear Rais' side of the story— but there are only three Compars there for forty-eight youngsters, and there's supposed to be four. Tell Merle I'm sorry, but Rais evidently hasn't been listening to her."

Before Phil hung up, Bren lied to him and told him Rais had telephoned from Puerto Rico and was on his way back to the States. I knew Phil didn't believe this, but he gave Rais two more weeks, and that would be that.

Whatever happens, it can't be worse than my two weeks in St. Noir and the Daemon Gotterdammerung. Gabrielle met me at the airport, and I knew the minute I set eyes on her that if Rais hadn't talked my baby sister into bed (she was a gangling fifteen-year-old when I left), *she* would have dragged him into *her* sack. Listening to her as she drove to St. Michael's, I was not only uneasy with her philosophy, but I was jealous of her as a woman. She was the activist that Rais had tried to make of me, never quite successfully. "Rais is living in a shack near St. Stephen's beach," Gabby told me. "It's so crude you won't want to live there, so you can stay with me in St. Michael's. The kettle is boiling. Only George Holdam, Patrick Henry Orion, and myself know where Rais is. Granby can't pin anything on him, yet. Our smoke screen is that Rais is going to run against him in the next election. But Arthur has only a patchwork government held together with a weak coalition. If he makes one mistake—and we're going to help him make it—the government will fall. Then neither Ralph Clevis, a pussyfooter, nor Granby will be able to form a new one. Then Rais will move in fast."

As I listened, I began to suspect that Gabby was pushing Rais in the direction of a violent revolution; she was refusing to let him vacillate. As she fanned the flames with her writings in the *St. Noir Goat*, probably without too much objection from the publisher, George Holdam, she cast Rais in the role of the new messiah. Knowing Rais, I doubted if he wanted the role, or was equal to it.

Ten minutes after Rais had swooped me in his arms, and with his kisses and his big hands all over me was practically turning me into a screaming orgasm, it was apparent that Gabby and I would try to cut Rais down the middle each laying claim to what we believed was the true Rais.

Both George Holdam, who had been defeated in the last general election by Arthur Granby, and Patrick Henry Orion, who looked like a reincarnation of Che Guevara, watched Rais hugging me.

"Our boy certainly charms the ladies," Patrick said. He leered at me as if he wanted to be next in line to play feelies. "Rais, maybe we *should* wait for the elections. Every female I talk with on St. Noir is ready to toss out her old man and welcome you into her bed. If we could get the women to the polling booth feeling nice and sexy, you'd have it made."

"Sure, why not?" I said to Rais. "Gabby can run a centerfold of you in the *St. Noir Goat* showing you smiling and in the nude, ready for business with a big erection."

George Holdam thought that was funny, but Gabby didn't. "The hell with elections. The fat's in the fire. Any moment now something's got to give. Maybe it won't be what we expect, but it won't be what Granby expects, either. Although he's got the cane workers back to work, it won't take much to precipitate a general strike."

I kept waiting for Rais to tell her to go to hell, that he

was running things, but he just kept listening to her as if he were mesmerized.

Later that night I got him to admit that he had slept with Gabby. "Your sister's great, Merle; don't underestimate her," he said. The sheer nerve of him! Bren would call it *chutzpah*. He explained the meaning of the word by describing a man, who after he shits on your front doorstep, rings the doorbell and asks you for toilet paper. But *chutzpah* or not, I knew it would do no good to protest Rais' screwing my sister. With Gabby, fucking wasn't marriage. It was just friendly St. Noirean behavior.

I didn't underrate her. The only way I could attack her, at this point, was to suggest to Rais that he alone could cool her off. "Let her profit by your experience," I begged him. "The only way the established power can be uprooted is by using its own legal devices, not by simply stirring up popular fury. You've been down that road before in the States. Rais, don't you see that you're on the right track? Use the democratic structures they respect. Give the people a dream they can believe in; convince them of their own worth both as blacks and as a real melting pot of races. Make them believe in themselves, and they'll believe in you, too. If you did that, within a year the government could be in your hands."

Rais was gently making love to me, his erection embedded deep inside me, which, the second time around, wasn't in such a hurry. "You're right, Merle," he murmured. "I know that. Once we had control we could swiftly change direction, even use pseudo-legal means if necessary. We could complete the nationalization the trade unions have started. Then the guardians of the status quo would be caught with their pants down. They'd have no choice but to accept the People's Corporate Island of St. Noir. But I have an uneasy feeling that isn't going to happen. What do you want me to do—lie down in front of a steam roller? I'd like nothing better than to drive down to Harding Airport with you and fly back to Boston." Rais chuckled, but he sounded grim. "You want me to join Bren's revolution? How do you know that isn't another daydream? I'm beginning to wonder if human beings don't function better when they follow the slave rationalization 'Don't upset the applecart.' "

Merle Blanc. October, the first year of Premar. From tapes transcribed by Samantha Brown.

We talked most of the next ten days. The only place to get away from Gabby, who was busy with her innumerable schemes, was to join Rais in the hideout hovel in St. Stephen's parish. His one-room shack, built from flattened oil drums and refuse lumber, overlooked a warm blue-green Atlantic and the large northern horizon.

We made love under the stars and slept together on a rope bed that Rais had woven together. Covered with a tarpaulin and several layers of blanket, we'd wake in the morning with rope marks on our backs and sides. But I was winning; at least, I thought Rais agreed with me. In this age of power politics, I told him, with sufficient communications to mesmerize the people, revolutions with bloodshed were an anachronism.

Gabby had stayed with us several nights, acting like a loving sister and being very circumspect with her brother-in-law. I knew Rais was trying to cool her. So how could I object when she wanted to talk with Rais alone? And what could I tell my bitchy sister when she told me, "I love him, too, Merle. I don't want him to get hurt. He's such a dreamer. He needs a realist around."

I'm more realistic than either of you, I thought, but I didn't say it. I was sure that the right environment for Rais was with Bren; they needed each other. But what was momentarily more important to me was that I had discovered that Gabby wasn't any better in the sack than me. How am I sure? Because I asked Rais point-blank, while he was hugging me.

"There's no better or best in sex," he said. "The difference is in the jigsaw pieces of the human brain. I've already found the missing pieces of my puzzle ... and they're you, sweet potato. We may not win this game your way, but I know there isn't any other. Gabby doesn't seem to realize that the British, Canadian, and American investors in St. Noir hold the ultimate weapon. All they have to do is withdraw. When seventy thousand blacks on this island are starving to death, including you and me and Gabby, we'll have to be amenable to reason."

"Or beg Russia to help us," I told him. "And that'll get you nowhere." I knew Rais and Gabby had discussed the possibility of the Soviets coming to the rescue. Superficially, the idea of a People's Corporate Island was a natural for such support. But I was sure that Russian aid would defeat Rais' whole Utopian dream, and I didn't trust Gabby when she or her friends agreed with me. Anyway, I knew that the Americans or the British would defeat such a revolution.

But Gabby and her clique weren't listening, and with encouragement from them, on the morning of June 25 more than half the workers went on strike. Now, the workers were carried away by their long-repressed resentment against the foreign whites and the wealthier black landowners; and they were convinced by Gabby and her lieutenants that the deepening unemployment was part of an Establishment plot to keep wages low. Before the day was over, they were smashing and burning everything in sight.

If nothing else, thousands will have gleeful memories of their moment of power. By noon Radio St. Noir was in the hands of the revolution, police and army barracks had been invaded, and with the help of dissidents using government rifles and guns, disorderly groups had shut down the power plant, the telephone exchanges, and the airports. Supplies and food for the hotels, where there were more than a thousand white visitors, were hijacked on the island roads or turned back by angry mobs. "Let whitey starve a little," some of them yelled. "Let him sit in the dark and smell his own shit when the water don't run. Give 'em a taste of what it's like to be a poor black in St. Noir!"

Thousands in the jump-up atmosphere of a carnival were milling through the island roads, jamming the harbor town of St. Michael's. Smashing the store windows of white and black owners alike, they carried banners demanding the government cede its power to King Daemon. "Rais Daemon will save us! Rais Daemon for president of the People's Island of St. Noir!"

I tried to help Rais calm the crowds that were pouring into the shuttered streets, but it soon became apparent, for most of the natives, that Rais Daemon was just a name; they would not be calmed. This big, bearded black man, pleading hopelessly with angry and drunken natives to "cool it," was getting nowhere. I wondered if perhaps Gabby were right; maybe we did have leverage. Had the tide turned for us? The combination of the hotel workers, the dock workers, and the power-plant employees in a general strike had already brought Arthur Granby's government to its knees. The moment was ours! But Rais didn't believe it.

Early in the evening he located me at Gabby's house, which had turned into a command center. Despite my protests, he told me he was driving back to St. Stephen's in a car he had expropriated. "You can't run out now!" I told him. "You've got to see it through. You started it, and now you have the power to finish it."

"It's already finished, Merle. Twenty minutes ago Granby's soldiers recaptured Radio St. Noir. They've got it running on its own generators." Rais shrugged. "Damned smart. Granby hasn't much of an army, but he's controlling the place that counts." He turned on the car radio, and we listened.

"This is your premier, Arthur Granby. Radio St. Noir is back in the hands of your loyal government. At my request, British Fusiliers have landed at Harding Airport, and a Royal Navy Frigate will be anchored in St. Michael's harbor before morning. The uprising is over. Go to your homes. Let's have no more senseless bloodshed and destruction." The taped message was being run over and over again.

"Maybe he's lying," Rais said, "but it doesn't make any difference. It's over. I may have started it, but I can't finish it."

Back at our hotel, I watched Rais pack a duffel bag. "I'll take the recorder and the cassettes," he said. "A week before you came I calked up the old sloop my father used to go fishing in. I've got it moored in St. Stephen's bay. I've got a few bags of rice, some canned goods, and rum. I can make the Mons tonight, and then if the boat holds together, I'll sail on to Puerto Rico. You go back to Boston. Tell Bren I'll be back. Premar sounds interesting."

I listened to him, astonished. I couldn't believe my ears.

While I had been totally against the whole idea of the takeover of St. Noir, and I couldn't have cared less whether I ever lived there again, I kept thinking over and over that at the moment of crisis Rais was running out. The savior was tossing his followers to the British lion.

Confused and bitter, I started yelling at him. "You're just like all the rest of them on this island. Scared shitless. They'll all be back at work tomorrow bowing and scraping." I was crying even as I shouted at him. "I love you, you big damned fool. Why didn't you listen to me? Nothing matters really but us and the little joy we can get out of life."

"I know that." Rais touched my cheek. "I can't help what has happened here. I tried to warn Gabby." He looked at his watch. "She should be here. It's ten-thirty. I'll give her an hour."

"What do you mean, you'll give her an hour?" I screamed at him. "If you're really running out, I'm going with you, not Gabby."

Rais towered over me. The big ape was sailing to Puerto Rico dressed like a banana-boat worker. Barechested, his only clothing was a pair of cut-off dungarees secured around his waist by a huge black belt. In the dying embers of the fire, outside the shack, it was difficult to see his face, but his eyes were mirrors reflecting me, but not really seeing me.

"Merle," he said, "listen carefully. You heard Granby. Tomorrow there will be two or three scapegoats. Gabrielle Blanc and Rais Daemon, and maybe Holdam and Orion. Gabby and the others may already be in a feet-first position. If they aren't here in an hour, I'm leaving. If they arrive, Gabby will have to go with me. There's no other way, unless you want your sister and husband to rot in jail."

"You're running away. And I know Gabby. She wants you for herself."

"You don't make any sense." Rais flung his duffel bag over his shoulder and swooped me up in his arms. I knew he was angry, but he tried to kiss me anyway. "Sweet pie," he said, "I don't know how your mother ever stood all your yak-yak. She'd have done the world a favor if she'd cut off your tongue, and Gabby's too!"

"Let me down!" I screamed. I ripped my fingernails across his bare back. "It wasn't me that got you eight months in Walpole Prison. When you got out I begged you not to come here. Maybe all that talk in 'Walk Before God' about blacks inviting whites here on *their* island is just because you were thinking about yourself as Premier Stud, the big politician with the ever-ready black prick for rich, lonely white women, like that widow, Mrs. Fairleigh. If you weren't servicing her eight years ago, how come she left you a thousand dollars in her will?"

Rais was walking with me to the edge of a pig enclosure and suddenly he calmly dropped me between two pigs into a foot of black mud. "This is a new dress," I screamed. When I tried to climb out, he gave me another shove, and I slid back into the oozy slime.

"I'll tell you one thing, Merle," he said, towering over me. "You may be well acquainted with the spasms of my body, but when you get on one of your talking jags, you miss the spasms going on in my brain."

Wiping the stench from my face, feeling the mud slippery between my buttocks and crotch, I ran after Rais, following him down a path that led onto the beach below us. "Wait, Rais, please," I sobbed. "I'm sorry. You have to take me with you, too. They know I'm your woman. They'll arrest me, too."

Unable to run as fast as he was walking, I hung onto his belt. He had left the path and was thrashing through the underbrush on a direct route to St. Stephen's beach. Thorns and vines whipped against my face. Now I was getting mad. I lunged at his fly, ripped open buttons, and grabbed his cock. "It's mine!" I screamed hysterically. My words belonged to someone else; it couldn't be me, but it was, and I was coming apart. "You can't leave me. I loved you long before my fucking sister knew what a man was all about."

Emerging from the jungle of vegetation that girded the St. Stephen's inlet, ignoring the succubus dragging on her knees beside him, Rais plodded along the flat coral beach. My fingers still clutched his penis and balls in what must now have been a painful grasp. "If you don't stop and listen to me," I yelled, "I'll rip them off."

Rais looked down into my wet eyes. "If you don't let go, they'll be no damned good to me, or you."

I collapsed, moaning at his feet. He lifted me up, pulled my dress over my head, tossed it on the beach, and carried me into the phosphorescent, moon-gleaming water.

Then he actually laughed. "You smell like a St. Noir pig," he said, and I grasped him in a bear hug, kissing him wildly, my lips a mixture of mud, salt, and tears. When he tried to disentangle me, I hung on and pulled him under the water with me. Finally, spluttering and gasping, we surfaced. Up to my waist in the warm water, he held me limp against him. "I love you, Merle," he whispered. He washed away the mud between my legs and clinging in the cleft of my buttocks. "I should have listened to you and Bren. But, you have to admit, we've both been learning."

Back on the beach, he knelt in front of me, his arms clasped around my buttocks, and he kissed the hair at my crotch, and his tongue found my clitoris. I heard him laugh. "When you come right down to it, this kind of playing makes more sense than playing the fiddle while Rome burns. If man could see himself in perspective, he'd know that without this, there really is nothing—no need to be born, no need to live."

I lay back on the sand, still warm from the hot sun of the day. I could feel my labia slowly relaxing to the gentle pressure of his penis. And then, sobbing, I engulfed him. He rolled over so that I was on top of him. Kneading my buttocks, he crooned in my ear, "It's all right, blackbird, ride him." And I did, gasping and screaming my love and fear into his mouth, and then I cried, protesting my self- ishness and self-absorption. While I lay on top of him he caressed my back and behind, and he was still big inside me. "I love you, sweet potato," he said, "but I'm too screwed-up in my head to come. First I was hating this whole goddamned island. Then I realized that was very stupid. I was only hating it because I couldn't make it over in my image.

"I never wanted to go to jail again. Last year in Wal- pole there were times when I was a caged animal filled with rage. A man with a rage is always going to be a vic- tim, never a victor. He loses perspective. He can't act, ex- cept emotionally. That nearly happened to me again, and today I'm very depressed with myself because I've been hating the stupid blacks on this island more than I had ever hated whitey. I told myself that they're worse than kids, that they really don't want to work, don't want to grow up, that they just want to sit, or drink rum, or fuck, and when they can't drink or fuck anymore, then they gripe until they begin to drown in their own bitter gall.

Then, suddenly, my mind cleared and I laughed because I remembered that old joke about the kids and the neighbors' kids playing together in the cellar. It gets very quiet down there, and the mother rattles the doorknob and asks them what they're doing. 'Just fucking, Mama,' one of the kids yells, and mama sighs happily and says, 'That's nice, children—just don't fight.' In a nutshell, that's the white reaction to the black man. 'Just don't fight.' The only way to take over this island, or to get the Confamiliaum idea going, or Premar, from what you've told about it, is with a kind of joyous patience. Let them think you're just fucking, and then one day hand them a brand-new baby—with his hands firmly on the reins."

Rais Daemon. Parallel to Premar. July to September; the first year. From tapes received and transcribed by Merle Blanc in October.

This is the fourth day.

For the past two days U.S. Navy planes and helicopters have been searching the area. Skimming the shores of the Mons, they've apparently found no signs of survivors. Laura Stone and all other passengers of the ill-fated Pan Carib 707 flight from New York to St. Noir are officially dead, and early this morning the United States Navy finally gave up.

Mrs. Stone, are you listening? Since my survival depends on you, I can take God's point of view. Without fear of reprisal, since there are no witnesses, I can murder you. If there were an interested God, I have thwarted Him by pulling you out of the sea and saving you from certain death. So your life is now my responsibility.

You keep asking me why I didn't let you die. That's a question that obviously has deeper roots than your pain. You have no broken bones, the wound on your leg will heal, and sooner or later your swollen ankle will learn to support your weight. So have a swig of rum, Laura. Eventually you and I are going to have to tell each other why we were suicidal. But now, at least, I can tell that you really want to live. If you didn't, what would there be for you to be afraid of—that I might rape you? But how can you be sure that I haven't raped you already? When I stripped you I thought you were dead. Maybe, I'm a necrophiliac; think about that. It will give you some rage to cling to.

Go ahead . . . I applaud your decision to have a shot of rum. Get drunk. That's a good girl. With only two blankets, and that tarpaulin for a mattress, you might as well lie in my arms while I tell this tape recorder a bedtime story. We remind me of a poem by Robert Burns: "Oh, ye who sunk in beds of doone, feel not a want but what yourselves create, think but a moment on their wretched fate whom friends and fortune quite disown." It's amazing how insistent those cool winds from the north become at night. Can you really believe, Mrs. Stone, that you're in bed for the night, and it can't be later than eight o'clock? What would the ladies at your country club think if they could see your white legs wrapped around black ones? Laura Stone, society matron, sleeping belly-to-belly with a black man.

Yesterday, when I saw the cruisers on the horizons, I knew that if I carried you down to the beach below this cave and left you lying there stark naked, you would have been spotted. How could you explain to your rescuers that you alone of all those passengers had floated ten miles and then survived the rough surf crashing on the Mons? You tried to convince me that they really would believe you that, unaided by human hands, you had arisen from the dead.

So I asked you the first question they would ask. "Why are you naked, Mrs. Stone?" And you told me that you'd tell them that you had taken off your clothes to bathe, and they had floated away. You know, that's very funny. Mrs. Rocky Stone doesn't look like someone who would lose her clothes in broad daylight.

So unless I was willing to admit that I had stripped you, or you told them that you had been rescued by the infamous Rais Daemon, I would have had a new problem to solve, and that would have been beyond even me. So I gathered up our blankets, rolled our cans of corned beef, bags of rice, six bottles of rum, and this tape recorder in the tarpaulin, and hid them in the underbrush. Then I de-masted the sloop and levered it on its side so that it looked like an abandoned fishing boat.

And then, when I was working my ass off, you did a mad thing. There I was on the beach trying to conceal our existence from a curious world, and you rolled, hobbled, stumbled down the cliff to the beach below, trying, I think, to time your arrival with the first airplane to swoop over the island. What could I do? There wasn't time to get you back up the hill or into the jungle. I grabbed you and pulled you out into the water under an overhanging rock, and then I forced you under water. You must have a masochistic need to experience drowning. You really came pretty close.

After the first airplanes were gone, I dragged you to the beach and pumped out your lungs. You asked why I didn't drown you, and I answered that I didn't want to live here alone for years. Since God had provided me with a bedmate, I was not inclined to question His wisdom. My thanks were that you tried to bite me, you were so frus-trated and angry.

"You're a pain in the ass," I told you. "But you've made it necessary that we hide out in the middle of the island until the Navy goes away."

You didn't make it easy, Laura. Crying, clawing, sob-bing, you tried to maim me. Having a naked woman with a swollen ankle, who can't walk, in your arms, should be an erotic joy. Trying to clear a path through the jungle carrying a screaming harpy is something else again.

"Mrs. Stone," I finally said, "cut this shit out, or I'll make you stand on your puffy leg, and when you fall down, I'll drag you the rest of the way by your hair. You want to know why I stripped you? Because I was thinking it would be a great damned reversal of fortune for a black man to have his own white slave woman. But instead of a slave, I've got a damned incubus. For two days you've been a muling, puking child."

Well, why did I strip you? For a moment when I saw you lying there, unconscious, in the bottom of the boat with your eyes mascaraed and shaded blue, your puffy hairdo still pretty much intact, your face with the hard lines that etch the faces of women who drink too much, you looked like a rich Barbie doll—and I hated you. But I was turned inside-out by the horror and devastation of the crash, and I wanted you to live so that you could know you had survived it—and could wonder why. That it happened to you was your fault, for being rich. Poor people don't get blown apart five miles high in the sky. They can't afford to be there.

I don't trust you, Mrs. Stone. In a few days it'll be the Fourth of July, Independence Day. But for you and me, it's Dependence Day; we're stuck with each other because we don't trust each other. And that's the way of the world, here on the Mons, and back where whitey owns everything.

As I carried you deep into the jungle, I noticed that the ground was getting springier and spongy, and before long I stumbled into a clearing made by a small freshwater pond, and I sank, nearly to my knees, in soft, warm, black mud. I knew it was perverse, but you hadn't stopped yelling at me, so I just dropped you in that oozy gunk. Did I laugh hysterically? Mud is erotic, Mrs. Stone. I told you it would be good for your swollen ankle. But you wouldn't stop screaming. I put my foot on your back and tumbled you deep into it, and then, damnit, lying there, you looked so pathetic, with your face, tits, and belly mud-caked, I sat down in the mud with you and held you in my arms, and I patted the mud over your bruised body. Well, you slowly stopped sobbing, Laura, and I sat you against a tree on the edge of the pond and bathed you with fresh water. The sun filtered down through the tall trees, and I pretended for a moment you were Rima, my jungle girl. I packed your ankle in mud and told you that I would come back for you later, that I wanted to see what the Navy was up to. And finally you spoke like a human being to me for the first time.

"Rais," you said, and I was surprised you knew my name. "Don't leave me. I'll die of fright." You stared at the tangle of jungle vines and flowers and shuddered. "There may be snakes."

You looked younger. With the cosmetic paste of civilization washed away, I could see that a glimmer of the child-you, forlorn and yet somehow pretty, still existed. Maybe people are nice to each other when they finally realize they can't stand alone.

Why did I strip you? The question bugs me. Of course, it was amusing that someone like you, having lived thirty-eight protected years, would at last have been deprived of her physical privacy. Believe me, Mrs. Stone, that while I enjoy staring at your tits and ass and cunt, your nudity is a horrendous problem for me. If I ever dare to leave the Mons with you, you must have clothes; I can't take you back to the States wearing only a blanket.

Ha! I've used only fifteen minutes of the tape on this side. Maybe, if you're awake and I succeed in dredging out every last detail, maybe tonight my brain will stop re-dreaming those horrible dreams. If the god-with-no-name was trying to redress the balance of nature, then the sharks must have some cosmic purpose, too. Nothing is lost in the world, not even those macerated humans who already have been shit out the shark's anus into the clear blue water of the Caribbean.

It was as if there was no escape. The dread behind me on St. Noir seemed to be a prognosticator of the dread awaiting me.

Merle and I had passed beyond words. She swam out with me to my father's ancient sloop, which I had moored a hundred yards offshore. Like tonight, millions of galaxies were sharp trembling pinpoints of other worlds that had long ago disappeared, and their only reality was the image of light they had left behind. The air was listless, and we could feel the ominous, low pressure of the atmosphere.

I broke the silence as I told Merle I no longer believed Gabby was coming; now I was sure that she and George Holdam had alternate plans, and that they might even try to find a way to lay all the blame for the failing revolution on me. Then they would emerge as the patient ones who had preached moderation.

"I've got enough food to live on the Mons for a few weeks, and there are always fish to catch," I told Merle. "When things cool off, I'll sail to Puerto Rico and fly back to Boston from there. I'm a free man in the States, after all. Tell Bren it may take a few weeks, but I'll be back in Boston by August."

"Take me with you," Merle kept saying.

"Don't push it, Merle," I told her. Still, I was wonder-ing if I could make it myself. "It's a damned rough three-day sail to Puerto Rico, and I don't dare try it for another week, at least. When they comb the island and don't find me, the British may take a quick look around the nearby waters. If I get caught, I don't want to get you involved."

If you ever listen to this tape, Merle, there was another reason. At that moment, I was so depressed, I wasn't really planning to sail much farther than a point of no return.

After I had hauled the tattered sail up the mast, I sailed Merle back to shore. I almost weakened and told her to come with me, because I was afraid, too, and needed her. But I was most afraid to be less than she thought I was; I couldn't bear to be less than my tiny, strong-willed wife. If I were, how could I live with her?

I hugged her. Once again I felt her nipples erect against my chest. I pushed her onto the shore. "I love you, honey," I said. "I'm not quitting. See you in Boston." I flipped the tiller and caught the light breeze on a broad reach.

I leaned back against the railing, steadying the tiller with my toes, and tried not to think. And then I was thinking, not of Merle, but of my mother. Thank God the Merles of this world would never be a repetition of her. A toothless, grinning, shriveled woman who lived in a shack at David's bay. She was sixteen when I was born. I was fifteen when my father disappeared. A new man, Jamey, had moved in with her, and sired a new brood. Once, after I came back, I asked her about Daddy's boat, beached in front of her wattle-and-daub hut. She stared at me, the stranger who said he was her son, and replied, "Is you really Rais? My eyes ain't so good. Your brother farms in St. Philip's, but he fears de water. Jamey tried to sell de boat, but it's been there too long, full of holes. You rich now, Rais, with all that learning? Jamey says he'll fix de boat for you for five hundred bewees."

It wasn't worth it, but it got us here, Laura. Did you ever think you'd be sailing in a Bahamian sloop with a nigger? Remember that painting by Winslow Homer? No matter. When I was a kid, my father, a laughing man, took us fishing; then he sailed us to the Mons to get fresh water. Who would have believed that I'd ever come back with my own white slave? Laura, you can thank your stars that my daddy landed here. Most of the whites who cruise these islands in their yachts avoid this island because they know that there's a treacherous crossing between those coral reefs in the inlet. The place looks pretty inhospitable anyway. Why should they bother with the Mons when the Caribbean is full of beaches?

Have a slug of rum. Since you don't feel like communicating with me, you can listen to the story of your savior. That's a good girl.

Sailing an endless ocean on a black night with only your thoughts to entertain you can be boring. I had a transistor radio, but the only station I could get was Radio St. Noir, which was now, evidently, following Granby's instructions, playing an endless tape of rock music. I dozed, and about four in the morning, with the tiller lashed, and the sail set on a course to the Mons, the boom jibed across my head. I awoke in a hurry to save the boat from capsizing.

The sky in the east was jagged with thick rolling thunderclouds, their white edges reflecting the dawn. The waves were churning higher and spitting white, and I knew I would soon be in the middle of a squall. There was lightning and thunder, and even with the sail far over the starboard, traveling on a reach, I was taking more air than the boat could handle. The sail had no reefing points, but I couldn't have reefed her alone in that wind anyway. The mast was creaking and groaning, as if at any moment it would snap under the strain. Water was breaking across the prow and pouring into the boat. I tried to bail and hold the tiller at the same time, but it was hard going. At the speed the boat was traveling, bucking the waves like an empty barrel, I estimated my chances of making the Mons were about one in five. Overhead, lightning was cracking, followed by the long hollow roll of thunder. I was going to drown. I was going to die. And I wasn't mad at the god-with-no-name. I just yelled, "Come and get me, you bastard. I'm not afraid of you."

But it isn't easy to choose death, is it, Laura? Something perverse in you keeps fighting the odds.

I became aware of the monotonous susurration of a jet to the north as it prepared to land in St. Noir. Then, within the same split-second that I saw the plane—up about five thousand feet, its landing lights on—lightning zigzagged through the black sky and the jet burst into flames. Screaming in terror, feeling as if Jehovah had suddenly stepped out of heaven and I was being confronted with the final cataclysm, I watched the plane plummet through the sky, trailing fire. Very soon, with a terrifying swishing sound, it disappeared into the ocean.

I wondered if I had drowned and this was the final nightmare. A minute before there had been this man thing in the sky. Then, after a puff of flame from heaven, there was nothing. If there had been a crash, or if I were still dreaming—no matter—I was sailing directly toward hell. A mile or two ahead of me, death was having a come-as-you-are party. Was I the uninvited guest?

Even had I wanted to, I couldn't change direction, and minutes later I was in the middle of a horror world; Gustave Dore's drawings of Dante's *Inferno* had come alive. Now I was sailing in a bubbling cauldron. The nose of the airplane was ripped off. The fuselage—with the letters "Pan Caribbean" blistered by the heat—was half-submerged. Like a dead sea monster, it was undulating helplessly in the waves. The prow of my boat thudded against debris—blown-apart luggage and freight. I saw a jumbled soup of lifeless, floating torsos—arms, legs, and heads detached from their owners. They bobbed up and down in the black water, dyed even blacker by their blood.

Jibbing and coming about in the widening circle of devastation, I screamed at God. "Why did you do this? You Bastard of Bastards!" Then I realized that I was sailing into whole bodies. I saw the gray head of a man who seemed to be alive, and I lunged over the side of the boat. I had his hair in my hand for a second; then he slipped under the boat, and I'm sure that I heard him moan. I realized that the water was boiling with sharks. I was sailing over their backs while they slashed furiously at the human remains. Vomit was rising in my mouth.

I was dancing master in a zombie cemetery. Eight, maybe ten airline seats in pairs were floating nearly upright, their dead occupants bobbing up and down, curtsying to each other in a monstrous floating graveyard that swirled in a circle. I grabbed at one of the seats that held a woman; the seat beside her was empty. She was slumped against her seat belt, which I caught and held. Bent forward, she was a broken U, ready to fall into the teeth of the thrashing sharks.

Yes, it was you, Mrs. Stone. Why in hell I hung on, my arms being wrenched from their sockets, I do not know. I was certain that you were dead, but I dragged you and the double seats up onto the rail. Your pocketbook still dangled on the arm of the seat. I unflipped your seat belt, and you slumped into the foul, vomitous water slurping around the cockpit. The mainsail was gyrating madly, the sheet ropes were in a tangle. When at last I got the boat under control, we had blown well away from the carnage. I believed you were dead. But, God ... damn Him! I had saved one passenger from the bellies of those fucking sharks.

You were lying face-down on the bottom of the boat. The easiest thing would have been to toss you over the stern. If I sailed your body into the Mons and left you on the beach, the buzzards would get you. If I buried you, the worms would finish you. I wondered why I was angry with the sharks. Eating you would help them to live.

Then I saw the diamond on your finger. How much did it cost your husband, Mrs. Stone, fifty thousand dollars? I tried to wiggle it off your finger, but your fingers were swollen, and it wouldn't move. Then I had a most disgusting idea. Since I still thought you were dead and you'd soon be resting on the bottom of the sea, who would know, or care, if I cut your finger off? Why toss so much easy living into the sea? Half-crazed, as I ripped the cabin apart looking for my fish knife, I became conscious that I was wading over my ankles in water, and I couldn't help laughing. It would be poetic justice if we sank into the sea together while I was cutting off your finger—for a lousy diamond that might be fake!

As I flipped you over on your back and knelt beside you in the muddy water, I hated you for invading my life. I hated God! I hated me. To hell with the fucking diamond. And then—was I dreaming? I thought I saw you breathe. I put my head against your breast to see if I could hear a heartbeat. Nothing. Conscious that your dress was blue and it was buttoned halfway down the front, I ripped at the soaking wet material.

And then, screaming, I stripped you. It took only a minute. Using the fish knife, I slashed through your slip, your bra, your panty stockings, and the tiny white panties you were wearing under them. Naked, you just lay there with your eyes closed, and you were just as supremely composed as when you were dressed. I hated you, but not personally. I hated you because you weren't dead, and I was dimly aware that now you owned me. I put my ear against your left breast, and your flesh was cold, but your heart was beating. Jesus Christ! I had done it now! I had stripped a rich white woman naked. I might just as well have raped you or murdered you. The retribution would be the same.

Squatting, I screamed at you, "Live, you white bitch! Live! Open your eyes. When I fuck you, I want you to know it."

Did I fuck you, Mrs. Stone? God knows I was deranged and I wanted to. But I didn't. You were shivering, so I took you in my arms, and an hour must have passed. Now the storm had passed and the surface of the water was already glassy. In whatever direction I looked, there was nothing human. The ocean had swallowed its uninvited guests.

With the tiller lashed and the sail set on course to the Mons, which was at least a three-hour sail ahead, I held you, a moaning child, in my arms. I tried to rub some warmth into your body as I explored your flesh. While there were no broken bones, you were covered with welts and bruises. Finally I saw you watching me, and I knew that you knew that I was black. But you didn't scream, you just stared. By then I knew who you were, because I had dug through your pocketbook and found your credit cards and pictures of your son and daughter, and your husband, and fifteen hundred dollars. . . .

"Turn that tape recorder off."

"Laura, do you know what you're doing?"

"Mmmm."

"You'll get yourself fucked."

"I'm only giving what you could take anyway. Be careful of my ankle. It hurts like hell."

"It will be easier for you to come on top of me."

"Nice. If you snap off that recorder, I'll stay here the night. . . . Can you last? My God, you *are* hard! Older men are not so firm."

"Older women are usually not so tight."

"How do you know?"

"Skip it. Laura, you'll get pregnant."

"If I do, you won't have to worry. I'll kill myself."

Bren Gattman. Merle Blanc. Ellen O'Day. October, the first year of Premar. From a tape transcribed by Andrea Pillisuk.

" 'If you will it, it is no dream.' Theodore Herzl believed that, and so do I."

"Is this a private conversation, or is that damned tape going, Ellen?"

"Come on, Merle, of course, the tape is going. You know Bren."

"Yeah, everything for the Premars—even what the Compars think about when they're sitting on the john."

"Merle, relax. Lie down with us. What've you been doing?"

"I got lonesome, so I dropped in to watch you two screwing. What else? I'm beginning to think Premar is logistically impossible. How are we supposed to find time to work for a graduate degree, manage the monetary aspects of this place, and change the diapers of forty-eight kids as a daily routine? I'm pooped. If I take off my robe and lie down with you two naked jaybirds, Bren will think he's a sandwich."

(*Laughter.*)

"Hell, no. I'll be an éclair with vanilla frosting on one side and chocolate on the other. So, get in and stop complaining; you know you never had so much fun. What's more, I was just telling Ellen I feel it in my bones that Rais is coming back."

(*Pause.*)

"I don't know about Rais, but *this* is a dream, baby. If Phil could see us, he'd puncture your bubble fast. Am I interrupting your lovemaking?"

"According to Bren, he never stops making love, but I don't know whether he refers to human love. I'm sure of one thing; he loves turmoil. It's not just Phil I'm worried about. My father's about to boil over, and Bren doesn't seem impressed. Bren called him yesterday at City Hall and told him that Father Tim, Bren, and I wanted to talk with him. Daddy actually made the telephone vibrate in Bren's hands. If Dancer's daughter is going to marry a Jew or be a whore, he'd prefer the latter. As for Father Tim marrying us, Dancer is going to call the archbishop and get Father Tim straightened out. And Rais ... How about Rais? I was looking at a map of the West Indies and saw that St. Noir is three hundred miles from Puerto Rico. What makes you think he can sail that distance with your sister and not get into a storm? They could drown— assuming he doesn't murder Laura first.

(*Pause.*)

"My darling husband must have been pretty horny to strip your sister. Samantha told me Rais must be soft in the head. He should never have sent us those tapes. Then he could have finished the job and buried her on the island; only he would have known. Bren, it's my opinion Laura might screw with a black, but the conversion will never be complete. And something is fouled-up. Those tapes are over a month old. Where's Rais?"

(*Pause.*)

"If Rais doesn't come back, I want us to stay together."

"Ellen, you're balmy. You've got your man. Two's fine, but for the long haul a threesome can't make it."

"Why not? I'm involved with you, too, Merle."

"Look at the smug grin on Bren's face. He thinks he's a caliph with two harem girls ready to do his bidding. Well, I'm not going to contribute to his delusions of grandeur."

"I have no delusions. The kids are intrigued, though. Since they know I've slept with both of you, they wonder why you're not jealous of one another. I heard Lainey ask you whether you and Ellen ever made love, and why you weren't angry with Rais when you discovered that he was screwing with your sister."

"I told Lainey I do love Ellen but that I'm not bisexual. Women making love together may be normal, but they're sad, too. Who knows what normality is, anyway? I think we should go into this in one of the general H.V. meetings. Mary Jane Sherfey's book *The Nature and Evolution of Female Sexuality* disputes the Freudian idea of bisexuality. She believes that men and women aren't basically bisexual, and it's the male who must transcend his innate female anatomy. Bisexuality may be only a Freudian idea. I love Ellen as a woman, but my basic drive is for a penis buried inside me. I told Lainey that for a few moments I was mad as hell at Rais, but then I remembered that when he was in Walpole, he didn't complain when he knew I was making love with Bren. Lainey said, 'I guess you and Ellen have learned how to share a guy.' I told her she was wrong. Bren wasn't a piece of cake that Ellen and I could cut in half. Anyway, who really knows all the answers? I love you both—but if Rais comes back, Bren will have to give up his chocolate diet."

"Why?"

"I want my own man, silly, and maybe, occasionally, you, too, Bren. That's the only way open sex will work."

"Ellen is staring at you bug-eyed. Aren't you implying that if Rais returns she would sleep with him?"

"I wouldn't count on that. Remember me? I'm Ellen O'Day, a simple Irish lass who shouldn't be messing around with her emotions this way. Marion Swenson told me not to let Bren, or my father, or anything at Premar, get me hung up. She doesn't understand that I'm a chip off the old block. I just talk and don't listen."

"Are you afraid to sleep with a black man?"

"My God, Bren—I'm still trembling when I sleep with you! Don't you think I'm jittery right now? Look at yourself. You're even a little excited. You know that it wouldn't take much for you to break us down or for Merle and I to lead you on. Please, Daddy! Don't break down the doors tonight! Your daughter might be in the middle of an orgy."

"Sorry, love bug. I'm not an orgiast. If I climbed on you right now, what would Merle be doing?"

"Sitting on your face while you ate me and simultaneously screwed Ellen! Then we'd reverse positions until you were a limp jimp. That's what they do in the porno movies."

"It always looked pretty grim and depersonalized to me. Remember, we're teaching the kids the joy of extended intercourse. Tantric yoga. But I suppose that's what Phil Tenhausen is afraid of. If the Compars start messing around, they might not practice what they preach. With me he doesn't have to worry. I need you both—but separately. The voyeuristic mechanics of group sex would interfere with my mystic needs. Instead of escaping our egos with each other, we'd end up with no deep intimacy. We'd be no more than an assemblage of cunts, pricks, asses and breasts, and sucking mouths. Flesh machines—each in business for ourselves until the final abrasion. So, even if I look ready—and I really can't resist the compulsion to lean over and kiss your breast, Ellen, or yours, Merle— I'm a very wise sahib. *Being* with you like this, snuggling with you, enjoying your flesh contact, and your body warmth—*being* a part of your *being* is breathtaking enough. It's a wise man who knows when he has reached a sexual El Dorado."

"Did you ever fantasize yourself with two women?"

"Sure, you bet—when I was a kid, I was going around with a perpetual hard-on. I did nothing but think of the miles of vaginas I'd like to explore."

(*Laughter.*)

"Can Merle and I kiss you?"

"Sure, why?"

"Because I can tell from the expression on her face that she thinks you're too good to be true. We better never let you get away!"

"See, I told you. If you will it, it is no dream. Here I am—a humble, ordinary man, and two women love me. Funny, I'll take a bet with you: For the same reason you feel trusting with me, Ellen, you'll like Rais. Isn't that right, Merle?"

"Maybe. If Ellen likes big black Pooh bears. God, I wonder if Rais has discovered that Laura is your sister?"

(*Laughter.*)

"That's a cliff hanger. I liked Mohammed Hassan's reaction to Rais' tapes. 'Before the last soap commercial they can ask the question of the week. Will Laura Stone destroy Rais Daemon, or vice versa?' There's no doubt that my sister, without a stitch of clothing, prisoner of Rais Daemon, is beyond the laws of probability. Maybe there's a Great Father up there somewhere smoking grass and roaring with laughter every time that he tosses the loaded dice.

"I won't put her down completely. Somewhere buried in her wasted life there may still be remains of the child Laura. I had a glimpse of a potential Laura about five years ago. That was the last time I saw her. It was the spring after I took you home, Merle. Passover. In her late middle age, Rivke is trying to rediscover her roots by returning to Orthodoxy. No contact between *milchik* and *flaichik*, and a strict following of the dietary laws that seem designed to drive Abe out of his mind. Whatever she hopes to accomplish, she isn't rebuilding her family. She rarely manages to assemble more than eight or nine for Passover dinner, and three of those are Abe's sister Thelma's kids. Anyway, she did better the year that Laura and I were home.

"Rivke hasn't had such a big turnout since. You see, everybody knew that Laura, the wife of multimillionaire Rocky Stone, was coming, so not only the Jews, but all the goys in New Hope wanted to come to Passover. And there she was, being taken to the club and all the important homes in town. My sister, wearing Pucci originals, and her kids, Shulamith and David, overbearing, superior versions of their mommy and daddy. During the entire three days, whenever I was present, she never ceased wondering aloud when her younger brother was going to straighten up and fly right.

"If I'd believed in transactional analysis, I'd have wondered how in hell, with a nine-year difference in our ages, our Parent and Child tapes could have recorded such different messages. 'I'm okay, but you're not okay,' was Laura's unspoken attitude—not only to me, but to everyone she came in contact with. To no avail, I tried to convince her that not even the richest people could afford the luxury of their so-called integrity. At thirty-three Laura greeted the world indiscriminately with a grim you-smell-like-a-turd smile and a Dresden-china face fired in the kiln of her self-satisfied little mind.

"Because of a pending corporate takeover, Rocky hadn't been able to come with her. But despite her cool assurances that Rocky was 'so disappointed,' I suspected that life with the great conglomerator was not all sugar and cream. The night before we left, I waited until Shulamith and David were in bed in the downstairs guest rooms, and Abe and Rivke had gone to their bedroom. Then I walked into her room, which Rivke had kept for her and Rocky in honor of their occasional visits. It was about quarter to one, and I was stark naked. I found Laura sitting up in bed wearing a sheer pale green nightgown. She hissed at me so loud to get the hell out of her room that I was sure she must have awakened Abe or Rivke. I grabbed her and held my hand over her mouth while she thrashed and tried to squirm out of my grasp. By this time her nightgown was around her neck, and I felt in the mood to strangle her with it. 'You nasty bitch,' I whispered in her ear. 'I came to rape you. Before you left home your little brother couldn't get it up, but now he can. If you scream, I'll start yelling that you loved to play doctor with me when I was six, and made me into a sex maniac.'

"She bit my hand. When I let go with a yowl, she was grinning. 'You do have a long memory,' she said. 'But you've forgotten that even then you enjoyed being diddled. You really want to screw me? But I'm honored!'

" 'Even if I wanted to, I couldn't,' I admitted. My prick was quite limp. 'It must be because of your continual mother or sister act with me, not because I've been brainwashed against incest. The fact is, you turn me off.'

"Laura shrugged, and I was wondering if she would have screwed with her brother. 'Okay,' she said. 'You've had your fun. Get the hell out of here.'

"I pulled the covers down and forced my way in beside her. 'I'm not leaving your bed until you repeat after me, 'I'm really full of shit, and I know it.'

"Leaning on her elbow, she looked at me for almost a minute, and there were tears in her eyes. Finally she said, 'Okay, Bren—you guessed my secret. I'm really full of shit, and I know it.' She tried to smile. 'It's the truth, but I'm not going to tell anyone else. It's our secret. Now, why did you want to strip me?'

" 'Why do you put me down?'

" 'I'm bewildered by you. How can you be so sure of yourself?'

"How do you like that? Isn't that the acme of something or other. Married to Rocky Stone, an icicle of aplomb in his own right, and she, a mirror image of him. I discovered that Laura is really mixed-up. I doubt if she or Rocky have ever surrendered themselves to anyone. That night may have been the closest she ever came. 'I don't know any answers anymore.' That's all she would say. She sobbed in my arms for a few minutes, then patted my ass and said, 'Thanks, Bren. Go to bed. I don't know how to build bridges, but I'm glad you're here.' "

(*Pause.*)

"Did you make love with her?"

"My God, Ellen! Didn't I just tell you I'm a wise sahib?"

(*Laughter.*)

"I think your sister needed physical love."

"Sure, but not with her brother. She even mentioned that she was on the pill. And something else. The only man she had 'known' in her life was Rocky. I guessed that Rocky was pursuing other butterflies."

"What did you talk about?"

"Me. I admitted that I was often bewildered. I told her that sometimes I really wished that I could have been a simple, uncomplicated man. It would be easier to have simply fallen into the rut. Be Abe's son or jump on Rocky's bandwagon. Could I go home to New Hope? Could I take over the agency, sell Fords, marry a nice Jewish girl, join the club, invest in the market, be an upright citizen, duplicate myself (God forbid the Gattman name should perish!) in the womb of a loving wife?"

"I couldn't. I told Laura."

"Why?"

"Because I knew too much ... because I knew the happiness and sheer erotic pleasure and joy of tumbling in infinity—all as easily attainable and as simple as getting in bed with your sister, brushing the tears from her eyes, suddenly aware that she too was human. Or it's as mysterious as the blood pumping in your arteries, Ellen, and your will to have your heart pump. Or as wondrous as that another human being can open up your chest, and hold your heart in his hands, and create new pathways for the work it has to do. And it's as simple as the serene beauty on your face, and on Merle's face when we've pierced through the orgasmic cloud of lovemaking and arrived on top of the mountain. And we are deeply aware that we are no longer separate identities. We are beyond God. Or as Rais would say, we walked before God and He is delighted. It's as simple as taking a deep breath of air and feeling it all the way down to your penis and balls or clitoris and vagina. It's as simple as selling Fords, or running an IBM machine—if you know *why* you are selling Fords or programming a work flow. ..."

(*Pause.*)

"You're a brave philosopher, sweetie, but is the angry world out there listening? And Ellen and I are a little scared. We think you better turn the gas down before the stew boils away. For example, what are you going to do about those kids who've been hanging around here every afternoon? They aren't very old, but they sure look mean. Yesterday they were asking some of the girls if they were hookers or 'hos.' Kathy told Mohammed that a tough Irish kid offered her ten dollars for a 'quickie.' And what about the reporters? You told the kids not to talk with any of them about Premar. But somebody has been sitting across the street in a station wagon taking pictures of everyone who goes in and out of here."

(*Pause.*)

"We're going to have a confrontation. I was talking with Phil yesterday, and he says half the Premar communes are having some adverse community reaction. First there is incredulity, then shock, then anger. Before the anger turns into violence, we've got to get most of the people who live in Topham's Corner on our side. The reason I've been trying to persuade Bill Issacs to lend us the old Strand Theater is that we need it for a community forum. It's only a half-mile from here, and it's been boarded up for years. I told him that the Premars would fix the roof, and we'd paint it. He agreed to think about it."

"Bren, sometimes I think you're not for real. I fell in love with a Jewish angel. Floating through Topham's Corner playing your harp—aren't you aware that you are surrounded by Irish and Polish and black devils just waiting to strangle you with your halo?"

"Maybe not, Ellen. Maybe we can co-opt them. Mohammed told Billy Rainbow that the Premar guys all want to invite those kids into Blanc House to strip and take a bath. Then they could see all the girls naked. Billy says they'll be a lot less ferocious with their pants off. I told Phil that I was really amazed at what the Premar structure is accomplishing for the kids. Here, let me read you some of Joe McDonald's last journal; I read it to Phil, and he was impressed.

" 'At our Eight-Three H.V. meeting* last week, Bren didn't arrive until after nine. But with Ellen and Merle directing traffic, we examined how we can convince our

---

* Following the Premar Human-Values program, the students were divided into six groups of eight students for their daily H.V. meetings. Group Eight-Three comprised Andrea Pillisuk, Mohammed Hassan, Katherine Flaherty, Samantha Brown, Julie Howe, Chuck Ventrano, Lainey Franci, and Joe McDonald.

neighbors that Premar is a strong moral concept that can actually strengthen the family and revitalize religion.

" 'Bren says the thrust of our exploration should be first, to convince each of us intellectually of the worth of Premar. I don't know about intellectually, but emotionally I'm sure that there aren't many of us left who aren't avid believers. The amazing thing is how fast we've changed. The first few weeks, seeing each other naked, overcoming our guilt feelings that somehow it wasn't right to be sleeping with somebody whom you might never marry, discovering how to be whatever kind of person you really are, and not be ashamed of it, being surprised at how easy it is to care for someone, and love them, and slowly realizing that "I love you" doesn't mean "I own you"—all this is changing everyone here very basically. Two months ago I would never have known how to laugh with a girl like Andy. I'd have been so self-conscious—thinking I was ugly, or boorish—that we'd have never got to know each other. And I'd have never known myself. Now, when I know that Andy is having fun with some of the other guys and is responding because they like her, instead of being jealous, I'm happy for her. I can't explain it, or say why it's true, but Andy needs me, too. When she's living with Mohammed next semester, I think she may still occasionally want to horse around alone with me.

" 'Even Bren says that while Premar depends on structure, the structure must bend to experience. Anyway, we didn't get to the Synectic approaches he's interested in immediately because we had a dozen other things to talk about. One of the things that makes Premar a fast learning experience is that we are sharing, on a very intimate basis, the problems and the feelings of the Compars, who are not old enough to be our parents, and that helps. They may not know all the answers, but their conviction that there *are* answers and that we can discover them together creates a lot of enthusiasm and excitement.

" 'Merle called this "the wished-for sibling relationship"—the big brother or sister who, if they actually existed in our families, might have bridged the generation gap for us. Most of us didn't grow up in families where that kind of intimacy exists. If our parents knew how to be friends, which maybe means just being open and admitting that they are occasionally "fucked-up," too—and need to be loved, if for no other reason than

that they are trying—maybe we'd have some of the answers that Bren wants to communicate to the whole
Topham's Corner community.' "

(*Pause.*)

"Isn't that great?"

"The kids feel more secure than Merle and I do."

"The environment of love gives you security, Ellen. If
you'd marry me, we'd have one open hatch battened
down."

"If I marry you, I don't think I'll feel one bit more secure. Maybe less!"

(*Laughter.*)

"The environment of love that we'll create will give you
security. Even after Premar, we'll be involved in a community of interdependent people. You'll always have rein-
forcement, not just from your children or me, but from
your own peer group."

"Yes, but my problem is that I've been brought up like
most girls. Even Merle admitted that she wanted her own
man *and you*. I'm still hung up on the until-death-do-us-
part syndrome."

"I'm not the Don Juan you may think I am; I'm quite
capable of making a commitment. I'm ready to marry
both of you—till death do us part! Since Merle is already
married, a good beginning would be to formalize *us*. How
about it, Ellen?"

*Laura Stone. Parallel to Premar. September, the first year. From a tape transcribed by Rachel Silverman.**

Tomorrow, unless Rais has lost count or has cut too many
notches on the tree above this cave, we will have been on
this island ninety-six days. Whatever happened to Mrs.
Rocky Stone? That poor woman died in the plane crash.

---

* This cassette was given to Premar by Laura Stone. Chronolog-
ically it belongs here, but no one was aware of its existence until
March of the first year of Premar, when she gave it to Rocky Stone.

This female, lying here on her back, naked on the sand, her legs open, her feet perched over her head, her toes pushing lightly against the sensuous bark of a coconut tree while she rambles aloud; this woman who has had a husband for sixteen of her thirty-eight years, who is the mother of two children, who never before had an orgasm, who in three months has been transformed from a sex object into a sex machine who climaxes five, ten, fifteen times, not once, but twice or three times a day—this woman has gone crazy!

Is that the kind of talk you want on your machine, Rais? You've broken down just about every inhibition I ever had; so here's the real me, every man's dream of a nymphomaniac, pornographic maiden who walks right out of the sex books he's been reading and leaps onto his erect dick and tortures him with a slow rumba rhythm of her behind that keeps him forever on the edge, but never lets him tumble over.

Is that me? No. By no means! Laura Stone is not a maiden. Laura Stone is a dead old bitch. The blood and genes which survived in this body have been taken possession of by some primitive, malign force.

A few years ago the jet-set newspaper *W* published a picture of me, along with Melina Mercouri, Pauline de Rothschild, Lee Radziwill, Marion Javits, Pamela Harriman, and a lot of others. The 'juicy people,' as they called us. The juicy people are presumably high livers and big lovers. Of course, they didn't know that I, and probably some of the others, were no longer juicy in the right places.

But maybe we get juicier if we are whipped or have a plug stuck in our anus like that bitch in *The Story of O*, which intrigued my husband so mightily. But the sexual proclivities of the juicy people were only hinted at. The way you identify a juicy person is to see if he or she takes the first bite out of the center of the steak. Or, if he's male, when he folds his hand, does he automatically put his left thumb over his right?

Sick? You bet! Juicy means that after amassing a certain number of millions you then make a career out of being USELESS, in capital letters a block high. Have I really gone down the sawdust trail and experienced a conversion to reality? Is screwing my heart out with a nigger who hasn't got a dime more sensible than lying in bed like a rock with an aged tycoon who can't keep his erection? The person I was keeps asking: Can it last? Isn't that the reason for my ecstasy—the utter suicidal, last-supper aspects of it? By any mathematical laws of probability I should be dead. Am I at last being truthful to myself now that I have gone to bed with death and survived, and become aware for the first time that breathing and being was better than oblivion, no matter what the conditions of living might be? Did I fear that if I didn't screw with Rais, he'd have raped me?

Maybe I did on day one, and two, and three, but the fear diminished. Rais didn't take me with his penis. It was I—I who wanted his penis to substantiate the drawly melody of his voice, and the tenderness of his hands. I had to know if he was real, if I was really alive.

Bren, my stinking, know-it-all brother—are you listening? If you are, you can afford to laugh, because your fucked-up sister is dead! Down to now I've never said a dirty word in my life, aloud. So, if you find this tape, or if my mad lover mails it to you, make a copy for Abe and Rivke. Oh, and by all means, be sure to send one to my beloved husband. Let them all know that in the past eighty-four days I've become a sex fiend. With all his gentleness, it took the black man—with my hand firmly on his prick—twelve days to strike pay dirt. No, not dirt—a warm spring geyser. Stand in line, ladies and gentlemen, old faithful erupts on schedule. Svengali Daemon does it not with his tool, but with hypnosis—what else?

By rough count I've spent more hours fucking in recent weeks than I ever have in the last ten years of my married life. As for orgasms, that's a whole new world. So I've put my priorities in order. I finally dared to do it, because I died and went to heaven. Some heaven! There's bugs, and the food is *dreck*. But my lover and I eat a little fish and rice—and each other. Swill a little rum, and float away on a high that is interrupted only by laughter at our kooky necessities.

My man is on the rocks, fishing. I can see him from here. His rod doesn't flop against his balls, but rides on a permanent hundred-degree angle, and when he walks toward me, all I have to do is smile and it will rise to a forty-five-degree magnificence. And when he returns, he'll rub stinking fish oil over me—already I'm tanned only a few shades lighter than he—and I'll slither into his arms, clasp him with my legs around his middle. Transfixed, I'll ride my cock-horse to Banbury Cross while he trots me into the water. Out over our heads, we will submerge, joined together in a pale green fairyland and encircled by coral reefs.

Another fact is I'm a white woman, prisoner of a black man. One of these days I'll wake to reality, and then the jailer will have to murder the prisoner before the prisoner murders the jailer. I'm a white woman prisoner of a black revolutionist. Remember *The Ballad of Reading Gaol*, Rais—you can live it out. "Some kill their love when they are young, and some when they are old; some strangle with the hands of lust, some with the hands of gold, some love too little, some too long, some sell and others buy, some do the deed with many tears, and some without a sigh; for each man kills the thing he loves, yet each man does not die."

So you better do it, Rais. I'm not predictable. You're my prisoner, too! Laura Stone, who should have died in that plane crash, has been kissed too deeply by the Dracula of her past. The zombie keeps surfacing and screwing up my head. I hate myself for my unleashed sexuality. Laura Stone, forgetting some of the time, and yet horribly aware that you, Rais Daemon, *are black!* Laura Stone—Rocky Stone's wife—world-renowned among her peers for her "cool." Laura Stone, the frigid good sport who grinned and bore her husband's entrepreneurial fucking. Laura Stone has a black child in her belly!

Goddamn you, Rais! Get me off this island, back to the States or Puerto Rico. In another few weeks it will be too dangerous to get an abortion. Come hell or high water, I'm not giving birth to a black child, or any damn kid. I can still figure out how to kill you before you kill me. Some night when you're exhausted from fucking, and just want to sleep against your white mama, I'll roll you on your back and shove your fish knife deep into your heart. I'll have to kill myself afterward, but I'll do it! I'm not going back to the States and tell my husband that I'm alive and pregnant. Why do you want this child, anyway? You're as *meshugge* as my brother. In your right mind, do you think I'd grow fat with your child, while my brother was watching laughing because his snotty sister finally let her genitals rule her head?

And Merle? What about her? Do you think your wife would take kindly to a white woman blossoming before her eyes from her husband's sperm? Rais, I beg you, get me home before I'm officially dead and Rocky decides to marry some new and younger bitch. You can be rich, Rais. If I don't try to murder you, I'll just walk into the ocean and swim out far enough so I can't possibly make it back. Why not? What do I have to live for? Your black arrow? It's great, but it's not enough.

And Bren, you bastard, I'm talking to you! Are you happy to discover that your sister has been screwing with your best friend? Do you remember when you were six, and you were finally taking your own baths? I was fifteen. I used to sneak into the bathroom and wash your back, and you, you devil, with a tiny grin on your face, you'd lie back in the tub and let me play with your jigger. Too bad it never got very big; we might have had a good thing going. Seven years later I married Rocky. After that I never thought about you much, except when I'd come home and Rivke would be in tears, and Abe would tell me you were worse than Abbie Hoffman and Jerry Rubin; Abe was sure that *they* didn't take their shit seriously, but *you* did.

How can Jewish kids run the gamut from characters like Rocky Stone, a money gobbler, to you, Bren? You shithead, you probably are indirectly responsible for me taking the initiative with Rais Daemon. In the very early days here, while I listened to your friend talking to his tape recorder as if it were human and might answer back, telling it about his screwed-up revolution and implying that any minute he was going to rape me, I heard him mention you and Merle. Slowly, in my numbed brain, everything clicked into place. There absolutely couldn't be any other Jewish boy in the whole world with a Yiddish adverb for a first name. And, of course, Merle was none other than that black babe you brought to the Springdale Yacht Club and screwed in Abe's boat. I saw that Merle was now Rais' wife and that you were both screwing her. What happened to Lena Goldman? Rais says he thinks you have still another girl now.

I told Rais that God must have abdicated His throne and He was running things the way Rocky Stone did, with an Executive Committee. As Chairman of the Board, God had appointed a spade Chief Executive officer and was

chuckling in His beard. Otherwise, what kind of fucking
deus ex machina had dropped me into the Caribbean to
be rescued by your nigger friend? Okay, you don't have to
like my language. If Rais plays this tape, neither will he,
although he does have a sense of humor and likes to hear
me recite "Little Black Sambo." It gets us both dreaming
of one hundred and sixty-nine pancakes covered with tiger
ghee. Anyway, when I am in Westport or on the Riviera
or in Palm Springs, nary a dirty word passes my virginal
lips. I've heard too many of those upper-class matrons slip
into truck-driver garbage language.

Did I tell you my black lover has recaptured his jungle
skills? We drink rum and coconut water as a daily diet.
Who else in the whole damned world has a cocktail lounge
under a coconut tree and a naked male who can climb to
the top and toss down ripe coconuts? No wonder I've become hooked on sex!

Wake up, Rais, Bren! The haves and the have-nots are
as old as man, and you're not about to abolish them. Do
you know what Rocky Stone is really doing in St. Noir?
He's transferring his Nasasu corporations to Grand Cayman.

Rocky is thrilled by the Grand Cayman. You know
why? Because it's suitably devoid of law. Think about
that. The Grand Cayman Island has plenty of the kind of
law that protects the First National City Bank or the
Bank of Montreal or hundreds of other banks that now do
business in Georgetown, the island's boom town. What's so
good about Grand Cayman? Well, the British still own
that one outright. Lynden Pindling, the black big shot in
the Bahamas, finally shut down on the hot money pouring
into Nassau. But no half-ass black pride is going to fuck
up the money men. On Grand Cayman you can form a
corporation, buy and sell stocks in Manhattan, London, or
Tokyo, and through the simple process of not reporting
earnings in the United States, eliminate taxes. The rich always get richer, Rais, and you can't mount a revolution
that will stop that. Who needs superpatriots like Pindling
and Granby, unless they can be co-opted? Money gets nervous when the blacks are screwing around. You and Rais
are batting your heads against a rock wall. The national-
ists can murder a few ambassadors or governors, but the
Rocky Stones go on forever.

Poor people—not just black ones—have a masochistic,

yes-sir-fuck-me-please wish. And I'm not coming back to Boston with a converted heathen to live in a ménage-a-trois with your black woman, to save the starving poor! You can talk your damned head off about Confamiliaums, and how you and Bren planned to create viable living, learning areas in the inner cities. Fifty poor families, an average hundred and fifty people, pooling their energies and piddling resources is still one hundred and fifty times zero. Maybe it has some point for you, Rais, but what's in it for Bren?

Why not join the inner circle, Rais? Get me home, and I'll make you rich.

Here he comes, fish dangling from his belt, bobbing against his naked prick and buttocks, a mile-wide grin on his face. I'll help him clean them—no choice. If I don't, I don't eat. And this is our sex diet. *Kallaloo*, which Rais discovered growing wild—the lover's food, sour sop, which Rais says is a tranquilizer; coconut; bananas; and since the rum is gone now, we have homemade opium—something that Rais ground up from the inner bark of the mahoe tree. We smoke it in a pipe he made from bamboo. And then, the transformation and the night of endless lovemaking begins. With birds still peeping back in the jungle, night sneaking in overhead, streaking into the fiery sun, a blood bath on the horizon, Rais takes a last puff on the dream pipe, kisses my lips, my breasts, my belly, buries his face between my legs, and I nibble his penis. Salty. Nice. And then somewhere in the infinity of a starlighted night, I feel his penis hover on the edge of my labia. And hours go by as he says hello on my doorstep, tentatively entering, withdrawing, moving in such a delicate dance that I am moaning, crying into an ecstatic world I may never return from.

The day before yesterday, I managed to get the tape recorder turned off before Rais knew I had finally recorded my thoughts. He himself has lost interest in it, and I suppose the only interest I have in it is that I'm playing with fire. When both sides of this tape are finished, I'd better bury it. If Rais listens, the last hope that we may return to civilization may be gone. Which only addles my brain. Why do I want to go back? Rocky may already have announced plans to marry Jeanne Mechante or some other whore. My kids don't seem to need me. Maybe God is offering me a second chance here. Maybe I'd be happier decivilized—perpetually knocked-up. What would Rais think if I suggested that we sail to some other island besides St. Noir? With the money we could get on my diamond, we could live ten years. Or maybe we could buy an older home and advertise for winter guests.

Yesterday Rais caught me looking in my pocketbook mirror. "Yes," he said. "You are prettier than you were three months ago. The lines have gone. Your hair is brown, and your blue eyes are clear and brighter than the sky. And you have a new smile—warm, juicy, the smile of a woman who enjoys fucking."

"My God!" I told him. "I'm Alice and you're my black rabbit!"

"We need a change of diet," he said, "so let's sail into St. Noir and buy some canned stuff, maybe a few live chickens and a rooster, and a few gallons of rum. If I land at St. Michael's, I can tie up with the boats that are always sailing between the islands." He handed me the fish knife. "I've honed it pretty sharp." His cool grin was sexy. "Now's your chance, Laura, to hack off my beard or slit my throat."

I twisted the point lightly against his Adam's apple. "If I jabbed you, you'd yank the knife out of my hand and kill me before you bled to death. If I was going to murder you, boy, I'd have done it while you were asleep." The word "boy" did it. Rais grabbed me, squirming and yelling, and took a bite on my behind that still aches, and I'm sure will leave me permanently scarred.

When we had calmed down, he said, "Sometimes I think you really want me to beat you to death."

"I've changed my mind," I told him. "I've got a good idea. If you'll leave me in St. Noir, I can still make it back to the States in time. Rais, the time for fun is over. You saved my life. Now, for what it's worth, I want to go on living. The pregnancy is my fault. I wanted to screw with you, but sure as hell I don't want this baby! If you'll buy me a cheap dress and shoes, and a suitcase, I can fly back from St. Noir. I have over a thousand in cash. Here—take my ring. It's a down payment. I'll give you a hundred times as much when I get back."

Rais chuckled. "So you can finally take it off." He patted my cheek. "I'm glad you've still got your finger."

"Rais, do you hear me?"

He nodded. "I was wondering what you're ever going to do without your daily screwing?"

"Buy a vibrator, you shithead."

"To tell you the truth, I'm kind of looking forward to being a father."

"You're what?" I screamed, pummeling him again. He grabbed my wrist, and I dropped the knife.

"I guess I'd better cut off my own whiskers. You're kind of belligerent, rejecting your destiny and all that."

"My destiny is *not* to give birth to your brat."

"Your egg didn't feel that way."

"Goddamn you. Neither my eggs nor my cunt have any brains."

Rais had finally sawed off his beard and was now trying to shave himself with seawater and fish oil. "Give me that damned knife," I told him, "before you cut yourself to pieces." He was sitting on a sea-worn wooden barrel. Spread-legged, I sat on him. He was practically in my womb. Hopefully, his penis might stab out the fetus. He played with my breasts while I slowly pared off his whiskers.

"You look younger," I told him. "Like a boy." I was aware again that I was ten years older than he, and for a second I felt like an old lady assuaging her newly discovered and rampant sexuality with a man young enough to be her son.

"You aren't learning very fast. Don't call a black man a boy, even when you're transfixed."

"I just told you what I was thinking."

"That's progress," he said.

Yesterday we sailed out of the narrow passage that leads through the reefs surrounding the Mons. Jibbing and coming about, pointing so high into the wind that the boat stopped sailing, Rais finally had to jump out and tow the boat behind him until his head was nearly submerged. At last we were in open sea. He pulled himself aboard, triumphant at having navigated the rocky passage once again. Still naked, I was shiny with the stinking greasy stuff Rais had concocted from the remains of our fish dinners. I knew I smelled rancid, but lately even my nose is mixed-up; Rais has convinced me it's really a musky perfume and that I smell sexy.

Toward afternoon we first saw a yacht in the south

coming toward us, and Rais put on his dungarees. He brought the boat up into the wind and let the sail flutter. I guessed the yacht was coming out of Hamilton harbor in St. Noir.

"Okay, Laura," he said. "Lie down on that tarpaulin on your belly. I'm going to tie you up."

"The hell you are!"

"You had your chance." He patted the fishknife hanging from his belt. "You should have stuck it in my throat." He grabbed my arm. The boat was dipping and thrashing, occasionally shipping water.

"Moron," I yelled at him. "If it's the last thing I do, I'll get you put in jail for life. I'll tell everybody the only reason I screwed with you was that I knew you'd rape me."

I guessed the reason why he wanted to tie me up. He knew that if we came too close to passing boats or we finally got into St. Michael's, I was going to start yelling.

Rais just squeezed my hand and pushed my arm down inexorably until I thought it would pop out of its socket. I collapsed on the bottom of the boat. In less than a minute he had my hands tied behind my back and my ankles lashed together.

"I'm not going to gag you until we get nearer," he said. "With this wind, that should be in about an hour." He flipped the tiller until the sail bellied, and then we were sailing on a reach. Holding the tiller with his toes, he pulled me into his arms and kissed me. "There's something very erotic," he said, "about a woman tied up and helpless—especially one as beautiful as I've made you!"

"You bastard! Who do you think you are—Frankenstein?"

"No. Pygmalion. But with you as Galatea, it isn't easy."

A few boats passed fairly close, but nobody noticed me because I was flat on my back with the big black foot of my master on my belly. Before he gagged me, I appealed to him once again. "If you won't let me go, at least please buy me some dungarees or a dress." All the time I was thinking what the hell difference it all made. "Rais, I'm not giving birth to a half-breed baby. You can call me a racist or whatever you want; that doesn't matter. But if the story ever gets out that I lived with you on the Mons for three months, and I was pregnant by you, and I wasn't trying to put you in jail, then I would be tacitly saying that the wife of Rocky Stone enjoyed her island sojourn

with her black lover. Rais, for your own protection, I
have to hate you. Rocky may fool around with other
women, but the mother of his children doesn't have any
kind of lover, black or white. Not one she admits to. Rais,
please don't leave me."

He wasn't impressed. He locked me in the tiny cabin
and tossed a tarry, smelly tarpaulin on top of me. Before
he returned, I was nearly dead from heat exhaustion.
Then I heard the sail being yanked up, and in a few minutes we were bounding in open ocean.

Rais opened the cabin, took off the gag, and untied me.
He held a bottle of cold Coke up to my parched lips, and
he hauled buckets of cool water out of the ocean and
poured them over me. I was so grateful I sobbed my love
for him.

"I thought they might have taken you off to prison," I
told him. "Would I simply have died?"

"Laura," he said. "You haven't been listening. No matter what else, I'm not going to let you die." He tossed a
paper bag at me. "Here. If I were going to kill you, would
I buy you clothes?"

Maybe someday I'll buy dresses again from Bergdorf
Goodman or Bonwit Teller, but nothing will ever delight
me so much as those dungarees, and a blouse, and a dress
with huge roses on it, and two pairs of panties, and a pair
of sneakers. And every last one of them fit me! I was
overwhelmed. After I tried them on, I took them all off. I
didn't care if I wore them, especially when we were alone,
and the sky and the sea was our only witness. Rais was
watching me, grinning. "I thought you'd never get undressed again," he said approvingly.

I undid his belt buckle. "I guess I've gone native," I replied. "Take off your pants; be naked with me." On the
rough deck of the boat we made love while the boat
drifted, and the sun slowly disappeared into the sea leaving behind pinks, yellows, blues, and green smoky night
clouds.

Back on the island, Rais carried me up to our cave.
Propped against him, sipping rum and eating huge to-
mato-and-lettuce sandwiches, I watched his fingers playing
gently with my nipples.

"I mailed my two tapes to Merle today. Bren will hear
them. Our love idyll is nearly over, Laura."

"My God! Not Bren! What do I do now?"

Rais wasn't listening. "No one recognized me in St. Noir," he said. "Life's gone back to normal. Gabby's been sleeping with Arthur Granby. I felt like Rip Van Winkle when I heard that. Have you ever seen those paperbacks *Where Are They Now?* Pictures of the formerly famous." He laughed. "Fame is fleeting. Today you are headlines, tomorrow, who was he? In a few days, while we've still got plenty of grub, we'll sail to Puerto Rico and I'll find you a hotel. Then it will be good-bye, Laura Stone."

I cried in his arms.

PART THREE

Confamiliaum

We will live in a horizontal order, where men will again participate in the decisions that affect them. We will live in an open order, with everybody being part of, and moving freely within, a number of overlapping subsystems in which one's leisure, economic, cultural and spiritual life are organized. It will be an order based no longer on property, on power, or on sovereignity, for all these concepts are eroding under our eyes. And it will no longer be dominated by Judeo-Grecian-Roman values. . . . "Interaction" may well become the catchword to give a common denominator to many of our activities.

ELIZABETH MANN BORGESE

Ellen Gattman. November, the first year of Premar. From tapes transcribed by Samantha Brown.

Where do I begin?

With the headlines on the Boston *Globe* yesterday?

PREMAR RAID MAY HAVE FLUSHED OUT JET-SETTER! IS LAURA STONE STILL ALIVE? Betty Hurley, one of the floor nurses, left the paper on my breakfast tray with a grim wouldn't-you-know-it expression.

Three days after Laura came home, Rais and Bren were fighting for the existence of Premar. So I guess I'm the only one who can take a deep breath (wishful thinking?) and communicate with the Premars via tape. Why not? What else can I do? I'm in the University Hospital, and so far I've survived a team of doctors and nurses poking tiny tubes into my arteries and veins until they reached my heart. In my semiconscious state, the bewildering array of equipment made me feel as if I were in a space-travel fantasy. Catheterization, they call it; they're trying to discover whether I'm a good candidate for heart surgery.

How did I get here? Not exactly of my own free will! Oh, damn! One of the floor nurses just walked in. She heard me talking and guessed that one of the crazy Premar kids, who have visited me in a steady procession, must be hiding in the toilet. What kind of a dimwit talks to a tape recorder as if it were a friend who could talk back?

Sometimes I can't believe that six months ago I was living a quiet, say, boring life. I remember watching Haroun Tazieff, the famous volcanologist, on television. He was camping with a group of students in the crater of a volcano on Mount Nyirongo, in Africa. They were living a few hundred feet from the boiling firepit, and eventually Tazieff had himself lowered down into it. I knew that kind of adventuring, man against the elements, could never happen to me. I suppose most healthy people live pretty prosaic lives, yet I know now that adventure is still alive in this world. If you are female, all you have to do is get yourself involved with men like Bren and Rais. If you do, day-to-day living becomes a continuous questioning process, and when no answers are forthcoming, you are plunged into a turmoil. Even though I know I shouldn't be involved, it's impossible for me to stay out. It may be dangerous, but at least it's an improvement over hypochondria. Bren told me that the most valuable thing I can teach the Premars is my own discovery that each confused day I live is in reality a lovely, unexpected gift. The first priority of a joyous life is that you're actually breathing; the second is that you're really loving; and the third is laughter, mostly at oneself, that comes automaticallly.

I better get myself in focus. Is this only Friday? The police raid was on Halloween—Wednesday. "Ah bitter chill it was, the owl for all his feathers was a-cold." No—that's St. Agnes' Eve, which hasn't come yet. Back up to Sunday. Yes, Sunday. I still don't dare to think about last Friday. Did I really dare to marry Bren?

Well, Sunday! It was a lazy, leaf-smelling, smoky, dying-living fall day. A time-has-stopped kind of day, with a seventy-degree temperature that you knew would vanish by night. More than half the kids decided to hike with Bren to the Blue Hills, about six miles from Premar. Merle drove the truck with Mohammed, Kathy, Lainey, and Chuck, who came with us to carry the hamburgers, hot dogs, rolls, and me. The boys made a chair-lift of their hands and arms. I had tried to persuade them that it wasn't necessary that I come, but obviously I lost that argument.

Bren arrived about noon, on foot, with his singing, yelling, ragtag army, who were jumping up and down trying to touch infinity while they quoted Edna Millay. On the westward side of the hill they found a rocky slope concealed from the main footpaths by the foliage. Soon the girls were running around in panties and bras and the guys in shorts. The more daring girls, like Samantha, Andrea, and Rachel, along with a lot of the guys, simply took off their clothes. Laughing at Merle's and my protests, they were posing like nymphs and satyrs in the tall grass. Finally, when Able Anderson and Cheryl Jones told him they had brought a climbing rope, even Bren got nervous. Able wanted to make a swing and hang it on the bough of one of the tall trees. Purpose—to try intercourse in a swing, with Cheryl facing him; it seems they'd read about that in Alex Comfort's book. The girl embraced the guy, and together they swooned through the air—joined! The ultimate ecstasy? Bren told them even he hadn't tried that, and that while it was an interesting idea, they'd better not try it here on a public mountain. We'd have to forgo a floating orgasm until next summer. I didn't dare ask Bren where this magic swing would ultimately be erected.

Amazingly, we didn't get arrested for indecent exposure. Somewhere up there God must have been chuckling, knowing that we were going to get tested soon enough. After we got back to Premar, I plunged into some work I was doing in a seminar on people and environment, analyzing the kinds of buildings and homes we live in, and how this affects our emotional lives. Bren was at his desk making notes for his doctoral thesis, which he hopes to submit with Rais, since they originally worked on the idea together: *Confamiliaums: A Proposal for Cooperative Initiative and Expanding Personal Freedom.*

I really wasn't studying too hard, because I had a euphoric, everything's-right-with-the-world feeling, the kind of twilight moment you wish could last indefinitely. But then the phone rang. What was I thinking as I picked it up? Whatever it was, was jarred right out of my head by a beautiful English accent saying, "I wonder if I have the right location? I'm trying to reach Bren Gattman." The voice on the tapes had come to life!

"You're Rais! You're Rais Daemon," I exclaimed. "Rais, this is Ellen O'Day. My God, Bren! Rais is home! Talk with him while I find Merle."

Rais told Bren that he had a surprise for us out at the airport, and a half-hour later, Merle, Bren, and I were there. Merle did the driving, because she didn't trust a madman behind the wheel—Bren was so enthusiastic! He was certain his sister had come to Boston with Rais.

They were waiting for us in front of the Pan Am Terminal. Laura seemed embarrassed and was hanging back, but she finally hugged Merle and me before she got swung in the air by Bren. She was wearing dungarees and a sheepskin coat bought in a secondhand clothing store in San Juan. Her bright blue eyes were awash with tears. She made me think of a bewildered flower child who had survived the sixties, and now, older and confused, had retreated into her own fantasy world. She was tanned chocolate brown, making her light hair, hanging down her back, seem almost blond. If you glance at her quickly, she looks as young as the Premars. I soon discovered that Rais and Bren use all the forbidden ethnic epithets with complete loving abandon with each other. "You did it, Rais. You turned my sister into a jig," Bren said. He was hugging Laura. "I can't believe my eyes. What happened to Laura Stone? What happened to my *shrying* sister who was buried under a foot of makeup? Rais, you rubbed away the shit, after thirty years, she's here again, a vulnerable girl-woman, as fetching as a nine-year-old nymphet."

Sitting in the back seat between Merle and me, Laura said, "I used to look at white women with black men, and black women with white men, and think they must be sick." She smiled at Merle and rubbed Rais' neck. "A bitchy woman on the plane kept staring at me and making remarks to her husband. I finally told her that my ass was black even if my face wasn't and that if she'd like I'd bend over and she could kiss it. It's nice to know one isn't too old to learn. Merle, I probably should have stayed in Puerto Rico, but I was afraid a Spanish horse doctor might do the abortion. I think I'm beyond the suction-cup stage."

I saw Merle's eyes open wider than usual. Otherwise her face looked cool. "So, you're pregnant?"

"It doesn't matter. In a few days I won't be. Don't blame Rais. I seduced him."

Bren was jubilant. "My big sister is pregnant. Wow-ee! Unbelievable! Fantastic!"

"What's so unbelievable?" Laura added. "I have two children. Remember? You're just happy because you think I've finally been shot down."

"In a way you have, Laura. As you plummet toward earth spitting flames, maybe you're wondering how you'll explain this to Rocky, not to mention our parents."

"I'm not explaining anything to anyone. Tomorrow you can take me to a hospital. We'll tell them that you're my husband—I robbed the cradle and got pregnant. Within a week I'll be able to call Rocky. *Mirabile dictu!* His wife has come back from the grave to tighten the noose around his neck."

"Maybe you can't go home again, Laura. Maybe you should have the baby." Was Bren just teasing her?

But Rais certainly wasn't kidding. "Damnit, that's what I told her. Have the baby. What's five more months in your life, Laura? Merle and I will adopt it."

Laura set Rais straight. "You're both quite mad. I'm too old to have a baby. And if I'm not, it doesn't make any difference. This baby will be black."

"Is that a crime?" Merle demanded.

Bren was enjoying the conversation. "Maybe it would be nice if some jet-setter stuck her neck out. Presumably the upper class are buddy-buddy with black people in the arts, or sports, or wherever blacks have made it. I can see the newspapers now. Yesterday the former wife of Rocky Stone proved that she's never been racist by giving birth to a beautiful black child."

"What do you mean *former* wife?" Laura asked. "I don't think that's funny!"

"No, it isn't, and you might as well know what's happening. Rivke telephoned me yesterday to tell me your Will is about to be probated. The rumor is that you left your kids ten million bucks. How did you ever manage to squeeze so much out of Rocky?"

Laura shrugged. "He's fifty-three. He may never have been the faithful-to-one-woman-husband type, but he wanted to make sure that if he dropped dead that he'd prevent the Internal Revenue from getting it all. And, keep in mind, dear brother, that I'm not dead!"

"Rivke said Rocky is considering marrying again. I suppose he could divorce you."

"Don't worry. I'm suddenly a million-dollar publicity bonanza. Even Stone-Western Industries couldn't afford the news coverage I'll get when the world knows that I was rescued. One hundred and sixty people dead, but God saved me." Laura's words were spoken in a whisper, as if she still couldn't believe it herself.

"God didn't save you," Bren said coolly. "Rais Daemon did. When are you going to open *that* can of worms? The first question the press will ask is exactly how you alone survived. And why didn't Rais save at least one other person? Also, why did you stay on the Mons de Cytherea so long? And isn't it true, Mrs. Stone, that you and Rais are lovers? Why didn't he take you back to St. Noir? What did you do together for four months on your island paradise, Mrs. Stone?"

There were tears in Laura's eyes. "I encouraged Rais to wait until we could sail to Puerto Rico, because I knew he'd be arrested if he tried to take me to St. Noir."

"The United States could deport me," Rais said. "If that's your story, Laura, they'll ask you the next question. You must care for Rais Daemon, Mrs. Stone, isn't that so?"

"I love him," Laura said. "He saved me—from a lot of things."

Merle said, "That's nice . . . but there are other things to consider. When we bring you up-to-date, Rais, you'll realize that the last thing in the world Premar or you need is to have Laura Stone tell the world about her island sojourn with a former revolutionist, who is now in the United States running a sex commune with her brother. I think it would be better if Laura simply told the reporters that some unidentified native black family rescued her and nursed her back to health. Leave Rais out of it!"

Rais ruffled Merle's hair. "I'm glad to see you still love your old man."

"Horny old man." Merle shook her head, but her grim tone was loving. "Next time I'm not around, and the girl's not on pills, will you please tell her that you're only permitted to play *outside* her playpen?"

Laura laughed. "That would have been inhospitable, especially to a man who told you that your white ass was his spoils of the sea. Anyway, I'm paying for my sins."

"You don't have to pay with an abortion. If you want to have the baby, Rais and I will love it."

Laura touched Merle's cheek. "Merle, that's nice," she said. "As for me, I might accept the fact that my husband made love with another woman, but if she were pregnant, forget it."

"If Rais loves you, then I'm sure of one thing—there must be something pretty special about you." I couldn't believe that Merle really believed what she was saying.

"Thanks, but I'm pretty damned ordinary. I don't know the first thing about love. And if any of you think I'm going to hide out in Boston, or move in with you and have this baby, put it out of your minds. I'm not joining any sex commune run by Bren. I'm too possessive; I'm not willing to share a man. If you don't mind Rais wandering, and you can welcome him home after he's screwed around, you're out of my league."

Bren approved of the openness of the conversation. "Laura wants you for herself, Rais," he said. "We'll have to give you a Premar orientation, dear sister. It will take at least until Tuesday or Wednesday to arrange an abortion. In the meantime, you can live in one of Premar's privacy rooms. Maybe Merle will let Rais visit you on alternate nights. Or maybe we can find you another man and you can begin a new life in a group marriage."

"May I interject a practical thought?" I asked. "How are you going to explain this to Phil Tenhausen? If Rais gets too much sex-and-revolution publicity, I don't think Phil and Margaret will want him as a Compar. Then what happens to Premar?"

I really wanted to say what happens to *you and me*, Bren. And I was thinking this really is a man's world. Last Friday, hadn't I been as *non compos mentis* as either Laura or Merle about a man? All right, Phillip and Margaret Tenhausen, if the Topham's Corner Premar survives, you can rest easy that for better or worse Premar at last has two married couples directing traffic. I can't promise you we'll be strictly monogamous, although I have no yearning to go to bed with Rais. The first thing I have to discover is whether I just love being married, or if being married is really so different.

"The Pope will never forgive me," Father Tim told Bren. "If the Cardinal or Archbishop hears about it, they may excommunicate me. Or maybe one fine day I'll wake up and find myself enrolled in a monastic order—preferably on the moon." He put his arm around me. "I've known you since the day I baptized you. If you insist on marrying a Jew, Ellen, then we'll do it properly in the church, provided, of course, that Bren will make certain verbal commitments."

"Like what?" Bren asked.

"That at least once a month you'll come to Mass—with the understanding, of course, that Rabbi Perlstein would also enjoy seeing your shining faces at Temple Beth El from time to time. Moses and Jesus should both be a part of your lives. Marrying this way, the least you can do is to share each other's wealth."

Bren agreed—communion and all. "I really like St.

Anne's better than Beth El, especially when the organ is playing and it's twilight and no one's raving." He grinned at Father Tim. "It really would be a nice place to make love, by candlelight, with God smiling down on us through the rose window."

Father Tim enjoyed Bren's bouncing vitality. Arguing with Bren is like standing under a cool needle shower spray. He forces you into an alive, tingly state. Father Tim asked Bren what he planned to do with his life.

"Father, I'm doing it. I'm working at it. My whole life is aimed in one direction. While I realize it may take a miracle, both the Pope and I believe in miracles. I want to be the first Jewish Pope!"

Father Tim crossed himself. "God forgive me . . ."

With the main doors of St. Anne's barred, and all of the Premars admitted into the side door and sworn to secrecy, Father Tim married us. I feel shivery when I think about it. Bren changed the ceremony slightly, and Father Tim agreed. Instead of "I take you, Ellen, I take you, Bren," we said, "I love you, Ellen, I love you, Bren. When I am flesh to flesh with you, I am merged with God . . . infinity. Will you be wife . . . husband? So that we may find the Way together?"

I know what Bren means. Joined with him, I too am suddenly free. My body disappears, and the essence of Ellen sweeps around the world in a second, or orbits the sun and the moon in two seconds, and I am God, and He's very happy with my discovery.

I love being married. Bren, have I told you that already? It's silly, but snuggling in bed with you feels different now. Maybe because I feel more secure. I don't want to own you. It's just nice to know that for some beyond-belief reason you need me. Surprisingly (though it hasn't happened since Rais has come home), I'm not jealous, either, that you and Merle can share that loss of identity too. Isn't it really a need to lose oneself, to vanish back to primal essence? If you can experience that with Merle, it's because she and I are really of one piece (does that make you chuckle?). Heads or tails, black or white, together we form a chord. No matter what, I promise you it'll always be a major one.

In our first five days of wedded bliss, the world has been too much with us. Would I be here, connected to computers and data-processing equipment to discover why my heart is still beating, if Wednesday night had never happened? Even without Premar, Daddy and I have been on a collision course. He'll never understand why I would rather die from the excitement of Premar than live to sixty and have my most intimate acquaintances be the characters on the afternoon soap operas. Actually, having the "problem" of Ellen has probably brought Daddy and Mother closer together. Isn't that sad? We can share each other's sorrows but we're suspicious of each other's joys.

Now that Daddy has tossed his hat into the mayoralty ring, nearly a year before elections, he's bound to run on his tested political platform—down with sex and up with morality! So, for the sexually fearsome, the biggest smudge on the Boston landscape today is Premar. And as Daddy has been saying for weeks, there are enough laws already on the books to take care of Premar, especially with the Supreme Court's new leave-it-to-home-town-talent attitude.

Daddy gave us plenty of warning. Two days before the raid he again attacked the sex communes in Dorchester at a meeting of the City Hall Council, which was broadcast on television. Mother cried when she talked about it on the telephone. "Daddy really loves you, Ellen, and he'll forgive you, but you must come home now."

"I'm sorry for Daddy," I told her. "I forgive him, though, for Bren says he knows not what he's doing." The biblical overtones were lost on Mother.

Halloween night, about seven-thirty, the kids were gathering in the dayroom for one of our twice-a-month dancing parties. It was Bren who had the idea to teach Premars a wide spectrum of folk dancing—Hungarian, Czech, Russian, Israeli, African, Caribbean, you name it— both the dance and the music as an ongoing process of full life.

A group of bouzouki players, drummers, and dancers from the Athens After Dark, in the first of four evening sessions, had agreed to teach us Greek dancing, as well as belly dancing and Greek-style dances for men only. A few months ago Merle had bought Serena's book *Belly Dancing Techniques* and had easily mastered most of the movements. Merle read us about *awalen*, the Middle East custom of having dancers portray sexual and birthing rhythms at weddings. Bren was anxious for Rais and Laura to see this kind of fun-learning experience, and

Merle, who wears sandalwood perfume when she dances and is very seductive in her harem costume, came on as trembly as a new bride about to show her husband a new, sexy side of his wife.

Knowing that the musicians wouldn't arrive until about eight-fifteen, I was still in the tubs, listening to Laura talking with about ten of the kids who were examining the slight protuberance of her belly and the darker aureoles of her breasts. I had a feeling that Laura wasn't really angry at their insistence that she should have the baby. "You kids can't be objective," she told them. "It's not a noose around your necks. Bren has arranged for the abortion tomorrow. I'm most certainly going ahead with it." Then she looked at me and said, "This is beyond belief. No one except Rocky and that damned Bren ever saw me naked before, even when I wasn't pregnant. I must have softening of the brain."

Then we heard the sirens. Before we were fully aware that the sickening bee-bop wasn't fading out but was frozen in front of the house, we were trying to put our clothes over our wet bodies. Almost instantly the room was invaded by a half-dozen young Irish cops, some of them looking as disheveled as the Premars. Smirking and delighted at the free flesh show, they goaded us and encouraged a couple of photographers who were snapping pictures to be sure and "get the broads." They herded us upstairs, and we saw the rest of Captain Jaimie Duffy's cohorts shoving the kids, yelling obscenities, out of the three houses toward paddy wagons waiting in the street.

Captain Jaimie greeted me with a disgusted shake of his head. "I'm sorry about this, Ellen, but you'll have to go down to the station with the rest. We've got warrants against all of you. Dancer told me that he warned you."

By this time I was weeping. On the front steps of Blanc House I saw Bren and Rais struggling against the forward motion of the police. They were demanding to know what the charges were, and Captain Jaimie answered, "Lewd and obscene behavior; unrelated couples living together under the same roof; conduct leading to the delinquency of minors; giving contraceptives to underage children; sexual intercourse between unmarried persons. We've got plenty of laws on the statute books in this state. Keep on moving," he yelled at the kids. "Cut out the clowning. You won't think it's so funny when we get you down to the station."

Laura had her arm around me. Bren and Rais, who both tower over Captain Jaimie, were walking with him between them. "You can let them go," Bren said pointing at Rais and Laura. "They're not involved with Premar, Jaimie, just visiting."

"My name is Captain James Duffy!" Captain Jaimie's voice makes up for his size; he'd have made a good hog caller. Suddenly recognition flooded his face. "Jesus Christ! I know you, you black bastard!" He grabbed Rais' arm. "You're the son-of-a-bitch who clubbed me at B.U. a couple of years ago."

"That's right, Massa Jaimie." Rais spoke with a heavy put-on southern accent. "Ah sure know you, but ah learned my lesson. I ain't gonna beat your ass again. No suh!"

As we were being shoved into the wagon, Laura boiled over. "These kids aren't hoodlums," she snarled at Captain Jaimie. "They're good Americans—probably the same age as your own children. No wonder the youngsters call you pigs. You have no human emotions at all. You're disgusting. Why don't you go after the real criminals in this city?"

One of the reporters was annoying Merle. "Print this in your goddamned newspaper!" she yelled. "Dancer O'Day is a fucking idiot! See her! That's his daughter, Ellen. She has a rheumatic heart, and she's almost in shock. Does Dancer give a shit? All he's interested in is his public morality, and getting elected! This wagon better get to a hospital before Ellen drops dead right in front of you!"

I don't feel any great love for Daddy, but I don't hate him. I wonder: How can he be so sure of himself? Does he ever wake up at night and have conversations with Danny O'Day, the boy he once was? This afternoon he came to the hospital with Mother just as Rais, Merle, and Laura were leaving. Daddy ignored them, of course. He stared at Bren, wondering aloud why he hadn't gone with them.

"I want to talk with my daughter alone," he told Bren coldly.

Bren shrugged and was about to leave. I couldn't restrain the tears. "Daddy, Bren is my husband, and he stays. Father Tim married us last Friday."

"Hi, Mom and Dad," Bren said. For the first time in his life Bren actually seemed shy.

Daddy's face had turned beet red. "You rotten son-of-a-bitch. I'm going to phase you out, and that bastard, Rais Daemon, along with you." He grabbed Mother's arm and shoved her toward the door. Before he left, he turned back and said in a controlled voice, "I just talked with your doctor, Ellen. You're a good candidate for a commissurotomy, but *before and after*, you've got to change your way of life, or you'll be dead. I can't believe that Father Tim would soil his hands with this marriage. But if he did, my friend the Archbishop will hear about it!"

This time I didn't faint. Bren was holding me in his arms. "I guess it's really whither thou goest, now." I told him. "You're stuck with a cripple," I sobbed. "Have you thought about that?"

He laughed softly. "Ellen, I love you. You're stuck, too—to save me from myself."

I listened to Daddy on the six-o'clock television news. He was speaking to reporters from his office at City Hall. "There's a story going around that I'm responsible for the raid on the sex communes in Topham's Corner yesterday," he said. "If responsibility means that I'm fighting a last-ditch fight to return morality to Boston, to stamp out smut and save the morals of the family . . ." Daddy was glaring into the television cameras. ". . . then I'll take that responsibility! The world needs a new Moses to whom God has committed the enforcement of the decalogue. I'm compelling people to follow the Ten Commandments. Is that such a bad idea? Those of you who know Captain Jaimie Duffy of Topham's Corner know that he's a God-fearing Irishman. He and Captain Henry Lord, who's a Black Muslim, made the raid on the sex communes on Felton Street. Like many of the good people of Topham's Corner, Jaimie and Henry have been well aware of the indecent behavior of these misguided young people. Captains Duffy and Lord bided their time while they gathered evidence from neighbors, and from conversations with innocent children who live in the neighborhood. We have actual witnesses. Six young men, three of them black, who live in Topham's Corner have told us that they were invited into the basement of one of the houses, and practically forced to take off their clothes and get into tubs where these so-called Premars—young girls and boys—bathe together naked. God knows what else they do. We've been told that these youngsters were harassing the

Premars. Now I ask you, who's harassing who? If those Premar girls have been accosted on the streets of Dorchester, who should be blamed? How far can any young man restrain himself if he's seduced by young girls who are encouraged to sleep with young men to whom they aren't married? What kind of women would parade around a house naked so that anyone could see them from the sidewalks?

"We've discovered that there's powerful forces, armed with plenty of money, among the intellectual muddleheads of this city. Pinheads who have actually given financial aid to this sex commune and several others like it in the metropolitan area. What's more, a group of fuzzy-brain college administrators are in the process of creating thousands of these—what they call premarital-conditioning environments. These places are hotbeds of sex maniacs determined to destroy the American system by corrupting it at its base. These communes will destroy marriage and the family and substitute orgies and sexual anarchy as a way of life. Let me call to your attention that in the Halloween raid, Rais Daemon, one of the commune leaders, was arrested. Who is Rais Daemon? He's the same ringleader who was involved in the Boston University riots a few years ago. After serving time in Walpole for assaulting an officer, he returned to his home, St. Noir, an island in the Caribbean. Last July he was involved in a communist attempt to overthrow a government that has always been favorable to the United States tourists." There were tears in Daddy's eyes as he finished. "The Boston newspapers, who are against my candidacy for mayor, are telling you that my daughter, Ellen, is one of the student leaders in this commune. Her mother and I warned Ellen again and again, but to no avail, to sever all connection with this vile corruption. Today Ellen is in the University Hospital recovering from the shock to her heart and from having been led astray in this Sodom and Gomorrah which has sprung to life in Boston. If you care about America and our good city, send Ellen a card tonight. Tell our daughter to save her own life, and her mother's too! Her mother is practically in mourning for her. Tell Ellen to take her doctor's advice. Ellen, come home to your parents, who love you."

Right now half the housewives in Dorchester and South Boston are writing me you-ought-to-be-ashamed-of-yourself letters. The way they scream over him at political rallies, I'll bet a lot of them are even fantasizing themselves in bed with my father. But Bren's right. We haven't time to hate Daddy or even be angry with him. And I refuse to die! Not yet! I have too much loving to do.

Bren Gattman. November, the first year of Premar. From tapes transcribed by Andrea Pillisuk.

I'm not sure that I can concentrate. I keep thinking Ellen could die, but I suppose that's true of anyone. She asked me to lie in bed with her last night, assuring the night nurse that it wasn't for sex, but for security and warmth. We talked about death. For some reason that I haven't managed to dig out of my subconscious, I've always been aware of death largely as something unpleasant that will stop me from completing my own idea of the dream called Bren Gattman. If I finally achieve my own completion, isn't that death? Most of us in our twenties and thirties don't give much thought to how contingent we are. Maybe an awareness of nonbeing, of how quickly the generations vanish, would make us more compassionate with each other. I know that awareness has molded Ellen's life, made her the kind of grateful-for-the day, loving person that she is. Laura's fantastic brush with death has changed her, too, softened her. But why hasn't Dancer O'day, at fifty-six, gotten the message? We need politicians who know they're going to die.

I went to see Gina this morning. (Ellen, this tape is for you, for loving me with your life itself.) Yes, I hugged your mother. First I let Gina give me a ten-minute display of Italian fireworks and some good old-fashioned moaning and cussing in Italian, and then I grabbed her and snuggled her face. She pulled back as if my touch alone might corrupt her. "Look, Gina," I told her, "Ellen's a fireball like you, she's not afraid of me, like you are of Dancer. Ellen says you've got to stiffen your spine and tell

Dancer off. Did you ever hear of women's lib? Dancer needs you as much as you need him, and you both need your daughter. Well, now you've got a Jewish son-in-law, and maybe I'm just what Dancer needs. Someone who dares to disagree with him, but still loves him."

I told Gina that she should shake Dancer up, tell him she had decided to visit Premar and see what's going on, that she might even take a bath with us. I told her to bring along one of her girlfriends and I'd wash their backs. In that way, I said, Gina could help us with the logical extension of Premar into a larger communal family. I told her that in the months before *Massachusetts vs. Premar* came to trial, we wanted everyone in Topham's Corner to visit Premar and see us in action as a living, learning, and loving community.

She said, "You must be cracked. I don't undress in front of anyone," but she couldn't repress a smile. She wasn't believing, but she was listening.

Your ma has lost confidence in herself, Ellen. She thinks you can't be fat and sexually appealing, too. I was wondering how you restored a middle-aged woman's belief in her femininity.

"It's about time you took your clothes off," I told her. "All the great Italian painters liked plump women. Have you ever seen any of Tintoretto's great beauties? You could be a reincarnation of the best of them—only prettier. Let's start right now by having coffee together in our birthday suits."

Gina was laughing. "I had a good body once, but only Danny ever saw it, and that's the way it should be. So don't think I'm buying your nonsense. All this flaunting of nakedness is disgusting."

Ellen, I wonder if your father ever listened to your mother. She has a good mind, and she's almost as argumentative as you are. Believe me, being naked isn't all we talked about, and now I'm sure that being accepted into your family isn't a lost cause. Eventually Gina will take off her clothes, too, if only to prove to Dancer that she's not completely owned by him.

In the past two days, with Phil and Margaret Tenhausen and various people from the consortium, we've thrashed out a plan of action while I've kept the tape recorder going. Rais agrees that the salvation of low-income urban areas will be to involve the people living in them with a Premar style of continuous learning experience, as well as with new approaches to community. A grass-roots restructuring of life styles for diversified groups of low-income people, without destroying their ethnic needs, would give their lives a strong axis and new purposes and goals. They'd have a future, a tomorrow to look forward to—something they now lack.

But Phil thinks Premar is a big enough bite and doubts we should waste time or energy on Confamiliaum. Yet, he's intrigued. Phil may think so, but even I'm not a complete dreamer; I know that the idea of blending Premars throughout the country directly into the community, and involving thousands of people from youth to old age in such a continuous education process, may not be achieved in a year or even ten. But I am sure it will happen. The limits to growth, the growing shortages of natural resources, the boredom of working to produce plastic junk that gives no creative expression to the workman who makes it or the person who buys it, the questioning of lives devoted to acquiring "things"—all will prepare the way for a world where men and women, interacting, learning, and discovering together, find the key to a joyous, fulfilled life.

Last night, Ellen, you wondered aloud if I ever cried. You quoted Kahlil Gibran. "He who has not looked upon sorrow will never know joy." I think that's silly—a grown-up conundrum. Do human beings gain new depth, become more compassionate, because they have suffered? Maybe, but only if the pain is in moderation. Are blacks or Jews more understanding because they have been persecuted or whipped with racism or anti-Semitism? Not that I've noticed. On the other hand, what is more joyous than the pleasure of a young child who has never known suffering? Isn't it closer to the truth to say, "He who has lost his innocence will never know joy?" Your suffering, Ellen, because your blood won't flow through a clogged artery, is quite different from your suffering because of Dancer O'Day's manmade tragedies.

Still, I must admit that Wednesday, while tears weren't running down my cheeks, I was close to crumbling. I guess the only thing that saved me was what Rais calls the leader syndrome. When the center threatens to collapse, there's always a new dervish ready to whirl into place.

Someone will always raise the flag and yell charge. Rais says he proved to himself in St. Noir that he can't provide that kind of leadership. I disagree. If St. Noir isn't ready to walk before God, maybe Topham's Corner is. In either case, banging your head against a wall will only soften your head.

The police finally released all of us, including Laura. We were booked on charges of lewd and obscene behavior and for breaking laws forbidding unrelated adults to live and cohabit under one roof. All fifty-two of us walked the two miles back to Felton Street. Merle was singing with the kids, " 'Give me ten men who are stout-hearted men, and I'll soon give you ten thousand more!' . . . Here comes General Gattman with his musical-comedy army," she yelled at me.

It was eleven-thirty when we got back to the dayroom. I knew that we had to give the kids a feeling of confidence. Some of the girls looked a little shattered. "First," I told them, "when your parents hear about this, cool it with them, play it down. Most of you are adults and can make your own decisions. If you're afraid of Premar, leave because *you're* afraid, not because someone out there is predicting a terrible fate for you. Tomorrow Premar continues as usual. Go to your jobs, go to your classes. If any of your employers or friends or teachers want to discuss what's happened, there's one thing we aren't going to do. We're not blaming the fuzz." I grinned at Mohammed and Samantha, who had locked arms with Kathy Flaherty and Julie Howe.

"Bren's message is simple." Rais laughed. "We love those motherfuckers."

"Who's leaving Premar?" Chuck Ventrano demanded. "Let's give Bren, Rais, and Merle a vote of confidence." The kids yelled their enthusiasm. Billy Rainbow contributed a song: "You may think we're suckers, but we love the fuckers. Mothers, we love you one and all." I finally quieted them down.

"What about Ellen?" Andrea Pillisuk asked. There were tears in her eyes. "Without Ellen it isn't Premar."

Standing there trying to bolster their morale and assure the kids that the demons plaguing us could be conquered with love, I kept hearing a voice inside me saying: Why the hell are you taking on the world, Bren? Why don't you get your priorities in order? You've found the only essential person in your life is Ellen O'Day. Without Ellen everything else is secondary. Without her pixie smile and the warm laughter twinkling around her eyes and lips, without the look of wonder in her face—when she's lying close to me—without you, Ellen, I am lost.

Rais, standing beside me in the police station, seemed despondent. "Revolutionaries are doomed men, Bren. Death is their only reality. Victory is only their dream. Bakunin and Che Guevara said it. Huey Newton says it. Revolutionary suicide is a way of life. Trouble is, Bren, that we have no island to run to."

"We don't need one," I told him. "Remember what Thomas Paine said: 'From what we now see, nothing of reform . . . ought to be held improbable. *It is an age of Revolutions in which everything must be looked for.*' Revolution is a way of life, not the end of life. Revolution keeps man from selling his sou to the devil and living forever in the purgatory of Utopian security. Anyway, Premar isn't really revolution, Rais. It's rebellion. Rebellion is like a torpedo boat compared to a battleship, a fighter compared with a bomber. Revolution can't manipulate. Rebellion can."

You were listening, Ellen, standing in line, while the police fingerprinted us. "How can you be so calm?" you asked. "How can you philosophize? Daddy did this to us, and I hate him! I hate him!" I couldn't quiet you. Holding you, I suddenly felt your full weight against me. "Oh, Bren," you sighed, and slumped unconscious.

Even Captain Jaimie was frightened. "If Ellen dies, it will be on your head, yours and her father's," I told him as he drove the cruiser car in a hair-raising, mile-a-minute clip through traffic to University Hospital. You had regained consciousness, but you were gasping like a long-distance runner. My "I love you," even though you tried to smile reassurance at me, wouldn't restore the normal rhythm of your heart. We waited at the hospital until a resident cardiologist told us that your fibrillations were under control and told me I could see my wife the next day. My wife!

Halfway back to the Dorchester police station, Captain Jaimie abruptly asked, "Did he say your wife?"

"Yes, I guess he assumed we're married," I told him. I was hoping he wouldn't get to Dancer with the story before we would.

"You better keep your mitts off Ellen," Captain Jaimie said in his usual antagonistic way. "And don't give us any crap about this being the police's fault. Ellen was a nice girl, and healthier, until she got mixed up with you."

Of course, Laura too was being pushed around by the cops, but in the situation, I couldn't help her. Afterward she insisted that she was going ahead with the abortion, and I assumed when she got out of the hospital she'd telephone Rivke and Abe and let them in on her resurrection.

When the kids had finally drifted off to their rooms, I found her lying on our bed staring at the ceiling with a kind of hopeless expression on her face.

"Here comes Christ Himself," she said, and grinned at me in a halfhearted way. "I have to admire your guts. The world's caving in, but you're either an incurable optimist or you're too stupid to know it. Oh, Bren, what in hell am I going to do? I'm scared. No one in this whole damned world cares whether I'm alive or dead. After shedding some cr codile tears, Rocky will wonder why he had waited for fat —why he didn't divorce me long ago."

I lay down beside her. "If you go home to him in this gingham dress that Rai bought you, with no makeup and your hair askew, the old boy is going to think he's got a sexy new bride. For the first time in your life you're a woman, not a plastic doll. You were girlish when you were fifteen; you didn't wear a rubber mask then. Don't put it on again, ever. I like the open Laura; you're daring to be a child again. Rais likes you, too; and you did something for him. After St. Noir, you helped him to like himself. Merle understands and knows that he cares for you. If he didn't, he wouldn't want the baby. You discovered aspects of yourselves that you didn't know existed. So you've got two people who love you."

"Who else?"

"Me. For a few years, when Rivke was too busy, you were my loving mother. Though I might have rejected you, you imprinted yourself on my brain."

"Oh, crap! You're my brother, and Rais has Merle. He's with her now. To him I'm only the white woman he always wanted to screw."

"Don't kid yourself. Rais got rid of that hang-up on St. Noir when he was eighteen."

"Yes, he told me that. If you screw with a guy for three months on a desert island, you get to know him inside and out. Well, I'm leaving as soon as I get released from the hospital. If I stayed, I'd only mess Rais up."

"It may not be easy for her, but Merle won't love Rais any less if he goes to bed with you. She likes you."

"Bren, you're immoral! I'm not sleeping with Rais *ever* again, no matter what the circumstances." Laura was sobbing. "Oh, God! I wish I were dead. Why am I alive, anyway? From now on life will be just a repetition. I've done it all."

"Life has its own reasons. Why don't you do something none of your birdbrain jet-setters has done yet—have a black child?"

"Goddamn you! You think it's hilarious that I've been knocked up by a jig."

I slid down the zipper on her dress. "Amazing. How come you're not wearing a bra? I can see you now. In *Vogue*. Mother of the Year. Laura Stone nursing her black child on her teen-age-firm white tits, while her husband, the famous Rocky Stone, admiringly looks on. Rocky Stone told *Vogue* reporters today that his maternal grandmother was an African princess, which accounts for the color of their premenopausal child. Hey! It s twelve-thirty. Are we going to sleep together? Or are you retreating to one of Premar's privacy rooms?"

Laura was blushing as she pulled her dress over her head. "Those damned cops didn't give us time to get dressed," she said. "This bed's big enough. Do you mind? I'm too jittery to sleep alone."

I pulled off my Levi's. "Yippee. I'm going to sleep with my unwashed sister tonight." I kissed her cheek. "There's a million things you haven't done."

Laura shrugged. "Big deal—sleeping with your sibling." I was suddenly conscious of her as a naked woman. Her shoulders and her clavicle bridge were amazingly fragile and feminine. Her sun-bleached pubic hair floated on a warm chocolate sea of breasts, belly, and legs. I wondered how she would look in bed with Rocky, who sagged a little in the belly.

Laura's hand brushed against my middle. "Nice! My brother has an erection for me!" She laughed sweetly, almost secretly. She held my penis and said, "I suppose you'd make love with me, if I let you."

"You're practically insisting."

"What the hell, I'm getting a housecleaning tomorrow."

That sounded like an invitation, but I ignored it. She still held my hard-on, but her grasp was cool.

I touched the pronounced curve of her belly. "Your problem is that you've never experienced insecurity before. If Rocky leaves you, so what? You have a good piece of his millions. You have your health and a new *you*—which you could easily develop into breathtaking woman."

"I'd trade it all for someone I could hold onto. You don't believe me, do you? When we were sailing to Puerto Rico I offered Rais this diamond to hock somewhere so we could go back to one of the small islands, where I'd have the baby and maybe another. I lived thirty-eight years and finally slept with a laughing man." She was silent for a while.

"I can't believe that you're really so damned altruistic," she went on. "How did you ever get the way you are? Abe never gave a damn about how the other half lived. Who are you rebelling against? You don't have to enjoy insecurity. You could leave this Premar business, and the even more Utopian Confam. That, Bren, is a daydream, a pipe dream. You're asking people to share the miserable income they have, but they'd rather play the lottery all their lives. *The Game*—dream of the jackpot. You'd better wake up. You armchair liberals keep talking about community and sharing, but that's not for you. No one wants to give up their privacy. Maybe you can con the kids, but you won't live to see the day that Ellen's mother is sitting in a communal tub with Captain Jaimie, Rais, and her best friend from the church sewing circle. Wake up! You're sitting on a time bomb. Lighting another isn't going to stop the fuse from burning on the first one." Laura kissed my nose. "You big dumb bunny. I'll tell you what I'll do. Get out of this now and I'll give you a million dollars. You and Ellen can join the jet set and fuck your way around the world."

"You better stay and see the fun," I told her. "A million dollars would only screw up my life. Why not give it to the consortium? It's a drop in the bucket to what they need, but God knows it would help. Right now, for example, we need a couple of Winnebago trailers—the kind that sleep six. The kids are on a rough schedule. If we could let twelve of them take off on occasional weekends, they could go skiing or to New York."

Laura looked at me incredulously. "You're not listening to me."

"Sure, I am." I grabbed a report, *The Educational Significance of the Future*, off the night table. "Hère, a guy named Harold Shane, who teaches education at Indiana University, wrote this. Since we're evidently going to stay awake all night, I might as well read you a couple of things. . . . But first, let this trickle through your brain. It seems to me that the happiest time you've had in your life was when you discovered how to be intimate with another person and learned to accept your interdependency. You're one person who can afford privacy until it comes out of your ears, but what has your privacy given you? Loneliness. There's a lot of people in the world who are discovering that they'll be happy to compromise. Read Ivan Illich on convival production. Do we have to devote our lives to producing junk? Rich people buy condominiums. All they get back are privacy and loneliness. What a deal! Poor people will be able to buy into a Confam, and in return they'll get economic and social security—the security of a caring group. Imagine the world with hundreds of thousands of Confamiliaums, and the knowledge that as a member of a Confamiliaum you can change your residence, or take a vacation and live in another society of people with common objectives." I knew that I was haranguing Laura, but she didn't seem to mind. "Anyway, I find it emotionally more satisfying to chase the pot of gold at the end of a rainbow than have it in my hands."

"How can you say you've done it all, Laura, when the whole civilized world is in the throes of constructing new human relationships? It's an exciting time to be alive. If you really wanted to, you could be in the thick of this excitement, fumbling for answers with a lot of people who care. What do you want? To be like Jackie Onassis—another of the bored rich who waste their lives away? Listen to this. Here are Shane's ten major problems confronting society." Laura was shaking her head in amazement as I read to her.

The crisis of crises: Among the ominous socio-political and economic indicators are the threat of bankruptcy in some U.S. cities; sustained international breaches in law and order; many forms of dissent, inflation, unemployment, racial tension. *The credibility*

gap: Even the most legally constituted authorities—
the President, law enforcement agencies, parents,
teachers—have had their authority ignored, denied
or threatened. *Institutional overload*: The growing
inability of institutions such as schools and courts of
law to adapt to their new roles. *Disagreement over
the "good life"*: Lack of agreement as to the best
quality of life—the nature of the "Good Society."
Economic, political, ethnic, ecological, industrial,
religious and business cleavages run deep. *The value
crisis*: Today there is a violent value crisis which
leaves many people bewildered as to what is "right"
and "wrong," with respect to such matters as drug
abuse, pornography, the role of women, the sexual
mores, the functions of the church. *Equity versus
Equality*: Is merely equal treatment fair and just, or
does justice reside in different treatment for the gifted,
the disadvantaged, the culturally gifted, the handi-
capped, the very young, and the very old? *Rejection
of egalitariansim*: A large majority conceive of democracy as a foundation for upward mobility; a
means of rising above one's father's station in life.
Neither democracy nor U.S. education has an adequate coping doctrine with which to confront the
inevitable resentment when they begin to realize that
they have failed to find room at the top. *Lack of a
future focused role image for youth*: Too little has
been done in family life and schooling to help children
and youth develop a satisfying personal-vocational
self image. *Insensitivity to changing patterns of survival behavior*: Our survival today depends on an
increasing degree of mutual understanding, empathy,
ability to reach agreement through inter-action and
reasonable compromise rather than by resort to force.
The haves and the have nots: The world *have* nations
are on a collision course with the impoverished Third
nations. We must recognize that there are limits to
affluence, to technological exploitation and to population increase.

Laura was leaning on her elbow, her breasts dangling,
watching me and listening. "You really are crazy," she

said. "No one, not even Great God Gattman, can straighten out this fucked-up world."

"I can't help myself. I believe in rainbows." I kissed one of her breasts and then tasted it. "You don't taste like a sister," I told her. "But you do taste sweaty."

"That's not just sweat." She laughed. "That's salty gut-twisting fear. While you were gone with Ellen to the hospital, a female reporter, an old bag from the *Globe*, cornered me. She asked if I was a Compar, and if not, what was my function in the commune. Endless drivel and crap that I tried to counter. Then she took another tack. 'You have a lovely tan, Mrs. Gattman.' She purred, 'You *are* Bren Gattman's wife, aren't you?'

" 'I'm his sister,' I told her. There was a glint in her eye, her ass was wiggling like an alley cat about to pounce. 'Funny,' she said, 'despite your modest dress, you look different somehow. Not low-income Dorchester. I keep thinking I've seen your face before. Bren Gattman had a sister who died in an airplane crash, last July, didn't he?' 'Sweetie,' I said, 'you're on the wrong slalom. I'm a stripper in the Combat Zone. Bren and I were fucking. The police had to pull us apart.'" Laura giggled. "Boy, that popped her arteries. Right now I'll bet she's in the *Globe* morgue comparing photographs of me. If I had the nerve, I'd pass up the abortion and get the hell out of here tonight." Laura changed the subject. "I don't see how you ever make love with anybody. You yak so damned much you could never stay erect."

"Don't kid yourself. I can do two things at once."

"Would you really make love with your sister?"

"I'm going to have to if you keep playing with my prick."

"Should we go down to the tubs and wash first?"

"I think I'd enjoy you better sweaty." I kissed her lips, and as I did so, I expected to see Rivke come charging into the room.

She snuggled against my neck and said, "What the hell!" Then she climbed on top of me and guided my penis inside her. She looked down at me like a bad kid who couldn't believe she was really doing what she was doing.

"Who's laying whom?" I laughed, and matched the rhythm of her swinging buttocks.

"Oh, Bren, you do feel good. It doesn't matter, does it? Would Ellen be shocked?"

"Honey, enjoy, enjoy. It's not a bad thing to like your sister or your brother. You're not evil, you're Laura, who finally dares to surrender herself. If you get that message across to Rocky, he'll spend more time in bed with you than he does making money."

She climaxed wildly, and lay flattened out on top of me. "Did you come?" she whispered.

"Only a holy tantric guru could withstand that assault. It was nice, Laura." I rolled her on her side and held her in my arms.

"Maybe tomorrow I'll fly back to Rocky in New York," she said. Her eyes were closed. "Maybe I'll just tell him the whole story before that mouse on the *Globe* discovers that Laura Stone is alive and well and in Boston. Jesus, what would Mother think? I made love with my brother. What would my kids think?"

I kissed her nose. "Stop bugging yourself. You made love with your brother, and you've made love with a black man. Making love isn't like killing someone."

From the journal of Kathy Flaherty, December, the first year of Premar.

I'm miles behind in this journal, so thank the Lord that it's a cold, rainy Sunday and I can do some writing. Trying to relearn my life and discover how to be intimate and trusting with a man isn't enough. But on top of that, keeping pace with the Human Values seminar would leave anyone gasping. And Merle, Keeper of the Premar Journals, hounds us to turn them in on time. The theory of learning which Premar pushes is that the best way to assimilate our interpersonal growth as well as make the H.V. seminars part of our lives is first, by "teaching" (or talking with) our roommates and our friends, and second, by being forced to correlate and evaluate what happens to us by writing it down.

Meditation might be another way. Bren is always pushing tantric meditation, but Ellen laughed last time he did

and told us even he can't last long enough to achieve nirvana the tantric way. As if we didn't have enough to read,
Bren bought four copies of *The Art of Tantra* by Phillip
Rawson and gave them to Premar. The book costs too
much for each of us to have a copy, so Bren asks that we
all read it, by couples, in twelve weeks. Which, I guess,
makes some sense, since the book is the study of an ancient Hindu religion which extolled the female principle
(Sakti) and used sexual intercourse—with a man and a
woman merged for hours at a time without climaxing—as a
way of experiencing nirvana.

Despite the fact that our Human-Values book this week
is *The Urban Wilderness* by Sam Bass Warner, Jr. (a
study of American cities to give us perspective on Confam), Rais thought we'd understand the need for Confams
better if we'd read Vance Packard's *Nation of Strangers*;
also *The Mating Trade*, by John Godwin; and *We, the
Lonely People*, by Ralph Keyes. (None of these are basic
Premar books.) On top of all that reading, Mohammed
has gobbled *The Art of Tantra*, reading it in utter amazement in two days. Now, though he admits he doesn't understand it all, he's my happy teacher. I told him I can't
imagine any woman who wouldn't be a delighted pupil!

"The idea," he said, "is that I insert my penis very
slowly and we stay together for hours. Without moving,
we float off into infinity." Lying beside me, Mohammed
had shown me the many pictures in the book. They made
his point beyond any doubt. "Of course, you have to be
moist enough to let me in."

"Now what?" I asked, enjoying the fullness of him. I
was kissing him wildly.

"Not so passionate." He sighed. I could tell Mohammed
wasn't going to last any hour. "Kathy, you've got to be
cool."

"With you kissing my breasts?"

"You're right. Just close your eyes. When you look at
me like that, I'm not sure I won't pop off. We're not supposed to excite each other. Tantra means a weaving together, so that we slowly feel the essence of each other, so
that finally I don't know me from you, and vice versa."

I gathered that weaving in the tantra sense didn't mean
moving my hips. After a few minutes I told him, "If this is
tantra, I like it. I'm falling asleep."

"That won't work either," Mohammed said.

"Why?"

"Because I'm not a yoga yet. I can't tell my mind to keep my big bamboo erect."

So I didn't weave, I undulated. But neither of us could stand that. Then, after a while, we gave up and climaxed together. Mohammed says he never feels so good as when we make love at least twice a day, so we agreed to try the system again in the afternoon.

"I've got a lot of reading," I told him. "Maybe this afternoon you should keep your mind on garbage." Gosh, I really like Mohammed. Every time he looks at me with his brown eyes, merry dancing question marks, I want to hug him. He still says that he's going to be a doctor. Rais convinced him that the sanitation job he's doing is related to medicine and he should approach it creatively. Doctors should be concerned with the future of garbage and sewage. Rais told Mohammed about the Odessa Project. Conceived by an M.D., Dr. Geoffrey Stanford, the plan is to refertilize the plains of Odessa, Texas, with the city's own waste products and create a new topsoil by plowing cellulose materials which have a special kind of organism in them into the garbage and then fertilizing the whole thing with sludge, a product of sewage, and eventually transforming the desert into huge fertile forests and gardens. Mohammed became so interested that he borrowed the Premar Econo van and six of us toured all the sewage and disposal plants and dumps in the vicinity of Boston. Now Mohammed isn't sure. He thinks maybe he should study to become a sanitation engineer.

Reading books, waiting on tables at Howard Johnson's (my thirteen-week work schedule before I start secretarial school in February), making love, and meeting each day with the kids in the Human-Values seminar isn't a dizzy enough schedule. Now Bren has asked all the Premars to participate in the Confamiliaum interviews. Our Human-Values meetings are temporarily oriented around the whole area of community. Can our psychic needs for community and sharing be merged with our needs for privacy? Aren't a great many of our privacy needs conditioned into us by a capitalist society? Rais used the word "indoctrinated," but he withdrew it until we could explore the kind of people we really are. How do we climb over the walls we erect around ourselves? Can we live healthy lives without sharing ourselves?

We agreed upon a target date—the week after Thanks-giving—to complete the family interviews. By that time, working in two-couple teams (Mohammed and I are paired with Samantha and Julie), each team would have interviewed four of the families living in the tenement houses on Warren and Benson roads. Before we started, we were given a one-week in-depth study of the Confamil-iaum proposal. Mother of God! I've got so much stuff whirling in my head that I'm jumping ahead of myself. Maybe I'd better back up and start from the beginning.

Saturday, after the police raid, Margaret and Phil Ten-hausen arrived with some people from the consortium. I think Phil wanted to have a private go-around with Bren, Rais, and Merle, but Bren insists that we air all of our problems together. "If the Premars aren't involved and don't have faith in what we're doing, we won't survive anyway," he told Phil. "I don't want to have any discussion behind their backs."

"Some of the consortium think the Topham's Corner Premar Commune is already hanging by its thumbs." Phil's eyes wandered around the dayroom as if he were speaking to us individually. "We're not worried about the charges of immorality. Topham's Corner may have the distinction of being the first Premar to attempt to exorcise the sex devils, but we are well prepared to fight the legal challenges. As you know, you've all been released on your own recognizance. Yesterday our lawyers asked the court to dismiss all charges. A more dangerous situation is that you, Bren, seem to be involved in a personal vendetta with Dancer O'Day." Phil was smiling, but he was pretty seri-ous. And several others from the consortium looked grim. "You're being attacked as a Jewish Svengali who is work-ing hand-in-hand with Rais Daemon, the communist leader of an aborted revolution. If that isn't enough, your sister, who had been reported killed in an air crash—the wife of a very wealthy man—was flushed out of the tubs the night of the raid. In the past few days the local papers haven't had room for war, violence, or politics on the front page—only sex. Yesterday, furthermore, you had the *chutzpah* to tell me on the telephone that you're planning to involve the Premars with your Confamiliaum proposal and are going to try to get some residents of Topham's Corner to participate. It seems to some of us, Bren, that instead of putting out the fire, you and Rais are throwing gasoline on it."

"Not really," Rais responded. "While I've only been here a week, I'm really quite impressed with Premar. I know you think Confam is a backhanded way to try some of our own theories, but in any community of working-class people, if Premar and the outraged middle class are even going to meet, it will be on the pivot of Confam. We believe that Confamiliaum is a way of life that will appeal to many Americans. For many of them it could be a re-birth, a new lease on life, and an assurance of economic survival.

"But first, we can put out one fire. Bren's sister isn't here. The day after the raid, she flew to her family's home in New Hope, New York. Eventually, I'm sure she'll tell the reporters what happened—that I rescued her from that plane crash. We were amazed to discover that we had a common friend, her brother, Bren Gattman. It was only natural that we flew here from Puerto Rico rather than to New York."

Margaret Tenhausen was obviously entranced by Rais' clipped British accent and his powerful six-and-a-half-foot body. "That doesn't explain the three-month hiatus," she said.

Rais shrugged. Raising his eyebrows so that the kids would know that he was lying, and hopefully wouldn't sab-otage him, he said, "Laura was badly injured. We landed on a nearly deserted island north of St. Noir. A black family nursed her back to health. As for me—and what-ever unfortunate publicity my activities have given Pre-mar—you knew about 'Walk Before God' before you telephoned me in St. Noir. What happened on St. Noir is over the dam. I'm not the kind of radical who be-lieves in bloodshed, or I wouldn't be here. The community concepts of Confamiliaum are embedded in my proposal for St. Noir." Rais laughed. "The world wasn't ready for a new kind of Caribbean island. It may not be ready for Confamiliaum—or Premar, for that matter—but that isn't stopping the consortium from trying."

"You win," Margaret said. "We've got more than enough problems nationwide with Premar without spend-ing all our time on this one. Maybe it's a good idea to invite some of the neighborhood husbands and wives to your Human-Values sessions, but for God's sake, don't try to sell them communal nude bathing. That would be too much."

"Don't worry," Merle told her. "We've decided that we need an open neighborhood forum—a public platform not only to counteract Dancer O'Day and his cohorts but also to show Premar in action. Bill Isaacs, who owns the old Strand Theater, agrees with Bren that it should belong to Topham's Corner. Fifty years ago it cost nearly a million dollars to build. It couldn't be replaced for three million today. He's willing to sell it for forty thousand dollars. One focus of the forum will be to raise the money for a theaterowners' cooperative to belong to the people of Topham's Corner. The other will be to show them the video movies we're going to make of Premar." Merle chuckled at the shocked surprise on Harry Littleton's face. He's attorney for the consortium. "We have to show them the tubs, Harry, and the naked bathing. It's too late now to try to conceal our communal baths. But in the next couple of weeks, if we can make our preliminary probe into the families on Benson and Warren roads, we may be able to announce some enthusiastic interest in a parallel concept to Premar-Confamiliaum, with the tubs on a purely voluntary basis." Merle grinned.

Marion Swenson said, "All of you have so damned much energy! The consortium should be thrilled. My only advice is to underplay sex, particularly the Premar roommate system. I haven't read your Confamiliaum proposal, but I'll warn you in advance, if the Confam community involves sexual exchange, then forget it. You'll never sell that to Topham's Corner or Middle America."

"Don't worry," Bren told her. "For the older generation Confam is based on community and monogamy, with very little relinquishing of familial privacy."

"I don't like the glint in your eye when you say 'older generation.'" Margaret Tenhausen laughed. "So just make sure it stays in your eye." She asked Bren whether he and Ellen were married.

"I am now a Catholic-Jew," Bren answered her. "If you don't believe me, ask Father Tim O'Hara. And don't worry. Ellen will be out of the hospital next week. We're going to make her dean of the bedchamber—her own—and keep her very much subdued. She goes back to the hospital in February for a commissurotomy. The doctors

believe they can open up her artery and that they won't
have to use an artificial valve."

But nobody associated with Bren can stay subdued very
long. Ellen wasn't home from the hospital more than a
day when she heard the tape Bren had made after the police raid. Like me, most of the kids were shocked when
they discovered that Bren had made love with his sister.
Incest is scarier than living unmarried with a guy. Ellen
asked whether Bren was just an exhibitionist, flaunting all
the rules of society. I guess I wouldn't have been so cool
as she was. After all, she had been married to Bren
scarcely a week, and he's off screwing his own sister. It
bugged Merle, too. All of us spent one evening discussing
it in an open Human-Values session. Merle led off with
the key question. "Basically, Bren, I want to know what
the hell you thought you were trying to prove by telling it
all on tape. If you did screw Laura, and long ago Ellen
and I guessed you had a thing about your sister, why did
you have to advertise it?"

When he answered, Bren was unusually serious. "It could
be, Ellen, that you and Merle are right. When I was three
or four and Laura was twelve or thirteen, I really liked
her. But a few years later, after my mother started aiming
Laura toward a rich marriage, her personality changed.
Or maybe the age difference began to separate us. Anyway, by the time she married Rocky, I really disliked her,
not because I was jealous of her sexually, but rather because she never failed to sit in judgment on me—'her
completely mad messiah brother.'

"Then she arrived here with Rais. To me it was as if
she had experienced a conversion—not to religion or God,
but to her own reality. Maybe it happened because she
held hands with death, or as I'd prefer to believe, she had
discovered the joy of giving love. Over and above the fun
and exhilaration of sex with Rais, she discovered that she
could really care for a black man. Laura has finally become a woman." Bren stopped, lost in thought for a moment. "Okay," he said finally, "I'm not avoiding the fact
that I had sexual intercourse with my sister. And I'm not
going to try to make a case for incest, though I believe it's
a common experience. Why are we afraid of a naturally
sensuous feeling between parents and children or brothers
and sisters? Isn't it a good thing if we can guide a young
person through his childhood without denying his erotic

needs? If a sexual experience occurs willingly between a brother and sister of nearly the same age, why should it be so tragic? Because of the potential of pregnancy? That's the only sound reason. But sisters and brothers are young girls and boys, too, and the knowledge that they should be given of birth control at an early age is a new factor in a potential sibling relationship."

Bren shrugged, again pondering his feelings. "At a particular time in her life my sister needed to lose herself in a warm, protective male embrace. I can assure you that my tape doesn't convey how distraught Laura was—is. I think she wants to keep her baby. For Laura, the plane crash and being pregnant have the inevitability of karma, something that is written in the stars. On the other hand, she's trying to cope with something that every one of you in Premar has to come to terms with. You are, or will be, living in close proximity with a black person. Should you decide to marry a friend of the other race, would you be willing to have a child, knowing the problems of adjustment the child will have and that you would have as parents? Many people believe that creating two separate worlds, a black one and a white one, they won't have to answer questions like that. But Premar believes that if you avoid these questions you will have less understanding of yourself and hence be relatively more ignorant. This goes beyond Socrates' 'Know thyself' and adds the dimension 'Free thyself'. Not to do your own thing, but to dare to stand alone.

"So it would have been possible, I suppose, to respond to Laura's need by being a grim moralist. While I was lying beside her, for the life of me I couldn't figure out any good reason for not giving her the affection and support she needed. That this culminated in the merger of my penis and her vagina did no harm to Ellen. Not loving Laura wouldn't have stopped Ellen's heart from fibrillating. I held Laura, and she held me. Maybe it was a way of temporarily escaping reality. But isn't that way better than alcohol or other drugs? Later, when we reached a climax and were wondering about ourselves, I told her that I loved her, and I loved Ellen, and I, too, was insufficient to myself—that I had come close to the breaking point. So, I'm not ashamed. I don't think Laura's ashamed, either. Momentarily we were providing each other someone to lean on. She knows that two men really like her. Rais and me."

While Bren was talking, he was sprawled against the big sofa in the dayroom with one arm entwined around Ellen's legs. Ellen was propped up on pillows behind him, and all the kids could see the warm expression of love on her face, and the tears in her eyes. She managed to smile at him and ruffle his hair. "Oh, Bren," she said, "when we arrive in hell, make sure that we stay close together. I don't want to miss the conversation when you try to convince the devil that you're in the wrong place."

Gosh, if I don't skip some things, especially writing about making love with Mohammed, I'll never get caught up in this journal. But since he's lying in bed, concentrating on that tantra book again, I guess the best and most sensible thing to do is *do it*, and not write about it!

Excerpted from stenotapes made and transcribed by Kathy Flaherty, November, the first year of Premar.

We did it! In less than two weeks our twelve teams have interviewed all the families on Warren and Benson roads. What's more, Bren was right. When we compared notes in our H.V. meetings, only the Dohertys, who live in D-10, and the Lees, who live in L-36, were really upset about Premar or thought we were completely whacked out. Some of the other families might not be waving flags for a Confam, but there was plenty of interest. Most of the families were intensely curious about Premar. Some of the mothers didn't object, especially because at first they thought their children would be near home. We had to tell them that with only two exceptions, myself and Samantha Brown, all the other Premars came from different cities and towns, the reason being that Premar represents a definite nest-breaking time in a young person's life, and this was a lot easier when father and mother weren't on hand to moralize. What's more, the theory of Premar was that all youngsters should have an opportunity to live in different cities from where they were born. Samantha and I were exceptions—me, because I had no family, and Samantha, I guess, because hers didn't count for much. It's funny, most of the fathers are against Premar—especially for their daughters. They thought a girl would get completely screwed-up if she went to bed with too many men. I think they're really afraid that women may get to think they have as much right to sexual variety as any man. But the Premars had been warned not to argue too much. "Most people don't want you to agree with them one hundred percent," Bren said, "but if you want to convince a person, go along with him at least eighty or ninety percent."

I guess I better get these pages in sequence. When Bren discovered I had taken a course in stenotyping in high school, he borrowed a stenotype from a local school "to keep me in practice," and so I could prepare transcriptions of the Human-Values meetings on Confam, the idea being that we would have the typed pages for immediate reference. Yesterday, after I was late in getting home from HoJo's I rushed up from the tubs with only a towel wrapped around me. Rais says he's sure I'm the only person in the world who has stenotyped naked. But the damned towel wouldn't stay in place, and the boys yelled foul when I tried to cover myself. Bren said he enjoyed the serious concentration on my face—a sort of minor-key melody in contrast with my bobbling breasts.

The weekend after the raid, Bren, Rais, and Merle worked in the dayroom with street maps and air photos of Topham's Corner. They were already pretty much convinced that the sixteen tenements on Warren and Benson roads, which intersect into a thoroughfare on Felton Street and form a huge T with the Premar buildings at the head of it, has a good topographical relationship to Premar that would make it the ideal location for Confam #1, Inc. Rais pointed out in the photographs that he and Bren had taken, and which he showed on our opaque projector, that the back yards of these houses, separated by about thirty-five feet, or the length of one house, were boarded up wastelands of junk, straggly gardens, and heaven trees. The front porches face into a similar row of tenements. All of their front porches face across the narrow street toward each other. Both sides of Benson and Warren roads are lined with automobiles day and night. A few straggly trees planted by the city are ready to give up and die. Altogether, it's a kind of ugly, barren place.

"If we can get the people in Topham's Corner interested," Rais said, "we could redesign the whole area. We could create central parking and then we could dig up a lot of these intersecting streets and plant trees and create walking paths and game-playing areas in front of the houses. We could have curling, and bowling greens and bocci and horseshoes and croquet, and for the older kids, volleyball courts and basketball courts. In the summer the older people who didn't feel too active could sit on their front porches and watch each other and their friends and young people playing together. Kids would have a place to congregate and not have to end up hanging around the Papa Gino's and Howdy Burger franchises. In one portion of these back yards we could teach the families how to nurture the earth, revitalize it, like we'll be doing this spring in the Premar back yards. The members of a Confamiliaum could raise a lot of their own food."

Bren cheered Rais on. "A great idea," he said. "Who knows, we may be able to resurrect the old front-porch canvas hammock and swing. In the summer, when the old folks have gone to bed, the teen-agers will be able to discover each other—lying together in a hammock. Ellen, have you ever made love in an old-fashioned hammock? We've got to try it. It's a nice erotic idea."

Ellen shook her head in helpless wonder, while Merle carried pins to puncture balloons. "Someone must have ripped off your brains," she said. "We haven't even tackled the interviews with these families, and the two of you are tearing up Topham's Corner and rebuilding it to your daydream of some Massachusetts paradise. You're both far-out."

Bren laughed. "We're going to create human living environments so that people can learn again how to interact with each other. Let the middle class have their suburbs, we'll have the best of both worlds. When our Confamiliaum members come home from work, they'll enjoy their home environment so much, be so involved in it, that it will become a central point in their lives. Getting in an automobile and driving long distances to amusement areas

MEMBERS OF TOPHAM'S CORNER CONFAMILIAUM #1

FLAT	NAMES OF ADULTS	AGES Adults	AGES Children	RELIGIOUS OR ETHNIC BACKGROUND	NATURE OF JOB AND HIGHEST SINGLE INCOME AFTER TAXES	
A-1	ABUCEWICZ, CHARLES-GRACE	32-30	2-3-5	Polish	Secretary	9,000
A-2	JOHNSTON, MARY	37	7-9	Anglo	Clerk	7,500
A-3	BAMBETA, THOMAS-HELEN	45-40	16-18	Greek	Filling Station	8,500
B-4	SCALESE, JAMES-PATRICIA	30-28	2	Italian	Data Processing	9,000
B-5	INGRAHAM, NEIL-DOROTHY	59-52	0	Anglo	Guard	8,000
B-6	MAHONEY, DANIEL-CHARLOTTE	60-55	0	Irish	Welfare	4,000
C-7	McKENZIE, THOMAS-GLADYS	42-41	12-15	Scotch	Postman	10,000
C-8	GODFRY, RICHARD-GERTRUDE	40-38	6-8-10	Afro-American	Mechanic	9,000
C-9	GROSSMAN, HELEN-ABRAHAM	36-37	8-9	Jewish	Salesman	9,500
D-10	DOHERTY, NANCY-HENRY	36-39	6-8-12	Irish	Bartender	10,000
D-11	DALEY, JEROME-FRANCES	52-50	17	Irish	Telephone Co.	10,500
D-12	ADAMEK, MARY	67	0	Polish	Welfare	4,000
E-13	CHAN, ROBERT-SALLY	29-27	3-6	Chinese	Salesman	8,500
E-14	IVANOWSKY, WALDO-MARGERY	65-58	18	Polish	Social Security	6,500
E-15	YANG, CHARLES-YIN	39-36	5-8	Chinese	Waiter	8,000
F-16	FITZGERALD, HENRY-MARGARET	50-50	15-18-19	Irish	Electrician	11,000
F-17	BARONE, RUTH	2?	3-7	Italian	Welfare	4,000
F-18	JURKEWICZ, PETER-JOAN	36-34	3-8	Polish	Janitor	9,500
G-19	DELISA, ANTHONY-MARGERET	70-68	0	Italian	Social Security	5,000
G-20	BERKOWITZ, GLORIA-MICHAEL	59-53	0	Jewish	Postal Worker	9,000
G-21	GIUSTI, SALVATORE-MARY	38-36	1-4-6	Italian	Airplane Loader	10,000
H-22	CARNEY, MARGARET	42	10-15	Irish	Welfare	4,000
H-23	O'LEARY JAMES-ETHEL THOMAS-HENRIETTA	60-65 36-35	8-12	Irish	Truck Driver	9,000
H-24	CAYMAN, HENRY-ROSE	28-24	3	Anglo	Plumber	12,000
I-25	CAREY, RICHARD-ALICE	45-36	6-12	Irish	Postal Worker	10,000
I-26	LEVY, SAMUEL-ESTHER	39-37	8-10	Jewish	Gas Company	11,500
I-27	O'TOOLE, WILLIAM-MARY	51-48	15-18	Irish	Bus Driver	9,000
J-28	KAMPARADES, THEODORE-NINA	35-30	6-8	Greek	Barber	10,000
J-29	BALUKUNA, ROBERT-ALICE	65-60	0	Polish	Social Security	6,000
J-30	McCARTHY, HENRY	74	0	Irish	Social Security	4,500
K-31	ALVAREZ, JOSE-ANNA	39-34	4-6-8	Puerto Rican	Sales	12,000
K-32	BAKER, HARRY-KATHERINE	37-35	6-9	Jamaican	Carpenter	9,500
K-33	CALMAN, HENRIETTA-SOPHIA	41-65	8-12	Afro-American	Mechanic	7,500
L-34	BAKER, DOROTHY-ANNA	39-31	10-15	Afro-American	Typist	8,000
L-35	GOULD, MARTHA	28	3-5	Jamaican	Welfare	4,000
L-36	LEE, ROBERT-MARTHA	58-54	15-17	Afro-American	Steam Fitter	9,500
M-37	HOULIHAN, JAMES-MARGIE	45-43	13-16	Irish	Pressman	9,000
M-38	MAHONEY, ELLIOT-MARY	32-28	3-4	Irish	Salesman	9,500
M-39	DUGGAN, WILLIAM-ANDREA	71-68	0	Irish	Social Security	5,000
N-40	DeROSA, PETER-MARIA	45-36	6-12-13	Puerto Rican	Baker	10,500
N-41	DONOVAN, JOHN-MARY-THERESA	39-36-60	8-5	Irish	Salesman	8,500
N-42	MARCHITELLI, ANTHONY-RITA	37-38-70	5-9	Italian	Clerk	7,800
O-43	SANTA, LILLIAN	36	6-8-10	Puerto Rican	Welfare	4,000
O-44	DOMINGO, JUAN-SEMINA	46-40	12-14-15-17	Puerto Rican	Cook	8,500
O-45	NAZZARO, FRANK-FLORENCE	44-40	12-13-15	Italian	Mechanic	9,000
P-46	McCARTHY, WINIFRED	68	0	Irish	Social Security	4,500
P-47	DOYLE PATRICK-MARTHA GEORGE-HELEN	45-44 75-73	15-16-17	Irish	Fireman	12,000
P-48	DONOVAN, JAMES-BERTHA	29-27	2-3-5	Irish	Trucker	9,500
	TOTALS	94	87			$384,800

CONFAMILIAUM #1
TOPHAM'S CORNER

and parks crowded with strangers they can never know will be dull by comparison."

Merle shook her head. "Bren, you sound like an old-time revival preacher. Before we walk the sawdust trail with you, will you please tell us where you're going to park all the automobiles that clutter the streets today?"

"Easy," Rais said. "We'll get Dancer to introduce a bill into City Council which will close off Topham's Corner to all through traffic. Thousands of automobiles traveling through here are headed for homes in the suburbs. When we've got that traffic eliminated, we'll close off the main thoroughfare, Franklin Road, and use it for automobile parking for residents of Topham's Corner only. From the parking areas we'll run minibuses which will drop people off near their houses. Minibuses and bicycles will be the only form of transportation in the area."

Merle threw up her hands when she heard Dancer O'Days' name. "Okay, be skeptical," Rais replied. "Dancer's got sex on his brain, granted, but he's running for mayor, and Topham's Corner represents some of his constituency. So maybe we'll have some leverage against him. But meanwhile we'd better concentrate on Confamiliaum Number One.

"Billy Rainbow has worked hard to check out the ownership of these sixteen tenements, and found out that only two are owner-occupied." Rais passed out a mimeographed sheet to all of the Premars (see pages 262–263). Headed up "Confamiliaum #1, Topham's Corner," it showed the location of the houses with a listing of the families living in the various flats. The tenements were lettered from A through P, and each flat in the total group had been given a number. "By using a street-directory census and comparing this with the telephone book, we've been able to identify the families and the approximate number of adults and children in each of the forty-eight flats. The house lettered E is owned by a Polish family, Alice and Robert Balakuna. They live on the second floor. Interestingly, the families on the third and fourth, floor E13 and E15, are Chinese. Usually Chinese congregate. Maybe the Chans and the Yangs are rebels. Anyway, we don't want to lose them. The house lettered J is owned by Henry McCarthy. He's a widower and is seventy-four years old. All the other houses are owned by three different realty companies that rent the flats at rates averag-

ing one hundred and fifty dollars a month. Little or no re-
pairs have been made to most of these premises in the past
five years.'"

"We live in a profit society," Bren explained. "Until we
find some other way for people to function together—equit-
ably, according to their abilities—the basic areas of food
and shelter must either be socialized or profit must dominate the tenant-landlord relationship. Hundreds of years
ago the landlord was a squire or a baron or an Earl. He
obtained his land through birth, or through valor in service
of the king, or through political influence. At first, he
might not have charged the tenant rent to use his land,
and he permitted the tenant to build his own cottage on
it. The tenant's obligation was to provide the landlord with
food and serve in his army, presumably for mutual protection, but more often to aid the landowner in his military
conquests. The tenant sold his freedom for security. Today
the tenants—you and I—still trade our labor for security.
But even more than our great-great-grandfathers, we are
owned by the landlords, because our forebears at least still
had the skills to live off the land and grow and kill their
own food. They had no 'learned' needs like soap and
toothpaste and deodorants, for example, so they were much
more independent. In essence they could tell the landlord
to fuck off!" Bren has unexpected ways of grabbing the
kids' attention, and those words brought down the house.

"Today the economic system has made us practically totally interdependent. A few people try to drop out and go
back to the land, but no one is really prepared to live so
primitively. Even if they were, the availability of wild
game as a main source of food is strictly limited. The landlord is now called the Establishment, but the Establishment isn't easy to define. The landlord has expanded his
wealth to include buildings and machinery. And now he is
partially dependent on you, the tenant, to buy his 'things.'
To make you willing robots, unable to live without his
'things', he indoctrinates you by advertising—thousands of
impressions a day. And this is a game that you've been
told you can play, too. Your security needs make you dependent on the Establishment, but your desire for things
makes you part of the Establishment. You finally *become*
the things you need. So the landlords, who own the land,
and own the buildings, and the machinery, hire managers
who give you a job making all these things. They not only

provide the house you no longer know how to build, but the food you haven't the faintest idea how to grow.

"To make matters worse, while the new-style landlord depends on you for his wealth and power, he's less dependent on you and me, as individuals, than the old earls and barons were on their serfs. The reason is that there are many more millions of producing units like us than there were tillers of the soil like our forefathers. From a capitalistic, production point of view, each of us is little more than an interchangeable part, and now the parts bin is overflowing, overpopulated. Even when the landlords manage to destroy millions of us in wars, there are still more than enough parts remaining. Subtract a billion of us, and those who remain can produce more things than all of us together can trade for our labor. Of course, you may not have all the food and shelter and things that you personally need, but neither the landlord alone nor he and you working together can satisfy all your learned need for 'things.' Not even if we worked eighty hours a week. If somehow the landlords could figure out how to distribute the money so everyone could have all his needs fulfilled, that wouldn't work either, because then no one would strive hard enough. To keep the system functioning, the tenant must be dissatisfied.

"The money that the landlord gives you is simply a unit to measure the amount of your labor that you sell him, plus a profit in return. But the landlord is caught on the treadmill too, because unless he keeps paying you more, and keeps your productivity growing, and helps make the gross national product larger each year, and can outprice his competitors, his profits will disappear and he will go bankrupt. So, while a few million of the landlords in the United States may have enough money to buy all the things they want, most of the landlords soon discover they haven't time, won't live long enough to enjoy all these gadgets and things. Finally, the landlords end up in as big an emotional stew as their tenants. They too begin to wonder: Why in hell are we living this way?"

Bren laughed. "Merle was asking about automobiles. The landlords have designed our working environment so poorly that millions of working men need an automobile whose sole reason for being is to get one person from his home to the place where he works, and home again. Does that automobile give the working man any enjoyment?

Ten to fifteen percent of after-tax income is spent for that 'second' automobile. To pay the depreciation, the excise taxes, the gasoline, and the insurance for this vehicle that contributes nothing to his life, the working man actually endangers his life by trapping himself in an avalanche of other human beings all caught on the same treadmill, and he must work ten percent of his annual working year, at least twenty-eight full days, for no joy whatsoever! How much of your life do you want to waste working for a vehicle that does nothing but take you back and forth from work? Right now Americans owe forty-eight billion dollars on the automobiles they are driving, and most of them are paying eighteen percent interest to pay off the loans. Is that pleasure or slavery?"

We were listening intently to Bren, wondering when we'd find out what in heck Confamiliaum was all about and what we were supposed to ask in these interviews with the families on Warren and Benson roads. "A few years ago," Bren was continuing, "when I bought one of these tenements, Rais and I developed a theory that families working together in small cooperative groups could not only own the roofs over their heads, but they could create a more caring, joyful environment to live in—an environment that was realistically work-oriented and did not promote the old Judeo-Christian ethic that work was a salvation or a duty. Rather, work would be seen as a means to an end, something that must be done to make life more pleasant. While some jobs could be made pleasant and self-fulfilling, most work could only be made joyful because it allowed you to achieve other purposes. We believed that we could define 'the pursuit of happiness' in terms that made sense to millions of people. Basic to this happiness is our belief that the cubic space that an individual or a family occupies is more important than things. But this space must be *his* or *their* own living space. No Utopian communal living proposal can divert that need. If an individual, or preferably a family, owns the roof over their head, it becomes a creative extension of the people living in it. Many communal efforts come apart because they try to force a presumedly common environment on the entire group."

Bren paused for emphasis. "That's the reason that mass housing—huge apartment and highrise rookeries—are such a vast failure. The environment makes it impossible for the individual to adapt himself to his own needs. Furthermore, as a tenant he has no vested interest in these buildings. A request to tear a wall down between rooms, for example, because at a particular time his family's need for certain kinds of space varies, becomes a bureaucratic nightmare.

"We believe that there is another approach to living. You've all got copies of 'Confamiliaum: A Proposal.' Any salesman worth his salt has to believe in the product, and in these sessions we're going to give you a thorough understanding of how a Confamiliaum could work. In the process, we think you'll agree that any family joining a Confamiliaum becomes an adventurer—just as you Premars are adventurers—with little or nothing to lose, and possibly much to gain."

Bob Jefferson was waving the proposal over his head. "Man, some of these peckerwoods are going to think we're on the pluck. Do you really think that four of us Premars are going to ring a guy's doorbell and talk sanely with him when most of the people around here already think we're sex maniacs? Now they'll think we're running off at the jibs."

"Am I supposed to report these asides?" I asked Rais.

"Sure, and maybe you should translate them, too." Rais was laughing.

"Don't have to," I told him. "We're not poot-butts anymore. We're blood. Mohammed and Billy are teaching us to converse with the brothers. My worry is that most families in Topham's Corner are going to be mighty shocked when they find a white guy and a black girl, or a black guy and a white girl, standing in their doorway trying to convince them of the joys of loving one another."

"That isn't all," Mohammed said. "Kathy doesn't like my fronts. She thinks this suit is funky. I like it, man. It's got class. My uncle sent it to me. It cost fifty bucks."

"I have to agree with Kathy," Billy Rainbow said. "You look as if you were mackin' your roommate."

"He means pimping," I said to Bren, who looked a little bewildered. Mohammed's suit is a style that only black kids or pimps wear. A flashing neon sign around his neck wouldn't attract more attention. His suit came from a company that specializes in selling way-out clothes by mail. Called the Stud, it's made of red polyester with gold studs down both legs and studs bordering the jacket as well as the collar. His chest, in a long narrow V, is bare down to his belt line. His bellbottom slacks measure twenty-six inches across, with a four-inch cuff. When Mohammed is fully dressed he wears a white felt hat called the Fly. It has a three-and-a-half-inch brim and a red feather sticking out of it. I think he looks pretty sharp in his suit when he wears it Saturday night and we walk around Park Street in Boston. I know the brothers think I'm his "ho," and it's kind of funny.

Mohammed pointed out that the Compars talked about creativity and expressing oneself, but when it comes to clothes we all wear the same student uniform—jeans. He said, "I like to dress up and look sharp. Even if Kathy and I are just going to a movie, sharp clothes make me feel different. Bren says you can change the mood of any environment with the kind of music you play. When I'm wearing this suit, I'm a new me."

Merle agreed with him. "I like your new suit. But blacks have to play the image game. Superintellect confuses the devils; they don't know how to react. But if you look like Super Prick, whitey responds quick and cuts off your balls. Premars should look like black WASPs. And that means you black girls, too. Some of you have been wearing dresses that are so tight you can see the crack in your ass and the hair on your pussy. We don't give a damn what you wear inside the houses, but outside you play it straight. The Premar uniform is jeans and shirts, or simple dresses, and no big afros, and no wigs. If you think about it, a clean, crisp black look is pretty exciting. Make it work for you."

"Okay," Bren said. "We're off the main ball. Before we get into the interview, we're going to concentrate on Confam. A Confam is a group of from five to fifty families who have voted unanimously to incorporate themselves under a Confamiliaum agreement into a nonprofit corporation. The basic purpose of the Confam corporation is to provide food, shelter, and limited mutual responsibility. A Confam will create an environment for living that offers privacy but simultaneously satisfies the genetic and psychic human needs for community. In any incorporation of five to fifty families the adult members of each family will singly or jointly own a hundred shares of stock in the corporation, and there will be no unissued stock. Thus, each original participant in a Confamiliaum venture will be guaranteed that his hundred shares can be inherited by his children, or sold to individuals who did not originally participate in the Confam agreement, or can be offered for repurchase by the Confam, which can also vote to resell units of purchased stock or permanently withdraw them from sale. Each one hundred shares of stock in the Comfan entitles the owner to a husband-and-wife bedroom and individual bedrooms for two children under twenty plus a living room, kitchen, and utility or hobby room. Since the needs for space will vary with the changing size of the family, as members grow older the bedroom space they require will contract. Thus, a family that had six rooms when all the children were living with them could be expected to shift to other locations within the Confam as their space needs contracted.

"We want to propose the Confamiliaum idea as an experiment to the people in these tenements. The agreement entitling the stockholder to his stock would require that each family contribute half of the wages of the highest wageearner in each family after taxes. This money, forming the main source of revenue for the Confam, would be paid to the treasurer weekly, and payments would continue as long as a stockholder remained in the Confam. The families would elect from their members a president, vice-president, secretary, and treasurer and would empower the corporation to purchase the sixteen buildings from their present owners."

"I'm getting lost," Able said. "Where does the Confam get the money to buy the buildings?"

"Since the general approach comes under the area of low-income housing," Rais said, "we think we can get the Department of Housing and Urban Development to work with us on a thirty-year mortgage at somewhat advantageous interest rates. But first, let's see if we can put together the kinds of resources a corporation of forty-eight families has to work with. While we don't yet know the exact income of the families in this grouping, it's not difficult to approximate it. We have estimated the average income of these families, including those who are on social security or welfare, at $7,000, after whatever federal and state taxes they may now be paying. Times forty-eight, this equals $336,000. Half of this, or $168,000, plus any other sources of income the Confam can generate, becomes the total operating income of the corporation.

"Now, let's assume that we can purchase this group of sixteen houses for $20,000 each. This would mean that the corporation would need a loan of $320,000, which, in effect, would be guaranteed by all the families. The repayment of this loan at seven percent interest, based on a thirty-year mortgage, would run approximately $2,129 a month, or $25,548 annually. This repayment includes both taxes and interest. The corporation could deduct the interest as an expense, just as the individual homeowner deducts his mortgage interest. The total city taxes on these buildings now run roughly $12,000 annually. Thus, the Confam would spend $37,548 yearly for the total of mortgage, interest, and taxes on these buildings. Unlike the rent the individual families are now paying, the payments these families would be making would build them an equity value in their one hundred shares. Keep in mind that each family would actually own their living space to the maximum, as we have mentioned. The values of Confam shares would appreciate, first by payments on the mortgage; second, by the increasing real-estate values as the members improved the buildings; and third, even more, by the financial benefits that would accrue to any family living in a Confamiliaum. Some of the benefits we foresee is a nationwide—ultimately an international—network of Confams whose activities would be coordinated by an International Association of Confamiliaums. Among other things, the association could coordinate job transfers of members and arrange inexpensive vacations for members to Confamiliaums in different parts of the United States and the world. Eventually, the Confam network might become financially more powerful than union organizations, and thus emerge as an important horizontal political force.

"Everybody's waving his hands ready to ask a thousand questions." Bren's eyes were dancing. "I'm jumping with joy that we're reaching you, but first let's get some more facts out, aimed specifically at Topham's Corner and this group of forty-eight families. Rather than limiting ourselves to $320,000 for a mortgage, we would borrow an additional $100,000. This would increase the rent-tax to approximately $45,528 annually, based on the seven-percent, thirty-year payback, and would leave the Confam $123,000 a year to feed its members. But let's leave food aside for the moment. You'll note that on the drawings we have made, these houses we've proposed have a one-story building running down the middle of the present back yards for approximately half their length. This building would house a heated swimming pool, and adjoining the pool there would be communal bathtubs. In the far end of this building, in a separate section, would be a communal dining area capable of seating about one hundred people, or about half the people in this Confamiliaum, at a sitting. The communal kitchen would serve this area. Both the dining area and the pool area would be designed so that they could be transformed with seating to serve as meeting areas or as an auditorium, or for card and game playing, or to show movies. The additional $100,000 would be used to build this as a 'do-it-ourselves' Confamiliaum project.

"The physical environment this particular Confam has to work with, and the nature of these one-hundred-year-old tenement buildings, give a greater potential for community than highrise dwellings do. Three-story buildings are an environment that human beings can relate to physically and mentally. We don't believe that's true of most low-income highrise apartments. The use of these buildings makes this first Confam all the more valid because we would be saving a good urban environment from the developers, who would otherwise, eventually, turn it into oversize stone-and-glass dormitories.

"We have determined that there are ninety-six adults and eighty-four kids under eighteen living in the sixteen houses, or a total of one hundred and eighty people. We believe that with some family regrouping into underutilized areas, it would be possible to free all the floors in the buildings we have marked D and E and use these for Confamiliaum purposes. The first floor in building D would be used for a Confam cooperative which would buy all the food and sell food specialties such as ice cream, candy, cookies, and delicacies which the members might wish to have available, as well as wine, beer, and liquor. These items and toiletries would be sold at supermarket prices and profits would go to the Confam. The second floor of building D would be minimally supervised dorms for teenagers who wanted a change of pace from living at home. The top floor would be for the offices of the Confam and a study area for teen-agers.

"The first floor on building L would be a family pub that

would sell beer and wine to members. It would have television and would be arranged to create the homey, conversational atmosphere of a typical English pub. The second floor of building L would also have a Confam TV area capable of handling several groups of twenty to thirty people watching different programs. The third floor of building L would be a library and study area. During the day the second floor, and the dining area in the new building, would double as a day-care center. The actual family regrouping to free these areas would be worked out by the members. Remember that each flat now has a big kitchen area which can be put to other uses, since most members will probably not do much private cooking. Also, a Confam laundry will be established in the basements of buildings D and L.

"Keep in mind that the Confam requires some membership interresponsibility that will not be paid for in money. Thus, day care of children by older retired members would be reimbursed in kind by sick care of older members. So far as possible, the Confam would care for its own and not depend on outside institutions for human love and affection. Members on welfare and social security would be expected to be deeply involved in work such as gardening, bartending, house painting, running the food co-op, day care, nursing care, and so on. As in Premar, *all* members and their children would assist in food preparation and serving, and this would be a week-long duty for each person about once every four weeks. The other three weeks a member would have the luxury of being served his food at tables for four and six couples. Teen-age children would be served in similar groupings.

"We estimate that a Confam of this size could feed each member for one dollar and a half per day, or less than two thousand dollars per week. Thus, the cost of food for the corporation would run approximately ninety to one hundred thousand dollars annually. We are also assuming that as inflation continues the percentage relationship between food costs and an average member's after-tax income will remain relatively in balance, since wage increases will bring these factors into line. Food management and dietetics in an area where the Confam will concentrate to combine necessary protein with more independence from meat. We believe that there are many approaches to group food preparation, as evidenced in books like

Recipes for a Small Planet, by Ellen Ewald, and *Feast*, by the True Light Beavers, and *The Kitchen Garden Book*, by Stringfellow Barr, which we use in Premar, and which offers well-rounded diets. We believe also that the environment of eating, good conversation, good lighting, wine, etc., particularly for the evening meal, is as important to total enjoyment as the food that is served. Members will quickly discover that eating in their own dining room is not only a great deal less expensive than eating in garishly lighted, plastic food emporiums such as McDonald's and Kentucky Colonel, but that the quality of the food and the friendly community experience will make the evening meal something they look forward to with added zest.

"Assuming that we keep in these guidelines, this particular group would have an excess income of approximately twenty-five thousand dollars. While smaller groups could function without any paid officials, we believe that a Confamiliaum of this size should pay the president and the treasurer an after-tax income of seven thousand dollars each. The president and the treasurer should be a male and female from different families. In this Confamiliaum Number one, a woman on welfare might make a good treasurer or president, since she remains closer to the area because of her responsibility to her children. But whenever possible we have to free mothers who can work away from the premises by providing day care for their kids. Whether some of this day care can be paid work for Confam members remains to be seen.

"The long-term goal of the Confam would be to build a surplus, hopefully at the rate of ten to twenty thousand dollars annually. One use for this surplus would be a credit association for members or to purchase low-cost group travel for Confam members.

"Okay," Bren said. "I'm coming up for air. We haven't covered half of the possibilities open to a Confamiliaum. The main thing we want to accomplish is to convince you that it's an approach to a new, exciting, cross-generational style of life which could help people live fuller and more exciting lives. We believe, for example, that Confam with mixed ethnic groups such as this one has a great potential for sharing the cultural aspects of different backgrounds, such as cooking. In the swimming-pool areas, where the Confam should permit nude swimming, and in the communal baths, where members can gradually be encouraged to enjoy communal bathing, naked, the great hurdle of sex education—the physical difference of the sexes—can become a normal unembarrassing part of life."

"I don't know," Rachel Silverman said. "A Confam sounds like a kibbutz. Even in Israel most people don't want to live in the kibbutz. They don't want to share. They'd rather suffer."

"Rachel's right," Joe McDonald said. "My father believes that most people don't want to work. They're lazy and they'd rather go on unemployment insurance and welfare. He would never give half his money to anyone."

"How much does your old man make?" Able asked.

Joe shrugged. "I don't know. Ten thousand, maybe twelve."

Billy laughed. "Your old man is brainwashed. He's poor and doesn't know it. If you got kids, twelve thousand is poor. My old man owes everybody. Every time he gets his paycheck, instead of two hundred twenty dollars, after his Blue Cross, union dues, taxes, and social security are deducted, he's lucky if he's got one-sixty-five. Ma gives him twenty bucks and budgets the rest for food and rent and payments on the car, the refrigerator, the TV set. What's more, the apartment we live in in St. Louis isn't as good as these tenements."*

"During the next H.V. meetings," Merle said, "we'll cover the economics of operating a Confam as well as the interpersonal problems of a sharing community and the opportunities for each person to participate in a democracy of their own making. Now, if Bren and Rais don't mind, I'll wrap up this meeting comparing Premar and Confamiliaum with other approaches to communal living. First, the kibbutz. Most kibbutzim are agriculturally based. The kibbutzniks grow their own food and sell their surpluses in the marketplace. The money obtained in this

* Kathy's transcription of her stenotapes of the human-values meeting devoted to Confamiliaum represents more than two hundred pages of questions and probings by Premars. Many of these are covered in other Premar journals which appear in the following pages, but since the final answers on Confamiliaum will be arrived at only by experience, at this moment in time you, the reader, can amuse yourself with the pros and cons, and the inevitable economic pressures, already casting their shadows before, which will make Confamiliaum-style living inevitable for millions of middle- and low-income people.—BOB RIMMER.

way not only buys whatever supplemental food they can't grow, but lets them purchase farming equipment as well as some of the amenities of life. The surplus income of the kibbutz is used for the good of all the members, presumably on consensus rather than specific vote. Each member has some limited discretionary income paid to him by the kibbutz.

"In both Confam and Premar, *some* work is assigned to the members, particularly food preparation and serving and maintenance. In the kibbutz, *all* work is assigned to the members, and the members are expected to work within the kibbutz an eight- to ten-hour day. In a Confam, as in Premar, assigned work shouldn't average one hour per day a year, and possibly less. Of course, members are not paid for performing assigned work. In a Confam, a member's equity grows, and he may cash it in by selling his shares or willing them to some member of his family. In the kibbutz, if you leave you do so more or less empty-handed. Of course, Premar is a short-term setup for its members. But the members who have Premar training may, on their own option, organize a Confam around some of the basic approaches of Premar." Merle laughed. "This, of course, is not for publication in Topham's Corner just yet. We have envisioned Confams where the members have learned how to cope with their jealousies and enjoy some sexual variety, in addition to the original, monogamous pair-bonding. However, this is for people much more experienced in interpersonal relationships.

"In a Confam, the money to provide food and shelter and heat is derived from the economic system itself. Member families contribute half of the highest income, after taxes, earned by one adult member in each family. All other income earned by a family or individual adult member is theirs to use as they wish. In a Premar commune a larger portion of your income is given to the commune, but by capitalizing on the system's need to have a constant flow of trained young people, and by pooling your resources, you are forcing the system to give you an education. Both Premar and Confam *use* the capitalist economy to gain more independence from it than would be possible for individuals functioning alone.

"Many people are suspicious of communal living as a 'dropout' philosophy. This was true of many of the communes that flourished in the late 1960's and now have largely disappeared. The people involved failed to take into consideration man's mutual interdependence, and thus failed to use this for their benefit. Instead, many tried to find products they could manufacture and sell to the larger society, or tried to live off the land. This requires an unnecessary return to primitivism. While communes like Oneida in the 1800's could prosper by selling the goods they manufactured, and the kubbutzim can function in the particular environment of Israel, it is impossible to turn back the clock. No commune or small group of farmers can produce a product, or food, as economically as our modern industries or mechanized farms.

"Some communes have tried free love and a sexual exchange based on the moods of their members. But no organization that lacks structure can survive. Perhaps man realized that his dreams of anarchy are not compatible with his need for interpersonal involvement. If Robinson Crusoe on his desert island hadn't created a strict daily regime for himself, he would have deteriorated mentally and physically. The reason Englishmen dressed for dinner in the jungle was not really to impress the natives, but rather to avoid a natural human inclination to measure oneself against the lowest common denominator, especially in situations where social pressure is absent. As you know, the Premar communes are highly structured. While each of you has a great deal of freedom, you do operate within rules that cover many aspects of your life, from the amount of discretionary money you have to the cleanliness of your rooms, to your agreement to abide by and live with the roommates of our choice—not yours. In a Confam, again structure—previously agreed upon by the members—forces each one of them at various times to be involved in community work. And it is—will be—policy to involve the older people with the community and not only keep them active and viable but to assume responsibility for those whose families no longer exist or whose families are not interested in them. Unlike retirement communities and condominiums, Confam believes that cross-generational involvement, even up to three generations, is the key to mental and physical health. In truth, we believe that Confam, for those who are too old to start their lives as Premars, can open doors to *achievable* goals. And having a reason for living means that they no longer have to pursue happiness, they will have captured it. And that's our revolution, kids, and we believe it can change the world without bloodshed."

Rais was listening to Merle with a big, loving smile on his face. "You can double that in brass, sweetie. Premar and Confam will change the world because they are yeasayers. Technologically, and as loving human beings, we can recreate the environment man lives in and find the answers *Beyond Freedom and Dignity*. But we don't do it by overthrow, or by takeover, but simply by building an entirely new structure on the old one. Maybe the old commie, Khrushchev, meant to say that when he said 'We'll bury you.' Leave the old ways to the archaeologists; we'll build new cities on top of the old, or right in the middle of them, and bury them!"

"In his backhanded way, Rais is trying to tell you that B. F. Skinner's book is on the Premar reading list a few weeks from now," Merle said. "If by any chance you are running out of things to read, I can issue copies immediately."

Bren laughed. "It's too damned late to read. Eleven-thirty. Time to hop in the sack with your roommate. Unless, of course, you are at sixes or sevens with him or her, in which case, hang around, Merle is counselor first class this week, and ready for consultation, day and night."

From the journal of Joseph McDonald, December and January, the first year of Premar.

I remember writing in one of my journals that I'd really like to be a science-fiction writer, but I've never read any science fiction that got me so involved as the day-to-day reality of Premar and Confamiliaum. My father thinks Premar is a maniac's daydream, because normal people love only themselves, not each other. A lot of people who live in Topham's Corner probably agree with him, but they *are* aware of us. Most of them aren't belligerent, but are grinning in an embarrassed way, as they might do with people from another planet. Bren told us that we weren't strangers in a strange land; rather, we are people of to-morrow living today. But sometimes I feel like the carpenter walking with the walrus. "Such quantities of sand. If only this were cleared away, it would be grand." I told Ellen, and she laughed and said, "Maybe we'll surprise the oysters and eat them."

I was a little bit scared when Andy and I and Chuck and Lainey started interviewing. I could imagine how my father would react if we arrived at his door, or even worse, if I walked into his house with some of the black kids. The families assigned to us were the Giustis, the Balakunas, the Dohertys, and the O'Learys. Not only were we supposed to get the exact names of all the adults and kids in each apartment, but hopefully to get them so interested in Confam they wouldn't mind telling us the gross pay and take-home pay of each working adult. We were also supposed to see what their initial reaction would be to the suggestion that they join a Confam.

"The idea," Rais told us, "is to talk about Confamiliaum as if it were a reality. After the interview, give each family a copy of the Confam proposal, and then invite them to the Strand Theater on January 12 for the Neighborhood Open Forum. If all these families will make the experiment, eventually we'll get other families in Topham's Corner who will want to try. Father Tim is going to talk about Confam next Sunday in church, and since about half of the families on Benson and Warren roads are Catholics, they'll be expecting you."

Andy was dubious. "How much do we tell them about Premar?"

"The truth," Merle said. "You are roommates who care for each other. You study together. You sleep in the same room. You're earning your own education. Contrast Premar with what you might be doing if you never came here. If they're scared or shocked over males and females being naked together, invite them to come to dinner with us. Before we eat, they can bathe with us in the tubs."

Chuck thought that was hilarious. "I can image my old man's reaction. For Ma's benefit he'd act horrified, but then he'd get you aside and tell you he was only pretending, and he'd ask if he could come alone, without her."

Merle was grinning. "That's your clue. Most guys enjoy

seeing young women naked. Women often say that naked men don't turn them on, but they aren't so uninterested as they may pretend. If a husband and wife will bathe with us together in the Premar tubs, a Premar couple will baby-sit for them—not only the night they come to Premar, but another night, too. Free."

Ellen was enthusiastic about the baby-sitting idea. Practically all the families had kids. In one of our H.V. sessions we voted unanimously, whether Topham's Corner families came to visit us or not, that Premar roommates would volunteer to baby-sit. At least six couples would be available in any one week. The price would be a token fee of $1.50 an hour. Money that Premars earned baby-sitting would go to the Premar Commune Entertainment Fund.

Maybe it's our baby-sitting service, maybe it's because most families are lonesome, and there aren't many ideas that a husband and wife can talk about together; maybe arguing for or against Premar or Confam gives them something more interesting to share than the current junk on the tube. Whatever it is, suddenly we're no longer a bunch of kooky outsiders. Already a lot of people know us and are waving at us, saying hello, and best of all smiling at us.

Our interviews with our four families were fun. Sal Giusti is thirty-eight and his wife, Mary, is thirty-six. They have three kids: Giuseppe, six; Giacomo, four; and Sophia, five months. Sal is an airplane loader at Logan Airport, and he hates his work. "It's a complete shitass bore," he told us, "but what else can I do. I only net one-sixty-five a week, but I don't know anything else. I'd like to take off for Alaska or Timbuktu. But I love Mary and the kids, so this is my life."

Andy was sure that Mary would never come to Premar, but last week Sal and she arrived while Chuck and Lainey minded their kids. "He threatened to come alone," Mary said, "so what could I do?" Sal can't stop talking about it. He sat naked in a huge tub surrounded by a lot of teen-age girls. "All the girls—you too, Mary—look better than any of those broads in *Playboy*," he said. "Hugh Hefner never had it so good." Andy and some of the girls washed Sal's back, and I helped the guys soap Mary until she was about to slide down the drain with embarrassment. But after a while she relaxed and enjoyed it. Sal had a little erection, but no one paid much attention to it. "It was hysterical," Mary admitted. "I might even go back sometime if I could trust Sal with all those young girls." Mary doesn't have to worry, because she's in good shape for a mother with three kids.

Alice and Bob Balakuna are sixty and sixty-five. Their kids are all married and have moved to the suburbs. Alice, who weighs close to two hundred pounds, hasn't come to the baths yet, but she keeps telling Bob, who is Jack Spratt compared with her, that one day she'll visit Premar, "if you're sure that they've got my tub size." We introduced them to the Giustis. They could have thrown a stone and hit each other's houses, and they even nod to each other at Mass, but they had never really talked. I think they're pretty lonesome.

Before he was retired, Bob was a pipe fitter working at the General Dynamics Shipyard in Quincy. The Balakunas own the tenement they live in, and he's not sure that they would want to sell their house to the Confam. "Our kids have no room for us," he said. "We don't want to end up in one of those homes for the elderly." Bob thinks that the economic basis of Premar—kids earning one hundred dollars a week subsidized by government and business—won't work. "The unions won't let your consortium get away with it. Kids would be taking the jobs away from men and women with families." We tried to explain to him that the government is subsidizing education and jobs right now. If Premar finally becomes a way of life, instead of giving money to kids or lending it to them or paying taxes to subsidize state universities, young people at seventeen would be expected to *work and learn* over a period of from two to four years after they graduated from high school. Millions of crap jobs that need to be done in the area of services would be done by young people. Rather than bumming their way through college, living off the family, or saddling themselves with loans, or, worse, never getting any further education at all, young people would be involved in the society at an early age and would be a hell of a lot happier because they were contributing something. "For example," I told him, "if all the kids in Topham's Corner were involved in a Premar-style education and were paid a hundred bucks a week, they could turn this community into a paradise by painting all the houses, doing maintenance, planting trees and lawns, and flowers and vegetables, clearing away snow in winter. Instead of

giving the money to the schools and colleges and the Job
Corps, business and government pay it to the kids for services, and then the kids pay it back to the schools for their
education." I wanted to tell him that Premar education
was a new-style convivial, like Ivan Illich proposed in *Tools
for Conviviality,* but Bren warned us not to push all the
Premar ideas at once on our new friends.

Hank Doherty is a big easygoing, guy, six-feet-six, who
drinks too much beer and has a protruding belly. His wife,
Nancy, is skinny and very religious. She's shocked that Father Tim is so tolerant about Premar, and she's heard a
rumor that he married Ellen to Bren Gattman. A Jew?
Nancy's mouth curls in disdain. How could Father Tim be
a party to that? The church really was in trouble when
they didn't get rid of priests like Father Tim. "He gets
away with murder," she said, "just because he's young and
handsome. And he thinks he's sexy. The way he stares at
women when he talks to them is disgusting." Nancy isn't
so shocked that the Premars sleep together. "Kids will do
that anyway. Still, why make it so easy for them?" What
bothers her is that Premar practices birth control. "The
only sure way a girl can pin a boy down is to let herself
get pregnant. Those Premar boys will never marry you,"
she warned Lainey.

Hank is a bartender at Sully's, an all-male barroom in
Topham's Corner. He's enthusiastic about joining a Confam, and Nancy thinks it might be all right. If they ever
actually had "*those naked Jap baths*" in the Confamiliaum,
she wouldn't make a fuss, she said, because "if people are
going to hell, that's their own business—it's just that I'm
not going with them." The Dohertys have three kids—
Billy, twelve; Susan, eight; and Kathy, six. Lainey asked
her if she was going to have any more, and Nancy told
her that's up to God—but she is helping God with rhythm
and lots of refusals to Hank, who, she says, "has sex on
the brain."

The O'Learys have two kids—Gretchen, twelve; and
George, eight. Tom's mother and father, who are sixty
and sixty-five, live with them. Henrietta, who is thirty-five,
is plump. She weighs about one hundred and fifty, but
she's very breezy. She has more freedom than Nancy and
Mary, because her kids are older and Tom's mother is always home. Henrietta's whole body—big breasts and
swaying behind—are in motion when she walks; she's a

ship in full sail. She came to Premar last Thursday, during the day, by herself. Only a few of the kids were around when Merle and Ellen took her to the baths, but Able was there, and Bill Cusik, and Cheryl. Henrietta let Able and Bill soap her up and hose her down. Able likes her. "I always wanted to see what a woman looked like after she had kids," he said. "Not bad. Henrietta might not win a beauty contest in a bathing suit, but her round belly blends together with her roly-poly tits." She played Ping-Pong with Able naked, and was laughing so hard she was almost in tears. Her husband is built like a five-by-five wrestler. Tom drives a truck for United Parcel Service, and he thought it was a big joke that Henrietta had been to Premar. He's coming next week.

I haven't written anything for the past two weeks, mostly because, at first, I agreed with Cheryl Jones that what the Compars didn't know wouldn't bug them,* but I want to remember us being together, and writing it down is the best way. It sure was fun. I wonder what Merle and Ellen would think if they knew that Cheryl and I broke a Premar rule by making love. Not once, but every single day in Christmas week! What's more interesting is that Cheryl's future roommates are Bill Cusik, Chuck Ventrano, and Bob Jefferson. Mine are Kathy Flaherty, Samantha Brown, and Lainey Franci. So, in the next two years, at least, Cheryl and I aren't scheduled to live together. One of these days, I'd like to bring the subject up in an H.V. meeting. If you sleep with another girl (or guy) in addition to your roommate, who, for twenty-six weeks, is like a husband or wife, is that adultery? I won-

* Cheryl and Joe agreed not to write any journals which revealed what happened the evening they baby-sat for the Giustis. But Joe did eventually. He gave us this material, which he had saved for more than two years. In fact, more than half of the roommates broke the twenty-six-week rule and had sex with at least one other Premar in particular twenty-six-week periods. The Compars were aware of this, but since they too were stretching the Premar regulations, they didn't take issue with some of the Premars who actually recorded the episodes in the journals they turned in. Amazingly, however, though many Premars "strayed" out of the succeeding twenty-six-week commitments at various times, all of them continued to live with, and eventually have sex with, the particular roommate to whom they were assigned. Problems of jealousy occurred only infrequently.—BOB RIMMER.

der how Andy would react if she knew. Damn, I still enjoy making love with Andy, too. But Cheryl is different, not so serious, kind of laughing, crazy. Maybe two years from now, if I settle in with one girl—or if we decide after four years to get married—we'll both like somebody else so much that it would be natural to make love with them, too. Can a marriage like that work? Open marriage? We've talked about it in H.V. meetings. Bren, Rais, and Merle have lived that way. Will Ellen be able to? She only smiles when we ask her. "I'm not much more advanced than a Premar," she told us. "I don't have the answers."

Jumping jelly beans! Who'd ever have thought that I, Joseph McDonald, the most scaredy-cat character who ever graduated from Springfield High a little more than six months ago, would already have made love to both Andrea Pillisuk and Cheryl Jones—one white, one black! Both of them pretty and sophisticated. Yet, I don't feel bad.

Cheryl's pretty smart. She went to high school in Atlanta and she was in a lot of high school plays, and she wants to be an actress. If she were white, Cheryl would seem like a dumb blond. That may sound silly, but it's true. She's plenty sexy, especially the way she walks and talks, but she stares at you vacantly sometimes, as if one of you isn't there. That's because she's supposed to wear glasses, but she won't. And sometimes she really puts you on by answering you in a simpery way, as if she's agreeing that you're really a big man and smarter than any mere woman, but you know damned well that she's got a quick mind and can absorb stuff faster than a lot of Premars.

Anyway, neither of us is remorseful. How can we be when it's so much fun? Even the first time in the Giustis' apartment when we almost got caught, and Giacomo saved our lives. Jiminy! Was that only three days before Christmas? It would never have happened if I had gone home. Three days before Christmas most of the Premar kids had hitchhiked or taken a bus home for the holidays. But there were about ten of us, including Cheryl, who stayed. I had invited Andy to come to my house in Springfield, to stay through Sunday. At first Mom was against it, saying there wasn't enough room. Where would Andy sleep? With me, I told her, just like she does in Dorchester. Neither Mom nor Dad has really absorbed that. Finally Dad reluctantly agreed. But then Andy's mother insisted she come out to Chicago. So I called Ma and told her that there had been a slight change in plans and the girl I was bringing for Christmas wasn't my roommate. But it was okay, she'd sleep with me. I must have told her Cheryl is black, because I heard a scream of dismay on the phone. "Don't have to ask your father!" Mom's voice was shrill and hysterical-sounding. "I'll tell you! You can't bring a black girl here. There's no Negroes in this neighborhood. We may not be rich, but we've kept them out. What would our neighbors think when they found that the McDonalds were entertaining a Negro for Christmas? I think it's disgusting that you would even think of the idea. Oh, Joe! I pray you are not really sleeping with them."

Holy mackerel! I had walked into a buzz saw. Cheryl is a girl who happens to be black, and I could be Joe McDonald, who happened to be black, white, or yellow. I asked Mom what the hell did she care about the neighbors. What had they done for her lately? I tried to tell her that Cheryl Jones was seventeen years old, just a kid whose ma was dead and whose aunt, that had raised Cheryl, had her own family. I didn't say that the guy Cheryl's aunt lived with wasn't her husband and was in the numbers racket. But it wouldn't have mattered anyhow, so I finally told Mom to hell with it, I wasn't coming home.

I didn't feel like listening to sister Maggie's troubles anyway, and Bren and Rais needed all the help they could get to put the old Strand Theater in shape. The Compars told the kids who stayed in Dorchester that we'd all pitch in and have a big family Christmas dinner. I think Ellen was hoping that her parents and brothers, who would be home from the University of Massachusetts, might even come over Christmas Eve. But that seemed like my kind of daydreaming, because Dancer was still shooting off his mouth, on radio and television, about sin in Topham's Corner.

Bren told us he loved to sing Christmas carols. "Jesus was a nice guy," he said. "How did he know that Mark and Luke and Matthew and Paul would go overboard? Jesus really said he was *a* Son of God . . . not *the* Son of God. The guys who translated the Hebrew caused all the confusion." Bren told Father Tim that all of us sons and daughters of Jesus would go caroling on Christmas Eve, and he'd wager that after the first meeting of the residents on Benson and Warren roads next week, a lot of them would join us. Father Tim had borrowed a portable organ for the occasion. I could play simple chords on a guitar, and so could Rais. So staying at Premar sounded like more fun than going home. And at this point, I didn't know about the frosting on the cake—what was going to happen between Cheryl and me.

Tuesday, three days before Christmas, Ellen asked if any two of us would like to baby-sit for the Giustis. Mary and Sal had to go to a company Christmas party. I said I was willing to volunteer, but one of the Giusti kids, Sophia, was still on the bottle. "I'm not a male chauvinist," I said, "but to me, feeding infants is a female job."

Cheryl said she'd sit with me; her roommate, Able Anderson, had gone home to Ohio. Of course, I'd horsed around with Cheryl in the baths, and I had talked with her a few times in H.V. meetings. But I had never been alone with her. And there we were, walking in the front door of the three-decker the Giustis lived in. In the downstairs hall Cheryl flipped out of the long wool coat she was wearing and walked up the three flights ahead of me to the Giusti flat. Her pale yellow dress hung just below her crotch, and I was admiring the warm curve of her cocoa behind, barely covered by her yellow panties, and holding my hand in my pocket, pressing my dork against my thigh so that Sal and Mary Giusti wouldn't see that my mind wasn't really on baby-sitting.

Sal Giusti's eyes popped when he saw Cheryl. Her dress crisscrossed over her breasts. About a third of them were visible, soft, edible puddings. As she bent over to hug Giacomo, Sal and I were grinning at each other in anticipation that they might flop loose. In a few seconds Giuseppe and Giacomo were climbing all over her and she was snuggling them. "I like kids," she told Mary, who was showing her the kitchen, where she could warm up Sophia's bottle. "After school I used to work in a day-care center. Joe and I will take good care of them." Mary's only worry seemed to be Sal, who was babbling and smiling at Cheryl and giving the impression that it would be more fun to baby-sit with her than go to a Christmas party with Mary.

They promised to be home not later than one o'clock. We could look at television, and there was ice cream and soda pop in the refrigerator. Cheryl mentioned a book that we were reading called *Pleasure*, by Alexander

Lowen, and told her that we would probably read it together. I could see from the expression on the Giustis' faces that they thought the book must be a sex manual, and Sal was probably wondering how anyone could sit beside Cheryl and concentrate on reading. So was I!

We played with the kids and then maneuvered G & G into their beds. But Sophia woke up. Cheryl held her in her arms while Sophia nursed on her bottle. When the baby was fussy, Cheryl laughed and said, "This brown lady ain't my mama."

"She'd like a taste of yout tit," I remarked. "Why not let her try it?"

"There's no milk, dumbbell, hence no milk odor. A baby won't suck a dry nipple."

"I don't know," I said. "If I were a kid, I'd give it a whirl."

Cheryl grinned at me. "I think you're still a kid." She had permitted her dress to slide away from one of her breasts; it looked firm, brown, and perky. The nipple wasn't sleepy; it was erect, ready to be tasted. We were deliberately playing a sex-tease game. Sophia ignored the nipple for a moment; then her mouth touched it, and her reflexive sucking started. "Lord!" Cheryl exlaimed. "That does feel nice. I think women want to have babies because nursing feels so warm and sexy." I felt she was reading my mind and knew that I wouldn't mind having a suck myself.

I said, "You do look interesting with a white baby on your tits."

"It's nothing new," Cheryl said. "I bet my great-grandmother nursed plenty of white kids." She lifted up her arms. "Pull my dress over my head before Sophy dribbles on it."

So there we were—Cheryl sitting in the Giustis' living room wearing nothing but her yellow panties, holding Sophia while the kid first took a swig on the bottle and alternated with a contented coo on Cheryl's nipple. And me sitting beside them watching while my sugar stick grew to the size of a big salami and poked so hard against my jeans that it actually was aching a little, like when you swallow too much ice cream and your skull feels as if it's about to crack open. I curled up on the sofa and tasted Cheryl's free tit. It was erect, too, and felt very nice in my mouth.

"Now, I've got two white babies," Cheryl said, and didn't seem displeased. Finally, Sophia, her belly full, conked out. I followed Cheryl into the bedroom and watched her put the baby in the crib. Then, still naked except for her panties, Cheryl moseyed around the flat, looking in cabinets, poking in some paperback books—detective stories, westerns, and a few gothic romances. Then she flipped through piles of phonograph records, all the while singing in a low voice. " 'Such were the plans I made . . . You know I was made for a night like this.' " She was smiling at me, and still singing: " 'Ride—c'mon baby ride.' Lord, that song makes me feel real loving."

How could I resist that invitation? Everyone in Premar is practicing Tantra, so we didn't hurry. Anyway, we had a lot of discovering to do; I was her second white boy, but she was my first black girl. We spent at least a half hour looking each other over for the physical differences, and could only find there weren't any, except male and female, of course. And that was just great. Cherry— my love name for her—is very sensuous. Her body arches to my touch like a purring cat, and her fingers are erotic floating question marks asking the kind of questions you want to have asked for hours, while maybe you only murmur, "Yes, yes . . ."

I can't compare Cheryl to Andy. How do you compare a violin concerto with a piano concerto? Maybe a symphony and a ballet? But I'm not sure who is which.

In the Premar library there's a big book called *The Golden Book of Love.* It's subtitle is *600 Coital Positions for Human Efficiency,* each one of which is illustrated by a drawing showing how. Cheryl and I remembered the Pounce, the Cut Blossom, Farewell Call, Sun Cup, Joystick, Sweetmeat, Flat Pass, Fulcrum, Express, Forward Squat, Snorkel, and House-Call, which isn't bad for one night. Two hours and several laughing orgasms later, Cherry was sitting in my lap transfixed, and we were looking at television, when Giacomo appeared in the room.

"I need to pee-pee," he announced. He didn't seem bothered by our nudity or our unusual position.

Cheryl slipped off my dork, and just as calm as if she were fully dressed, took Giacomo's hand and led him into the bathroom. She aimed his considerably smaller gellung at the toilet, and kissed his head while he had an enormous piss.

Before she tucked him back in bed, I was fully dressed. "Holy cow!" I said. "You've got nerves of steel. What if he tells Sal and Mary?"

"He won't. Kids never tell their parents anything they learn about sex. Why should they? They don't have to get very old before they discover that their father and mother aren't coming clean with them."

Her words were still floating in the air when we heard Sal and Mary, an hour early, outside fiddling with the door. Cherry grinned as she picked up her dress and shoes and disappeared into the bathroom.

"The party was a bore," Sal said minutes later. "They gave us two drink tickets. Half the guys were making up to anything in skirts."

"And you were no exception," Mary snorted.

"Sometimes I think Premar isn't so far-out," Sal said as Mary disappeared into the kitchen to talk with Cheryl. "But you kids haven't solved afterward. What about some stray stuff after you get married?"

While I was waiting for Cherry to shake loose so we could go back to Premar and try some more positions, Sal tackled me on Confamiliaum. "It's not really so new," he said. "There's a Tenants' Council that's trying to sell the idea in Boston. If the tenants own their housing, they won't wreck it like they have some of the housing projects around here."

Bren and Rais had discussed these proposals with us. "Sure," I told Sal. "The trouble is that when the landlords are finally willing to give up, and the city doesn't know any other way, they grab at the only last resort and offer to sell it cheap, if the tenants will rehabilitate housing that's practically bombed out. The trouble is that tenants, without a common goal, like in Confamiliaum, and working with little or no leadership, can't make it by themselves. They can't get mortgages, and who's going to lend them money, anyway? Bren says it's like trying to introduce democracy into Vietnam or most of the African nations—nobody knows what the hell it's all about. Even Americans, who should know how to make democracy work, act as if they can't live another minute until they get a big white father in the White House who'll tell them what to do."

I was spouting Premar stuff and wondering what in hell Cheryl and Mary were gabbing about in the kitchen. Finally Cheryl appeared—still cool and unflustered. I wondered what Sal and Mary would have thought if they could have seen us a half-hour ago trying the Cock-Eyed Wobble in their rocking chair.

Walking back to Premar, Cheryl was bubbling over. "Joe, you won't believe this, but Mary was telling me some gossip she heard at the party. Her cousin Betty Marchioni lives on Beacon Street in back of Boston University. Every Tuesday and Friday, Dancer O'Day spends the afternoon in the apartment of her neighbor, Martha Casey. Martha's a widow; her husband was shot a few years ago."

I grabbed Cheryl and swung her into the air. "Yowee! The dirty rat gets Premar raided, and all the time he's screwing some dame who's not his wife."

"What are we going to do about it?" Cherry demanded.

I shrugged. "Who'd believe us?"

"Should we tell Bren and Ellen?"

"What can Bren do? Dancer is Ellen's father."

"Maybe we could hang around this Casey woman's apartment Friday and see if it's really true."

"Maybe we could hide under her bed and then pop out and catch Dancer and her bare ass—"

"And take their picture!"

"Who's got a camera?"

"Able! Able has!"

"Maybe . . ."

Julian Howe. January, the first year of Premar. From tapes made at the Premar Open Forum. First half transcribed by Samantha Brown.*

---

* In April of the third year of Premar, aware that we were gathering material for the story of Premar, Julian Howe revealed that six of the Premars—Andrea Pillisupk, Joseph McDonald, Cheryl Jones,

Good evening, ladies and gentlemen. I am Julian Howe.

Here we are standing in front of the Old Strand Theater in Topham's Corner, Dorchester, Massachusetts,
U.S.A. Yours sincerely and his lovely roommate, Samantha Brown, are greeting the people as they arrive for
this unprecedented community event. Parked in front are
Premar's two new Winnebago motor homes, a gift of
Bren's sister, the wealthy Laura Stone. Tonight they are
being used by the Compars to entertain local big-wig
members of the National Premar Commune, and Dancer
O'Day, Premar's candidate for mayor of Boston, who is
expected to arrive momentarily.

A few weeks ago I told Bren that someday I'd like to
be a disc jockey or break into radio and television. J.
Howe—*The Man Who Knows How!* Though I'm about to
switch from my first thirteen weeks "on the books" at
Emerson College, where I will major in broadcasting, to
my first bread job as third assistant shipper at the Barton
Shoe Company, Bren suggested that I was overlooking an
opportunity to get some practical experience. Hang one of
the Premar portable cassette recorders from my neck, he
told me, and pretend that I am Douglas Kiker of NBC reporting this Open Forum. An on-the-spot happening, as

---

Able Anderson, Samantha Brown, and he—had agreed to keep a
secret which would explain Dancer O'Day's sudden conversion and
public acceptance of Confamiliaum and Premar the night of the
Neighborhood Forum at the Strand Theater in Topham's Corner.
Keeping their agreement, none of the Premars ever wrote about the
blackmailing of Dancer O'Day in their journals, but Julian made a
cassette recording which covered the events themselves, interspersed
with the story of Dancer's entrapment. Because the tape covers
much of what transpired the night of the Open Forum, it was decided to transcribe it and show it to Ellen O'Day as well as the
other Compars. Three years ago, Ellen, who was preparing to have
heart surgery, might well have been shocked to discover that her
father had a secret love affair. Now she was only amused. "Mother
is a very different person from what she was then," Ellen said. "I
have a feeling that Gina is now confident enough of her own potential that she might laugh at the Chaucerian aspects of Dancer's
Doomsday. Of course, Premar has helped broaden her vision, too."
When the transcription was given to Dancer to obtain his reaction
to possible publication, he only shrugged. "Every nut is writing
about their sexual lives these days. Alongside some of those bums,
I'm strictly minor league. My people won't read your book anyway. If they do, I'll tell them it's a pile of crap . . . malarkey to
sell the book. My people believe me. Even if they don't, a lot of
gals in Southie and Dorchester will be tickled skinny to know that
Dancer can still get it up."—BOB RIMMER.

seen through the eyes of one of the participants. The result could become an important historical document.

So welcome to a new world. It's seven-thirty P.M., a brisk, snow-sputtery Wednesday in January. In a half-hour, for the first time in ten years, this famous old landmark, boarded up and mostly forgotten, but now refurbished by the Premar kids, will reopen its doors so that the people of Topham's Corner can see Premar in action—on videotape—and decide whether we're children of Lot about to be turned into salt, or whether they will slowly welcome Premar into their daily lives.

When this theater first opened, more than fifty years ago, it was the heyday of the silent film. The grandmothers and grandfathers of Premars, who weren't much older than the Premars are now, came here on foot and by streetcar. At least once a week, on Friday and Saturday nights, here and in thousands of other movie houses across the country, neighbors exchanged hellos with each other, before they sat together in the darkness and wept and laughed at Laurel and Hardy and Greta Garbo and Lon Chaney and John Gilbert and Clara Bow and Conrad Nagel and Lillian Gish and Joan Crawford and hundreds of other movie stars whose lives they followed and "knew" more intimately than people know their neighbors today.

And after the silent movies, in 1929, came the talkies, and people stood in line to see Clark Gable, Betty Grable, Fred Astaire and Ginger Rogers and Cary Grant, James Cagney, Edward G. Robinson and other stars. Little restaurants opened in Topham's Corner where people could eat together before they went to the movies, and the stores stayed open until the last show started, and a lot of people in Topham's Corner knew each others' faces. But then came television and shopping plazas, and people didn't look at each other anymore. They moved to the suburbs to little icky-bicky houses, and when they went outdoors they buzzed around alone in little tin boxes, and were actually afraid to look at other people who were driving their little tin boxes, because they might run into each other. And people got used to seeing thousands of tin boxes whizzing by them, and not paying any attention to the people inside them, unless they whacked into each other's boxes. And the only people they ever stared at were shadow people on glass tubes. And of course these robots never looked directly back at the idiots watching them. Finally, everyone, not only in Topham's Corner but everywhere else in the world, forgot how to look directly at another person or smile or say "hi." It was easier to look away and not get involved and pretend that most other people didn't exist at all.

But tonight something is happening at Topham's Corner! Everyone is looking at everyone else! They're grinning and maybe feeling silly for coming here, but you can see by their faces that they're not mad—just curious and maybe a little embarrassed. Are they really going to show movies with the kids running around ballicky?

Yes! Tonight the people of Topham's Corner will see boys and girls cavorting in the Premar tubs and horsing around the Premar commune. Premars, in the flesh, naked and blithe—a nice word. That means beautiful and kind and gentle and friendly all at once. And they'll meet all the Premars and their roommates on videotape, and they'll see the Human-Values seminar in action. Inside the theater, right now, cameramen from WGBH, Boston's educational television, are setting up their cameras, because before and after the Premar movies, which will run about forty-five minutes, and will be simultaneously shown on television, WGBH will televise the speeches of Bren Gattman, Rais Daemon, and Dancer O'Day. Yes, ladies and gentlemen, I am predicting that tonight Dancer O'Day will do a complete turnaround. But more on that later.

"Are they going to show us naked on TV?"

Those words you just heard, good friends, were spoken by my roommate and erstwhile companion for the first twenty-six weeks of Premar—the lovely Samantha Brown. I have a public confession to make: I'm in love with her, and you would be too, if you knew her.

Yes, Samantha, there is a Santa Claus! WGBH believes that naked Americans of both sexes are a lot less dangerous to look at on television than John Wayne or Godfathers popping off Indians and bad men. Imagine, millions of Americans for the first time will see young men and women naked, soaping each other, playing the hose on each other, sitting in hot tubs together, and playing Ping-Pong with titties flopping and dangles waving. But that's not the only precedent-shaking event that will be seen here tonight.

During the second half of the program Rais Daemon

will tell the residents of Topham's Corner about Premar and Confamiliaum. He will also announce that forty-eight families on Warren and Benson roads have voted unanimously to form the first Confamiliaum in America. Depending on whether Rais and Bren can raise the mortgage money, these families will soon own their own homes and be participating in an experiment in cooperative living that will be watched eagerly by community planners around the world. And that's not all! Tonight, in this theater, Dancer O'Day will walk up to the stage and before a live and a televison audience endorse Confam and at the same time—can you believe your ears?—state that he has had second thoughts about Premar and that he now believes Premar may well be the turning point toward a new egalitarian world of social, mental, and sexual relationships.

That delighted laughter you just heard is Samantha. We have just entered the Strand Theater. The noisy background is the enthusiastic crowd milling about as they find their seats. I would estimate there are well over twelve hundred people present. Only bona-fide residents of Topham's Corner have been given free admission tickets. Had we opened the doors to the general public, there would be lines all the way to downtown Boston. Samantha and I are now sitting in the last row of the orchestra, where we can survey the entire theater. All the other Premars are sitting in the first five rows, intermingled with the first Confam families of Topham's Corner. On stage are twenty chairs for Compars and distinguished guests, including Captain James Duffy and Captain Henry Lord of the Boston police; Margaret and Phillip Tenhausen, Marion Swenson, and Harry Littleton, from the National Premar consortium; Father Timothy O'Hara and Rabbi Samuel Perlstein and the Reverend David Dobson.

Dancer's wife, Gina, is sitting between her daughter, Ellen, and Bren Gattman. Incidentally, ladies and gentlemen, we're happy to tell you that Dr. John Meserve, the well-known heart surgeon at University Hospital, has stated that Ellen is a good candidate for heart surgery. After much discussion with Ellen, he finally acceded to her wish to delay her operation until Valentine's Day—four weeks from now. What a lovely Valentine present Dr. Meserve will give Bren, and Ellen's father and mother, and her brothers, and the Premar students, and her many friends—a heart that pumps blood through open arteries. Man loving man and performing miracles.

"What if Dancer doesn't come tonight?"

Samantha, Dancer will come! Can you believe that he doesn't want the little gift which we have agreed to make him immediately after the forum?

"Andrea, Cheryl, and I gift-wrapped it this afternoon. Maybe we should have packed it in a shoe box to make it look more substantial."

But as you and I both know, Samantha, big things sometimes come in little packages. And, as you and I have observed, some big things, even when they're nearly fifty years old, don't show any signs of wear.

"Baby, you're right, and that *is* worth remembering. And I hope your big thing stands up until you're eighty. Julie, do you think we should be talking like this on tape?"

Good friends, while the Premar movie is being shown, I want to think about Samantha's words. Obviously, this conversation between us has suggestive overtones. It should either be erased, or we should come clean. Tell all. If I tell all, I suppose I would be breaking our promise to Dancer. On the other hand, *this is my tape*, and not my journal. Didn't a former President of the United States, whose precepts all good citizens should follow, claim executive privilege? Why can't I? Anyway, whether *The Old Politician's Tale* is on *my tape* or in *my head*, it's still a secret, isn't it?

"I'm not sure about that, Julie. No one can stick your head in a tape recorder and play it."

That's true, Samantha ... but think of the posterity. Chaucer told "The Miller's Tale." Joe McDonald thinks that "The Tales of Topham's Corner," if they were ever told, might be even more interesting. Geoffrey Chaucer Howe, they'll call me.

I'm sorry, ladies, and gentlemen, the story of Dancer O'Day's Doomsday must wait. Dressed in gray slacks, a pale green sports jacket, and a tie, our leader is now walking across the stage. The Premars will scarcely believe their eyes. Is this really the infamous Bren Gattman? Or as Phil Tenhausen remarked a few moments ago when he visited with us in our Winnebago mobile home, "Bren, are you really you or are you disguised as a loan officer of the First National Bank?" Bren laughed as he answered, "Yes!

Yes! It's really me. But blame Ellen; it was she made me do it."

Kiss me, Sam-Sam, hold hands with me while we record Bren's message of wisdom.

"Good evening, friends and neighbors of Topham's Corner. I'm Bren Gattman. I could only wish that for a second, at least, you could see your faces through my eyes. Next to the day that I married Ellen O'Day, this is the most exciting moment of my life. There must be more than fifteen hundred of you out there . . . mothers and fathers, and young teen-agers, single adult people, a beautiful mixture of black, white, and brown faces. Americans. Questioning, maybe. Dubious, maybe. But willing to listen to the other guy's story and make your own judgment. In a few minutes we're going to show you a video movie which we have made ourselves. It's called *A Day in the Life of a Premar*. After the movie and before we open the forum to discussion, we also want to orient you a little bit, give a little background on Confamiliaum #1, Incorporated, which is very close to becoming a reality in Topham's Corner. We hope that many of you have read our Confam proposal, which we have distributed to every household in Topham's Corner. The trouble with writing about things like Confam is they often don't come through when you read them. They sound like jibberish. So, after the movie, Rais Daemon will talk to you for a few minutes about what's going on in the cities of America, and give you an overview of the kind of crazy world we are living in. A world where the people who control the wealth are building huge hotels and highrise banks and insurance companies in the inner cities, while the little guys who live on the fringes and who pay most of the taxes live in hundred-year-old, decrepit, bombed-out housing, or are offered low-income housing in massive projects where they will be compressed into nonhuman beings by architects who design buildings not for people who will live in them but for the investors, so they can make their miserable profits at your expense.

"After Rais' short talk, if we hold to the schedule, it will be about nine-thirty. And then it will be your forum. If you don't like what you hear tonight, we hope that you'll let us have it straight from the shoulder. There's been a lot of talk about Premar and Confamiliaum being the daydream of kooky left-wingers, hippies, and revolutionaries. If we accomplish nothing else tonight, we want you to know that we're Americans, and we love our country, too. We think that the United States has moved into the future at least twenty-five years ahead of the rest of the Western world. Americans will have to come up with the answers that will make it possible for all men to exist on this planet. If we're all going to survive, one thing is certain, the little guy, you and me, the guy they call 'Joe', the hard-hat, should get a little more out of life. While this nation is pretty screwed-up in some areas, we believe that all of us working together—white Americans, black Americans, Italian Americans, Greek Americans, Irish Americans, Polish Americans, Puerto Rican Americans, Chinese Americans, Jewish Americans, you name them—have got to blend our ethnic backgrounds a little and share the good things in our various cultures and remember that we're Americans first, and that means we come from people who dared to gamble, who took chances, who dared to try new things, who gave birth to the Franklin Roosevelts and the Malcolm X's. And we've got to understand that the little guy in this world, whether he's black or white, is only one or two steps ahead of slavery. If you're black, look at whitey sitting next to you. Remember, it wasn't his great-grandfather who was running the slave ships a couple of centuries ago. If you don't believe me, read how the Irish and the Jews and the Poles and the Chinese came to America. Read about the poverty and slums they lived in when they arrived here. They weren't treated as people. They were just cogs in the Industrial Revolution—cheap labor. Your great-grandfather and your great-grandmother came to America to escape agricultural slavery and discovered they had traded off their lives for another kind of economic slavery—the Industrial Revolution—in which they were little more than an extension of the machinery they operated.

"Rais Daemon will amplify on these approaches later in the evening. For a moment, before the Premar movie begins, let me focus on you as parents and kids. In the past few weeks we've been called socialists or communists, or just simply sex maniacs, out to destroy marriage and the family. Some people have accused us of running orgies on Felton Street. Well, I can tell you, speaking not only for myself but for Ellen O'Day, Merle Blanc, and Rais

Daemon, with whom I run this Premar commune—we think that screwing around with a lot of different people, half-gassed on alcohol or dope, with nothing on their minds but getting themselves off, might be fun for some people for about a half-hour, but very soon becomes a game for morons. At Premar, we believe in love. We believe that every human being needs' to be able to express love deeply in affectionate sexual contacts with a member of the other sex. We realize that the idea of young men and women living together unmarried and ultimately having intimate physical contact with at least four members of the other sex *before* they marry, may be shocking to you. But keep in mind that we are trying to create a new kind of marriage and a new kind of family, based not only on teaching young people how to love, acquiring this knowledge not only through books, but learning to love by loving and actually living with different human beings and ultimately discovering how to interact with another person in a lifelong relationship.

"Is this happening in the United States or Western world today? Of course. But mostly by trial and error. Fifty percent of those who marry each year stay married—monogamously. Maybe in some cases they aren't happily married, but they do prove the rule that monogamy is here to stay. The real tragedy is that we live in a world where the divorce rate—we have nearly a million divorces a year—is fifty percent of the marriage rate—two million marriages. Just think of all the tragedy and trauma and hopelessness growing out of so many failures. Can we create a premarital and postmarital society where marriage, based on making good pairs from the beginning, has a better chance of lasting a lifetime? Premar believes we can. Premar believes that we can create a world where intimacy and sexual varietism exist within the boundaries of strong primary family relationships.

"But we must have the courage to start young. We must create a world where young people and their parents can really communicate. Do you know that suicide is now the third most common cause of death, after accidents and homicides, among youngsters fifteen to twenty-four years old? Can you remember when you were young and idealistic and the greatest need of your life was someone in your own age group with whom you could really talk? If you were male, that person couldn't be another male. If you were female, that person couldn't be another female. Men and women need each other. But month after month, year after year, when you were young did you ever find that person of the other sex with whom you dared to express all your pent-up sexual and biological needs to be a loving man, or if you were female, to find sex combined with romantic love?

"We believe that this kind of youthful suffering is unnecessary. We believe we can create a world where loving is natural and normal from early childhood. A few years ago in Philadelphia a seventeen-year-old high school student committed suicide. He was a brilliant boy, a leader; people looked up to him. He was a straight-A student, a National Merit Scholarship semifinalist. But he had never found anyone with whom he could share all his youthful doubts and questionings of life. He wrote a poem which he probably never dared to read to anyone.

It seems a shame / To feel so old / So young / Yet sometimes / You feel the loneliness / You feel the despair / You feel the uselessness / Of standing at the crossroads / Of dead ends.

"And this boy had a girlfriend for a little while, but he couldn't reach through to her either, and she left him. After his death by carbon-monoxide poisoning, they found this poem in his desk:

How Is it / If Love is Blind / It always / Sees me coming / And if Love is giving / I always seem to get taken / Yet We laugh and cry / And turn away / But I know / We almost had something / More than rainbows / For rainbows hold the sky / And we embrace / Each other.

" 'And we embrace each other.' Do you remember the movie called *Joe*? It tried to tell the story about an average guy, a hard-hat steel worker, who hated the long-haired generation and didn't know how to give much love himself. The movie ended with Joe and his friend killing his daughter and all her hippie friends. If we don't create a world where fathers and mothers and their children have really learned how to love, we will always end up with tragedy. Here's the true story of a man whose name isn't Joe. His real name doesn't matter. You may remember reading about him in the newspapers. He lived in Detroit. His sixteen-year-old daughter had left home and was living with a young high school drop-out named Scott. A black boy, Greg, who was working days and studying nights at the local high school, and another boy, Tony, also lived in Scott's apartment. The kind of tragedy people can create in their lives is revealed in the father's own words:

" 'I knew my daughter was in there with Scott. I broke down the door to apartment nine with my right shoulder. I was carrying a flashlight in my right hand. They were both nude. I pulled out my .38 revolver and struck Scott over the head with the gun as hard as I could. The weapon discharged, killing my daughter, who moaned and fell back.' " (His wife had come with him to Scott's apartment to find their daughter.) 'My wife screamed, "You killed my baby!" I told her that it was an accident. After I knew my daughter was dead, I shot Scott in the head two or three times. I don't remember shooting a colored man named Greg, who was in bed in the same room, but I remember thinking he was probably taking turns with my daughter. I remember seeing blood on Greg. I put the .38 in my belt and pulled out the Luger and walked into the other room and shone the flashlight at Tony on the couch, and I shot him, I believe through the forehead. I believe that he was having intercourse with my daughter also. They all ruined my daughter.'

"His daughter was seventeen. The three boys were eighteen, seventeen, and sixteen.

"Were these kids evil because they were trying to find some meaning in their lives? Are the thousands of young girls who get pregnant in their early teens guilty of anything except trying to find love? And the hundreds of thousands of youngsters who run away, many of whom virtually disappear each year—is it their fault they are bewildered and confused? Or is it ours? Each one of us who refuses to create healthy loving environments for kids to grow in?

"A father kills his daughter. A father kills his son. Why? Here is a true story which you can read in a paperback book called *Richie*. Richie Diener was seventeen years old. He was a good-looking boy, personable, but he didn't make friends easily. He was shy, withdrawn, like most of us are in our teens. Richie was interested in science and ecology, but he didn't have anyone with whom he could share any interests. His father was remote, busy with his own affairs and earning a living. Richie didn't care for his father's hobby, which was practice shooting at the Levittown Rod and Gun Club. His mother was a mother. She loved him, but she wasn't a friend. At seventeen, Richie had never found a girl he could share his dreams with. Do you remember what it's like to be lonesome? To be over-flowing with a need to love and not know how to express it? Richie was noncommunicative, and this irritated his father. To find out what his son was thinking, his father taped Richie's phone conversations. To his father's shock, he discovered that his son had experimented with drugs, such as seconal and quaalude. The tension between Richie and his father often built into corrosive arguments between them. One afternoon, in a fit of anger, Richie picked up a kitchen knife and threatened to kill his father. The argument between them was most abusive on both sides. His father ran upstairs and got his gun. Would Richie have stabbed his father? We'll never know. His father was so aggravated by this monster, his child, that he shot him between the eyes. On one of the tapes his father had recorded, Richie was talking on the telephone with a girl, Sheila, whom he knew but had not made love with. 'I only got three Christmas cards this year,' Richie told her. 'How many were you expecting?' Sheila asked. 'Fifty?' 'I don't know, at least more than three.' 'Who sent you the cards?' 'You,' Richie answered, 'my grandma, my aunt.'

"All right. Enough of man creating his own tragedies. Now, as you watch the Premar movie, ask yourself: If these were my sons and daughters, and I opened my heart to them, and I rejoiced in their search and discovery of love, and I dared to be the loving human being that is the essence of me, but which I'm so afraid to expose to day-light, would the number of Christmas cards matter?"

Julian Howe. January, the first year of Premar. From tapes made at the Premar Open Forum. Second portion transcribed by Andrea Pillisuk.

"Julie! I just saw Dancer walk down the aisle; he sat down in the third row!"

Sam-Sam, he knows what's good for him. If he doesn't root for our team, it'll be his ass.

"Julie, I'm getting jittery. Who knows what'll happen now? Suppose he gets up on that stage and tells everybody we're blackmailing him?"

Then a picture of old Dancer, stark naked with a hard-on with his girlfriend, Martha Casey, also naked, will be hanging in every police station in Boston. Happy O'Day!

"I don't think Ellen could stand it. Stealing from people and grafting is one thing, but if a politician tells everybody he hates sex, and then turns out to be a lecher, the voters will fry him."

Good friends, if you're still listening, this is your friend J. Howe and his girlfriend, Samantha Brown. Don't you honestly think it would serve Dancer O'Day right to be fried? Or maybe boiled in oil would be better. That would make him happier. Then he could be made a saint. Saint Vitus Dancer.

The Premar movie is now running, and the good people of Topham's Corner are watching it in silence. Though Sam may finally convince me to erase this portion of the tape, it's a good opportunity to review the secret life of Dancer O'Day. Just four weeks ago Mary Giusti's cousin, Betty Marchioni told Mary that she'd bet that Dancer had been screwing Martha Casey ever since—and maybe before—Martha's husband was murdered. Martha wasn't exactly a close friend of hers, but why else would Dancer arrive faithfully twice a week at her apartment? To have lunch. Lunch wouldn't take four or five hours, and Dancer never left until late in the afternoon. Anyway, he could have gone home to his wife for lunch and a quickie, too, if he was that horny.

Mary told Cheryl that if Dancer was really two-timing his wife while he was acting so saintly about sex and sin in Boston, then he deserved the worst.

But as Joe McDonald told Cheryl, there wasn't much anybody could do about it. Anyway, as Cheryl pointed out, even if some oily, nasty gossip leaked out, Dancer would deny it; the dirt would only rub off on Ellen and Ellen's mother, who might never go to bed with her husband again. She might even divorce him. That's the way "grown-ups" reacted to sin—and not only in Topham's Corner. A lot of people might eventually accept the idea of premarital sex, but fooling around after marriage was a one-way road to hell—if you got found out. No one knew this better than Dancer. Cheryl said the really neat trick would be to get the goods on Dancer, prove he and Martha were lovers, and then threaten to pull the rug out unless Dancer agreed to endorse Premar and maybe even Confamiliaum.

Cheryl not only convinced Joe, but overnight she uncorked a secret yearning of Joe's which he had never revealed to anyone. When he was a kid he had always wanted to be a Royal Canadian Mountie. Sergeant Joe promised, now that his fantasies were out in the open, that he'd live up to their motto. He'd "*Maintenir le droit*" and "get his man." But he needed help. Andrea and Able would be back in two days, and four heads were better than two. In the meantime, Cheryl and he decided to check and see if Betty's story would hold up.

Sure enough, at one o'clock on Friday Dancer arrived on Beacon Street and took the elevator to the fourth floor. He ignored the seedy character in the elevator with him. Sergeant Joe got off on the fifth floor and reported back to Cheryl, who was nearly frozen from the long wait outdoors. In the next few hours, our heroes, waiting for Dancer to leave, were kicked out of the lobby of the apartment by the janitor, who rightly suspected them of skulduggery. Finally, huddled in a doorway across the street, they watched Dancer depart at four-thirty in his blue Chevrolet with the "City Official" sign on the windshield.

When they got back from their Christmas vacation, An-

drea and Able agreed with Cheryl and Joe that all they
had to do was give Dancer a shove and he'd fall down in
his own shit. Able, whose hobby is photography, has taken
beautiful black-and-white nudes of everyone in Premar.
Some of the kids even gave eight-by-ten photographs of
themselves, or nakedly embracing their roommates, to
their parents for Christmas presents.

Good friends, if such a Christmas present shocks you,
you should know that Able is a student of George Hester,
whose book *The Classic Nude*, in the Premar library, in-
spired him to create poetry of flesh with his camera. The
photographs he took of Sam and me, for example, are
songs of life in black and white.

It was a good guess that Dancer and Martha hadn't
been discussing the philosophy of city government. Still,
what was needed was a photo to prove the point. A week
was wasted on the expanding daydream of getting a picture of Dancer and Martha belly-to-belly. Sergeant Joe
kept murmuring that this would be the perfect *prima facie*
evidence. My suggestion, made later, was that it would be
prima gentilium, and *prima mirabile,* if we ever managed
it. At the very least, it would prove, in the words of
Rachel Silverman (my new roommate, beginning in
April), that Dancer was really an old *kocker.*

At this point only Joe, Andrea, Cheryl, and Able knew
that Dancer had dirty linen. But they still hadn't been able
to dream up a way to help him wash it in public. Sergeant
Joe by this time was determined to prove his mettle as a
Mountie—not a bareback lover, but a Canadian in a red
hat. He decided the best approach would be to enlist the
aid of the unknown but informative Betty Marchioni. She
would help us to catch old Dancer with his pants around
his knees, and he'd never be able to say they fell off while
he was doing an Irish jig. By now the spirit of the chase
was changing Joe's character from timid to outright fool-
hardy. When the other conspirators said they were too
chicken to call on Betty, Joe undertook the mission himself. Betty was shocked that Mary Giusti had mentioned
her name as the source of the gossip about Dancer, and at
first she denied that she knew anything, and anyway, what
Martha Casey did was her own business. So Joe let her believe he might burst into tears if he couldn't find some
way of saving Premar from the bastardly Dancer.

Betty, who is in her late thirties, hasn't gone to seed,

and she's quite sympathetic to Premar. She told Sergeant Joe that she wished she had slept with at least one other guy before she got married. "I don't know Martha too well," she told Joe. "She moved here after her husband was shot. If a man loses his wife, and he's in his forties, he can find another woman. But when a woman is a widow at that age, it's not so easy, so I don't blame Martha if she's getting a little bit of loving. Hurray for her, I say! That Dancer O'Day is quite handsome."

For a moment Joe thought he was losing the scent. Betty was sending out signals that maybe, given the opportunity, she'd hop in the sack with Dancer, too. "But on the other hand," Betty told Joe, "I sure hate those smug politicians who tell you to do one thing while they're merrily doing another. Funny thing. A few days ago I was cleaning the apartment—my husband and I are going to visit his parents in Jacksonville during the holidays—and I found the key that Martha gave me to her apartment last July. It's still there in that old green flower vase in the front hall. Martha was expecting a new TV set and was going to be away for the day, and asked if I'd let the delivery man in. Well, a lot of things happened just about that time, and I must have forgotten to give the key back to her. I should really knock on her door tonight and give it back to her."

Sergeant Joe was ogling the vase as if it held the key to Ali Baba's cave. "Why don't you give it back when you come home from Florida?" Later, Joe told Able he was nearly stuttering, because a mad idea flashed through his mind: He would swipe the key, and one of them—Able, of course, since he was the photographer—would crawl under Martha's bed. At the right moment—before he was beaten to death by the hammer blows of the descending springs—Able could roll out, snap the belly-to-belly picture, and run like hell.

"You must have been sniffing glue," Able told Joe. "If you think I'm going into that apartment alone, your head is really screwed on backward. Bren says that Dancer used to be a two-gun cop, and he's bigger than me. Anyway, maybe they don't make love in bed. Maybe they like the floor better."

Sergeant Joe had not yet solved the problem of how to borrow Martha's key from Betty. The idea haunted him. He couldn't sleep, and for three days he couldn't even make love to Andrea. "If Betty and her husband are going to Florida for two weeks," he told her, "all we have to do is to get into Betty's apartment, then we'd have a command post."

"But then you'd need two keys," Andy pointed out. "Betty's and Martha's." Andy was sure that Joe was cracking up.

But intrepid Sergeant Joe convinced his Wonder Girl, Andrea, to come along with him and meet Betty. If nothing better developed, at the very least he might be able to pluck Martha's key out of the front-hall vase. This time Joe tackled Betty like an old-time con man. "I told Bren Gattman and the other Compars how nice you were to me the other day," he told her. "Andrea and I got their permission to invite you and Vinnie to our Open Forum with your friends the Giustis. It'll be on January 15, after you're back from Florida. And if you'd like to come to the Premar baths with the Giustis and have dinner with us some night, we'd be delighted."

Joe was laying it on pretty thick, and Andrea was leading Betty on to show her the apartment. "Oh! You have two cats," Andrea bubbled. "I just love cats. Fluffy and Muffy. What nice names! And all those plants. Who's going to take care of them for you while you're gone?" By this time Joe had checked the vase and slipped Martha's key into his pocket. And then, presto! The wheel of fortune slowly ground to a stop on their number.

"Now that you mention it," Betty said, "I asked the janitor if he would feed poor Fluffy and Muffy and water the plants, but Bill drinks a lot, and he's not very reliable. If you and Andrea could drop by every other day, I'd be happy to give you ten dollars." Betty beamed at them. "And Vinnie and I would really like to visit Premar some evening."

Of course, Sergeant Joe would have gladly paid Betty for the privilege of feeding her cats. Unbelievably, he now had the two keys in his hot little hand, and Dancer's goose was ready for the oven. What's more, Joe was positive that Betty knew she had helped him pluck Dancer's feathers.

But, having the keys to both apartments was still far from surprising Dancer in his birthday suit. And Able wasn't one bit more enthusiastic about the project. Either Tuesday or the following Friday, after Betty and her husband had gone to Florida, the three of them and Sergeant

Joe (according to him) would camp in Betty's apartment and wait until Dancer arrived next door. Able wanted to know what happened if the lovers weren't in bed when they burst in on them. What if they were just sitting there, playing chess or something? And if they were in bed, which way was the bedroom, for Christ's sake? By this time even Cheryl was beginning to feel a little hopeless.

But Sergeant Joe had crossed the frozen Arctic of Boston in search of his man, and he wouldn't quit now. "All we have to do is to bug Martha's bedroom," he told them. "Then we can wait in Betty's apartment while we wait for the sounds of action. It would beat Watergate all to hell."

Now, good friends, I hope you are still listening to this rambling remembrance of things past. Things like how you get a bug into Martha's bedroom, or where you get the money to buy the necessary electronic equipment to tune into it, are easy to write in a story, but damned expensive and nearly impossible to accomplish in reality. To do the job, they'd have to sneak into Martha's apartment when she wasn't home. Joe quickly solved that problem. He knew the day. In his first conversation with Betty when she was rooting for Martha, she told him: "Martha's really a nice person. She spends every Saturday and Sunday with her invalid mother in Waltham."

Time was running out. Bugging day had to be the next Saturday coming up. But who knew how? J. Howe, of course, *The Man Who Knows How*. Able told Joe that I was a whiz at electronics. Just last week hadn't I rewired the whole Premar stereo system? So, now there were six. At the rate they were going, I told them pretty soon all the Premars would be on hand to greet Dancer the Prancer. "When Dancer Prances with me . . ." Holy Gee! Almost paralyzed with laughter, we slowly calmed down and began planning our caper more seriously.

I studied the Radio Shack catalog and found just what we needed—a simple, tiny microphone that hung under a window frame. Martha's late husband, whose picture was on the wall of her bedroom, watched us grimly. It took us a half-hour to run a wall-concealed thin wire from the mike out the top of the window, where Joe and Able, standing on the fire escape, strung it around the corner of the building into Betty's apartment.

Then Andy and Joe flopped on Martha's bed. "On Dasher, Up Dancer, Up Prancer, On Cupid, Comet, Donner, and Blitzen." Andrea laughed so hard it sounded like Lawrence Welk champagne music. "Screw me, honey. Make my eyes pop!"

Alas, good friends, the continuing story of Dancer O'Day must wait, for the Premar movie is over. The noise you hear is cheering and applause. But stay tuned! Rais Daemon, dressed in a pinstriped suit, looking even more like the Establishment than Bren, is walking across the stage. Let's listen to his words of wisdom. . . .

Rais Daemon. January, the first year of Premar. From tapes made at the Premar Open Forum, transcribed by Merle Blanc.

Good evening. I'm Rais Daemon, and like Bren, Ellen, Merle, and all the Premar kids, I'm feeling very enthusiastic. After the Premar movie, we hoped you'd still be smiling, and you are. That proves what I've always believed: The man in the street, the little guy—you and I—who are the salt of the earth not only in America but the rest of the world, has a lot more sense than the bosses and politicians give him credit for. Some of those smart-asses who live in hundred-thousand-dollar homes in Connecticut, New York, and Los Angeles and prepare all that stupid, degrading advertising that appears on TV—one day they'll get the message. And those people in Washington and right here in Boston who fawn all over you to vote for them—not to help you, but so that they can get their hands in the money box—one of these days they'll all wake up too and discover they've lost power and that you and I have inherited the earth.

The newspapers tell you that I'm a wild-eyed revolutionist who screwed up St. Noir—Rais Daemon, the Black Castro, they call me. Well, it's not true. Most of you have never been to the Bahamas or the West Indies, so let me use this opaque projector and show you some pictures of

St. Noir. Here, for example, are photographs of some of the miles of beautiful beaches there. Look at all those pink and white hotels! Their owners are mostly white millionaires from the United States and Canada, and they own the beaches, too. Here and there the black people are permitted to bathe, but not where they might make the tourists nervous. Who are these tourists who can pay fifty to one hundred and fifty dollars a day to live in these hotels and gamble in these casinos? Have *you* ever had a winter vacation on St. Noir, or in Nassau, or Antigua, or any of the hundreds of Caribbean islands? Not likely. You're lucky if you can afford a vacation in Atlantic City or Coney Island. Now, here are pictures of shacks like those in which most of the black families of St. Noir live. As you can see, the people who live in them are barely existing on the fringes of a very rich world. So what was I trying to do?

I wanted the people to gradually take over their island and create a new kind of tourism—a family-style vacation—to make St. Noir into a place where *you* could take *your* family, by jet, for a week or two weeks, and live in inexpensively simple housing, with the black people, and eat their food and enjoy their hospitality and dance and sing in the sun and under the warm starlighted, unpolluted skies. Black and white people sharing their lives, instead of a few black people being corrupted by the rich Americans' money, and the majority living in poverty.

I hope you have read "Confamiliaum: A Proposal," which we tried to deliver to every flat and house in Topham's Corner last week. Later we will be rapping together about this idea, but for a few minutes I want to show you how Premar, Confam, and the idea of a democratic communal St. Noir are interrelated and converge. Perhaps, as I'm talking, you will also understand that none of us are yelling slogans and waving guns. Rather, we believe, if all of us pull together, we can reinherit the world. We'll take it back from those who are draining it, because we have learned how to make the system work *for us*, and because we have learned how to love one another.

So tonight we're going to tell you how we think that all of us working together with a common objective can create a new Topham's Corner, and make it a forerunner of hundreds of thousands of small communities—green islands within the city where man can rediscover his dimensions and where we can give new meaning and purpose to the urban area. Once again using the projector, I want to give you a fast tour of some of the major cities of the world. Here is East Berlin—the Russian-controlled sector. Look at these miles and miles of highrise apartment dwellings. Are these really places where human beings can live, or were they designed for robots? Imitating the Americans and the Europeans, the Russians show their lack of vision in these huge projects where people are huddled together in stone-and-glass prisons. To be happy in Russia it would be better to be in Siberia. At least there you could breathe the life and vitality of a snow-covered world. Scientists have made extensive studies of rats, and they have discovered that when they are crowded together, some become apathetic, some die, and the tough ones become vicious and attack each other. Are humans different? Here are pictures of Pruitt-Igoe, the housing project in St. Louis. Ten years ago, when it was built at a cost of millions, Pruitt-Igoe was supposed to be the best in low-income housing. As you can see, the people who formerly lived in it destroyed it. Pruitt-Igoe was bombed out, and the housing authority has now torn it down. Here, in our own back yards, in Cambridge, are Roosevelt Towers, where the crime rate is so high that it has become impossible to live there. Stabbings, rape, drunkenness, are a way of life. If you walk into the empty tower building, you can't stand the smell of shit and piss.

There are hundreds of other such projects I could show you. Housing such as this ultimately turns the occupants into suicidal savages fouling their own nests. These places soon become homes for terrorized humans who stay there only because they must have some roof over their heads, even if it is just a garbage-pail cover.

In Europe and in Russia and in the Russian-controlled countries like Hungary and Czechoslovakia, the people are even more complaisant than we are here. Look at these pictures. These tiny one-room cottages and the flowers and vegetables growing on fifteen-feet-by-fifteen-feet plots is the low-income European's feeble response to herding. On the fringes of practically every major European city, these tiny vacation garden plots are the city dwellers' pathetic attempt to escape the highrise jails they live in, and recapture man's instinctual need to touch earth.

Do our leaders and the presidents of industry and the

banks care about you and me? For thousands of years billions of black and white and yellow consuming, taxpaying units, you and me and our forefathers, have lived and died and accomplished one purpose on earth—to consume products and provide services. Through the medium of money—a paper exchange for your labor—the owners and managers of wealth who keep a portion of your labor can still retain their power. The power they once claimed as their divine right is now money, and with it they control your lives. Why do we have an economy that depends on four firms producing eleven million new cars each year? Why do we have a way of life that depends on you and I owning two automobiles—one to get to work and one for our families to get to the shopping centers or drive kids to school? Why have our so-called planners used your tax dollars to build tens of thousands of miles of high-speed highways? How often do you personally use these highways for pleasure? Or is their purpose just to get back and forth to work? If you occasionally use them to go on a vacation, do you really enjoy the illusion that you are going somewhere, driving seventy miles an hour, to another city that looks just like Boston? Maybe you're only trying to escape to where there's some earth or sea still left. Do you need superhighways for that? These highways were built with your dollars—not for you, but for the profit of the owners and managers of wealth who clutter them with their huge cross-country trucks while they personally fly over them in airplanes. The reason our railroads weren't improved to carry freight between cities, instead of using trucks, is that it was more profitable to build highways.

Why do we have this kind of world, instead of a world where every family has a chance to live in well-designed communities, in homes and apartments which would give each of us space to expand and express ourselves as creative human beings? The reason is that the real-estate men, the investors, and the politicians who have their fingers in the pie can't make money by selling you a simpler kind of life. It isn't profitable to let you touch earth or make it easy for you and your family to coexist with green growing things. So they've created synthetic environments where you are scarcely aware of the changing seasons or your own bodily rhythms vibrating to the earth rhythm as a normal part of your life.

The owners and managers have jammed vast numbers of the low-income people into standardized highrise apartments, and now they've learned how to prebuild and stack your housing in inhuman, prefabricated modules. And what do the politicians do who told you they would help you if you voted for them? When they are elected they pass laws which permit these rich investors to borrow money at very low rates. Then they tell you that they're really very public-spirited citizens. They've built needed housing, haven't they? You bet—stone-and-glass asylums where the human spirit slowly turns to jelly. Rooms with a view on what? Housing for the mindless. Do the builders of these inhuman jungles and the few million rich Americans want the people who live in them to be happy? Of course not. If you were happy in your home, and you found a full life in a community of friends, you'd no longer be so mobile—you wouldn't spend half your life in an automobile escaping from these human rookeries. You wouldn't be buying so much gasoline and oil or eating the ersatz food sold to you in the endless hamburger, pizza, and fried-chicken franchises. It's important to keep you mobile and restless, because the job you are doing may suddenly be eliminated by technological change. If you were happy where you were living, you wouldn't want to move to another city. If lots of people didn't move every year, there would be a shortage of human cogs to fit into the machinery. That machinery isn't designed to come to you. You have to go to it.

Now, let's look at some of the cities of the world and try to discover if the designers are people-oriented, or if the modern architects and city planners are really more interested in creating monuments to glorify their own ingenuity and immortalize themselves in some freaky way, like the Egyptian monarchs did with their sphinxes and pyramids. As you watch these skylines projected on the screen, note that all of these cities have skyscrapers erupting in all directions. Why skyscrapers? The architects' answer is that it saves space for people. That, in plain words, is crap. The real reason is that designing cities where people live in such congestion automatically increases the value of land in central-city areas. The owners of these buildings can rent office space for twenty dollars a square foot or more. Here is the skyline of the new city of Boston, which has been created in less than fifteen years. Note, as we switch from city to city, that the fifty-story and higher towers mostly belong to insurance companies, banks, or investment companies. The white-collar office factories have three things in common. They cost money, someone made a profit from them, and they are glossy work-oriented areas occupied during the day by people who have driven into the city from the suburbs and leave it as fast as they can maneuver their cars through the traffic at night. For a very large percentage of these workers, the city—whether it be Boston or any other city—is not a place to spend their leisure or enjoy the potential cultural offerings of music, art, theater, and people mingling together. If it weren't for the black people and low-income people, and—in the case of Boston—a very large student population, the city would be deserted at night. What joy is there in walking through the lonely plazas of the Prudential Center and standing in the shadow of John Hancock Tower at night, or wandering across the empty windswept plaza of the Government Center, or staring idly at the people-less Christian Science Plaza dominated by a huge pool that wasn't built for swimming or wading?

These areas don't glorify man. They are monuments to the emptiness in the minds of the men who conceived them. Did you ever stop to wonder why man builds exquisite environments for his fellow man to work in, while the homes many of us live in and in which we raise our families are old, decayed, crowded slums? I'll tell you why: because we live in a world created by leaders who believe in Work—not in God or Joy and Love and Humanity.

Here is a picture of John Portman, a man you probably never heard of. He's a famous architect, a builder of hotels, and he is interested in the inner city. Here is a picture of Portman's famous Regency Hyatt Hotel in Atlanta. Here is his Regency Hotel in San Francisco, and here is a picture of a new one in Times Square. You can see that Portman is not designing hotels for people like us. Though it may be nice to take a glass elevator to the top floor, and no matter which floor your room is on, it's quite spectacular to look down on the lobby, hundreds of feet below you, I'm sure that *you* can't afford to pay forty dollars a night for a room in these hotels. Yet, most architects and city planners agree that John Portman is having more impact on the city than any other architect in the country. And Portman has said to the owners and managers of wealth, "You've got to take space and merchandise it for human use and human activity. We try to see what man likes in his environment and then crank that in—that's cranking in success."

The success that Portman is talking about is not success for you, because he's not concerned with how or where you live. On the screen now is an advertisement for a new condominium, Chestnut Towers, in Newton, a few miles from here. Note that the bathrooms are all of imported marble from Italy. If you have the right credentials, the brokers will pick you up in a Rolls-Royce and drive you out to see it. All you need to buy one is seventy thousand dollars up to two hundred and fifty thousand dollars. It's rumored that a few years ago one of the developers of Chestnut Towers was a slum landlord in Detroit. Such developers are not interested in you and me. They can't crank in success—which means money—out of poverty.

Never mind! Let Portman and other architects give you a World's Fair, a Walt Disney hodgepodge of glitter and gimcrackery. Will he or any of these architects create an environment for you and me—middle-class and poor Americans—to live in? No, because they measure buildings only in rental yield per square foot. They can't rent homes to you and me where we can have families and try to build a strong America for our children. Why? Because we can't pay an annual rental of twenty-five dollars a square foot. Measure that in your head—that's twenty-five dollars for twelve inches by twelve inches of space. The only time you're going to be worth that much rental is when you're dead. Some of these architects and developers love man so much they are now building "Death Hiltons," million-dollar skyscrapers—you can see the first one, in Nashville—where they bury you in style. Your relatives pay even more than twenty-five dollars a square foot so that you can finally rest in peace.

About fifteen years ago in the West End of Boston, the city fathers had a chance to develop and rehabilitate a thriving ethnic community. What happened? Herbert Gans wrote a book about it called *The Urban Villagers*. All the human-dimension turn-of-the-century buildings were torn down. When you ride by now on Storrow Drive, you can see how "success was cranked in." The community was destroyed to accommodate the rich who can afford to pay six hundred dollars a month or more for a view of the Charles River and Boston harbor.

Here's a picture of the city of Atlanta as it is proposed for the year 2000. Note the plazas, all overshadowed by huge office buildings and store complexes. All a person can feel in this environment is a complete lack of individuality. Architects and developers agree that letting you express your humanity isn't profitable. Here's an architect's drawing for a new central Chicago. It's called Chicago 21 because it's supposed to prepare Chicago for the twenty-first century. It will cost fifteen billion dollars to build. Part of it will be a new town in the South Loop of Chicago, with three thousand dwellings built on terraces over sixteen acres. You can bet that this won't be low- or middle-income housing. Here's a picture of the Houston Center in Houston, Texas. In the words of one of the developers: "While the profit motive was uppermost, the deeper we got into this, the more we realized the significance this development could have in Houston. We realized that we had a responsibility to the community."

That, friends of Topham's Corner, is pure bullshit. What kind of community? For the little man? The guy like you and me who survives by borrowing at an eighteen-percent interest rate from the banks and finance companies? The only community that the owners and managers of wealth are interested in is the community that gives them a profit on their investment. Building environments where you and I can realize ourselves as human beings and raise children who won't begin to wonder why they were born isn't profitable. Creating mechanical robots who ask no questions is what makes the world of wealth go around. The salt of the earth is everywhere, so you can't make much of a profit buying it or selling it.

Here's the World Trade Center in New York City, one hundred and ten stories high. One hundred and thirty thousand people work here. The architect, Minoru Yamasaki, believes that his towers "humanize the art of skyscrapers, inspiring the occupants with pride and a sense of nobility." Look at the tiny plaza surrounding his monstrosity. Trees planted here are like withered weeds. The theory dominating architecture is that we must build up to keep the land around us open and free. This is ridiculous. Man is open and free only when he can touch earth. Do you remember the story of Atlas, who held the sky on his

shoulders? With his feet off the ground, he was a weak-
ling. These buildings don't humanize man. They diminish
him, and alienate him, and weaken him.

Here, quickly, are skyline pictures of Paris, Hong Kong,
Montreal, Hamburg, London, Los Angeles. Do these cities
look warm and inviting? No, these stone-and-glass skyscrapers and apartments have a boring similarity. Cranking in
success limits human imagination! Here's an artist's con-
ception of the skyline of Jerusalem in another twenty
years. The skyscrapers have erupted like a pestilence. Today's architects and developers and their bosses—the owners and managers of the world's wealth—know what the
Egyptian monarchs knew: Man is dwarfed and humbled
and his spirit crushed by mighty structures that extol the
power of the ruler.

If you ever get rich enough to afford a room in one of
John Portman's hotels, after you've got over the initial
awe and shock you'll realize that the very sophistication
and impersonal gaudiness of this kind of environment pro-
hibits people from communicating as human beings. Along
with other guests, you'll have to play a role, put on your
mask, pretend to be what you're not.

Fifty years from now your grandchildren will wonder
what madness obsessed the owners of the world's wealth
to create cities with buildings reaching one hundred and
fifty stories in the air. They'll wonder whether the banks
and insurance companies that were trying to impress the
citizens with their wealth and power weren't run by impotent old men expressing their frustrated sexuality in huge
symbolic stone-and-glass penises, men who had come so
far away from the reality of life—of being born, living,
eating, making love, and dying—that they devoted their
lives to immortalizing their shrunken phalluses in sterile
stone images.

Your grandchildren will have to figure out how to tear
these huge buildings down. By that time man will discover
that he is only human when he lives close to the earth,
and by then it will no longer be feasible to waste the energy to run the elevators or to air-condition these mauso-
leums. Kids of the next century will wonder why in the
1970's man didn't create some sane working environments.
Human-scale one- and two-story factories and office buildings surrounded by open country and trees and homes
from where the working people could walk to work, and

hear the birds singing, and smell the burgeoning spring, or feel the brisk sting of winter making their blood run and renewing their lives. An environment that would not only let man feel less cramped at his work, but closer to people and unafraid to develop intimacy and be open and self-disclosing with his friends.

You and I—like millions of little people—are jammed into the rim of one of these cities. We live in former suburbs, in old and deteriorated housing and ghettos that separate the inner city from new suburbs. But now an important change is happening: We here at Topham's Corner have the opportunity to create a warm, life-giving community, right in the core city. From our little island, fingers will extend right into downtown, will begin to turn it green and to humanize it. But we can only do it on the terms that the owners and the managers of wealth understand. We'll crank in success, we'll buy our way into the system on the Establishment's terms. We'll give the owners a return on their investment and a repayment of their principal, and at last our children will own their own land and the roofs over their heads.

In the lobby you have seen a model of this island community—your Topham's Corner. Here on the screen is a retouched photograph of our Central Square. Note that the square is no longer jammed with automobiles. Note that Franklin Road, just below the square, has been closed off and turned into a parking area. Note that the sleazy, screaming neon signs that now dominate the square have been removed. Each store and bank has just one simple sign over its entrance. Note the sidewalk cafés, which will be enclosed in the winter. Note that, in the central areas, Franklin Road has been dug up and replanted with trees, and there's a central pool for wading in the summer and skating in the winter. Now, go further and visualize the square as a huge oval surrounded by shops, banks, stores, and little theaters. Visualize the present narrow intersecting streets turned into rambling walking alleys. Visualize that all of the families in Topham's Corner have combined themselves into ten to twenty Confamiliaum groups. Visualize all these Confams in friendly competition with each other—joining in open meetings like this one, creating an exciting new style of living for each and every one of you. Now, before we open the forum to general discussion, I'm happy to tell you that last night the families on Warren and Benson roads met in the Premar dayroom and voted unanimously to incorporate themselves into the first Confam in America. We have the saddle and the reins on a new Topham's Corner—and eventually a new America! Come along with us as we ride into the twenty-first century!

Julian Howe. January, the first year of Premar. Third portion from tapes transcribed by Samantha Brown.

The cheering is gradually quieting down, and the Open Forum on Premar and Confamiliaum is about to begin. Before long our friend and yours, Dancer O'Day, will make a public retraction of his attacks on Premar and, to the amazement of just about the entire audience, will hop on the Confam and Premar bandwagon. Since the acoustics here and the limitations of this recorder make it impossible for me to record the audience participation in this Open Forum, let me, at least, finish the story of the capture of Sitting Bull and his subsequent conversion.

When we finished bugging Martha's bedroom, we explored the apartment. There were five rooms: a living room, an extra room with a small bed that Martha was using for a sewing room, a bedroom, a kitchen, and a bathroom. In the living room there was a framed enlargement of Martha and Dancer taken beside the swimming pool of what looked like a Holiday Inn. There were also pictures of Martha with an older woman, who must be her mother, and pictures of a couple of kids with their mothers and fathers. Some letters on top of her desk revealed that these pictures were Martha's children and grandkids. Andrea was fascinated. "Martha Casey must be about forty-seven," she figured. "That makes her about the same age as Dancer, only to be a grandmother she must have got married sooner."

Martha's husband looked down at us from another photo in the living room. His crew cut made him look like a popeyed porcupine wearing a police uniform. From another picture we discovered that Martha used to have dark hair before she dyed it blond. We found out later she has big soft breasts and a forest of very black pussy hair.

The bedroom door opens out into the living room. Sergeant Joe pointed out that if Martha left her bedroom door open when she jumped in the sack with Dancer, Able would have to start taking pictures about two seconds after we opened the front door. "However, Joe said, "My guess is that Martha Casey is like my old lady. When she goes to bed with my old man, which isn't often, even if no one is in the house, she locks the bedroom door." That got us into an extended discussion about parents and screwing. We took a poll and found out that none of the guys would care if their kids caught them making love. Cheryl agreed with them, but Samantha and Andrea weren't so sure. "At least, I wouldn't want my kids standing around watching me," Samantha said.

"Maybe they don't make love at all," Able said. "My father is only three years younger than Dancer, and the way Ma looks at him, I'll bet he's not making it with her more than twice a month."

"Martha isn't Dancer's old lady," Cheryl pointed out. "Maybe that makes the difference. They're not used to each other."

"Anyway," Joe said, "we won't crash until we're sure they're in bed. I'll hang around down in the street until Dancer arrives, and the rest of you can wait around Betty's apartment. When I finally show, you'll know Dancer is here. Then, Able, and you, Julie—be ready for action! I'll open Martha's front door. Julie and I will be right behind you, Able; don't worry!"

On Tuesday, Able was still worrying, and so were the rest of us, except Joe. By eleven o'clock in the morning all of us except Joe were in Betty's apartment. We had tried Martha's phone, and she answered it very politely. "No, you have the wrong number," she told us. "This isn't Uncle Wiggly's Market."

At quarter past one Uncle Wiggly still hadn't arrived, and we were all so nervous that every ten minutes one or the other of us was taking a piss. Able had brought six joints, made from grass he had grown in flowerpots last summer, but the few drags we took, instead of turning us on, made us all morose, and we got to thinking this was a hell of a thing to be doing. It was stooping almost as low as Dancer did when he got Premar raided and then denied he was the instigator.

At quarter of two, Joe burst into Betty's apartment out of breath. He was dancing up and down with glee; he had cornered his man. "He's here! He's in Martha's apartment right now," Joe said, and sniffed the air. "It smells like a moldy hay barn in here. For God's sake, you creeps have been smoking grass! Snap out of it! We need alert minds."

A half-hour later we were still all crammed into Betty's bathroom listening at the other end of the bug, but the only words we had heard were Martha's. "Make yourself comfortable, honey," she had said. "I'll be with you in a minute."

"I think she's fixing her hair," Cheryl whispered.

"You don't have to whisper," I said. "This isn't a two-way bug."

"Maybe she's getting undressed." Samantha was grinning.

"Maybe they're going to make love in the living room," Andy said.

"You can count me out," Able said. "This is getting too complicated."

Joe's brow was furrowed. "If they're running around bare-ass, maybe we can get a picture of them from the fire escape."

"Not this kid," Able said. "I'm not climbing four flights of fire escape in this weather."

"Maybe we should just go down to City Hall tomorrow," I offered. "We could tell Dancer we took the pictures from the window, and that if he doesn't lay off Premar, he won't be able to run for dog catcher."

"No, no!" Joe said. "Dancer would burn you at the stake. He's got to see in black and white that we've got him cold."

Somewhat later Samantha said, "I don't think this is very nice. Bren and Ellen and the people from the consortium would have diarrhea if they could see us." Then our little speaker cracked to life.

"Oh, Danny, Danny. I missed you."

"I missed you too, hon. But it was hard to get away during the holidays."

"Yes! Danny, yes! Yes! I wish we could do this every day."

Sergeant Joe was on his feet, shoving Able and me. "They must have undressed in the living room," he gloated. "It's now or never!"

Andrea shook her head. "You should have a search warrant."

"Jee-zus!" Joe looked at her disgustedly. "I'm a god-damned Mountie. Remember? Mounties can make out their own warrants." He was edging Able and me toward the door. "If Dancer's clothes are in the living room, we've got him by the short hairs. When we open the door, I'll grab his stuff and toss it in the hall. You girls collect it fast and run back here to await developments." Joe laughed. "Bren always said that a naked man isn't a fight-ing man. Now we can prove it."

After Joe had unlocked Martha's door, we discovered we were in luck. She hadn't put the night catch on, and Dancer's pants, coat, shorts—everything—were in full view, draped over a chair. The bedroom door was closed. Tiptoeing quickly into the room, Joe collected the clothing and handed it out into the hall.

A second later we heard Dancer say, "I thought I heard something. Did you leave the radio on?"

I yanked the bedroom door open, and Able started shooting pictures, lighting up the place with his electronic flash. Dancer was naked, very white, his prong big but flopping. He jumped out of the bed roaring like a wounded lion.

Martha screamed. "Danny! My God! Who are they?" Trying to cover herself with the sheet, she cowered on the bed.

"I got them!" Able yelled. "Let's get the hell out of here."

"You're not going anywhere, you son-of-a-bitch," Dancer yelled, and charged. "Give me that camera!" As Able was backing away, his face frozen in horror, expect-ing Dancer would pick him up like a bag of smelly shit and hurl him out the window, I knew it was up to me. I stuck my foot out and shoved Dancer from the rear. He staggered off balance and crashed against a coffee table that crumbled under his weight. White ass up, he lay sprawled across it, cursing and panting, and I was afraid that he was having a heart attack. So was Martha, who had left the bed and, heedless of her nakedness, was crooning over him and holding his beet-red face against her breasts. "Danny, Danny, it's going to be okay," she said. "They're only kids."

Their curiosity was too much for Cheryl, Samantha, and Andrea, and by now they were in the living room too, cowering against each other. Shocked at the destruction we had wrought, they stared down at the fallen gladiator and his sobbing mate.

"Give me my clothes, you rotten little bastards!" Dancer's breathing was still heavy. "I know who you are. You're those goddamned fucking Premar kids! You won't get away with this!"

"Neither will you, Dancer." Sergeant Joe had recovered his poise. "This is a citizen's arrest."

"Bullshit! I'll have you all in a home for juvenile delinquents by morning." Suddenly aware that three girls were looking at his shrinking penis, Dancer covered himself with one of Martha's silk sofa pillows. But Bren was right. Suddenly conscious that he was naked with three husky guys dressed in jeans towering over him, Dancer felt he didn't have a chance. Tears were running down Martha's cheeks and dribbling on her breasts. "Please," she sobbed, "what do you want from us?"

"Both of you get up on the sofa," I told them. "We don't like this any better than you do. We'll let you get dressed in a minute."

Sitting beside Dancer, her hair askew, her eyes red and swollen, Martha was trembling. Did Joe, Able, and I look that mean and nasty? Did Martha think we were going to beat them up?

"You aren't even as old as my children," Martha remarked as she wiped her eyes. Looking at the girls, she said, "Why are you letting them do such a terrible thing to us?"

"We're sorry, Mrs. Casey." Andrea choked, and I thought she was going to cry, too. "But Joe says it's the Code of Hammurabi. An eye for an eye and a tooth for a tooth."

"It's very simple," Joe said. "Let me bring you up-to-date, Mrs. Casey. Dancer has been sabotaging Premar any chance he gets. He doesn't even care enough about his own daughter to lay off. All we want to know is: Why does Dancer think adultery is okay, and premarital sex isn't?"

"I'm not discussing our business with a bunch of hippie freaks." Dancer was clutching the pillow against his balls.

"I'll give you two seconds to get my clothes and get the hell out of here."

Joe shrugged. "If we leave, you'll have to borrow one of Mrs. Casey's dresses to go home. Won't your wife think it's kind of funny that you've taken to wearing ladies' clothing? But don't worry, you'll get your clothes back eventually. We'll hand-deliver them to the mayor, along with enlargements of the pictures we just took. And we'll make enough prints of Dancer the Sex Pot to send them to all the city councilors and your police buddies and the newspapers."

"What do you want us to do?" Martha looked terrified, and his predicament was slowly sinking into Dancer's head.

Cheryl brought Martha a blanket to cover herself. "Look, Mrs. Casey," she said, "right now we're the only ones who know for sure about you and Mr. O'Day, and we don't care whether you make love together. In fact, we hope that when we get married that we can still make love with someone besides the person we're hitched to. We don't like Mr. O'Day much, but we're not mad at you."

"Sure." Samantha smiled at her. "We think it's great you've got a guy who likes you. Even if he's not a nice guy, he could be nice to you."

"So here's the pitch." Sergeant Joe butted into the feminine chatter. "You get your clothes back, Dancer, and everything the six of us know stops right here. Not even Ellen, or your sons, or your wife will hear about it from us."

Dancer's face was grim, but his huff and puff had switched out; we had blown his house in, and in seconds he had turned into an old man. It had evidently not occurred to him before that his kids would be more than a little shocked to hear that he was a big bag of sewer gas. "How much money do you want?" Dancer finally asked.

"You haven't got the kind of money we want," Joe said, "because we wouldn't take a million bucks, not even if you had it. All we want is a gift of love. The night of the Open Forum, on January 15, you're going to get up on the stage of the Strand Theater and tell everybody in Topham's Corner, and everyone who's listening to you on Channel 2, that Premar and Confamiliaum are great, and that anyone who votes for you votes for them. If you'll agree to do that, we'll give you your clothes right now, and when you've made the speech, one of us will give you a little present—the roll of film that Able has in his camera. And none of us will say a word about this."

"You've got three weeks to think it over," I said. Able, who had been snapping pictures all the time, finished the roll with a shot of Martha with a sheet around her and Dancer with the pillow crushed against his balls.

"You've got one hell of a fucking nerve!" Dancer shouted. "If you think I'm going to crawl for a bunch of long-haired junkie kids who are still wet behind the ears, you've got softening of the brain."

"Okay. If that's the way you want it." Joe shrugged and grinned at us. "Let's go, junkies."

"Wait a minute," Martha pleaded. "Dancer, do you love me?"

It was a question that Dancer didn't want to answer in front of us. "Oh, Martha, for Christ's sake!" he complained. "No kids, with shit still in their diapers, are going to blackmail me. I'd look like a goddamned ass backing down on Premar. Anyway, Premar is sick. These kids don't know what love is all about."

"Do we know what it's all about?"

Dancer stared at her, and amazingly there were tears in his eyes. Finally he turned to us. "Give me my clothes. I'm not promising you a fucking thing. How do I know you'll keep your mouths shut, anyway?"

Andrea and Cheryl had already brought Dancer's clothes back from Betty's apartment. They dropped them in a chair in the front hall.

"Okay, Dancer . . ." Sergeant Joe was smiling from ear to ear. With one leg in the stirrup, he was ready to mount his horse and ride away into the sunset. "We'll see you the night of January 15. Mrs. Casey, you are invited as a guest of Premar. Make it good, Dancer."

Good friends, you are about to witness a conversion. Bren Gattman has just announced that Dancer O'Day has requested permission to respond to some of the questions from the audience about Premar and Confam. Hold your breath, here's Dancer!

"Neighbors, Topham's Corner is my home town too! I guess you all know who I am. Like you, I've listened with interest to this young fellow, Rais Daemon. And having read his Confamiliaum proposal, I'm proud that we've got men like him—not only in Topham's Corner, but in the city of Boston, and in this great country of ours. Now, you may be wondering what I'm doing on the stage of this famous old theater on this particular evening. Are you wondering if Dancer O'Day has gone off his rocker? A few weeks ago, wasn't I telling you that Rais Daemon was just another crazy-ass, hopped-up black man out to wreck America? Well, I'm going to tell you something. I was wrong. Yes, Dancer O'Day has made a mistake. They say we all make mistakes, so maybe mine proves at least that I'm human. The mistake happened because I was jumping to conclusions. That's the trouble with most of us white people. We hear the black folks complaining, but we don't listen. Well, I listened tonight, and you and I know that here's a black man with a good idea. Now, I'm not sure that you can mix black and white folks up in these Confamiliaums, but then, I'm not sure you can mix up the Irish and the paisans—even though I've been happily married to a paisan for thirty-two years. But I want my black friends in this city to know that when I'm elected mayor this fall, I'm going to create a special Confamiliaum department in the city of Boston. And you can believe me, the new officials of the city won't feather their own nests. We'll work together in every way to give low-income people—and I'm one of them—a chance to survive and live a decent, law-abiding life in this city. And you won't have to worry about crime or being attacked on the streets or having your children exposed to filth and corruption."

"Julie, this is a funny kind of speech."

It's a political speech. He's damning with faint praise.

"How come he's praising Rais and not Bren?"

There aren't many Jews in Topham's Corner, but there's a lot of blacks.

"But Bren is his son-in-law, and we told him to help Premar."

He's not finished yet. And Bren is a harder pill for him to swallow.

"Why?"

Because he still believes that Ellen wouldn't have sex with a black man.

"Do you think she will?"

Damn, Sam-Sam, listen to his speech."

"And you can take it from me that some of the politicians in this city are no better than the owners and managers of wealth that Rais told us about. The only reason many of them want elective jobs is so they can get their hands in the till and play footsie with the big-shot rich Boston Brahmins. But they wouldn't be caught dead in Topham's Corner, because no rich people live here. But no matter what else you can say about Dancer O'Day—even that he likes women—now I ask you, is that so bad? Would you want some kind of pansy ... fruitcake representing you in this city? I just want to tell all the gals who go down to the polls and vote for me—rain or shine— I do like you. I love you! And your old man doesn't mind that I love you, because you both know the *big* truth. I'm one of you. Well, I grew up in Topham's Corner. After the big war I came back here, and I walked these streets and I watched out for your homes. And all the time I was on the force, I never took a dime from anyone—not even to fix a parking ticket. I'm clean, and I'm proud of it, and when I'm mayor you can count on it that I'll stay that way.

"Now, I want to talk with you a few minutes about this place called Premar, and I'm going to be damned honest with you. Tonight Ellen's mother and I were more than a little shocked to see our daughter running around naked on this screen. I haven't seen her that way since she was five years old, and the only way I could look at that screen was to pretend that this was some other woman. I felt it just couldn't be my daughter running around with her husband and all those college kids stark naked. Now, I don't want to be pig-headed about Premar, but I can only say that I may be more right than I'm wrong. Still, I've decided to withhold judgment, because, after all, I'm not God; I'm only Dancer O'Day, a humble Irishman. Now let me explain my wait-and-see attitude. A few weeks ago, a friend of mine invited six of the Premar students to a little private discussion on Premar. For better or worse, we wanted to find out directly what was going on in those tenements on Felton Street. My friend understood that I didn't want any publicity, and we agreed that no one connected with the press or TV would be told that I was there. Hell's bells, after all the commotion, if some of the reporters had heard a story like that, you'd have been reading it in the newspapers. Dancer O'Day was skinny-dipping last night with the Premar kids! Well, you can bet your ass—life, that ain't going to happen. If you want to accept their invitation to visit these Premar tubs and sit around in your skins from now on, it's all right with me. But don't expect to find Dancer O'Day giving you a political speech in his birthday suit. Anyway, what I want to say is, not one of these kids, in the past three weeks, have opened their mouths about that meeting. So I know one thing, the Premar kids may like skinny-dipping, but they're honest and they're honorable. And there may be worse things than young girls and boys sleeping with each other. In the old country, a girl used to sleep with a boy to get pregnant; that way she was sure to get a husband. Now girls sleep with boys and they tell everybody they don't need a husband. Maybe my generation are too old to be honest about sex. Gina and I went to the movies the other night, and you know, they don't make them for people our age anymore. The theater was packed with kids. And here on the screen was this actor George Segal, who is married and has a couple of kids, taking a woman, Glenda Jackson, who is a mother and also has two kids, for a weekend in Spain. I won't tell you about the language in that movie, and some of the sex stuff, but even though George and Glenda are a lot younger than I am or Gina is, they were both plenty sneaky—scared to death of getting caught playing fast and loose. In that respect, they weren't much different from you or me. If you go to Premar for four years, I guess afterwards, when you get married, sex is no big thing. Now, I'm not saying that's good or bad, but maybe being sneaky isn't the best way. Well, I'm nearly fifty years old, but Gina and I still keep each other warm on cold winter nights, and we didn't have to go to Premar to learn that. So while I won't endorse Premar— and I honestly can't believe that any good will come of mixing religions, or letting black and white sleep together—I admit that the world today is a whole new ball game. And I wouldn't want it written on my grave that Dancer O'Day wouldn't even sit in the bleachers to see who was going to win—and who strikes out."

"Julie, did he do what we wanted him to do?"

Listen to everyone clapping.

"He didn't say anything nice about Bren."

He didn't say anything bad. That's progress for Dancer. Look! He's walking down in the audience. There's Andrea, hugging him; I'll bet she's slipping the film in his pocket!

"Ellen is hugging Dancer. Oh, I think I'm going to cry. What's he going to think when he opens that film and finds it's completely blank?"

I don't know, Sam. Maybe he'll cry too when he reads our note: "Dear Dancer, this was the film that was in Able's camera. The pictures came out beautifully, but Martha was crying, and they were too sad to keep. So we voted to toss them back in the developer. Maybe we only learn from overdevelopment. Signed, The Silent Six."

From the journal of Mohammed Hassan, March-April, the first year of Premar.

Ellen was released from the hospital last week, but she still has to stay in bed a few hours every day. All the kids have admired her "miracle scar," which curves from her back under her arm to just below her left breast. Meanwhile, Bren has been meeting with banks and city officials. So far neither Rais nor Bren has been able to arrange a mortgage to get the Topham's Corner Confam off the ground.

One thing about Premar, it never settles down. Bren says that Utopias should never be achieved, nor should we ever accomplish all the goals we project for ourselves. If our reach exceeds our grasp, life will never be boring. When one of the Compars opens the tap on an idea like that, one them immediately jumps in the churning water and yells for the rest of us to join in. Ellen has been reading Erich Fromm's theories on aggression and violence, and at the first Human-Values meeting since her operation, she refused to be calm. She said, "God, it's nice to be able to think of something besides myself for a change." Her eyes were sparkling. "Listen to this: 'Among the answers to the questions of how violence and drug consumption can be reduced, it seems to me that perhaps one of the most important ones is to reduce boredom in work and leisure. This requires drastic change in our social, and economic and moral structure.' Fromm goes on to say, 'Man is a passionate being, in need of stimulation; he tolerates boredom and monotony badly, and if he cannot take a genuine interest in life, his boredom will force him to seek it in a perverted way of destruction and violence. I believe that the further study of what has become the illness of the age—boredom—could make an important contribution to the understanding of aggression.' " Ellen was looking at Bren. "Isn't that what we're working on—life styles that are a continuing self-renewal, an antidote for boredom?"

We'd all agree on one thing: Premar isn't boring. As Rachel Silverman, who's Julie's new roommate, told Bren, "Premar doesn't give you time to be a *kvetch* with your roommate. Before you really get him under your thumb, some other *shikseh*'s got him." The week before we went spring skiing we had the first Great Roommate Exchange. Two weeks later, my own secret poll revealed that about half of us aren't yet adjusted to our new crib companions. On the big day, Joe McDonald moved in with Kathy Flaherty, while I transferred my junk into Andrea Pillisuk's room. For the first game of musical chairs, we tossed a coin who would have to move. The guys lost, but in our next great switch, we'll stay put and the girls will move.

Kathy and I talked with Ellen and Bren before the switch, because neither of us wanted a new roommate. I really care for Kathy; she's my *good* friend. "Kathy and I really love each other," I told the Compars. "When you've got a good thing going, why screw it up?" Of course, I wasn't being honest. The few times that I've talked with Andrea, I got the feeling that she thought she was pretty superior stuff. Andrea has a fresh-scrubbed-white-innocent look. Watching her in the tubs, knowing that if I survived twenty-six weeks of Premar, I'd be rooming with her, a kind of violent feeling came over me, as if I were in silent confrontation with a racist. I wanted to slap her perfect white ass until she agreed to stop swishing it around, giving the guys the impression that all they had to do was reach out and grab.

How's that for being zapped out? I was jealous of Andrea, and I don't really know her. I suppose what bugs me and Kathy is that she's one of the Premars who's always the center of attention. Even last fall, before I knew him very well, I felt sorry for her roommate, Joe McDonald. He seemed like a little old hound dog, hanging on her footsteps, ready to lap her hand, even though she just whipped him. But after Christmas, something happened. A new Joe McDonald crawled out of the skin of the old Joe, and suddenly Andrea was his "lick". (Rais says that's St. Noirean for adoring girlfriend.) Now Samantha and some of the other kids are calling him Sergeant Joe. Did living with Andrea do that for him? Or maybe the Premar philosophy is working, and Joe isn't afraid of losing the poontang he never could own.

Ellen was sympathetic to the idea of Kathy and me remaining together, but Bren wasn't. "You haven't lost each other," he told us. "Both of you are going to be right here—learning and experiencing and discovering yourselves with other Premars."

"Yeah," I said, "but maybe Kathy doesn't want to go to bed with Joe." Kathy had been listening kind of quietly, and finally Ellen asked how she felt about having a new roommate. "I don't know." Kathy blushed. "I guess I was thinking . . . during the first weeks it wasn't easy for me to make love, and I haven't changed that much. Yes, I've learned how to enjoy making love with Mohammed, but starting all over is different. I'm not sure I can just jump into bed with Joe or any other boy and make love with him, because I really don't know him. And maybe I'm jealous of Mohammed. After he's been with Andrea, he may never want me again."

Bren hugged her. "Kathy, stop worrying. All of us are learning a new loving sensitivity toward another person. You and Mohammed aren't alone. A lot of the kids are frightened about experiencing their new roommates, not only as bed companions, but as friends."

"Even me." Ellen was smiling, but she had tears in her eyes. "I told some of the girls the other night that I'm just as innocent of knowing a second male as they are."

"That's the point," Bren said, looking at Ellen. "Suppose Hassan and Kathy had met outside Premar and had lived together for four months or a year. Then, what if they got married, and were still under twenty—as they would be— and then, what if one of them met another guy, or another girl, and one or the other thought this other person was the real thing? What would happen then?"

Kathy shrugged. "It would be messy."

"Well, that's part of what Premar is all about. Premar gives you a living, learning environment that lets you discover, with a minimum amount of interpersonal friction, the kind of man or woman who will really parallel your own emotional and intellectual needs. And, equally important, it gives you an emotional growing time to discover whether the ego needs you now have are realistic or not. We're happy as hell that you love each other. Now you're going to learn how to share that love and make it intrinsic, while at the same time you'll develop a new kind of self-confidence so that your love for each other never becomes a duty, but rather is a lifetime expression of your joy in each other's *being*."

I was bewildered. "What happens in two years?" I asked. "After we've roomed with four other people, who decides whether Kathy and I will really live together, and maybe get married?"

"You and Kathy do."

"Suppose Kathy discovers that she prefers Joe or some other guy, and I still prefer her."

"If Joe prefers Kathy, and after four years, the feeling between them is mutual, we think you'll not only be able to cope with that, but you'll still care for Kathy." Bren laughed. "We're living in a new world where people may not be expected to forsake past loves. If you finish Premar, perhaps you'll move into a Confam with Kathy or some other Premar girl. A Confam, partially composed of young people who have experienced Premar, would have the challenge of evolving both a complete community as well as an interwoven family structure that could offer a lifetime, postmarital, Premar adventure." Bren never misses a chance to speculate on Confam.

One of the keys to the roommate shift is that both roommates must either be on the work circuit or on the study circuit. The original pairings gave us all thirteen weeks of the same basic work-to-study structure. But at the time of the first Great Roommate Exchange, everybody still had three weeks to finish up their work or study program. Rais said this was deliberate, since from now on we should get to know our roommates in both the work and study phases of our Premar lives.

Andrea and I had three weeks to go on our study program before we rejoined the ranks of the working Premars. Of course, if you consider the Human-Values seminar as studying, no one ever stops learning something. Sometimes the reading load gets insane, especially when we get a book like John Galbraith's *Economic Goals and Public Purpose* as the book of the week. (We dug through that one a week ago, and Rais and Bren seemed determined to turn us into worthy opponents of Paul Samuelson and Milton Friedman, whose theories we now contrast with Galbraith's, as if we were economic experts.)

The book we're reading now, *Humanistic Psychotherapy,* by Albert Ellis, makes more sense, because it's where some of us are at (me, at least) after this roommate switch. The first night of the great switch, Andrea, who is studying computer programming at Northeastern University, and I, who am taking a whole bunch of freshman garbage from math to chemistry to English for a B.S. degree, weren't really communicating with each other.

Finally, I broke the silence.

"It's funny, we've been here almost five months, and you and I are still practically strangers. Goes to show, you don't know a dame, even if you've looked up her squish."

She just shrugged. "We've been in different groups. You spent most of your time with Kathy and other kids."

"Did you sleep with Joe every night?"

"No."

"Every other night?"

"It's really none of your business."

"Why isn't it? The easiest way to find out how you are in bed is to ask."

"Did you make love with Kathy every day?"

"Sure. Sometimes twice."

When a guy is bursting, he gets to the point, so I asked her, "Are you going to sleep with me tonight?"

Andrea shook her head. "I'm not a sex maniac. It takes me a little while to make up my mind that I'm ready to relax and enjoy it. Joe and one other guy, who just wanted any female to dip his wick into, are the only guys I've ever known. Maybe girls are different. I don't look at a guy and think I can't wait until he screws me. If I like a guy, I might just want to hug him and that's all."

"You think guys are different?"

"Sure, you're made different."

"Well, you're wrong. When Kathy and I were rooming together, I never gave the idea of screwing another girl a second thought."

Andrea laughed. "No wonder. Kathy took good care of you."

Even though the weather was cold, Andrea slept naked. The first few nights, when she'd come back to our room from the john, I'd watch her coolly toss her Turkish-towel robe on the foot of the bed. Her ass, in the air as she turned down the covers, was white and sassy. I could see her pubic hairs dangling in little curls between her legs. Finally, before she slid beneath the sheets, she'd turn and grin at me. "Good night, Mohammed." And that was that! Was she thinking I was going to beg her—or rape her? Man, she could sweat in hell! I could still pile the fuel on my going-to-sleep daydreams, and six times out of ten have a wet dream. To hell with her snotty white ass!

But I couldn't stand it, and a few days later I complained to Merle. "Andrea's sexy enough," I told her. "I asked Joe McDonald. She may not be as eager as Kathy, but she's not turned off, at least by white stuffing."

I knew Merle wasn't very happy with me. "You know, Mohammed, the way you're talking, I don't think you like Andrea—or maybe even Kathy, or any woman. All a female is for you is a way of getting your rocks off."

"That's shit talk," I told her. "I'd never screw with anybody who didn't like me, and I don't think Andrea likes me. I got to face it that she probably never wanted to room with a black."

Merle shook her head. "You're one of the few blood around here who makes me color-conscious. Until I talk with you, I just think I'm me, not some color, and so does everybody else. I thought you had got rid of your hang-ups with Kathy. You loved a woman because she was a woman, without thinking she was white or black."

"Andrea isn't like Kathy," I protested.

"Maybe she is. And maybe this conversation is like one you and I had about her a long time ago. Let it happen to you. Flow with the current. Stop fighting it. Here, in these houses, at least, whitey's not out to get you."

I wasn't so sure. But I was sure that the great world out there wasn't changing that much. A few miles away in the Dorchester High School, black and white kids were rioting. Premar was whistling in the dark. Black-dark!

I was wrong about Andrea, just as I had been wrong about Kathy, but it took me another week to find out. In the meantime I had sunk into one of my depressed moods. Joe and Kathy seemed to enjoy being together, and I kept thinking about Kathy, and I could imagine her snuggling

in bed with Joe. I guess she was happy to finally be with
one of her own kind. Funny, I was embarrassed to discuss
my sexual frustration with Bren or Rais, and I knew that I
wouldn't get anywhere with Merle, so I tackled Ellen.
Anyway, the night that she read to us Erich Fromm's theories on boredom I wanted to disagree, even though in
front of Andrea I knew my motivations were too obvious.
"I think Fromm isn't telling the whole story," I told Ellen.
I had corralled her in bed. "Maybe boredom turning into
aggression happens to a guy when he isn't having a good
sex life. If young guys involved in violent crimes would
tell you the truth, you'd find they are kids who never had
any loving in their whole lives. Jerking off with Playboy or
Penthouse in one hand isn't the answer, either. No matter
what the sex books say, masturbation doesn't give you that
warm, singing, its all's-right-with-the-world feeling that
you have when you make love with a girl who loves you."

Ellen propped up on pillows, taking her post-operative
bed rest, was smiling at me. She was wearing a pale green
nightgown. Her breasts were clearly visible, but Ellen
never makes me feel horny. I just want to tell her I love
her and hug her. "Mohammed, I agree with you," she
said. "I told Daddy, yesterday, that when Premar becomes
a way of life, law and order will be a much lesser problem." Ellen took my hand. "Lord—you have lovely strong
fingers." She stared into my eyes for a second. "Andrea really likes you. She told me yesterday. But you've got to
remember one thing—she comes from a poor white section of Detroit. Her mother raised her to fear black people. You're not helping. You probably scare her half to
death. Beneath the belligerent mask, you insist on wearing,
you're really a softy. How do we persuade you to take it
off? Have you been reading Albert Ellis?" Ellen pointed at
the book on the night table beside her bed. "Ellis's Rational Emotive Therapy gives you a good frame of reference. Ellis would say that you're at situation A. Andrea
rejects you. Then you jump to point C, and conclude her
rejection of you is because you're black and worthless, and
then you're angry with yourself and depressed. But if you
back up to point B, and rationally think about what is
happening to you and Andrea, you'll begin to understand
that you are insisting that Andrea respond to you in a particular way that caters to your own ego needs and your
own beliefs as how she "should" or "ought" to react to

you. Because she doesn't, isn't the end of the world." Grinning, Ellen handed me the book, *Humanistic Psychotherapy*. "Read that page to me."

I shrugged and read.

The main irrational ideas that all humans seem to subscribe to in order to manufacture their own states of panic, self blame and self doubt appear to be:

1) The idea that it is a dire necessity for an adult to be loved or approved by virtually every significant person in his community.

2) The idea that one should be thoroughly competent, adequate and achieving in all possible respects, if one is to consider oneself worthwhile.

3) The idea that human unhappiness is externally caused and people have little or no ability to control their sorrows and disturbances.

4) The idea that one's past history is an all-important determinant of one's present behavior and that because something once strongly affected one's life, it should indefinitely have a similar effect.

5) The idea that there is invariably a right, precise and perfect solution to human problems, and that it is catastrophic if this perfect solution is not found.

6) The idea that if something is, or may be, dangerous or fearsome, one should be terribly concerned about it, and should keep dwelling on the possibility of it occurring.

The main irrational ideas that men and women seem to endorse in order to create their own states of anger, moralizing and low frustration tolerance are these:

1) The idea that certain people are bad, wicked or villainous and that they should be severely blamed and punished for their villainy.

2) The idea that it is awful and catastrophic when things are not the way one would very much like them to be.

3) The idea that it is easier to avoid than face up to certain life difficulties and responsibilities.

4) The idea that one should become quite upset over other people's problems and disturbances.

"Okay," I gave her back the book, and I couldn't help laughing at Ellen's serious expression. I kissed her cheek. "You're getting to me. It's nearly Easter. Where's Calvary? I'll carry the cross." I found out later that Andrea asked Merle to switch us, so no former roommates would be sleeping in the same Winnebago.

We left at six, and Andrea was sitting beside me as I guided the mobile home through Boston's evening traffic. I asked her why she didn't want to be in the same Winnebago with Joe and Kathy.

"Use your head," she said. "Do you want to listen to Kathy whimpering while she makes love with Joe?"

This was intriguing. "How do you know she whimpers?" I asked, but Andrea didn't answer. Anyway, with Rais and Merle sleeping in the bunk over the wheel, and Rachel and Julie in the bed at the back, leaving Andrea and me to share the middle bunk, it looked as if somebody was going to be listening to somebody.

"I guess you'll finally have to sleep in the same bed with me," I said, and smiled at her impassive expression. "We could try tantric sex—no climax, no yelling."

"Who says we're going to take our clothes off?" Andrea was watching my reflection in the windshield. "If we don't find a camp ground to plug this box into, it's going to be colder in here tonight than a deep freeze."

"I borrowed an Arctic sleeping bag big enough for two from Bren," I told her. "We'd be really warm in it, sleeping naked, belly-to-belly."

Julie and Rachel, having weathered the Great Switch, were curled up together in the back of the trailer, while Rais and Merle sat behind us on the fold-out sofa. We could hear them discussing plans for renting skis and stuff and fooling around on the lower slopes of Wildcat Mountain. Then Rais said he had brought two gallons of St. Noirean rum, and Merle asked if he was feeling homesick. "Not really," I heard Rais say, "just the music and the dancing. Tomorrow night we'll make rum flips and hot rum toddies. Julie and I will play some calypso music on our guitars, and we'll teach the kids how to limbo. Very good exercise for the leg muscles."

"Oh, great! Then we can have an orgy," I said, muscling into their conversation and being antagonistic.

Merle laughed. "Someday I'm going to arrange an orgy for you, Mohammed, and let you get it out of your system. How many girls do you want at once? Three? Four? They'll lap you all over, and play with your big black putz, and eat it and shove it in them. Then they'll tie you down like the pygmies did Gulliver, and two of them will rub their titties in your face while one squeezes your dong and the other one rims your asshole. And in about two seconds, when you shoot your load, they'll do it to you all over again, and you'll be their sex slave. Rais and I will write it all down, and we'll call it *The Story of M,* and it'll be flakier than *The Story of O.* Would that make you happy, Mohammed?"

I could see Merle's face in the rear mirror. Her eyes were laughing, warm, affectionate. Her voice was like a throaty lullaby. She's the nice, friendly sister I haven't got. But I didn't want to give in too easily.

"Maybe it would be more fun than Premar. Once you get quiff off your mind, you can concentrate on more important things."

"Like what?" Rais asked.

"Like running a revolution," I said.

Rais was grinning. "Shit, man! *We* are a revolution. If you think all of those other revolutions and civil wars and world wars are important, just pick up a history of the world and see how many thousands of wars have been waged and millions of people have killed each other, and nobody gives a good goddamn. Do you really give a crap about World War II, or the Korean War, or the Vietnam fiasco? Of course not! And I care even less about those who died in World War I or the Civil War or the Revolutionary War. Six of us—sitting here in this bus and loving each other—are more important than any of those fucking insanities. Did any war ever fought make people love each other more? Making love, prying your real self out of your own selfish protectionist skin, is the only revolution that will save man. It starts with us, and it can grow exponentially, and one day there won't be any more wars." All the time Rais was raving he was smiling, and his words were like music with an upbeat that makes me want to yell and dance. I think he should run for president of the United States.

We got to Wildcat after ten, found a camping ground, parked the Winnebagos side-by-side, plugged into the electricity, and warmed up the pizzas we had bought en route. We all gathered in the Winnebago I was driving, and at

one o'clock we were still arguing about everything from
who was making breakfast tomorrow, to how the Great
Roommate Switch was working out, to how to shuss and
slalom, with Samantha, who has never skied, giving us expert advice and pantomines, to Merle and Rais teaching us
how to limbo, both stripped to the waist, while we all sang
with the music from a cassette tape, "Limbo-limbo like
me," passing under a ski pole we had erected and challenging Merle to try it naked, with the pole only three feet
from the ground. That was Joe's idea, and Kathy called
him a voyeur. I think we were all aware of the good feeling between us—twelve people, interacting easily with
each other, because we dared to like each other. Andrea,
who was sitting pensively beside me, kept playing with my
fingers and examining them like a baby with a new toy—a
black erector set, she told me later. But she was in charge
of the erection—not me!

Finally, with a consensus that we really should get some
sleep, the other kids went back to their Winnebago and I
put out the lights. Fumbling around in the dark, I whispered to Andrea, "Now you're just as black as me." She
was sitting on the foldout bed, in her ski clothes, as if she
couldn't make up her mind what she should do. We could
hear Julie and Rachel in the rear bunk undressing and finally smothering their giggles under a pile of blankets.

"Can two people really sleep in that bag you brought?"
Andrea spoke so softly I could scarcely hear her.

"Bren told me he slept in it with a girl when he was in
college."

"It's a beautiful moonlight night. Come with me for a
walk and bring the bag."

Andrea led the way to the door, past Rais and Merle.
"We're going to look at Mount Washington by
moonlight," Andrea whispered to the black air.

"Okay," we heard Rais mumbling. "Don't freeze your
asses."

Outside in the cold night air, Andrea grabbed me. "Mohammed, I'm sorry that I've been so bitchy. I wanted to
make love with you all last week, and then we got stale-
mated. Like both of us were determined not to make the
first move. Then, when I signed up with you for this weekend, I forgot we wouldn't be alone, and I suddenly realized that I couldn't in the Winnebago—not enjoy it,
anyway."

We were walking over the crunchy snow past rows of trailers and mobile homes toward a pine grove on the edge of the park. A mile above us, clear and remote as a mountain at the North Pole, Mount Washington, snow-covered, pale green and ghostly white, was moonlighted against the black sky. It was so cold that when I took a deep breath I could feel it deep in my lungs. I wondered how in hell we were going to get undressed and crawl into that bag naked without freezing. Ahead of us we saw a tall pine with branches hanging to within two feet of the ground. At the base of it, beneath the branches, there was no snow. We crawled under and spread the sleeping bag on a deep cushion of pine needles. Lying on top of it, Andrea wiggled out of her ski pants and jacket. She was na-ked under them. "I took off my bra and thermal under-wear an hour ago," she gasped as the cold air bit at her flesh. Then she slithered into the bag head-first. I kissed her disappearing behind. "Hurry, Mohammed, before you freeze it off," she said.

In ten seconds flat I was beside her, zipping up the bag, facing north to her south. I could hear her giggling as I bit her toes, which were poking against my face. We were both still shivering, me worse than Andrea. Then, while I couldn't see her, I knew she was arched over my face, her behind making an enclosed tent out of the bag. I could feel her warm breath on my shrunken, frozen penis. Somewhere near my knees I heard her voice. "I can't see him, but this poor baby needs help. You nearly froze him off." I tasted the silky hairs on her warm vulva. "Are you muff-diving, Mohammed?" she asked, but my mouth was too busy to answer.

Andrea turned and burrowed her way into my arms, kissing my lips. "You're okay now—too big a mouthful! I'm not afraid of you anymore, Mohammed."

"Why were you?"

"I don't know. Because of my mother, I guess. She read about those Boston hitchhiker murders. You know, those six girls—most of them were college girls. They were stran-gled, and their bodies left naked in the woods. They think a black man did it. Then, there was that girl that the black kids set on fire after they made her pour gasoline on her-self."

"What about the white guy in Texas who murdered all those white boys?" I asked.

Then Andrea was silent for a while as she nibbled my lips and brushed her hand over my belly. "Gosh, I like your pubic hair. It's no nice and prickly. Oh, Mohammed, Rais is right! You and I, loving and talking together, is the most important thing in the world. Come inside me! But don't come . . . yet."

I lay on top—me deep inside her—and we balanced on an orgasnic cliff for an hour, talking, kissing, floating, undulating against each other, until finally Andrea whispered in my ear. "You never asked me why I couldn't make love in the Winnebago."

"Because you didn't want anyone listening?"

"Worse than that. Oh, honey, I can't help it, but when it happens, I yell and scream and sob and scratch."

"We're two firecrackers in the same package," I told her.

Ellen O'Day. March, the first year of Premar. From cassette tapes transcribed by Rachel Silverman.

Oh, Bren, I love you. It's only two weeks to spring, and I'm alive! Breathing! This blood is flowing easily in my veins! My heart has a new, lovely rhythm. Sometimes I even forget what it was like, before. Five weeks ago today, at eleven o'clock on a snowy Tuesday morning, Valentine's Day, John Meserve, whom I shall love all my life, held my heart in his hands. And now my encrusted mitral valve may not be a brand-new expressway, but some of the bumps in the old road are patched. The tough weeds that were growing through the concrete are cleared, and my heart is no longer working overtime pumping my blood through the amazing cloverleaf of arteries that is me. Laura and I were talking about death today and how unimportant "things" suddenly become after you've walked through the valley of the shadow or lived on the precipice as I have. Promise me, Bren, if I ever complain or am petty about life, and people ... remind me, I could be dead.

But I won't forget. I promise you! Each day I wake to morning, I'll thank whatever gods may be. I'm new! I'm overflowing with love! First, I'm singing—doing somersaults in my head; and then, a minute later I'm blissfully floating. I look in the mirror at the long scar curving under my arm, stopping just below my left breast, and I can't help smiling and touching my breasts. Oh, dear me. It's been too long. They need you! When I told you that my scar would always look terrible in a bathing suit, you kissed it and called it "a smile of wonder." Bren, why can't a man who performs such miracles to save his fellow man create a world where all men and women love each other? Maybe Premar is a beginning. Maybe we can teach our children to stop reenacting the same ancient *self-created* tragedies. Maybe we can teach new generations of men and women that laughter at oneself is a better cure for bruised egos than anger and hatred toward others.

A few hours before I was finally released from University Hospital, John listened to my heart and examined my "wounds" to see how I was healing. As he silently bent over me, wrapped in his professional barricade, I wasn't able to contain my tears. I not only told him that I loved him, but I tried to put my feelings into words. For me, he was as wondrous as the primitive tribal medicineman—a saint who had known how to touch me with his fingers so that I could breathe normally again.

John smiled at my torrent of words and brushed my cheek affectionately. "I'm not ready to be canonized, Ellen. I'm just a reasonably good mechanic—a heart surgeon—for which I'm well paid."

"But you love life," I told him. "If you don't, what impels you to work so hard—probing into muscles, veins, and arteries—to preserve it?"

John laughed. "I like 'impels.' It presupposes someone out there—God, you name it. And why not? Whoever, whatever, holds the carrot or whips the donkey is determined that the life cycle doesn't stop. Maybe for me it was simple environmental conditioning. When I was a kid, I was always collecting living things. Bugs, frogs, snakes, hamsters, gerbils, wounded birds, and starving alley cats. I was mad as hell when one of them died. The driving need of the organism, whether it be animal, fish, vegetable, or human, to live out its full life cycle—often succeeding against impossible odds—was etched on my subconscious."

I showed John the book Bren had bought me. A beautifully bound, four-hundred-and-sixty-five page yearbook of the twenty-fifth reunion of the class of 1904 of Yale University, with individual photographs twenty-five years later. Some reading for a hospital patient! Bren had paid twenty-five cents for it at a secondhand book sale at Lauriat's. His eyes were filled with dancing laughter at my bewilderment when he handed it to me. "They belong to us, Ellen, all three hundred and seventy-six members of the 1904 graduating class. Some of them were already dead in 1929. Killed in World War I. Look at those who were still alive in their golf knickers and caps and white flannels and straw hats. Look at their stiff necks in their tight Hoover collars. Look at their determined, self-assured faces. Imagine the undeviating, unrelenting minds behind those frozen confident expressions. Those who survived World War I, in June 1929, at their twenty-fifth reunion, were the leaders of America. Here they are at the height of their careers. October and Black Friday on Wall Street and the Depression was yet to come. Read all these good old New England names. And look here. There was one! One black man in their class. Read the catalog of their successes and achievements. Between the lines, you can fill in their daydreams and failures." Bren was really entranced with his new responsibility. "No one alive in this whole world," he told me, "except you and me, cares whether these men ever lived. All of them are either dead or over one hundred years old. Only you and I can give them any reality at all. Wouldn't they be surprised if they knew that the man who is trying to unpry their dead hands, still clutching at a world they can never see again, is probably one of the few persons alive who would spend twenty-five cents to rescue them from oblivion."

When I repeated Bren's conversation, John was really amused. "Maybe Bren is trying to tell you that human life doesn't amount to much. We have no time to honor the dead heroes who led us up to our necks in quicksand."

"I think Bren wanted to simply dramatize, for the kids at Premar, how transient we all are. Which is at least one good reason why we should love the living. Those not yet born may have good reason not to love us." I grinned and squeezed his hand. "I love you. For whatever reason, you gave this organism, Ellen, a new shot at living. It's a great gift. I can't disappoint you."

"Pay your Blue Cross." He laughed. "I enjoy my luxuries."

But I should go back. The trouble with unloading your mind on tape is that you ignore continuity. Since this is for the Premars, it's necessary to know where I've been to understand where I am. Physically and mentally! Bren says that all of us have so many ideas exploding in our heads at any one time that we need to set aside the time to recapitulate. It helps give us new perspectives. So, Bren, sweetie pie, let me give you the jitters. I haven't been to bed with Rocky Stone . . . yet; but he's asked me. Oh, hell, I'm too wedded to the one-and-only traditions to ever want anyone except you. When some of the kids who were dead-set, a few weeks ago, against changing their first roommate, listen to this, they'll be sure I'm a hypocrite. But God knows I'm sailing on uncharted seas, too.

Okay, I'm backing up to three weeks ago, Saturday. The day you drove me to New York to stay with Laura. I really didn't want to come here. But being me, the first day home from the hospital I was immediately poking my nose into the day-to-day excitement of Premar and Confamiliaum. I can't help it. My Irish temper has a low boiling point. I get mad! It isn't enough that you and Rais haven't been able to convince any banks to give Confamiliaum a mortgage loan, or that you can't get any reply from the Department of Housing and Urban Development, or that the president is talking out of both sides of his mouth (as usual) about federal appropriations for low-income housing, but now Daddy is backtracking on both Confamiliaum and Premar, and wondering out loud if the only "real" solution to racism and core-city housing problems is segregation "until the black people learn to live up to their responsibilities."

While I was foaming at the mouth at Daddy's stupidities—determined that, if he wouldn't visit me at Premar, I'd beard the lion at City Hall and stand up at one of the weekly Council meetings and tell the great Dancer O'Day, if he wouldn't work with us, then at least he could stop undermining a really viable solution to the central-city housing problem, namely Confamiliaum—Bren tricked me. Yes, you did, Bren. Your story was that Laura telephoned you from the Stones' Park Avenue co-op apartment and desperately needed a friend.

Rocky hadn't been in the United States since last November. In their only encounter since the air crash, Rocky told Laura that he was delighted that she was alive and well. When she told him that she was also pregnant, he managed to swallow that, too. He could understand how that might have happened under the circumstances. Rivke told us the whole story when she came to Boston with Abe to meet me. I wasn't black, but Irish and bad enough already. Rivke was sorry, but I should understand that some of Bren's relatives might never speak to him again. To add to their troubles, Laura was adamant: Come hell or high water, she was going to have the baby, and if Rocky divorced her—as he said he would if she didn't have an abortion—she'd tell everybody it was Rocky's child. Hadn't he traced his ancestors to Algeria? That was Africa as far as she was concerned. Anyway, a lot of people who looked white had black blood, and Rocky was no Scandinavian blond beauty. The way the world was going, what difference would it make if one of the heirs to Stone-Western Industries was black? Abe was appalled at the very idea of being *zeyde* to a *schvartzer* grandchild! *O, yeder not zich zayn pekl.* Laura was acting even crazier than Bren. He was certain that God was mad at him, but he couldn't figure out why.

Furious, Rocky had disappeared, and Laura guessed he was living in Cannes with Jeanne Mechante. According to Laura, at any moment he might die of a heart attack—working to be richer than Onassis while trying to get his limp dick to rise to the occasion. Certainly he would never stop trying. Rivke reported that Shulamith and David were cold to the idea of having a black sibling and that David had told her, "Mother, you really are too old to enjoy a civil-rights pregnancy."

Anyway, according to Bren, Laura, depressed and frightened, with no one to cheer her up, was holed up in her huge apartment. Except for her doctor and some of the co-op staff, who delivered groceries, she had seen no one for months. Despite the pleas of Harry Bacon, her doctor, and assurances that if she persisted he would enlist the aid of some interns and kidnap her in an ambulance,

Laura was determined to have the baby in her own bed and not in any damned hospital.

Bren and I consulted with John Meserve, who thought I was going to New York to be a companion to a happily pregnant woman for a few weeks. John agreed that it would be just fine for me to take it easy in such a nice, calm environment and said he wouldn't need to see me again for a month. On the telephone Laura told me she expected the baby about March 13. After we arrived in New York and had been cleared by the uniformed security guard, I quickly discovered that I wasn't as much Laura's companion as she was mine. My fairy godmother, with her swollen belly, was religiously doing her breathing exercises with a to-hell-with-it attitude. Laura still couldn't believe she was alive. If this wasn't a dream, she asked me, then why was she the only survivor of that air crash? She wondered aloud whether she was meant to have this baby as expiation for a useless life.

Standing naked in this glass bubble that covers the roof of Rocky Stone's penthouse, and watching Laura swimming in the rooftop pool, I find that by turning my head slightly I can also see the tootsie-toy automobiles on the streets and ant people of New York plodding back and forth between work and home. Have they any idea that thirty floors above them, on top of this glass-and-stone tower, Rocky Stone has one of his several homes? Probably most of them never even heard of Rocky. If they had, would they be surprised to discover that four thousand individuals control half or more of all the wealth and raw materials in this nation? But what does it matter?

Two years ago, before this building was finished, Rocky decided that he needed a new apartment for October and November, the only months he could tolerate the city. Finally he bought the top floor for $600,000. Below this apartment are twenty-nine others, none of which were sold to the owners for less than $250,000. Isn't that unbelievable? The entire mortgage that Bren has been unable to obtain, and which would be guaranteed by forty-eight families, isn't much more money than the price of this one apartment, which up to now has never been occupied for more than eight weeks in a year.

On our arrival, Laura hugged me; there were tears in her eyes. "Thanks for coming," she said. "Living on a desert island in the sky isn't much better than living on one in the middle of the ocean, especially without a man." Then she took us on a tour of the rooms—4,800 square feet of space—over three times the area of a flat in Topham's Corner.

"We have four bathrooms with bidets and two extra toilets." Admitting that she hadn't really talked with anyone except Rivke for the past few months, Laura was seeing the overwhelming grandeur of the place through our eyes. She sounded like a tour guide to the White House.

Bren was shaking his head. "What do you need all the toilets for? People who live here don't actually shit and piss, do they?"

"We don't usually admit it." Laura's eyes were sparkling. "The toilet paper costs about a dollar a roll, but if it's too scratchy, you can use the controlled-temperature bidets. Quite erotic—and ideal for spritzing assholes as well as cunts.

She opened the doors between the living room and library and we were in a room fifty-five feet long and forty feet wide. Oriental rugs were used as scatter rugs over the broadloom. The library was lined with leather volumes which Laura assured us were all classics, bought for decoration and not for reading. Oil paintings, soft Italian leather couches and chairs, a refrigerated "wet" bar, with running water and soda water, and a simulated fieldstone colonial fireplace, with gas logs, completed this section of the room.

Behind the bar, Bren opened a new bottle of Johnnie Walker Black Label and offered us all a drink. "Good God, Laura," he marveled. "This is great. Why don't you charter a bus and invite the entire Premar commune for the coming-out party on the weekend of March 13? None of them have ever actually seen a kid born, so you'd be helping with their education. The Premars could sleep on the rugs."

"Why not?" Laura's eyes were dancing. "The kids can give me moral support. Of course, it will shock hell out of the other apartment owners in this building. They'll think they have finally been invaded by Harlem and the Bronx. You can be sure that some of them will try to sue the owners of the building for invasion of their privacy. I'll warn the staff that it's going to be Watch Laura Stone

Have a Black Baby Weekend." From the tone of her voice it was impossible to tell whether Laura meant it or if she was being cynical. She led us into the master bedroom. "Rocky designed this room. He expected eventually the president might like to use the apartment when he came to New York. He might not be able to communicate with whomever he was in bed with, but he wouldn't lose touch with the world."

Laura wasn't kidding. A circular bed, ten feet in diameter, dominated the mirror-lined room. Telephones and intercoms were within easy reach in the curving headboard of the bed, which also had an instrument panel to control heat, air-conditioning, sliding curtains, television (an oversize screen in the ceiling angled for bed viewing), and a quadrophonic sound system. Running along one-quarter of the arc of the bed was a brass rail about four inches above mattress level.

"This rail was Rocky's special contribution," Laura told us. "Most modern beds have eliminated the footboard. Rocky's theory was that bed designers have forgotten that people screw in bed, too. As you can see, no matter who's on top, the rail gives toe and foot leverage, something to push against. Of course, Rocky was dreaming of his youth when he came up with that one. The only time we made love in this bed he needed a splint instead of a toe hold."

Bren was poking in the bathroom that adjoined the bedroom. It was completely lined with white marble. In addition to the glass stall shower, there was an oval sunken tub big enough to accommodate four people.

"Strip down, girls," Bren yelled. "This is great. We can bathe together and talk just like in the Premar tubs." Ten minutes later, up to our shoulders in wispy bubbles, all three of us were sitting naked in the tub, drinking French champagne from long-stemmed glasses. Bren and I both admired Laura's belly, and she told us the kid was kicking like hell and wanted to join the party.

Later, having been hot-dried by an overhead fan, we wrapped ourselves in rug-size Turkish towels and wandered into the library, where we all flopped on the floor. We watched the glow of the evening sun in a cold blue sky turning the towers of Manhattan into mysterious Easter Island phalluses. Bren finally broke into our fantasies. "When you sent us the postcard in February and told us that you were still carrying the baby," he told Laura, "we couldn't believe it."

"It was your damned fault." Laura touched my hand. "Bren told me that you know I slept with him that last horrible night in Boston."

"I guess it was a loving thing to do," I said. "Do you want to make it a way of life?"

Laura shook her head. "I don't know how you put up with him, Ellen. He probably talks so much he forgets what he came to bed for." Laura was silent for a long time, evidently remembering. "I haven't screwed with any-one since," she said. "But I accept that night for what it was—a *mitzvah*. I was frightened, lonely. Bren held out his hand." She smiled at him. "And finally your penis. No—it's not incest that fucked up my head. It was Pre-mar, and those fifty-two books you're shoving down the kids' throats. You'll make them all crazy. The day before the raid I was skimming through that required book, *Birth Book*—reading the hour-by-hour account of those whacked-out dames describing their at-home 'natural' childbirth. Jesus! What's natural? Isn't all childbirth natu-ral? Anyway, those pictures got me. Ecstatic women pho-tographed by their mates, squatting on their hands and knees with the heads of their babies hanging out of their cunts. On that island with Rais, I had discovered what deep, primitive, sexual involvement was like. I kept think-ing this baby was really conceived in love. When you were a kid, did you ever do something compulsive like not walking on the crack in the sidewalk, because you told yourself that if you did, something terrible would happen? That's the way I feel about this baby. Maybe I'll die in a lovely orgasm of birth, and the baby will live. Whatever happens, I must have the child. Here in this apartment. It's my destiny."

Listening to Laura, I thought it obvious that she was riding an emotional roller coaster, and I wondered if she would ever know how to get off. Unlike me, she didn't have a Bren to prepare her for her rebirth.

"Later," Laura said, "I realized that Bren was trying to con me with a rational-emotive-therapy approach. Who knows? Maybe it worked. Anyway, I'm over the hump. I've convinced myself that it isn't awful or tragic for a white woman to give birth to a black baby—just inconvenient."

Bren, lost in thought, was staring at Laura. She was

lying on her side, and her towel had slipped away. Naked, she was caressing the tight skin on her belly; she had an angelic expression on her face.

"Damnit—I never realized that a pregnant woman's body was so beautifully unified," Bren said. "You actually look ten years younger, Laura, and terribly fragile. And that's the point. I'm glad that you're going to have the kid, but not alone, here, with just a doctor and nurse. That's insane. What are you proving with natural childbirth? Despite what you say, it sounds to me as if you're still ashamed to have a black child. You may look like a twenty-five-year-old, but don't forget, you're damned near forty. If anything went wrong, you'd be in real trouble."

Laura shrugged. "I'm not worried. I've had two kids. This one will drop out."

"Honestly, Laura," I told her. "I think Bren is right. We use that *Birth Book* at Premar with the idea that a closely knit group of nuclear families such as Confamiliaum would enrich their lives and provide support for natural childbirth at home, but even so, mobile hospital care units would be standing by. With you alone, it's different."

"Don't worry," Laura said. "If I know Harry Bacon, he'll arrive prepared for any emergency. Oh, damn, what difference does that make? I really don't know what motivated me into this cul-de-sac!" Her voice was husky, and tears were running down her cheeks. The flames from the fire dancing in the shadows on her belly and breasts reflecting on her body made her seem ephemeral and terribly vulnerable.

I took her in my arms, and her face was warm and tear-wet against my breasts. In the midst of all this wealth, she needed affection and confirmation of herself. Finally she wiped her eyes and kissed my cheeks. "Maybe the real reason I'm having the baby is that I wanted to give Rocky a solar-plexus blow. If he's going to divorce me, anyway—or expect that I'm going to be good old faithful Laura, while he screws any young thing that takes his fancy—this is one way to penetrate his thick skin." She sighed. "I suppose it's perverse, but I had the romantic notion, too, that maybe Rocky would understand that being saved from certain death and having Rais' baby was all mixed up in my head. Oh, shit. I don't really care what happens to me. Sometimes I think I'd jump out if the windows in this building opened."

Late Sunday, after Bren had left for Boston, Laura told me that she was happy that I had come. She wanted us to have at least two weeks together, and it was to be a vacation for me, she did not want me to entertain her. We could make our meals together, and if I wished I could sleep with her in the master bedroom, which she hadn't been using because the circular bed was too lonely with just one person in it. I told her I was still determined to get my master's and had brought a lot of reading. But it didn't seem so urgent anymore; the road ahead was full of possibilities. Now I might have kids and live to be an old lady. In many ways my feeling toward her is like the Premars' attitude toward me—she's an older sister with whom I can really be friends. The first week we talked, day and night, about tiny, intimate details of our lives. Neither of us had ever dared to be so open with another person.

"I love Rais," Laura told me. "The amazing discovery for me is that I don't want to possess him. Wouldn't it be a nice world, if Rais and I could meet once in a while, maybe two or three times a year, and go to dinner together, and afterward go to bed? Then we could tell each other all the things that happened to us since we last met, and after we had made love, easily, like good friends, we could return to the main highway we had been traveling on, knowing that one day, again, we would relax and reach out to each other. Tiny vacations from marriage."

"Maybe that's the way Rocky feels when he's chasing butterflies," I said. "But don't you both need something beyond chance encounters? The guiding light of Premar is Martin Buber's words: 'The basis of man's life with man is twofold, and it is one—the wish of every man to be confirmed as what he is, even as what he can become, by men; and two, the innate capacity of man to confirm his fellow men in this way. That this capacity lies so immeasurably fallow constitutes the real weakness and questionableness of the human race; actual humanity exists only where this capacity unfolds.'" I laughed. "What Buber didn't mention is whether one human being can confirm another in a one-night stand."

Laura was silent for a long time. "I guess that hits the nail on the head, except that some people must be happy with little gifts and learn not to expect continuous confirmation."

Last Thursday night, about ten-thirty, we heard the elevator stop in the reception area; then Rocky walked into the library. Laura and I were sipping fifty-year-old Napoleon brandy from huge goblets. Every time I took a sip I breathed the lovely fumes in the confined area of the glass. Sitting there in shortie nightgowns, having finished half the bottle, we were both feeling giddy. Rocky looked at me with unwavering eyes, fixing me like a biologist's specimen. Then, grinning at Laura, he filed me away for further reference.

While Laura was probably startled, she didn't show it. "So the wandering Jew returns?" she said coolly.

"To a very pregnant wife." The muscles in Rocky's dark-brown weathered cheeks were rippling. He had the stance of a javelin thrower about to toss Laura across the field.

"How did you know I was here?"

"I just flew in from Saudi Arabia. A Stone-Western pilot was waiting for me at Butler Aviation. Fortunately, I telephoned Rivke. She told me you were here acting the spoiled brat, as usual."

"Why did you come?"

"Maybe to evict you. I'm not sure you have any marital rights left." Rocky's black eyes swallowed me. I wasn't sure whether I was seeing two of him, but I was sure that his wavy gray hair grew too low on his brow. "I'm Ellen," I stuttered. "Bren's wife."

Rocky laughed. "A *shikse* married to a Gattman? God help you!"

"Ellen is recovering from heart surgery. I asked her to come."

Rocky shrugged. "You're welcome. There's plenty of room."

"I'll sleep in the guest room," I said, wondering whether I should leave them alone.

"Don't bother, I'm sure that my wife doesn't want to sleep with me."

Laura scowled at him. "You'd need a long reach. I'm only available through the back door."

Rocky suddenly smiled. "Seems to me I tried that when you were carrying David and Shulamith. Afterward we held each other belly-to-belly."

"You've lost weight," Laura said. *"Your* belly has disappeared, and you look younger. Jeanne Mechante must have given you a lot of exercise."

I was thinking the same thing. Rocky Stone may be fifteen years older than Laura, but he's not bad-looking in a crude, overpowering sort of way. His cold, obsidian eyes never stopped searching our faces and bodies, as if he was imprinting us forever on his brain. I wondered if, later, like a warlock, he could summon up a complete image of a person and cast a terrible spell on him.

"Jeanne is off to greener pastures," he said.

"A few thousand dollars richer, I presume."

"You presume right. So what? I'm clean. I'm not giving birth to a Frenchman."

I shivered. That was a low blow.

"And I am giving birth to a black. By this time I'd have thought you would have filed for divorce."

"And miss the fun? If you think that you having some nigger's kid is any skin off my ass, think again. When Rivke told me, I couldn't help laughing. I also called Harry Bacon. He's sure you'll finally come to your senses and check into the hospital. Too bad, I'd enjoy watching the imperturbable Laura Stone screaming and squirming and grunting to bring forth a black child. Tell me about this Rais Daemon. What's he got, that you're so determined to have his kid?"

Laura laughed nastily. "I'm not having it for him. I'm having it for you, so you can watch the birthing—right plunk in the middle of your lovely circular bed. Merle Blanc, Rais Daemon's wife, is coming, along with a busload of kids from Bren's Premar. Merle's mother was a midwife on St. Noir. If Harry Bacon doesn't show, I'll have my child without his fat-ass assistance. It's going to be a circus, Rocky, so you'd better reserve front seats early. When it's all over, your bed will become a collector's item. But not because Rocky Stone slept in it!"

Rocky may not have been shocked—it was hard to tell—but he was momentarily trumped.

Laura broke the silence. "After the baby is born, if you still can't make up your mind, *I'll* divorce you."

"Make up my mind to what? It sounds as if you were expecting a miracle, that, somehow, I should forgive you."

"Fuck off!" Laura snarled. "You have nothing to forgive. You should have thanked God that I was alive."

Rocky grinned. "Funny damned thing—that's just what

I did. Maybe someone has to die before we can learn to appreciate them. To be honest, I really have missed your bitchiness. Especially on the rare occasions when you've been repentant and become a fawning bedmate for an hour or so." Rocky grinned at me. "What do *you* think, Ellen Gattman? We're all family now. You might as well take your turn at bat."

"I'd rather pitch," I said. "If you had any sense, you'd smash down the walls and hug your wife."

"Oh, la-dee-da! What do we have here—little Miss Pollyanna from the aulde country?" Rocky's sneery voice made me want to sock him. "Eighteen hours ago I was talking with Faisal's right-hand man. He was telling me about karama, the Arab sense of honor, dignity, and pride in his Islamic traditions. The Israelis must give the Arabs the opportunity to restore this pride. When they're preaching a *jihad*—a holy war . . . Ah, shit. I've had it today. Good night. I'm going to bed, not as a Jew and not as an Arab. I gave up the eye-for-an-eye philosophy when I was a very young man, but I'm hanging on to my karama." Rocky shrugged and picked up his traveling case.

During the last few days, ends and means have been the subject of an ongoing discussion between Rocky and me. While he denies that the imminent birth of Laura's child motivated his return, he isn't being entirely honest. Rivke finally admitted to Laura, on the telephone, that Rocky had been in constant communication with her in the past few months. "You're pushing him too far," Rivke warned her. "No man will put up with your nonsense. If you'd have the baby without any publicity and immediately turn it over for adoption, you could save your marriage." Laura repeated Rivke's terms to Rocky, and before he could confirm them, she told him that if that was the price of their marriage, he could rot in hell.

He continually follows Laura around the apartment, staring at her silently. "As if he's trying to look inside my womb," Laura complained to me. "Whatever you do, don't leave me alone with him." Try as I may, I can't seem to build a bridge over this insane kind of hubris. Rocky is still sleeping in one of the guest rooms. I would have moved into another bedroom, except that Laura insists that I protect her from Rocky, the inevitable midnight prowler. "If I ever go to bed with him again," she said, "it will be after the baby is born. But don't let me stop you. If you want to, it's all right with me. I'm sure he won't hurt you, and it might be an interesting experience."

Yesterday we were sitting in sun chairs under the glass bubble on the roof that allows the actinic tanning rays of the sun to come through. The warmth felt good on my scar. Laura and I had been swimming naked. Rocky, in bathing trunks, watched us. I suppose living in a house with two women who run around half-dressed or naked could drive a man crazy. Rocky admitted that he was astonished by Laura's new lack of modesty. He attributed it to the sinister influence of her brother's half-baked ideas. She didn't dare tell him what she had told me—that living with Rais Daemon three months like Eve in the garden had been so joyously erotic that she would never again give a damn about being dressed or nude, one way or the other.

Whatever his reason, Rocky seemed determined not to leave the apartment. Even Laura assured him that he wouldn't miss the "fun" if he went out for a while. Rocky only grinned at her. "I wouldn't want to miss even one second of it," he said nastily. They were like bad kids flaying each other with words—using me as an audience, hoping I'd take a side against the other. But beneath a current of seeming distaste that sometimes bordered on hatred, I sensed an inner need for each other. When that need became too obvious, they both quickly declared war again, and they seemed determined to achieve the impossible—deflate each other's ego.

Last night Rocky stood in the door of the master bedroom for a few minutes, sarcastically admiring us, "two potential lesbians," were his words, but probably he was wishing he could get in bed between us. Finally he reluctantly departed to the guest room. I told Laura I thought that if she could say to him that she needed him and really wanted the baby because God intended her to have it, he would understand somehow. Laughing, she hugged me. "Honey, my father has an expression for people like Rocky, 'vos me hot, vil men hut, un vos me vil hot men nit.' What we have we don't want, what we want we don't have. Rocky doesn't like variables. After all these years if I said something like that to Rocky, he'd be sure that I'd lost my marbles. Anyway, my little Irish *boobeleh*, dove, I don't believe in God. Maybe, like Bren, I believe this is my karma—*I have no choice.* Since Jews don't believe much in the devil either, maybe Rocky would prefer to think that a malicious dybbuk not only saved me from being killed in the crash, and later from drowning or being eaten by sharks, but the dybbuk made me lie there and get knocked up, and then he made me so *meshugge* that I wanted the baby." Laura was laughing and crying at the same time. She kissed my cheek. "Tell Rocky his only hope is to read the ninety-first Psalm over me and tell the damned dybbuk to get out of town."

Naked, sitting in a sun chair on the roof, thinking of Laura's reaction, and how impossibly complicated people make the simple process of self-communication, I was aware that Rocky's eyes were crawling up my legs and roaming around my crotch. I knew it's not nice to display myself, and that it was unhinging Rocky's mind to be constantly seeing two females naked, but he deserves to have his arrogance punctured. Actually, I was trying to concentrate on *The Central City Problem, and Urban Renewal Policy,* a book which I would eventually be using for reference in my master's thesis. From where he was sitting, his eyes concealed behind big, ominous-looking smoked glasses, Rocky read aloud the title of my book and laughed crudely. "Why in hell is a sexy, nubile young woman reading a goddamned government report? 'Prepared for the Subcommittee on Housing and Urban Development for the Committee on Banking, Housing, and Urban Affairs of the United States Senate.' Jesus Christ, that's a good example of how to waste the taxpayer's money. Pay a bunch of do-nothing scholars to write hundreds of pages of garbage. You shouldn't be worrying about such things, Ellen. You should be keeping house for some nice Irish cop and mothering his children. My brother-in-law will make you crazier than he is."

"My mother married a nice Irish cop," I told him. "And he has the same caveman mentality you have. You both think women are mental midgets. Galbraith put his finger on it. We're cryptoservants. Stay home and smoke your Virginia Slims, baby—you've come a long way. Just leave the real world to us men. We really know how to fuck it up."

I was proud of myself. A few more days in this ménage and I'd be as expert as Laura in sarcastic verbal exchange.

"You really should read this book, Rocky," I told him. "When you've finished it, I'll give you Bren's and Rais' Confamiliaum proposal. Confam may be the only viable answer to the future of the family and housing in this do-nothing world that people like you have helped create. At least it will give you something to think about besides the shape of my cunt. Maybe then we'll all have what is known as congruence—something to talk about."

Rocky took the book. "You're right. I was enjoying the sight of your downy nether lips. Maybe I was even think-ing about congruence." Enjoying his double-entendre, Rocky was grinning. "Sorry, but your genitals are in my line of vision, and Laura's are obscured temporarily by the new stomach she's wearing. Of course, if you girls don't like this conversation, or think it's too honest, you should wear pants!"

Surprisingly, Rocky stayed glued to my book all morn-ing. Later he asked for a copy of the "Confamiliaum: A Proposal." This morning, once again we were on the roof, enjoying the nearly spring sunshine, protected from the cold March winds. While Rocky was idly sipping his cof-fee, Laura mounted the attack. "It's not that Rocky's en-tranced with females, or your brains in particular, Ellen. It's a way of life with him. He likes to see females capitu-late—even his wife—and his approach is subtle. He depre-cates his wealth, which of course entrances any sane woman, and temporarily becomes the kind of man they've always dreamed of knowing. Watch out for him. Once he's carved a new notch on his gun"—Laura emphasized "gun" so there would be no doubt that I knew what she meant—"and you've helped him confirm himself, he'll quickly return to his first love, playing king."

Rocky just shrugged. "I'm not interested in appearing in history books, but Bren evidently is. Okay, Ellen. I'm ap-proximately where you are. Bren needs a half-million dol-lars, and the banks aren't standing in line to underwrite his daydreams. I get the impression he has submitted Confam to the Department of Housing and Urban Welfare. If he has, you can count on it that it will disappear under a pile of papers, on the desk of the tenth assistant to an assistant secretary. So what do you want me to do, give Bren the money, or lend it to him?"

I was so angry I could only stare. "Don't be so damned sure," I finally managed to stutter. "Bren doesn't give up easily. And I'll tell you one thing. If Confam never gets off the ground, he won't take money from some cynical millionaire—even if he is a brother-in-law."

Rocky laughed. "I'm glad you qualified the kind of millionaire, because that leaves room for negotiation. Whatever you think, no bank will touch this unless it's underwritten by the federal government or some other philanthropist. Banks don't want thirty-year, fixed-interest mortgage loans. Not until the good Lord assures them, personally, that inflation is a two-way street. On the other hand, Confam is a natural for some politician. If he can prove himself a benefactor by shoving responsibility back on the welfare recipient and the low-income families, they might elect him dog catcher pro tem. It's a great campaign idea. Get the low-income-housing monkey off the government's back. Return to the good old days and American initiative. If people could unite to form their own housing corporations, the only thing they would lose is their privacy. They still can pursue life, liberty, and happiness— just so long as everybody agrees with everybody else on what makes them happiest."

I felt like throwing my glass of orange juice at him. "It's easy to undercut an idea," I said. "I'd hate to work for Stone-Western Industries. When the Great Stone Face frowns, everybody frowns."

"Dear woman, we have entire departments headed by young men who devote their lives to proving me wrong. And I listen to them. If they prove to me a company or product has outlived its profit potential, I get rid of it just as quickly as I buy new ones which have their feet in the future. And Stone-Western doesn't make twenty percent before taxes just by satisfying man's needs. We create needs and then we satisfy them. But Bren doesn't like to think about profits. He's a dreamer. Confam may satisfy man's needs on one level, but it hasn't got a profit motivator attached to it. Confam has a basic flaw. It assumes that people can work together without a strong leader. According to this proposal, the corporation elects its president and treasurer from the membership. So they elect some good-natured jerk named O'Toole, or Ravioli, or Feinberg. You name him. He loves people so damned much, and is such a good fellow, they walk all over him. In a few months the Confam members are squabbling among themselves. First thing you know, the project is

bankrupt. What happens to the bank that gave the mortgage? Tough shit. How do you collect from forty-eight in-
digent families? Who wants rundown tenement houses?
Hopefully, there's insurance, because only a match will
save the deal. You tell Bren that men are happier hating
each other. What fun is it working together for their own
good?"

"Living here, I'm beginning to believe you're right," I
said.

"I'll make you a deal, Ellen," Rocky said. His eyes were
narrow and he had a cynical look on his face. "I can't believe that you're for real, but since Laura is in no condition to have me in her bed, if you'll sleep with me tonight,
I'll give Bren the half-million."

"Damnit!" I yelled. "Bren doesn't want a gift. If Confam is going to work, it's going to be because the people
believe in people."

Rocky held his hands over his ears. "Stop screaming. I
give up! I'll get Bren a showcase loan. Stone-Western
owns a healthy piece of the First Merchants Bank in Boston. I'll go the whole route and get the loan subsidized by
HUD on an experimental basis."

"Do I have to sleep with you?"

"Who says we're going to sleep?" Rocky grinned at
Laura. "I'm just letting Ellen pay in advance. When Confamiliaum collapses, even though J. Q. Umglik will pay
the bill, a little *shtup* with this *faigeleh* is going to be the
most expensive piece of ass I ever negotiated."

Laura wasn't any help. "You're getting older, Rocky. If
it isn't for love, it costs more," she said. I was obviously a
pawn in the game between them; Laura was only too
happy to use me as a trade-off to assuage her own guilt.
And me? Damn. The expectant way Rocky was staring at
me made me tremble. Was I tempted to help Confam, or
simply to satisfy my own curiosity? Whirling through my
head was the thought that making love to Rocky would be
like making love to my own father. Did I have an Electra
complex? I was irresistibly attracted to men like Rocky,
and Rais, and Bren, and Daddy. They needed the wind
taken out of their sails, at least some of the time. I was a
long way behind Bren in knowing different bedmates.
Anyway, if I capitulated and actually spent some time
alone with Rocky, I thought maybe I wouldn't actually
have to make love. Maybe I could talk to him about

Laura. See, basically, I can't help myself. I like to meddle. Maybe I imagined I could convince him she was the perfect wife for him and that he should love her and be happy he was going to be a father again. Even if he didn't plant the seed, the child would be his and Laura's because they loved it. I'd point out that if Merle could love a child that Rais had helped make, Rocky could love one that Laura had sheltered for nine months.

Even while these thoughts chased each other through my mind, I was seeing pictures of myself locked in a sex orgy with Rocky. Was I enjoying it? I couldn't decide, but I mustered up a sophisticated smile. "Thanks for the compliment," I told him. "But you're overlooking the fact that I've only been married a few months, and I'm very inexperienced in bed. Besides, I'm not at all sure that my stitches would hold together. And my broken ribs are only partially mended." I said no more.

Rocky shrugged. "Okay! That's life. Ellens and daydreams come and go."

I hoped he didn't mean Confam.

Merle Blanc. March, the first year of Premar. From tapes transcribed by Andrea Pillisuk.

Did last week really happen? Was I midwife at the birth of my husband's baby? Did I really go to bed with Rocky Stone? That's the setting for a Greek tragedy—or *High Noon* in the Age of Aquarius. But instead of two gunfighters walking menacingly toward each other, ready to pop off the other guy at the flick of an eyelash, all of us were singing hosannas to the birth of a child. And all the Premars had come to New York with us. We'll most certainly be reading their amazed reactions in their journals for the next month or so.

"That's the point," Bren told me yesterday as I joined him and Rais in one of the Premar tubs. He kissed my behind as I bent over to kiss Rais, and I slid in between them, enjoying the unsolicited attention at both ends. "There were fifty-five weekends last weekend, Merle. Your perspective is more emotionally subjective than anyone's except Laura's. You both navigated uncharted seas. It's important for Ellen and me and Rais, as well as the kids, to know how you avoided getting lost in the fog."

"Because I kept my eyes on the stars," I said. Billy Rainbow, Cheryl Jones, and Joe McDonald were in the tub listening to our conversation. The other tub was temporarily unoccupied. Ellen was upstairs working with the Meals Committee on menus for a month of ethnic dinners to which we were going to invite different families from the Confam.

I stretched out and floated in the middle, tickling their penises with my toe. "Tell you the truth, I'm beginning to feel like a guinea pig," I said. "Instead of injecting me and Ellen with untested serum, you dumped us into a situation which would blow the average female's mind. Question being researched: Could Merle and Ellen survive their jealousy or guilt? Would one wipe out the other?"

Rais put his foot between my legs and wiggled it against my crotch. "Whether it was you and Ellen, or Rocky playing volleyball in his own swimming pool with eight naked girls, black and white. I think we defused a racist. You haven't said much about your night with Rocky. Did you sit up and talk all night, or did you make love?"

How's that for insouciance? Sometimes both Rias and Bren need a pin stuck in their egos. "Maybe I had nothing to do with it. Rocky was already pretty amenable when we arrived. Why don't you ask Ellen about her night with Rocky? Or why doesn't Rais tell us about his night with Laura?"

Rais smiled and gently rubbed his fingers in my hair. "I held Laura in my arms and I told her that I was proud of her, and she cried and told me that it was probably a futile gesture. When the story got out that she had given birth to a black child, she would be tagged as just another jet-setter seeking new kicks. I told her that would depend on her. Anyway, we made friendly love together, enjoying each other's warmth and sympathetic ears—and the baby pushing at her cervix would occasionally stop and listen to us, and Laura said she was smiling,"

Bren changed the subject. "You implied that Ellen made love with Rocky, too," he said.

"I haven't told you that I made love with Rocky," I said. "It obviously doesn't matter to you if I did, but you must be hoping that Ellen didn't."

"For God's sake, Merle, that's putting words in my mouth. If you both slept with him, do you think I'd love either of you less?"

"I don't think we should pursue that trail without Ellen. The question that keeps rumbling through my mind is: Where are the four of us going? If we can't answer that, then the question of what happens to Premars *after* Premar is left dangling. Even Phil isn't sure that the family-style merger the Tenhausens have with the Abernathys will work for most people."

"We don't know whether there's life after death, either," Bren said. "But we go on living, searching for answers. Obviously, there's no one answer for everybody. As Phil says, Premar opens doors. Which doors you keep open, or which you close, is up to you. I love Ellen. I love you, Merle. Those are two inescapable facts of my life. Do you and Ellen and Rais have a similar feeling toward me? I hope so, but I can't make it happen."

"Do you mean for a lifetime?"

Bren shrugged. "We've already lived a third of our lives. If each of us reserves the right to chase an occasional rainbow or do some sightseeing—those are options we may use rarely, if ever."

"I don't know," I said. "The kind of rainbows you and Rais chase are scarier than the reality. Rais loving Ellen is nice. I love Ellen, too. Rais dreaming of Laura, or being involved with women like my sister, Gabby, or God alone knows who else—that makes me feel insecure. It's interesting that you, Bren, can't make me feel anywhere near so insecure as Rais can, yet I do love you and need you, too."

"Merle, Merle." Rais nuzzled my face and neck while Bren watched us with a big grin on his face. "It's just like we've been telling the kids. Eventually they'll find the person who reinforces and confirms them. You're the gal for me. Laura and the baby are my friends, too, but Laura and I may only exist as symbols for each other. We created each other, and with your help we saved a dream from becoming a nightmare."

I guess my problem is that I'm trying to force-freeze the four of us—past and future—like the figures on Keats's urn. "Forever warm and still to be enjoy'd ... Forever panting, and forever young. When old age shall this generation waste. Thou shall remain in the midst of their woe." Is that the kind of Rais or Bren or Ellen I want? No! All of them loving me in their own way is more challenging and more realistic than if they tried to gratify my possessiveness and image of them. In human relationships, congruence is better than merger! It's less stifling, and the individuality remains. I am you because the geometry of our lives makes the fit inevitable.

Last Wednesday, at dinner, Bren told the kids, "I haven't heard from Ellen, and that means Laura hasn't started labor. Anyway, the bus that we've chartered from Continental Trailways will be out in front tomorrow noon. Bill O'Toole, one of the Confam incorporators, who lives on Warren Road, works for Continental. When Laura told me she would subsidize a Premar four-day weekend in New York, I made the deal with Continental, contingent on Bill being our driver. Anyone who isn't here tomorrow by twelve-thirty, ready to go, gets left. We have to be back in Boston Tuesday night, so let's hope the kid gets the message and gets born while we're at Laura's. You're going to miss three days, and we expect you to study or work like hell to make up for it, and those of you who are working should show your appreciation to your employers.

"And now, since I'm playing the role of Big Daddy, I want each and every one of you to help us prove one thing—that fifty kids can occupy an apartment and not wreck it. When we leave, Rocky Stone, in particular, will think he dreamed us, because the place will be spotless; there will be no damage. Keep in mind, guys like Stone not only think your generation is freaky, but that you haven't got a brain in your heads. Let's show him that Premar believes in America—that we're not trying to destroy it, but to redivert it, and put our own energy to work for all of us. If we get alone with Rocky, we'll play that tune for him. While I'll predict it won't make him dance for joy, we'll reach him, anyway—with affection and laughter and love.

"There will be no mess details, so you can all cheer. Ellen is working out meals, and she'll see there are plenty of snacks. One evening we all may go on the town, together or separately. If Rais of I catch anyone smoking grass, we'll toss you on a Greyhound bus and you'll be back in Boston before you know what happened. You can get high on the birth of the baby. That's something none of us, except Merle, has ever seen.

"We'll have the run of the place—showers, tubs, the pool—and you can run around naked. As far as lovemaking goes, the floors aren't that comfortable, and you won't have much privacy, but when the lights are out, it's up to you."

By noon on Thursday every seat in the bus was filled with excited, chattering kids yelling at Bren and Rais to get on the road. Opposite the driver's seat, a special seat was equipped with a tiny desk, a microphone, and a cassette player hooked into the bus's audio system. Bren was tour director, by agreement, and Rais and I sat behind him. When Bill O'Toole finally maneuvered us out of the Boston traffic, and we were on Route 128 heading for New York, Bren turned on the mike. "Okay," he said. "You've all met Bill. He promised his wife not to get any bad ideas from Premar, but he's listening with bated breath. Bill didn't bring trunks, but he's looking forward to swimming in Rocky's pool. I telephoned Laura just before we left, and she says she's certain she'll be in labor within the next twenty-four hours. When she heard that Able is a photography bug, she told Rocky that if Able does a good job, *Laura Stone Giving Birth* will be entered at the Cannes film festival next year. The apartment is now fully equipped for filmmaking, and Laura just hopes that Able can figure out how to use all the stuff.

"To give you some idea of what Ellen and Laura have been thinking, Ellen sent us a tape which I just received Monday. In a few minutes I'll play it for you. It may give you some insight into what happens between people like Laura and Rocky when they don't dare to reach out to each other. It's an old story. There's too many Moseses in the world—each with his own Final Word from Above, inscribed on Unerasable Tablets. So it's up to us. Maybe we can get Laura and Rocky to listen, a little, to different drummers. Maybe we can make this most unusual birthday party a rebirth party, too."

Bren turned toward me. "When Merle was in her teens, she assisted her mother at the birth of at least twenty St. Noireans. During the past couple of weeks Merle and Rais have been reading and comparing the methods of Erna Wright in her book, *The Natural Childbirth*, with Lamaze techniques, and those of the American Society of Psychoprophylaxis in Obstetrics, with her own experiences on St. Noir. You've all read the *Birth Book*, published by Genesis Press. Maybe Merle has something to add."

I took the mike from Bren. "Frankly, I can't believe that Laura will go the whole route. When the contractions get rough, she may demand a cervical block. But no matter, at the age of thirty-nine she's still an adventurer—and she's sharing the adventure with us. Daring to have a biracial child, and exposing herself in the act of birth, makes Laura a special kind of gal. Many of the women on St. Noir never read a book on natural childbirth, but the midwife coaches them during the labor, and the breathing techniques are instinctive with them. According to Ellen, Laura has not only learned what to expect, minute by minute, but she has learned how to breathe during labor so that she becomes a flowing part of the birth process. The doctor will have his own nurse there, and while I don't expect to be much help, there's a lot of simple things I may be able to contribute, like perineal massage, which may even help Laura avoid an episiotomy."

"Do you feel funny about this?" Samantha asked. She was sitting on the aisle halfway down the bus.

"What do you mean, funny?"

"Jealous!" Ruth Voight yelled, and a lot of the girls cheered their agreement. "After all, Rais is your husband, and Laura is giving birth to his child. I wouldn't buy that!"

"I didn't buy it," I said. "It just happened. The question you kids have to answer, or so do Rais and I, and Ellen and Bren, is whether Rais or Bren could tolerate it if Ellen or I got pregnant by another man. Would our individual marriages be strong enough so that we still love our children, and each other, if we had children by opposite husbands? Keep in mind, if that should happen between the four of us, it will be a conscious decision, and we'll have estimated the risks. With Rais and Laura there was no unilateral decision against me or Rocky. It comes to this: If you had been rescued from drowning by a guy, and were trapped on a desert island with him with no pills or anything, would you finally have screwed with him even if it meant getting pregnant?" I ruffled Rais' head. "Especially if this was the guy."

After listening to Ellen's tape—by this time we were driving through Connecticut—we got into a free-for-all discussion of jealousy, and Bren was put on the mat by the kids who searched for his reaction to the possibility that Ellen might already have slept with Rocky. The key to jealousy seems to lie around the feeling of possessive ownership so common in marriage. At Premar things are different. None of the kids, for example, are jealous of former roommates, who are now sleeping with new friends. A benign environment creates its own security. Though none of us have asked her directly, Ellen avoids the subject of what happened between her and Rocky. Did she or didn't she? Only I know for sure, and it was Rocky who told me, not Ellen.

Little did I realize that a few minutes after we arrived at the apartment, Laura would drop me into the forge again, and hand Rais the hammer. Rais was becoming my blacksmith! Rocky came down to the lobby to meet us. He shook hands with Bren rather coolly. "The Mother of the Year has had a few contractions, but she's not in labor yet," he said.

I put out my hand to him. "Hi, I'm Merle," I said, and tried to penetrate his poker face. His eyes bored through my pale orange dress, making me feel like one of my ancestors being appraised for a slave auction.

"You really are a lovely French-African," he said. Did he mean that I'd bring a better price because I had white blood? Bren introduced Rais to him. "So this is the father of the child." Looking up at him, Rocky added, "If you're that big all over, I can understand why Laura was so impressed."

Rais smiled easily. "The way I hear it, Mr. Stone, it isn't size that counts."

"You're probably right. But fifty-four years does go against you." Rocky shook his head, a little bewildered by the kids milling around in the lobby like country cousins. "Okay." He waved for their attention. "There's two elevators. This gentleman here who looks like a four-star general is Henry Partridge, and he's in a state of panic. There are no teen-agers living in this co-op because the owners prefer French poodles or Afghan hounds. So take it easy on him. Since Henry doesn't have a good memory, he's got a badge for each of you. You'll have to show it to get in or out. And please, no more than eight in an elevator. After you get your badges, you can take the elevators to the thirtieth floor. It's five-thirty. You can have wine cocktails, courtesy of the management." The kids gave a big cheer. When Rocky smiled back at them, he didn't seem so formidable.

In the elevator, Bren said, "To be honest with you, Rocky, you and Laura are an amazement to me. I feel as if I've walked through the looking glass. A decidedly different Laura died in that plane crash. You've got a new wife, Rocky. What is equally surprising is you seem to have given her a long leash." I wonder if Bren believed that saying it might make it so.

"Wishful thinking is a way of life with you, Bren, and Laura was always a little balmy about things like tarot and astrology. So there's something with your family, right? Now she must have softening of the brain. She believes that it's written in her stars that she would marry a Leo, me, but that she, a Virgo, needed a Taurus, Rais, to fulfill herself. Somebody up there planned it this way. Therefore, she must give birth to this baby." Rocky's lips curled as he smiled his disbelief. "As far as I'm concerned, believing that there's some manifest destiny or teleological purpose, or a God who gives a good *kuk* about anybody, is a half-ass cover-up for mental weakness." Rocky shrugged. "In this world there's only one guidepost—what's the profit? All Laura is getting is a $750 income-tax deduction. On the other hand, I must admit that determined as she is to have a *schvartzer* kid, and probably busting her ass in the process, Laura is a most fascinating spectacle and tribute to human naïveté. Maybe she's right. She says that social mores change from the top down. A poor white woman couldn't afford to have a black child. When all the beautiful people are using black studs to repopulate the world, they'll build a monument to Laura."

There was no time to argue. Ellen and Laura were hugging the kids, who had arrived ahead of us. Wearing a pale blue, man-size Turkish towel tied behind her back so that the kids could admire her firm belly and breasts, she told them they could listen to the fetal heartbeat later. "Follow me and I'll show you the delivery room. Then Ellen, Bren, and Rocky will take you on a tour of the apartment, and Ellen and Rocky will tell you the surprise they have for tonight. Well . . . all right, so I'll tell you! You're going to eat at Luchow's and then go to the ballet."

In the master bedroom Laura pointed out the mobile oxygen unit and mobile cabinets filled with all kinds of instruments. "Harry Bacon has transformed my bedroom into a delivery room. He even said the mattress was too soft, and had a huge piece of plywood cut and inserted between it and the springs. He told me that I can't bear down on soft foam, and he's not climbing around me with a baby halfway out sinking up to his knees on a mattress meant for fucking." The kids were looking around in awe at the magnificent bedroom. "It was really nice of you to come," she said softly. "Maybe you think I'm being kind of silly to do this. And when I realize that you will all be watching, I feel kind of scared—because I've always been a private person who couldn't even go to the bathroom if I thought people were listening and would hear me, or worse, watch me piss or shit." Laura smiled at Rais, and there were tears in her eyes. "Then I held hands with death. Maybe all of this is a dream, but it's a dream that seems to go on. Maybe Rais is dreaming me, and when he wakes up I'll no longer exist. Whatever, he not only got me pregnant in his dream, but he let the sunlight in on the dark shadows of my obsession with my own reality."

Rais told me later that he asked Laura if having a baby in front of everybody was a form of penitence—like the Brahman sleeping on a bed of nails. Laura insisted that she was neither penitent nor trying to be a martyr. If it were a dream, she wanted to have Rocky and her family share it with her. Her child would be a bridge, and when there were millions of bridges, the world would be a more loving place to live.

While the kids were exploring the apartment with Rocky, Bren, and Ellen, Laura lay on the outer curve of her bed. "Close the door, Rais," she said. "I want to talk with you and Merle. And both of you, don't look so worried. I'm going to have this baby as easy as rolling off a log. Harry agrees that I'm in excellent physical health."

Laughing, Rais lifted her milk-ready breasts. "Boy, these sure feel nice. But you're not a youngster. Labor can last twenty hours or more."

Laura touched his cheek. "Poor you. You snatched an old lady out of the sea." She nuzzled his face and hugged him. "I'm glad to see that, like a good expectant father, you've been reading. But you forget, you big black teddy bear, that with age goes experience. Even though Shulamith was born sixteen years ago. I can still remember some things."

"You probably were doped when she was born," I said. "I can remember something too. Those mothers in St. Noir screamed so loud, I didn't stop trembling for days."

"I'm a tough cookie," Laura said. "Anyway, the die is cast. About an hour ago I had a 'show' and a weak contraction. I'm damned sure that when my cervix really dilates I won't be in labor for more than eight hours." She brushed the tears from her eyes as she hugged me and kissed my cheek. Then she was sobbing against my neck. "You've been so good about this. Would you do me one more favor, Merle? I told Rocky that I was going to ask you. I'm positive that the baby will be born by noon tomorrow. Would you let Rais stay with me tonight?" She smiled through her tears. "That is, of course, if he's willing. It's obviously not for sex, and I may not be much fun, but I just want to come full circle with Rais. After tomorrow we'll all be pursuing our own destinies. At the very least, I want us all to be friends, and that includes Rocky. I can promise you one thing. This child will not lack love."

I burst into tears. "Honey, I want Rais to stay with you. I'm as involved with you and this baby as he is."

Rais smiled awkwardly—like a big kid not knowing how to respond. "I guess you might say I'm twice blessed," he said finally.

While I wasn't aware of it until later, Laura assumed Rocky would ask me to sleep with him. But how could she or Rais be so sure that I'd jump into bed with an old man, even if he was a millionaire? Anyway, I couldn't believe that Rocky would go to bed with a black woman either as a friend or for intimacy. It seemed to me that his love style would be impersonal, noninvolved fucking.

Before we left for Luchow's, the kids were wandering in and out of the master bedroom, enjoying the sheer wonder of Laura lying naked in her big bed. Rais was propped up beside her on a pile of pillows, looking like a black maharaja. Laura had dug out Harry Bacon's stethoscope so the kids could listen to the fetal heartbeat. In the midst of the excited but subdued confusion, Able was arranging movie-camera equipment and insisting it would be better if he stayed with Rais and Laura "to get things under control." Two cameras on opposite sides of the room with zoom lenses were controlled by a master switch. He also had a hand-held camera. I finally convinced him that he had practiced enough and that all of us kids should leave Mommy and Daddy alone for a few hours. Rais heard me and tumbled me onto the bed between him and Laura. He kissed me. Laughing, Laura hugged me. "Mommy and Daddy sure appreciate our oldest daughter," she said. "Be a good girl tonight?" she whispered in my ear. I didn't give a second thought to what she meant.

After Bill O'Toole found a garage and parked the bus, Rocky and Ellen, playing the role of troop leaders, led their co-ed scouts through the streets to the restaurant where Rocky had reserved five large tables. "Tonight's going to be a prebirthday party," Ellen announced. "Rocky is taking us on the town. You can have beer or wine, but don't get too high or you'll fall asleep in the theater." Ellen seemed a little tense with Rocky, and I kept wondering if she had gone to bed with him to get the mortgage for Confam, but it was a ridiculous thought. I could visualize Ellen about to be ejected into a howling blizzard finally offering her body to save the old homestead. Ellen maneuvered the seating so that Rocky and I were at one table and she and Bren were at another. Rocky certainly didn't seem dangerous as he taught the kids German songs and danced a polka with Samantha Brown, who towered over him, and with Rachel Silverman, who was so ecstatic I thought she was having an orgasm.

On the way to City Center to see the ballet, Rocky sat beside me in the bus. The kids, still singing or yelling at each other in a high pitch of excitement, were scarcely listening to Ellen and Bren, who were trying to give them a little background on the ballet program.

"It will be a new experience for me," Rocky said to me over the din.

"You mean that you bought all these tickets, and you've never been to the ballet?"

"I don't mean the ballet. I mean this will be the first time I've slept with a black girl."

I was being very dense, and for a second I wondered if he had propositioned one of the Premar girls. Then the truth dawned on me, and Laura's words, "and that includes Rocky," fell into the jigsaw puzzle. "What makes you think I'm going to bed with you?" I asked.

"Your husband is sleeping with my wife."

"What's different?"

"That's different."

"Laura's at least ten years older than Rais." I was obviously unhinged.

Laughing, Rocky set me straight. "I'm at least twenty-five years older than you are. But there's still fire in the furnace."

"Oh, hell," I said finally. "I'm not talking about age." The thought had jumped into my head, but what I really wanted to tell him was that Laura and Rais weren't going to have a sex orgy. I squeezed his hand. "Thanks for the invitation, anyway."

Rocky had bought three center rows in the orchestra. Sitting beside me in an aisle seat, he seemed delighted at the enthusiasm of the Premars. Every time I looked at him, he was watching me with a bemused expression on his tanned, craggy face. How could I concentrate on the ballet? Especially when he touched my hand? Once, playing lightly with my fingers, he whispered, "Merle, I like the proud, regal cut of your face. You're a lovely woman."

Back in the apartment at last, the kids were in the kitchen gobbling cold cuts and cheese, milling around here and there, examining their surroundings, or stalking out their sleeping positions. Rais appeared in white boxer shorts—worn, I imagine, in deference to Rocky. "Laura is having contractions," he said, "but they're pretty irregular, and she's lost a little water. A couple of hours ago we sat in the big tub and drank a glass of your Château Lafitte Rothschild. She had some steak and fries, and then she telephoned the doctor. Bacon told her she'd last until morning. He's going to have breakfast with us at seven o'clock."

Ellen asked Rais if anybody could help. Rais shook his head. "Right now she's dozing. When she isn't napping or eating, she's griping and wondering what persuaded her to have this baby. And she says I'm a bastard because I seduced her." Rais smiled. "Then I'm breathing with her or holding her hand while she pisses. I assured her if she has a good shit, no one is going to try to give her an enema, even me, though I'm well acquainted with her rosebud. She'll either shit normally in the next few hours, I told her, or she'll shit when the baby is being born, and one of us will wipe her ass and love her anyway, and be glad that she can shit. She's also insistent that she can have this baby without an episiotomy, and she's marshaling her arguments to convince Bacon to wait until the last second." Rais waved good night. "Laura's quite a woman. And natural childbirth is a fascinating, learning, loving experience." He looked at me. "You're next, Merle."

Bren and Ellen disappeared into one of the guest rooms. Listening to Rocky talking with some of the Premars, I was about to lie down on one of the couches in the library, hoping he had forgotten me, when he saw me and said, "You're not sleeping out here." About twenty of the kids were drinking in his words about the infallibility of the laws of supply and demand. He said we either lived in a society where competition, price, and a reasonable profit regulated wages and the amount of material goods that a person could buy, or surrendered our freedom to a government that told us what wages we could be paid, and controlled prices as well as human freedom. "And as I look around tonight," he said, "the male-female supply-and-demand equation seems to be balanced. You know, supply and demand works as well with sex as with money." Rocky's eyebrows were a question mark, and I thought he winked at me. "Since Merle has agreed to sleep with me, and Rais is comforting my wife with her big belly, it's neither a buyer nor a seller 's market."

"It's a standoff," I assured the kids. "And it's going to be too short a night to pursue the subject."

I followed Rocky into a dimly lighted bedroom, and we shooed out a few kids who were already curled up on the floor. I was jittery and self-conscious, and I tried not to act surprised at the king-size feather bed with a canopy and a built-in mirror over it. "An amusing sleeping experience, with the right partner," Rocky said. "Have you ever watched yourself?"

"No. I'd rather lose myself," I told him. I stood in front of the fireplace with its beautiful burning logs that would never turn to ash. Rocky slouched in one of the Queen Anne lounge chairs which flanked a mahogany table with a built-in refrigerator bar. On a tripod beside the chair, a long gleaming white telescope was aimed at the windows, which are flush with the floor. The city outside was a cold, impassive diamond, refracting millions of nervous, evanescent, manmade sparkles. It was twelve-thirty.

"Does it give the great God Rocky Stone a sense of power to watch the world from his own private Olympus?" I asked. Rocky had opened a bottle of brandy and filled the bottom of two oversize goblets. Sipping my drink, wondering if my tit would fit into the glass, I watched him focus the telescope. A warm, lethargic feeling spread from my head to my toes. I felt very self-conscious and strangely erotic. Was brandy at midnight a rich man's aphrodisiac? I'm going to buy a bottle for Rais and me and glasses actually big enough to hold my breasts.

"We're too late," Rocky said. He offered me the eyepiece. "The performance is over," he said. "No. Watching doesn't make me feel powerful. Only sad. It gives me an awareness of transience, and the feeling of feeble gropings of people trying to love each other. What you're looking at is a housing project two miles from here. In the past couple of nights I've got better acquainted with that woman than with some I've actually slept with."

I gasped. "My God! If you were any closer, you'd be inside her skin." A woman about thirty and man were lying naked on a bed on their backs. His eyes were closed, and she was idly playing with his penis. The magnification of the telescope was so powerful that the gism, still seeping out of his penis and glistening on the hairs on his belly, was perfectly visible.

Rocky was amused by my astonishment. "Two nights ago, he actually got inside her, but he climaxed on her belly. From the stretch marks on her stomach, it's obvious she's had a few kids. But she won't use the pill, and she isn't taking any more chances." He sipped his brandy. "That's the way it goes. Rich man or poor man, after a while humans communicate with a little finger diddling, and not much conversation."

"I read a book about a voyeur," I told him. "The only way he could get an erection was to watch someone else doing it."

"Everyone's a voyeur," he said. "Why do people go to the movies, watch television, read books? Why do *Playboy* and *Penthouse* sell millions of copies? Because most people don't dare admit their emotional needs. They watch from the sidelines, they're spectators, not participators. A lot of men sublimate their sexual frustration watching

football or hockey. Think of all the people in my generation who felt guilty about their oral sexual desires. Even
today, after Kinsey and Linda Lovelace, do most men and
women feel free to talk about their desire to suck each
other's genitals? Even when they do lap and taste each
other, they're too embarrassed to talk about it afterward.
A division of Stone-Western—a company I picked up four
years ago—makes this telescope. The more highrise apartments they build, the bigger our sales. We live in a world
of tongue-tied people, staring dumbly at each other, not
even able to use sign language to tell each other they're
lonely. Look at Laura and me; we're the perfect example.
Or look at you—you're not being honest with me."
Rocky's laugh was sarcastic. "If you were, you'd tell me
that I'm a self-complacent schmuck."

"Maybe you're a diamond in the rough," I said. "Laura
doesn't think Rais is a revolutionist. She thinks he's a
teddy bear, which is just the feeling I get about you."

Rocky shrugged. "Bears only look lovable. They can be
pretty mean customers." He sloshed his brandy in his glass
and stared at it awhile. "Laura seems to have your husband domesticated, and now she's working on me. Well, I
suppose I'm learning. How many middle-income white
women do you know who have given birth to a black
child while their white husband applauded the performance? Sometimes I get the feeling that Laura is
playing power politics with me. She waited until I was at
an age in life where I might have to accept her on her
own terms. Do I want this marriage more than I want another man's child?"

"Why don't you divorce her?"

Rocky laughed. "I admire her tenacity. She's always
been a very determined woman. But, as fucked-up as her
motivations may be, for the first time in her life she's focused. You might not understand that, but it makes Laura
challenging to me."

"Laura isn't having this baby to get your ass. She's really discovering herself."

"If the situation were reversed, would you want me to
get you pregnant?"

"If I were you, I'd be careful. If I weren't on the pill, I
might have different motivations. Having Rocky Stone's
baby should be worth a cool million."

"Shall we go to bed?" Rocky took off his shirt and tie

and cufflinks. Very methodically he hung his suit and pants on a coat tree, dropped his shorts on the floor, and walked naked into the bathroom. I heard the shower running. Dillydallying time was over. It had to be yes or no. I shucked off my dress, panties, and bra and knocked on the shower door. As he soaped me and explored my body, while the water poured over his head, I told him I thought he was reacting quite normally.

I shook his hard jigger, and with a towel wrapped around me, I fled into the bedroom. "Should we pull the drapes?" I asked. Rocky had flopped onto the superthick mattress and partially sunk from view.

"It's up to you. With the drapes open we can lie here and look at the stars. Maybe there's someone in a fortieth-floor apartment who has a telescope and is watching us, or maybe God's out there floating by on a white cloud, chuckling in his beard, because he's happy that I'm about to taste your pussy." Rocky nuzzled his head between my legs.

"Do I taste like a black girl?" I demanded. I wiggled out of his embrace.

"Do black girls taste different?"

"How do I know? I never tasted a white girl or a black girl. But I've heard white male stories. Black poontang is supposed to be muskier."

"I'll take the witness stand. You taste like Merle Blanc. Very erotic."

Shivering, I pulled the sheet over us. "Can we talk? Maybe you're searching for your youth with young women? I hear Jeanne Mechante is in her twenties. Did you make love with Ellen?"

Rocky pulled me in his arms. "Last Sunday night Ellen lay here with me, and she never stopped talking about how much she loved Bren. I felt like her father—listening while his wide-eyed, innocent daughter told him how happy she was. How could I screw my own daughter when she was hugging me and talking to me like a starry-eyed angel? I was impotent. It was a magnificent con job. Could I tell her that she had to do something besides just lie there? She knew I wouldn't ask her to help me. Can you tell a child that Santa Claus' soft prick might come to life if she held it? The funny damn thing is, I think Ellen was disappointed. She may even tell Bren that we made very passionate love—but only because she's a little jealous of him and you." Rocky kissed my lips and breasts. "So here I am again, with another babe in the woods."

"I guess Jeanne isn't so naïve," I said.

"Jeanne's a sex mechanic. Her system is whorehouse efficient—'Come on, baby, fuck me, fuck me.' She never turns her engines off. A fine performer, but boring in the long haul." Rocky was gently teasing my nipples and then tasting them. With his eyes open, he was discovering black flesh.

I held his penis and told him he was the only white man I'd ever touched except Bren. "You don't seem to have a problem tonight," I whispered. "I read that older men, when they get it up, can last a long time. Come inside and make love to me long enough to tell me who you really are."

Rocky laughed. "I'd never come out again!"

"Why are you looking at me so strangely?"

"I'm admiring your black nose. I like it better than my curved Semitic one. Are you black? I suppose so. But far more important, you are easy to be with. What are you thinking?"

"That you and Bren have much in common. The protective, gentle, Jewish male. You're easy to be with, too. But I'm surrendering my vagina because I'm expecting you to surrender your brain. Tell me why you wanted to be richer than Croesus."

Rocky thought that was hysterically funny. Big inside me, lying on his side, he told me that when he went to the University of Pennsylvania he had been an overweight, aggressive, bull-headed, know-it-all neurotic who was self-conscious about his appearance. He had no friends, male or female. When his father died, in his junior year, he quit college and helped his mother manage the family store, which was a cross between a Woolworth's and a Kresge's. By 1940 the family business had expanded to four stores in New Jersey. At the end of the war he sold them all to a national chain for $300,000 and split the money with his mother. A fellow he had met in the army was looking for venture capital to manufacture a transistor he had patented. In five years Rocky's $150,000 had become a million dollars in stock ownership. He sold the stock in the transistor company and bought control of a small company that made cathode-ray tubes. A few years later he was able to use the stock of this company to acquire four other companies in both electronics and microwave components. Soon he merged them all together under the name Stone-Western Industries and went public. By the time he married Laura, Stone-Western owned a fleet of oil tankers, a chain of drive-in theaters, a distillery, two banks, and an insurance company. Stone-Western now had fifty-three divisions and subsidiaries.

"I learned how to buy and sell companies at the right time," Rocky told me. "Suddenly everybody loved me, and for a few years I was involved with more women than Bernie Cornfeld. Then my mother decided that before she died she should have grandchildren. Her brother, my Uncle Sam, became the self-appointed *shadchen*, marriage broker. His best friend, Abe Gattman, had a nubile daughter. I was thirty-six. Laura was twenty-one, just graduated from Bennington." Rocky smiled. "I really had no time for love. This is the longest time I've ever been inside a woman in my life. Your vagina keeps gently massaging me. How did you learn to do that?"

"I've had world enough and time," I told him. I could see by a digital clock on the other side of the room that it was 2:46 A.M. I rolled on top of him. "Okay, Big Daddy—talking time is past."

Did Rocky and I learn anything from each other? For a few hours we bridged two worlds, and maybe we discovered that, rich or poor, white or black, a man and woman can reach the essential being of each other, better than a man can with another man, or a woman with another woman. Maybe the male has been his own worst enemy. He created a male-dominated, patriarchal, homosexual-style world when he could function better in a fully heterosexual world. Human beings need people who like them without too many qualifications. Only men and women can do this for each other.

I fell asleep in Rocky's arms. Somehow, in the morning, he managed to dress without waking me. At a quarter of seven he was bending over me kissing my lips and breasts. "It would be more fun to get back in bed with you," he said, laughing at my bewildered where-am-I expression. "But I've been talking with Rais and Harry Bacon in the kitchen, and Laura is about ready to go into the second stage of labor. The show is on."

I jumped out of bed and hugged him. "Thanks for the evening," I told him. "Maybe our spouses will let us do it again sometime. And maybe you should let Laura discover the other Rocky Stone—the guy who'd rather be a snuggly bear than a big tycoon."

Rocky held my shoulders. His eyes were crinkly with suppressed laughter. "I'm only just discovering him myself," he said. He patted my ass. "But getting cozy in bed with a stranger isn't as dangerous as being snuggly with a wife of long standing."

As I dressed I kept thinking that maybe a woman like Laura, seeing the world from a new perspective, was like a living mirror. Not only could she reflect the world around her differently, but she could reveal a very different Rocky to himself. The rejected adolescent who still lived inside him might at last find a friend. And in the master bedroom, the transition between the stages of labor was slowly opening another perspective on the world for both Rocky and Laura. I hoped they could embrace it.

In the big bedroom, Able, standing on a kitchen ladder, was photographing the expressions on the kids' faces. Oblivious to me, they were all watching the scene on the bed. Her legs widespread, Laura was breathing one-two, one-two—holding her breath, and then panting, she expelled air. Rais and a tall thin man—the doctor, obviously —who looked like a rabbinical scholar were looking into her vagina. "The pelvic floor is thinning nicely," the thin man said. "Did you see the walls of her vagina move just slightly?"

"Wow!" Laura gasped. "I feel like something that just crash-landed from outer space. Every damned country cousin is peering at my cunt wondering if it has teeth. I must have been mad to allow this." She opened her eyes and focused on me. "Hi, Merle, I'm glad you're here. The bony guy standing next to you is Harry Bacon. Tell him to cut out bugging me. I finally had the damned enema. Harry wouldn't believe that just two hours ago I had a good shit. Rais even wiped my ass for old times' sake."

Bacon grinned at Rocky. "I remember when Laura would say, 'I have to go to the powder room.' She's been playing with a new friend."

Rocky was amused. "Her island sabbatical released her previous inhibitions."

Harry shook his head. "I still think you're being remarkably cool about this, Rocky," He looked at Rais with uplifted eyebrows. "The baby will no doubt be a healthy child, but it isn't going to be lily-white."

"When I was a kid," Rocky told him, "we had a bitch named Lulu, and some stray dog knocked her up. I didn't love her any less."

Finishing a contraction and panting, Laura heard the interchange. "You're a shithead, Rocky," she gasped.

"No, I'm not. I really loved Lulu's pups, too. I hated to part with any of them."

"Goddamnit, tilt that thing a little." Laura gestured toward a mirror that had been hung on an angle from the ceiling. "I want to see what everyone's looking at." She stared a moment and grimaced. "Nothing but the same hairy swollen slit. Harry, when this baby starts to come, I'm going on my knees. I can see the action better that way."

Harry grinned at her.

A plump woman in a nurse's uniform and cap introduced herself. "I'm Martha Weiss, Dr. Bacon's nurse. Mrs. Stone has gone through the transition stage very quickly, but I'm afraid she still isn't aware of what's ahead of her."

"Don't worry," I told Laura. "Every person in this room is in love with you—even Rocky." I decided that someone needed to put the words in his mouth.

Even I was amazed to see Rocky squeeze Laura's hand. He leaned over and kissed her perspiring brow. "You're okay, kid. It's a great performance," he told her.

"This is fun," Laura said. She had tears in her eyes. "I always wanted to be . . ." She stopped to breathe through her contraction.

I matched her breathing through the ascent, peak, and resolution. "Beautiful, you're doing fine," I told her.

". . . an actress," she panted. ". . . and such a lovely audience. Boy, I keep feeling that I want to push down. I've got a dull cramp in my stomach."

"No pushing yet," Harry said, and *he* was perspiring! "And you better not advertise this day. My patients have their babies on my schedule, with a damned small cheering section. This is like the zoo with all the monkeys jumping up and down and chattering."

"You," he said to me. "You're supposed to know something. Do you know what effleurage is?"

I nodded.

"Well, since we seem to have reverted to the days of

the midwives, go ahead, massage her belly. Her stomach muscles need to be soothed."

I sprinkled talc on Laura just above her pubic hair, and on the next contraction looped my fingers in a soft rhythmic curving stroke around her stomach.

"Aaah ..." she sighed when she could talk again. "That's real sexy, Merle. I like it. I think the contractions are getting easier."

"It's the calm before the storm," Martha said.

"I feel the head," Laura yelled. "God—it's pressing against my vagina like a hard rubber ball."

"Okay," I told her. "Don't tighten your ass. Relax those pelvic floor muscles."

"Aim the kid at me," Harry said; he was kneeling between her legs. "I can see the head. You can push—not hard, very gently, because there's no hurry. Let your uterus do the real work—that's its business. Well, well! You're beautifully dilated. I can tell this will only take a little longer."

Harry was enjoying himself as he told the kids they could walk by the bed and take a closer look. I watched the faces of the Premars. A lot of the girls were teary; the guys looked amazed. Some of the girls bent over and kissed Laura's cheek. Cheryl whispered, "Everyone here loves you, Laura."

Laura was by turns groaning, yelling, cursing, lapsing into silence, laughing, sucking on a sponge which I dipped in raspberry tea I had made for her, telling us all she loved us, thanking us for coming; she even sang a childhood song: "I wish I were a rhine-sah-rarius, a hippópotamiee, But since I am not, and never can hope to be ... I'm a june bug, I'm a beetle, I run and hit my head against the tree." Laura was still breathing perfectly in her contractions, but she seemed bone-tired.

"Oh, Bren, Bren, do you remember that song?" She smiled at him as the tears streamed down her cheek. "Rivke's father sang it to us when we were kids."

Bren caressed her, and so did Ellen and Rais. I guess even Rocky could feel the vibration of deep caring and affection for Laura. He sponged her face. "Okay, honey," he said. "You're proving you're a tough cookie. I'm with you."

"You're really a *mensch*, Rocky. Thanks for being here."

Rocky smiled at her. "I'm promoting you to president of Stone-Western. With the exception of me, you have more cool nerve than anyone I know."

"Not nerve." Laura grinned. "Balls."

"The hell with that. I've got balls enough for both of us."

Laura was on her hands and knees rocking back and forth. I told Harry that if he wished I could do a perineal massage. He shrugged. If Laura wanted to consort with witch doctors, what could he do about it? I scrubbed my hands in the bathroom; then Martha pulled sterile gloves over my hands. With the index and middle finger of my right hand well lubricated with jelly, I gently pulled up and to each side of Laura's vagina, massaging her perineum, which was amazingly loose and relaxed. Harry watched me with a tiny grin, and I realized that he now was sure that Laura's baby would be born without any tearing. Between contractions I continued to massage her.

At the height of the contractions the baby's head was appearing, and then it would disappear again. It was eleven-thirty.

"Another hour," Harry said. "You better relax, Merle. You're going to be as pooped as the mother."

"God." Laura moaned. "Get me some more water. I'm dying of thirst."

She lay on her side awhile. Then she stood up on her knees and turned and smiled at the kids. "All of you give a good yell," she said. "You've been so damned quiet, you'll burst."

The kids let out a huge whoop as Laura dropped back on her hands. Now her contractions were coming about three minutes apart and lasting a full minute. At twelve-fifteen the head, with crinkly black hair, crowned. Everyone in the room was involved and breathing in rhythm with Laura. Looking between her legs, Laura moaned. "Rocky, Rais, it's me! It's me! The baby and I are being born simultaneously."

Then Harry took over. With a gauze pad in the palm of his hand he held a steady pressure on Laura's wide-open anus, pushing the outer borders of her perineum down and in to relieve the tension. "You're going to make it, sweetheart," he said, "with no damage except a sore asshole." Now he unwound the cord, which was wrapped around the baby's neck.

Martha removed the mucus from the baby's mouth, throat, and nose. Laura was laughing and sobbing. "I never saw a purple cow, but I'm getting a purple kid. Oh, God. I can feel its head against my leg." Harry was still supporting her perineum. "He's turning. He's turning. His hair is tickling me." The right shoulder and a hand emerged, and with the next contraction Harry had the slippery baby in his hands.

"It's not a he. It's a beautiful little brown she."

"I did it! I did it!"

The baby, still connected to the placenta, was screaming her indignation. Harry cut the cord and clipped it. Martha wiped her slippery body. "Okay, sweetheart," Harry said. "Give it one of those luscious nipples, and help the placenta along." Smiling weakly at all of us, Laura held the baby against her breast. The wizened brown face was silent for a second, and then the baby started sucking.

"Imani. Dear Imani." Laura called the baby. "Imani Imara. That's her name."

"They're Swahili words," Rais explained. "*Imani* means 'faith.' *Imara* means 'strength.' Laura and I decided last night that this girl will need a little of both."

Laura looked at Rocky. "Imani needs a surname. Shall it be Daemon or Stone?"

She handed the baby to me. "Harry, I'm contracting again. No real pressure—just like a wave." Looking at the placenta as it streamed out of her, she said she had changed her mind and couldn't eat it after all.

Rocky shook his head. "I told Rais this morning that I married you for better or worse." He brushed Laura's hair back, and his voice was gruff as he tried to conceal his emotion. "Somehow, in a goddamn way I haven't stopped to figure out, this marriage seems to be getting better. If you don't mind, Rais, I'll adopt the kid. Imani Imara Daemon Stone," he said. "If names mean anything, she's got it made."

Rais Daemon. July, the first year of Premar. From tapes transcribed by Rachel Silverman.

Once again I'm on an island, Big Brewster, one of the more than thirty islands in Boston harbor, a far call from St. Noir or the Mons de Cytherea. Except for a lighthouse keeper, no one lives on these four islands. Big, Middle, Outer, and little Brewster, with a white-flashing beacon—they are rock-ribbed nesting grounds for seagulls, terns, egrets, and occasional great blue herons. Wild grasses, milkweed, daisies, mustard, chicory, buttercups, wild beach roses, nettle, chokeberries, bayberries, sumac, and poison ivy—all the vegetation thrives in the cold fogs and winter winds that sweep in off the Atlantic. Preserved by the state, the harbor islands are tiny escape worlds still dominated by sun and water, and tides and winds, and growing things and birds and insects and free-roving rodents, and thousands of copulating sea creatures pursuing their timeless destinies.

In the past two centuries, while the children of the Pilgrims were still fighting their revolutions and civil wars and world wars, when simpler methods of human destruction prevailed, these outer islands were armed fortresses. From the Brewsters, unwanted or attacking ships could be sunk, and the harbors mined to prevent the enemy from reaching shore. But man learned to fly over gun emplacements. And now, though man has fished most of the famous cod, mackerel, and flounder out of this harbor, and has polluted it with sewage and oil spills, and the gun mountings have eroded, and the cement on the fortresses has cracked and is filled with vegetation the microcosm of insects, birds, sea life, and plant life—which may have a sentience all its own—exists as it has from the beginning of time, oblivious to the world of man and his follies, as man is of this more ancient world.

Last night the Premar girls frolicking on the moonlighted rocky beaches were moonflowers waxing and wan-
ing on a menstrual cycle which had its origins in the same
life-loving forces that turned the tides and moved the
earth on its orbit. Bren told the kids that if we could comprehend all of the deep interrelationships of each one of
us with this sea world from which we emerged aeons ago,
we would have taken a long stride toward wisdom and
love.

Bren and Ellen and Merle and I agreed that in September, when the first hurricane brewing in the Caribbean
whirled its way to New England, we'd come back to this
island and make love in a howling wind, clinging to each
other, whipped by rain, and awed by the pounding sea and
the sky and the earth, which only seems to have been
tamed. The age of man's arrogance is fast receding, and
both wonder and joy in our common humanity are standing on the doorstep, patiently waiting to be invited back
in.

Sitting here a few hundred feet above sea level on the
top of Big Brewster, I can see a hazy, opalescent coastline
that extends from the tip of Provincetown to Gloucester.
For the next six hours the moon will coax the ocean back
on itself, and lay bare a world of bright starfish, pink sea
pork, purple sea urchins, and a sea carpet of anemones
and amphipods, ribbonworms, polychaete worms, periwin-
kle snails, nematodes, and chitons. Then the scene will become a dinner table for the gulls, an erotic symbiosis of
sun and sea and slippery algae and rich organic mud.

It's a lazy July day. Twelve months ago a white woman
and a black man discovered themselves on another island.
Maybe islands are an essential missing element in most human lives. Surrounded by sea or deep in a forest, or lying
in tall grass, or sitting under a tree, or touching and smell-
ing the earth, *being*, being anywhere where you can surrender your self-consciousness to the primal world, and
find a sense sublime—"that blessed mood in which the
burthen of the mystery . . . of his tunintelligible [man]
world is lightened: that serene and blessed mood in which
the affections gently lead us on, until the breath of this
corporeal frame and even the motion of our human blood
almost suspended, we are laid asleep in body, and become
a living soul, with an eye made quiet by the power of harmony, and the deep power of joy, we see into the life of

things . . . a sense sublime whose dwelling is the light of
setting suns."

So today is both a time for recapitulation and empathy
with worms. A few hundred feet below this eroding, vine-
covered Civil War gun emplacement, I'm watching,
through binoculars, the Premar encampment on the beach
below me. Mumbling into this machine, which is impar-
tially recording my poetic mood and the enraged squawking
of displaced seagulls, I can see the mile-long crescent spit
that curves toward Big Light and George's Island, and
Fort Warren.

The entire Premar commune and a half-dozen families
from Confam #1, about seventy of us, have been camping
here since last Sunday. Coming here was Ellen's idea.
"The kids need a change of scenery," she said. "The city
gets to be too much in the summer." We were short of
money, but Bren convinced the owner of a harbor excur-
sion boat to sail us out here for a round-trip cost of fifty
dollars. With only three boats to land us, and to carry
ashore our rented tents, food, and sleeping bags, everyone
who could swim jumped off the weathered sailing sloop
and swam ashore. A couple of hours after our water
transportation had left, the command tent and some
thirty-five pup tents had been set up. To a casual observer
it looks like a Scout encampment, except these scouts obviously have dorks and tits, and no one is concerned that
many of them are exposed to the sun and air.

A quarter-mile below, I can see Ellen on the beach waving at me. Most of the kids, naked, jumping, swimming,
tumbling in the shallow water have wandered out on
shell-covered Brewster Spit, a treacherous shore which will
be hidden at high tide by a few feet of water. Then it
seems like a clear expanse of ocean, luring mariners who
haven't read their charts and are trying to reach the harbor on a more direct route than the curving channels.

We warned the kids that while Dancer seems to be on
our side, he isn't exactly advocating skinny-dipping on the
Boston beaches. But the Premars don't care. "The police
boats can't come up on these shoals," one said. "Before
the cops could run the length of the spit, we'd have our
bathing suits on. 'Naked?' we'd say, 'Man, you must be
dreaming.' " Maybe Premar has seeded another revolution.

Ellen is slowly climbing the hill. Through the binoculars,
I can see her madonna face alight with some happiness

she wants to share. For a second Ellen is Laura, and I'm on the Mons, and memories and nostalgia flood back. My white mistress is approaching with undulating hips of love. Where is Laura? Where is Imani Imara? Where are the snows of yesteryear? Even after the long discussion the four of us had in March with Laura and Rocky, I can't believe that Rocky has managed such a complete about-face. Or has he? Sometimes I agree with Bren. Rocky Stone is a reincarnation of Sir Francis Drake—half-gentlemen, half-pirate, guided by a code of morals that only seem not to be self-serving. "Robin Hood would have lasted longer," Rocky told us once, "if he had incorporated and sold stock to the poor. The lambs were meant to be shorn."

When Bren told Rocky that, as important as we believed the Confam experiment is, under no circumstances would he permit Stone-Western to underwrite it, Rocky gave it to him straight: "Listen, I don't run a charity organization, but I'm going to get you the mortgage money. The First Merchants Bank, on my approval, will lend the incorporators what they need at reasonable market mortgage rates. Obviously, this will be no government handout, and that means the incorporators can't sit on their asses. Those who don't work in the regular employment market will have to justify their existence and support by the Confam. If they don't, I doubt if those who are working are going to be too goddamn pleased."

Rocky had gone over the figures with his Boston bankers. While they thought the members could handle the principal and interest payments, they advised him that the Topham's Corner Confam belonged in the area of public housing, and Stone-Western shouldn't get involved; the profit margins didn't warrant the risks. If the Confams went bankrupt, less than fifty percent of the investment would be recoverable.

"Fortunately, I don't listen to bankers," Rocky said. "For the most part they are followers not doers; a boring, uncreative profession. Centuries after Shylock, they're still insisting on their pound of flesh for collateral."

"I really don't understand all this," Ellen told him. "I didn't think Bren and Rais were thinking of Confam as a business proposition—something that succeeds or fails according to whether it makes money. What happens if these incorporators miss a mortgage payment? Will the bank evict them?"

Rocky laughed. "My dear Snow White, what happens today if these same people don't pay their rent or taxes? The sheriff will evict them. What's the difference? There's always a wicked witch hiding somewhere. I don't give a damn if the Confam is profitable or breaks even; all I care is that it meets its mortgage payments—even if the members have to starve a little to do it. That's the only pound of flesh the First Merchants will honor."

"Get us the money," Bren told him. "We're not going to fail."

"Great! I'm betting you won't. I'll ask the bank to send me a quarterly progress report, and if your Dorchester Confam survives, Stone-Western just might go in the business."

"What business?"

Rocky grinned. "In your proposal you envisioned a national network of Confams, but one thing you haven't wanted to face is that some people aren't going to be satisfied to rehabilitate substandard housing. If the Confam idea spreads—and with the new kind of world we're facing, with insufficient energy, there may be a hell of a lot of interest in pooling more things than automobiles—then middle-income people, grouping together as incorporators, will make condominiums old hat, something only the rich can afford. If we can make a profit, Stone-Western will go into the business of building brand-new, especially designed Confams. Woolworth's makes more money than Tiffany's." Rocky shrugged. "What's more, we'll probably be able to get Uncle Sam to bankroll us. I'm going to make you all rich in spite of yourselves. Or at the very least, I'll show you that the only way to 'green America' is to play the game. If you know how to play the game, you can even break the rules and get away with it."

Laura smiled. "I think Rocky will argue with the devil and try to take over hell when he gets there."

"I'll put it on a profitable basis," Rocky said, "or send the backsliders to heaven."

Merle laughed. "Be careful, Rocky, Bren and Rais are dangerous company. They may turn you into a charity institution."

Rocky continues to amaze us. Last Saturday we received a note from Laura together with copies of *Vogue* and *Women's Wear Daily*. "Thought it might be a while before these other-world reports seep down to *Time* magazine or Dorchester, Massachusetts," she wrote. "As you can see, Rocky is still being his sweetly sour self. Well, Imani loves him and wrinkles her nose at him, which entrances Rocky no end." The magazine and newspaper had illustrated interviews with Laura and Rocky. They were in Nice, en route, on Rocky's yacht, to St. Noir. Asked by reporters whether he was adjusted to being the stepfather of an interracial child, and what effect this was having on their marriage, Rocky told them, "I'm co-opting the counterculture, showing them how to stop sawing against the grain. I'm showing my brother-in-law, Bren Gattman, and Rais Daemon, who've been getting a lot of publicity with their new Premar and Confamiliaum life styles, how to dry themselves behind the ears. Bren thinks he'll co-opt me. Co-optation. Hell, that's an instrument of policy for Stone-Western! I've played that game when they were both in diapers. As for Imani Imara, Rais Daemon's daughter, Laura and I both love her. The rumors that your tribe persist in spreading that our marriage is on the rocks are sheer nonsense. All my business life has been devoted to proving that the best business for America is a strong conglomerate. Why shouldn't we have interracial family conglomerates?

"I've set precedents all my life," Rocky told the reporters. "One of our subsidiaries has just taken over a real-estate-development company that has been dredging and filling a three-thousand-acre cay off the western shore of St. Noir. Their original plan was to create a resort-style gambling area, similar to Freeport. Now, working with Arthur Granby, the president of St. Noir, we're going to build a family-style, low-income, live-with-the-people vacation area. That's an idea, incidentally, originally proposed by Rais Daemon. Eventually we hope that Rais and his wife will join us and perhaps take direct management of this project.

"Who knows," Rocky finally told the reporters. "My wife has set a precedent, and she understands that should the occasion present itself, I'm not too old to take advantage of it."

When Merle read that, her eyes twinkled. "You have permission to visit your daughter, Rais," she told him.

"But little Merle isn't going to be 'the occasion that presents itself.' My first child is going to be at least as black as I am. I wonder if Gabby is interviewing Rocky. Ha! There's an occasion!"

"You're a racist," Bren said.

"So is Ellen, but neither of us has made any decision, yet, about our *second* child."

Ellen is only a few hundred feet down the hill. Swinging her blouse in the air, she's wearing pale blue jeans, cut above her knees, and sneakers. The swinging pendulum of her breasts, free in the warm air, and the laughter hopping and skipping over her eyes, lips, and nose are combining into a soft summer adagio.

"Oh, Rais, aren't you proud of me? I did it! I climbed this hill, and I'm only puffing a little. My love, why are you alone up here? Ah, I see that you have a tape recorder for company."

"The way you are kissing and touching me, I think I should turn it off."

(Laughter.)

"Are you making this tape for the kids or for Laura?"

"Both, I guess, but mostly to hear myself think."

"Then I think you should let it run, so everybody can hear me ask you, Rais: Will you sleep with me tonight? There—I asked you. *You* didn't ask me, though I don't know why."

"Because I like you. Because I'm black. Because I'm not promiscuous. And because you're my friend, and that's more important to me than the joy of reaching an orgasm with you. But I must admit that you're so lovely half-naked, leaning back on your elbows, the cool wind teasing your hair, and making your nipples erect, that a man would be half-dead not to want to make love with you."

"I heard everything you said except 'because I'm black.' You're Rais. You're a dreamer. And I'm a patsy for dreamers. Can't we be friends after we make love? I asked Merle if she'd mind, and she's still laughing. She told me that I was something out of this world. I quoted Shelley to her. 'I never was attached to that great sect, whose doctrine is that each one should select, out of the crowd a mistress or a friend, and all the rest, though fair and wise, commend to oblivion.' Stop grinning! I believed that before I ever met you or Bren."

"I'll still bet you a kiss on your freckled cheek that Bren read *Epipsychidion* aloud to you."

(Laughter.)

"You get the kiss—but I married Bren with my eyes wide open. And I'm learning, too. Want to hear the rest of the poem? I'm going to recite it anyway. 'Though it is the code of modern morals and the beaten road, which these poor slaves with weary footsteps tread, who travel to their home among the dead, by the broad highway of the word, and so with one chained friend, and perhaps a jealous foe, the dreariest and the longest journey go.' One thing I'll not ever be to Bren is a chained friend, nor a jealous foe—not in sickness, nor in health. I love Bren— free to love and perchance to love me. But you haven't answered my question."

"What question?"

"I'm going to sock you."

"Sweet, of course I'll sleep with you, and we'll lie close together all night under the stars."

"And share our dreams? Begin now, Rais. You seem happy, but *il penseroso* happy. Why are you sitting up here alone? Are you pretending that you're God, and this sky and sea and islands and boats and people and birds and insects are your creation?"

"They are my creation, and now that you're here, they're yours, too. And I know that we can join our bodies in complete harmony because we know how to share each other's creations."

(Laughter.)

"I really don't know what I was thinking. On one level, I supose about Rocky and Laura and Imani, but on another level ... amorphous questions, like: Who are we? Where are we going? What will the world really be like in 1984? Will we—you, Merle, Bren, and I—have created a wobble in the spin of events? Is anything inevitable in this world?"

"Death."

"Are you sure? Maybe death is only a different side of the same coin. The heads can't see the tails. Hey! It just flashed through my mind that I helped create another human being and in July of the year 2000 she'll be nearly the same age you are now."

"Do you miss Laura?"

"Of course. I love three women. Merle, Ellen, and Laura."

"That's not in alphabetical order."

"It's in order of commitment. Your order is Bren, Rais ... is there a third person?"

(Laughter.)

"No, thanks, two's enough!"

"You know, there's something I've wanted to ask you. Did you make love with Rocky?"

"Didn't you listen to Merle's tape? Don't you believe what Rocky told her? Just a few nights ago Bren asked me the same question. [Laughter.] Rais, do you know something? You look awfully big under those jeans."

"What do you expect? You haven't stopped kissing me since you've got here. Your nipples are sticking out like gum drops, which I may start to nibble if you don't calm down."

"Ummm ... Bren says it's a common male fantasy to dream of the woman taking the initiative and arousing the man. Your lips taste nice. Am I being too aggressive?"

"I can't believe what's happening. I never knew you were a love bug."

(Laughter.)

"I'm not with everybody. I cooled Rocky by talking my head off."

"I'm sure you didn't kiss his belly, either, or unzip his pants."

"He had his pants off, silly. [*Pause.*] But he didn't have, anything like this."

"Ellen?"

"What?"

"This afternoon, and tonight, too?"

"Right out here in the sunshine?"

"Sure, Ireland and Africa finally discovering each other under the sun. We could lie under those sumac bushes over there."

"This isn't *poison* sumac, is it? Is the tape recorder still going?"

"Do you want it turned off? No—only when it has white berries."

"Leave it on. [*Laughter.*] But I may want to censor it afterward."

"We really should have a blanket."

"Spread out your jeans. Here. Use mine, too. God, you have a lovely body—and a big bamboo."

(Pause.)

"Rais, am I too heavy on top of you?"

"You're a warm white cloud."

"The sun feels nice, but what if I get a sunburn on my behind? [*Laughter.*] Oh, Rais, I'm not really aggressive; I was just acting like a sex maniac to gain courage. [*Pause.*] Don't look at me like that."

"Are you afraid now?"

"Oh, no! I don't feel strange with you at all. This is dreamy. I'm as high as a little bird can fly. I don't want to ever come down. Can you last?"

(Laughter.)

"Forever."

(Pause.)

(Laughter.)

"Rais, oh, Rais, I'm so very happy today. Do you want me to be passionate, or shall we just go on coasting? Do you know what I've been thinking? I'm realizing that everything is coming into focus. Premar has survived its first year, and ... I was reading a poem by Paul Williams— from his book, *Das Energi*. 'We are on a verge of a new age,' he says, 'a whole new world. Mankind's consciousness, our mutual awareness, is going to take a quantum leap. Everything will change. You will never be the same. All this will happen just as soon as you're ready.' "

(Laughter.)

"That's the point, isn't it, Rais? We're in the mainstream. We're ready. [*Pause.*] I think that being religious, being God, is the ongoing process of trying to put it all together. Seeing everything at once from every dimension."

"If we succeed, will it make any sense?"

"Maybe, after a lifetime of trying to correlate all the questions and answers, we'll discover the joy was in the search. Ellen, undulating her vagina—around the black penis of Rais Daemon—loving the dreamy expression on his face, and the feather-touch of his fingers on her breast and behind; Bren and Merle, and the four of us interacting, caring for each other; Laura and Rocky with their child; all those kids down on the beach, and the families daring to experiment with Confamiliaum; Leonard Woodcock, the president of the United Auto Workers, saying, 'We are challenging in effect whether human beings exist for the sake of production and profit, or whether we are engaged in production for the sake of human beings,' or Paolo Friere telling us in his book *Pedagogy of the Oppressed,* 'There is no such thing as neutral educational process. Education either functions as an instrument which is used to facilitate the integration of the younger generation into the logic of the present system, and bring conformity to it, or it becomes the practice of freedom, the means by which men and women deal critically with reality and discover how to participate in the transformation of their world.' We, and they, and thousands of others, each day, are taking the quantum leap. Nothing will ever be the same. But more people may be more creative and more joyous and more loving. Oh, God! Yes ... Yes! Rais, more loving!"

(Pause.)

(Laughter.)

"Wasn't that nice?"

"Ellen, Ellen! All by itself a simultaneous mental and physical orgasm is a quantum leap! Standing here naked with you in the sunlight, I'm me and you and the whole world. I am God. And I'm in love!"

Premar's First Fifty-Two

Because we live in a society where communication is dominated by the mass media, it can be safely assumed that the average high school graduate beginning his Premar education has not only already been indoctrinated in the Western work ethic and the confused sexual and interpersonal moralities of the late-twentieth century, but is also floundering in a world of constant change.

The "why" of individual striving and the purposes of existence as well as the ends and means continue to puzzle most people. For many "Who am I?" and "What's it all about?" become their own hollow echo in a dark tunnel that has no light at the other end. Worse—most of us never discover how to lean on each other, at least lightly, because we are afraid to admit our fears and questionings for fear of being judged weak or cowardly. The intermedi-

aries—the priests, the ministers, the rabbis, the psychia-
trists, and the medicinemen—often seem as confused as
we are. Except for the incurable optimist—singing "Jesus
Saves"—leaning on God is usually unproductive, and no
one has taught us how to walk before Him.

A good education, therefore, should not only provide
skills for economic survival, but simultaneously should give
the young person perspective so that he/she can evaluate
and choose a life style that fulfills him/her not only as an
individual, but also functioning as a couple. Despite the
hazards of self-disclosure to at least one other person,
most of us cannot survive a lifetime without personal confirmation in the form of love. In the past, liberal undergraduate education has provided, for a small minority, a
mass-media, mass-culture deconditioning process. But for
the most part the other undergraduate courses and vocational training perpetuate the status quo. If you include
the fifty percent who don't go to college, most people receive little or no "value appraisal" education.

Since the major goal of mass communication is to in-
doctrinate and condition the masses in the name of profit,
to accept everything from smoking cigarettes to taking vi-
tamins and tranquilizers, or using vaginal sprays, or
creating apathy toward political programs that include the
bombing of rural enemies, or justifying inflation, the particular leader's right to legislate personal morality, we are
desperately in need of a continuous counterbalancing education that separates the facts from the fictions, and gives
a much larger portion of the population the ability to
discriminate in broad areas of their daily existence. The
buyer needs the ability to stay clear of shoddy and useless
junk merchandise; the same person, in another situation,
needs to be able to determine whether many of the intan-
gible values being promoted by those in power really contribute anything to his self-fulfillment. The anonymous Big
Brothers who are running the Western world—the managers of the biggest five hundred multinational companies—
and their political henchmen, as well as the leaders of the
Communist world, must be forced to operate in the flood-
light of intelligent mass opinion.

While no society can achieve the millennium, the joy of
being human is that we must try. Thus, the Premar Human-Values seminars are aimed at the large majority of
young men and women who, whether they pursue immedi-

ate vocational training or undergraduate or graduate specialties and professions, are not ordinarily taught any interpersonal skills or how to question the value structures thrust on them from childhood—or how to search for new meanings that would make it possible not only to cope with the world they live in but to refashion it.

In the past few years transactional analysis (I'm OK, You're OK) has overlooked that the basic human transaction is not the relatively internal one between parent and child, but a very insidious and dangerous process of molding all citizens, young and old, into responsive robots who are too lazy or too tranquilized to question whether the old values fit the new world they must live in.

The following books, which are scheduled for the first fifty-two weeks of the Premar Human Values *reconditioning*, are not listed alphabetically, but in the order in which they are read by the Premars. It should be noted that students who complete the entire four years are exposed to more than two hundred books in this total deconditioning process. In the last three years the "required reading" expands the Premar's cultural horizons in every facet of living, and includes an acquaintance with the entire range of world music, literature, dance, and the arts, as well as exposure to the delights of quality food and wines and the joy of personal preparation of these. Thus, a graduate from Premar would be able to distinguish between the ersatz world of McDonald's and Colonel Sanders', and discover that *vin ordinaire*, a Greek salad, homemade bread, and Thou are no more expensive, and perhaps a more soul-satisfying way of dining than eating hastily in the plastic, aluminum, neon warrens of the food franchisers. At the same time, he/she might on occasion still enjoy Boone's Apple Wine, or Richard's Wild Irish Rose, and a little grass, as a harmless way to achieve a different-weighted consciousness in the company of friends. Thus, in a very real sense Premar education answers the fears of Clark Kerr and the last warnings of the Carnegie Commission about the Gresham-law effect that has been occurring at the college and university level. Don't underestimate Premar. This kind of approach to life *can be taught*—because this is what the great low-income class is yearning to achieve.

Some of the first fifty-two books, such as *Word Power Made Easy*, are used continuously by Premars; other books are read rapidly, a few are skimmed, and some are really studied. While a book a week may seem heavy, the Premar environment, with the roommate system and the brother-sister relationship of Premar to Compar, puts the Human-Values seminar in the form of a life experience rather than in that of structured learning. There is no testing or grading in Human Values—simply exposure to a world of widely different values and the opportunity to select, reject, and argue. And most important, there is no finality about this particular first-fifty-two listing. Over a period of years more timely books will be written. But let the reader be forewarned. These books are intended to begin a process of radicalization. If you are afraid of that work, keep in mind the real meaning of the word. Radical: "forming the root, basis, or foundation; going to the root origin; touching or acting upon what is essential or fundamental." On that basis, a joyous life is a life lived radically!

Nobody who plows through these books, reading them with his or her roommate, and who is involved with ideas in the Synectical approaches of the Human-Values seminar, will emerge apathetic. The test of the Premar education will be whether the driving curiosity and wonder still carried over from childhood by the teen-agers has been revitalized and combined with a new, mature awareness of human possibility. Premars will have acquired a drive-to-know, a need-to-ask-why that is figuratively injected in their bloodstream. If this goal is only partially achieved, Premars—for the most, youngsters who would never have experienced this world of wonder and why—will be better educated than a majority of the young people attending conventional colleges and universities, or trying to discover their sexual selves in the confused, nightmare world of what now passes for the sexual revolution.

In a very real sense, Premar is "open admission" for all young people to the kind of education that is fully integrated with their economic lives. Unlike most state and city universities offering open admission (but gradually giving up in the face of continual inflation) Premar education *knows* what it is trying to accomplish: To create a human soil where self-actualization and interpersonal communication and deep human intimacy can flourish.

While some Premars will actually be working toward specific undergraduate degrees in the arts and sciences, most will be taking specific vocational courses in everything from data processing to plumbing. Thus, if Premar has any fixed premise, it could well be that we must create a society where there is no difference in status or human value, between the man or woman who runs the filling station and the president of any of the top corporations.

Until Premar has been in existence for a century, social differentiation through money may still be the carrot that energizes the donkey. In the interim, a large majority of men and women will be taught that too many carrots lead to satiation—even as Premar creates a world where the enjoyment of beauty, human and nonhuman, does not depend on how much money one has. This will be a world where the mechanic will enjoy ballet, opera, rock music, country and western—and will *participate* in new kinds of sports instead of watching professionally controlled spectacles as an increasingly bored spectator. A world where the engineer, as well as the plumber, understands world economics, and the bricklayer and the surgeon are as interested in communities and urban problems as the banker and the politician. A sophisticated society of men and women, who have vast areas of communication *beyond* their work specialties, will mean a world where husbands and wives have thousands of interpersonal bridges to cross over to each other. Islands to share.

If it's too late for you to experience the interpersonal growth of Premar living, you can still, if you dare, expose yourself to the Premar deconditioning. All of these Premar first fifty-two are available in low-priced editions. Begin today. You have nothing to lose but your chains!

1. COMFORT, ALEX. *The Joy of Sex* and *More Joy*. Crown. New York, 1972, 1974. The wide circulation of these books in paperbacks probably means that many high school youngsters have turned the pages and admired the idealistic drawings of lovemaking. But in most cases the books have probably not been read, and shared, in the ongoing roommate experience of the Premar environment. In the Premar library a companion volume titled *The*

Atlas of Sexual Pleasure by Gunther Hunold has over 130 full-color photographs of a happy young couple in the act of love. This book, which is priced too high, is available from John Amslow Associates, Post Office Box 2369, Culver City, California 90230. Eventually many photographers and film-makers will discover how to blend the bodies and minds of lovers, young and old, as they engage in joyous, fun-loving, awe-inspiring flesh contact. When this happens, sex and religion will be close to a merger.

2. LEWIS, NORMAN. *Word Power Made Easy.* Pocket Books. New York, 1972. Ludwig Wittgenstein pointed out: "The limits of my language mean the limits of my world." This vocabulary-building book is in use throughout the Premar years. Interaction between Premars and Compars and between the youngsters themselves rapidly expands the Premars' reading ability—and the limits of their world!

3. DAY, BETH. *Sexual Life Between Blacks and Whites.* World Publishing. New York, 1972. Beth's book and Grace Hasell's *Black and White Sex*, Fawcett, New York, 1972, and Joseph R. Washington's *Marriage in Black and White,* Beacon Press, Boston, 1970, are read by different Premar human-values sections and then compared back and forth. Ultimately Premars encompass all three books. Beth Day and Grace Hasell are white women. Joseph Washington is a black male. Together they provide the "deconditioning" mental process for interracial mating.

4. GORDON, DAVID COLE. *Self-Love.* Penguin Books. Baltimore, 1972. Since their interpersonal sexual selves are in a continuing development in the Premar program, Gordon's book provides Premars exceptional insights into the human sexual-growth process.

5. KNIGHT, RICHARD, and THOMAS WRIGHT. *Sexual Symbolism, A History of Phallic Worship.* Julian Press. New York, 1957. This book has the complete text of Richard Payne Knight's *A Discourse on the Worship of Priapus* (1786) and Thomas Wright's *The Worship of the Generative Powers During the Middle Ages of Western Europe* (1886). Premars may eventually return to the folds of their family religions and expand these religious horizons, or they may prefer to embrace a humanistic, man-based religion, but whatever route their lives may take, they learn the common bond between religions, all of which have their roots in a reverence of the generative powers. In the process, Premars may discover the validity of a return to symbolic praise and exaltation of the penis and vagina as a mystical element in a new theology.

6. VAN VLECK, DAVID P. *The Crucial Generation.* Optimum Population, Inc. Charlotte, Vermont. This pamphlet covers the limits to population and economic growth. Dedicated "to my children and my children's children," the pamphlet is an ex-

cellent summation of "where we and the world are going." Available from the publisher for $1.00.

7. PRINCE, GEORGE. *The Practice of Creativity*. Collier Books. New York, 1972. Human-values Synectic-style encounter which occurs daily between Premars and Compars during the entire four years of Premar is outward-looking rather than inward-looking. Prince's book is better and more comprehensive than its predecessor, *Synectics*, by W. J. Gordon, Harper & Row, New York, 1963. Both books point the way to a new kind of T-group interaction that not only develops creative, metaphorical thinking but just as importantly could be developed as a tool in "fitting" different kinds of brains together in an exciting new approach to interpersonal understanding. Prince's book is a key Premar book. Aristotle pointed out that "the greatest thing by far is to be master of the metaphor." Developing the ability to think metaphorically is an ongoing Premar experience.

8. FROMM, ERICH. *The Art of Loving. An Enquiry into the Nature of Love.* Harper & Row. New York, 1956. This book, of course, is a perennial favorite that actually should be required reading in high school, but is even more a source of insight in the Premar environment.

9. JOURARD, SIDNEY. *The Transparent Self.* D. Van Nostrand. New York, 1964. This book and Sidney Jourard's *Self-Disclosure*, John Wiley, New York, 1971, are key Premar books. The how-to of self-disclosure and the ability to give and to receive deep intimacy from another person is the cement of all interpersonal relationships and is the high road into a community of loving, joyous humans.

10. VINCENT, CLARK E. *Sexual & Marital Health.* McGraw-Hill. New York, 1973. Contrary to some opinion, Premars do not spend their lives watching how-to-do-it sex demonstrations or reading sex manuals. Very quickly "sexism" as a way of life disappears. But even as Premars become loving, human men and women they need plenty of "between-the-ears" sex guidance. Vincent's book was written for physicians, who, as society is now constituted, are often the only sympathetic ear the average man and woman can reach with his or her sexual problems. For this reason, reading a book that counsels doctors on how to assist their patients gives Premars a two-way perspective on themselves. This book is used in conjunction with the book *Human Sexuality*, prepared by the American Medical Association and available from them at 535 North Dearborn Avenue, Chicago, Illinois 60610.

11. GOLDBERG, B. Z. *The Sacred Fire. The Story of Sex in Religion.* Horace Liveright. New York, 1932. Yes! For Premars to come to terms with their psychic needs for wonder, eventually they must build the groundwork for a new religion. A Premar theory is that a religion based on the sheer joy of

human beings—joined in a never-ceasing sexual dance—has
more validity than separating one's genitals from his spiritual-
ity.

12. CRAVERI, MARCELLO. *The Life of Jesus*. Grove Press. New
York, 1967. While many Premars are Jewish, this biography
of Jesus will give any young person, Jew or gentile, black
or white, a new perspective on Christianity and religion as a
whole. Compars can use this book in conjunction with John
Allegro's *The Sacred Mushroom and the Cross*, Bantam Books,
New York, 1971.

13. ILLICH, IVAN. *Tools for Conviviality*. Harper & Row. New
York, 1972. Illich's definition of conviviality meaning "auton-
omous and creative intercourse among persons, and the intercourse of persons with their environment—in contrast with the
conditioned response of persons to the demands made upon
them by others" makes his theories a key Premar concept.

14. RAWSON, PHILLIP. *The Art of Tantra*. New York Graphic
Society. New York, 1973. Also available in a shorter form,
Tantra, The Indian Cult of Ecstasy, Avon Books, New York,
1973. Either of these two books is read by Premars to give
the flavor of the Indian background of tantra. But the key
introduction to tantra which puts it in full perspective for Premars and shows them how to incorporate it into their full
sexual life is *Tantric Sex*, by Robert K. Moffett, Berkeley-
Medallion, New York, 1974. This book points the way both
to a new religion and to a new society where the priorities
of loving take precedence over acquisition as a way of life.
Since young Premar males are capable of several orgasms in
any lovemaking encounter with their roommates, the tantric
art of extended sexual intercourse becomes perfectly feasible
for them, at least after the first ejaculation. One of the Premar
theories is that extended sexual intercourse is the perfect environment for joyous, intimate communication of oneself—
self-disclosure is easily attainable when orgasm is not the
immediate goal and the physical blending can often become
a peak experience of wonder and mystery. While the idea of
tantra is a key Premar concept, Premars learn to adapt tantra
to their own needs, and they are aware that the extensive
rituals of Indian maithuna, or the elimination of orgasm for
the male, as was attempted by the followers of John Noyes
in the Oneida community, may be tried as an occasional loving experience, but for the most part Indian tantra has only
esoteric historical interest.

15. WATTS, ALAN W. *Nature, Man and Woman*. Pantheon. New
York, 1958. In this book, and in many of his writings, Alan
Watts exalted the male-female relationship and extended the
boundaries of interpersonal communication. Compars are expected to give further glimpses into Watts's philosophic con-

tributions, and many of Watts's tapes are available in the Premar dayroom.

16. *The Autobiography of Malcolm X.* Grove Press. New York, 1966. By the sixteenth week, black and white Premars are now living in close intimacy. Both the black and white students must try to grasp the "black experience" in depth. Through the four years of Premar, many of the exciting young black writers are read and studied. Malcolm X's life story, and speculation on where Malcolm X might have led his people if he were alive, is one of the Premar mind-opening experiences.

17. FANON, FRANTZ. *The Wretched of the Earth.* Grove Press. New York, 1968. Using Fanon as a point of departure, Compars in the human-values seminar explore colonialism, earlier black freedom writers, and the entire history of man enslaving his fellow man.

18. WARNER, SAM BASS. *The Urban Wilderness.* Harper & Row. New York, 1972. Since the Premar concept is not only related to a new kind of approach to urban problems but also to how the cities of the future can be restructured, all Premars are exposed to the history, development, and varying nature of cities throughout the world. Sam Warner's book is an excellent overview of American cities. Sam's book *Street-Car Suburb, The Process of Growth in Boston, Mass. 1870–1900*, Atheneum, New York, although he is unaware of it, is specifically oriented around the Topham's Corner area. There are many other books on urban problems in the Premar library. Some of these are among the books listed following this chronological listing of the first fifty-two.

19. MILLER, HERMAN. *Rich Man Poor Man, Who Gets the Money and Who Doesn't.* Crowell Company. New York, 1971. This book, in conjunction with *The Myth of the Middle Class*, by Richard Parker, Horace Liveright, New York, 1972, begins the Premar exploration of the "affluent society." In the continuing inflation of the 1970's the average annual earnings of various income groups have increased but the percentage distribution of wealth remains static. The thrust of the Human-Values seminar in these weeks is how the emphasis on continually increasing economic growth in our society is used to reinforce the work ethic and how, in contrast, low- and middle-income people, by cooperative living, can improve their share of the total wealth and eventually modify the theories that continuous expansion of the gross national product is to their advantage.

20. MEADOWS, DENNIS. *The Limits to Growth.* New American Library. New York, 1973. This is a look into the future and the frightful consequences of exponential growth which the Premar generation must actually come to grips with. It rein-

forces the ultimate validity of the Premar and Confamiliaum
life styles.

21. GARDNER, JOHN. *Self-Renewal and the Innovative Society*.
Harper & Row. New York, 1963. Gardner reflects the basic
Premar optimism toward the American system and Western
society, and the belief in our combined ability to create a
world oriented toward wonder and discovery and self-realization for the individual. Compars use this book in connection
with Charles Reich's *Greening of America* on the premise that
Premars must learn how to retain a large measure of their
youthful idealism or their lives will become self-negating.

22. LAING, R. D. *Interpersonal Perception, A Theory and Method
Research*. Perennial Library. New York, 1970. As Premars
move toward the first roommate exchange, emphasis in the
Human-Values seminar shifts to a heavier concentration on
interpersonal behavior. This book, in conjunction with Erving
Goffman's *Relations in Public*, Basic Books, New York, 1971,
helps give Premars a greater self-perception. For additional
perspective, *Women's Sex Talk: What Every Woman Wants
Her Lover to Know*, by Dr. Jane Calder, New American
Library, New York, 1974, becomes an additional book that
Premars and Compars can use to gain comparative insight on
how human beings, without the Premar experience, fumble
toward sexual rapport.

23. ELLIS, ALBERT. *Humanistic Psychotherapy. The Rational
Emotive Approach*. Julian Press. New York, 1973. This summation of Albert Ellis's most important contribution in the
area of self-discovery and self-realization, and the principles
of rational emotive therapy, is a key Premar book, and is used
in conjunction with *A Guide to Rational Living* by Albert
Ellis and Robert Harper. Wilshire Books Company, 12015 Sher-
man Road, North Hollywood, California 91605.

24. MASLOW, ABRAHAM H. *Toward a Psychology of Being*. D.
Van Nostrand. New York, 1972. Interwoven through the entire
Premar fabric is the belief that the hows of self-actualization
can be taught to all young people—if we create challenging
learning environments and if the academic establishment wakes
up to the fact that the fundamental approaches of all non-
vocational education should be interpersonally oriented.

25. SLATER, PHILIP. *The Pursuit of Loneliness. American Culture
at the Breaking Point*. Beacon Press. Boston, 1969. Slater's
book reinforces the Human-Values-Seminar approaches of
flushing out the meaning behind much of our antipeople behavior.

26. SKOLNICK, ARLENE. *The Intimate Environment. Exploring
Marriage and the Family*. Little, Brown. Boston, 1974, and
Intimacy Family and Society (ed. by Arlene and her husband,
Jerome), also published by Little, Brown as a companion
reader to this textbook, are used by Premars—with separate

Human-Values groups using David Schulz's *The Changing Family, Its Function and Future,* published by Prentice-Hall and *Marriage, Personhood and Partnerships,* by David Schulz and Stanley Rodgers—who then compare their findings in the Human-Values seminars. While there are many other excellent books on the changing character of the family and marriage in the Premar libraries (see listings ahead, and other listings in Bob Rimmer's *Thursday, My Love* and *Adventures in Loving,* New American Library, New York, 1973), these particular books, written for undergraduate courses in marriage and the family, deserve much wider reading. Since Premars come in close contact with Confamiliaum members, in their various localities, they too are encouraged to read the Skolnicks' and David Schulz's books to broaden their perspective on the new kind of expanded community family which Confamiliaum can become.

27. MUNCY, RAYMOND LEE. *Sex and Marriage in Utopian Communities.* Indiana University Press. Bloomington, 1973. With this book Premars and Confamiliaum members discover that they are the children of a long inheritance of American, French, and British Utopian activists. The essential difference is that Confamiliaum and Premar are not "no-places" but are easily achievable "good places."

28. BETTLEHEIM, BRUNO. *Children of the Dream, Child Rearing Techniques in the Israeli Kibbutz.* Macmillan Company. New York, 1962. Bettleheim's book and Melford Spiro's book *Kibbutz—Venture in Utopia,* Schocken Books, New York, 1963, which is in the Premar library, are essential reading for Premars and Confamiliaum members and reveal their parallels to the kibbutz in the areas of economic sharing and a search for new kinds of communities which foster self-development.

29. NEWFIELD, JACK, and JESS GREENFIELD. *A Populist Manifesto.* Warner Paperbacks. New York, 1972. Premar and Confamiliaum are political. This excellent book, which should occasionally be revised by the authors, is a national program covering many phases of politics, economics, and government which a strong leader of the people could very well make his modus operandi. This is a key book in the Premar "deconditioning" process.

30. SENNET, RICHARD, and JEREMIAH COBB. *The Hidden Injuries of Class.* Alfred A. Knopf. New York, 1972. An open window into the psychological differences money and education make between people, and the new kind of class society that the United States has become. This book is based on interviews with low-income people in an area of Boston, that is equivalent to Topham's Corner. Premar youngsters eventually should be able to avoid these human booby traps.

31. NEIL, A. S. *Summerhill, A Radical Approach to Childrear-*

ing. Hart Publishing. New York, 1960. To avoid conflict with the more regimented style of Premar, Neil's famous book is not read until the thirty-first week of Premar. It is then possible to relate Summerhill to Premar as a step beyond which A. S. Neil did not believe it was possible to go, perhaps largely because he wasn't sure the British public would accept a Harrad- or a Premar-style continuation of Summerhill.

32. *Work in America.* A Report to the Special Task Force to the Secretary of Health, Education and Welfare. M.I.T. Press. Cambridge, Mass., 1972. This book, which has been praised and reviled, depending where one stands economically in the establishment, together with Harold Sheppard's and Neal Herrick's *Where Have All the Robots Gone? Worker Dissatisfaction in the 70's,* The Free Press, New York, 1972, and *Worker's Control,* a reader on labor and social change edited by Gerry Hunnius and published by Random House, New York, 1973, are used by Compars in the Human-Values sessions to kick off discussions on the nature of work and leisure in the world of tomorrow.

33. LOWEN, ALEXANDER. *Pleasure.* Lancer. New York, 1970. One of Lowen's most stimulating books. Many of his approaches to a full life are key Premar concepts.

34. BECK, ROBERT (Iceberg Slim). *Pimp, The Story of My Life.* Beck's autobiography, which continues through four other paperback volumes, is a fascinating story of a black man literally pulling himself up by his own bootstraps. While Beck is not political, his black experience, covering the past fifty years, is a valuable learning experience. These books are available from the Holloway House, 8060 Melrose Avenue, Los Angeles, Calif. 90046. Holloway has also published many other "nonliterary" books written by black people. Prices are approximately $1.50 each. During the Premar years all Premars read a considerable body of writings by black people from all income levels.

35. LANG, RAVEN. *Birth Book.* Genesis Press. P.O. Box 877, Ben Lomond, Calif. Price $6.00. Raven didn't write this entire book. Rather it is a very informal chronology of young women giving birth to their children—for the most part without medication and, often, without the necessity for episiotomies. The book is replete with photographs which have been taken by husbands or friends during the birth process. Over and over again the photographs convey a sense of mystery, awe, and wonder. A companion book used by Compars, unillustrated, is Erna Wright's *The New Childbirth,* Pocket Books, New York, 1971, and also Thomas and Ellen Phillips' *The Natural Childbirth of Tara,* Frederic Fell, New York, 1973. A delightful story of Ellen's pregnancy and the birth of their child in Mexico. Premars, of course, are given the opposing view to so-called "natural childbirth" in books like *Confes-*

sions of a Gynecologist (anonymous), Bantam Books, New York, 1973, and *Women's Doctor*, by William Sweeney III, M.D., William Morrow, New York, 1973.

36. HOLBROOK, DAVID (ed.). *The Case Against Pornography*. The Open Court Publishing Company. Lasalle, Illinois 61301. A collection of essays by well-known writers which reveals the lack of human values in much pornographic writing and illustration. The consortium's attitude toward pornography is that a healthy society could simply eliminate the need for it by ultimately creating an environment where the experience of human beings being naked together and copulating together is a joyous fact of everyday life.

37. GALBRAITH, JOHN KENNETH. *Economic Goods & Public Purpose*. Houghton Mifflin. Boston, 1973. Can young teenagers read and understand this book? Yes—with the help of Compars who will use it as a jumping-off point to compare the economic theories of other societies. If we are slaves, tied to either a socialistic or capitalistic economic wheel that must keep turning, or if it doesn't we'd all starve, then it is vital we understand the nature and kind of slavery we prefer. An equally valuable overview book used by some Premar communes is *The Future of Technological Civilization*, by Victor Ferkiss, published by George Braziller, New York, 1974.

38. WRIGHTER, CARL. *I Can Sell You Anything*. Ballantine Books. New York, 1972. This exposure by a professional advertising man of how the media, and particularly television, can brainwash even the most sophisticated is an eye-opener for young people from lower-income families, who often are unaware of how their purchasing decisions are being motivated. Compars use it in conjunction with *Subliminal Seduction*, by Wilson Bryan Key, Prentice-Hall, New York, 1973, and Issac Baramesh's *The World Is Full of It*, Delacorte Press, New York, 1974.

39. BARR, STRINGFELLOW, and SHEILA STANDARD. *The Kitchen Garden Book*. Lancer. New York, 1956. The essay in this book on small-plot gardening by Stringfellow Barr is a classic. It is especially important reading for young people reared in the asphalt jungle. Since a Premar and Confamiliaum concept is to literally green the cities, both in the Premar communes and the Confamiliaum communities, this book ties in with popular cookbooks used in the Premar communes, such as Ellen Ewald's *Recipes for a Small Planet*, Ballantine Books, New York, 1973; *Feast, A Tribal Cookbook*, by the True Light Beavers, Doubleday & Company, New York, 1972; and *Home Comfort, Life on Total Loss Farm*, New American Library, New York, 1973.

40. SKINNER, B. F. *Beyond Freedom and Dignity*. Bantam Books. New York, 1972. Whether or not B. F. Skinner would approve of the Premar or the Confamiliaum concept, their thrust is

toward creating environments to make human dignity possible. Skinner's book is a key Premar book.

41. FRANCOEUR, ROBERT and ANNA. *Hot & Cool Sex*. Harcourt Brace, Jovanovich. New York, 1974. While Premars in their fortieth week have already discovered a whole new kind of nonpossessive, loving, sexual-value orientation, the Human-Values seminar now weaves Bob and Anna's excellent survey into the discussion to create the groundwork for self-disclosure and deeper understanding of whatever emotional hang-ups may still be occurring. As Premars approach the end of the first year, and in another twelve weeks will be involved with their third roommate, this book and a few other topical ones are interwoven into the Premar reading program.

42. DOXIADIS, CONSTANTINOS. *Between Dystopia and Utopia*. Trinity College Press. Hartford, Conn., 1966. Six lectures given at Trinity College by the famous creator of Existics, the science of city planning. Doxiadis is one of the first "builders of cities" who proposed in his "entopias" (his own word) an approach to small human communities within the big cities—and a total human environment that each of us aspires to where a person can "achieve the realization of his own dreams within the framework of the common dream."

43. ADAMS, LEON D. *The Wines of America*. Houghton Mifflin. Boston, 1973. Premar communes and Confamiliaums buy grapes wholesale and make their own wine (and perhaps eventually will grow their own marihuana). However, an awareness of that unsurpassed quality of many American wines is a part of the educational process which can't be learned at McDonald's or Burger King, or in the average low-income restaurant. Even though they may occasionally enjoy Ripple and Boone's Apple Juice or Richard's Wild Irish Rose, poured over ice, as a fun drink, Premars will also be able to savor the difference when they drink a Cabernet Sauvignon or a Pinot Noir or a good Zinfandel.

44. BENNELLO, GEORGE C., and DIMITRIOS ROUSOPOULOS. *The Case for Participatory Democracy*. Grossman. New York, 1972. While this may seem a more difficult book for teen-agers, it is an excellent diving board into the kind of world they must help create. Note that for the three preceding weeks the Premar reading load has been at a much less intensive level.

45. FRIEDMAN, IRVING. *Inflation, Worldwide Disaster*. Houghton Mifflin. Boston, 1973. Since we will probably live in a world dominated by inflation for many years, it is important that Premars are aware of the whys and wherefores and how inflation could ultimately regiment their lives under a dictatorship. Friedman's book is used in conjunction with Robert Lekachmann's book *Inflation, The Permanent Problem of Boom and Bust*, Vintage Books, New York, 1973.

46. SCHRAG, PETER. *The End of the American Future*. Simon

& Schuster. New York, 1973. Chapter IV, in the *Province of History* section of this book, is a summation of lower- and even middle-income destiny which, without Premar and Confamiliaum, has a ring of future shock. While Premar beliefs in man are far more optimistic than Schrag's, it's instructive to listen to the nay-sayers.

47. MOOREHEAD, MARIO C. *Mammon vs. History, American Paradise or Virgin Island Home?* United People's Party, Square Deal Printer. St. Croix, Virgin Islands, 1973. At the request of Rais Daemon this book by Mario Moorehead, which raises many of the problems that Rais Daemon covered in his article "Walk Before God," is included in the first fifty-two Topham's Corner Premar books. Mario wrote this book in the Lewisburg Federal Penitentiary. Unlike Rais Daemon, Mario Moorehead, of course, is a United States citizen by birth. The problems on the Virgin Islands, however, parallel the problems of St. Noir. The book is available from the United People's Party at a cost of $10.00, and it's obviously only the beginning of much writing Mario Moorehead will do in this area.

48. RICHARDSON, HERBERT. *Nun, Witch and Playmate. The Americanization of Sex.* Harper & Row. New York, 1971. This book is a fascinating study of the changing sexual attitudes of Americans and particularly the American male. It gives the Premar student an excellent historical perspective.

49. PEARCE, JOSEPH CHILTON. *The Crack in the Cosmic Egg.* Pocket Books. New York, 1973. Compars will use this book with Premars to search out the crack in their own cosmic eggs. This is an exciting and controversial book for the Human-Values seminar.

50. HUTSCHNECKER, ARNOLD, M.D. *The Will to Happiness.* Cornerstone Library. New York, 1972. A valuable book exploring the relationship between mind and body and how a purposeful, goal-directed life can develop into a healthy and successful one. The book has been recommended for medical students but it is not beyond the scope of Premars.

51. HERRIGAN, JACKIE and JEFF. *Loving Free.* Grossett & Dunlap. New York, 1973. An open look into the sexual life of a married couple in their late thirties. No aspect of their physical and their interpersonal feelings is left undescribed. While Premars have proceeded intellectually and emotionally beyond most of the problems the Herrigans encountered, many of the Premars' parents have not. Compars suggest to Premars that their fathers and mothers should read this book.

52. KAHN, THEODORE C. *An Introduction to Hominology. The Study of Whole Man.* Charles C. Thomas. Springfield, Ill. This approach to the study of man was developed by Professor Kahn, who teaches at Southern State Colorado College. Unlike anthropology, "hominology," a word coined by Pro-

fessor Kahn, does not have any academic boundaries but utilizes facts from all of the disciplines in order to develop an integrated study of human behavior. This book sets the groundwork for the second year of Premar Human-Values sessions.